ALAS, POOR LADY

Persephone Book N° 65
Published by Persephone Books Ltd 2006

First published by
Jonathan Cape in 1937

Endpapers taken from an early twentieth century
bargello tapestry in a private collection

Typeset in ITC Baskerville by Keystroke,
Jacaranda Lodge, Wolverhampton

Colour by Banbury Litho

Printed and bound by Biddles, King's Lynn

ISBN 1 903155 55X

Persephone Books Ltd
59 Lamb's Conduit Street
London WC1N 3NB
020 7242 9292

www.persephonebooks.co.uk

ALAS, POOR LADY

by

RACHEL FERGUSON

✳✳✳✳✳✳✳

PERSEPHONE BOOKS
LONDON

ALAS, POOR LADY

CONTENTS

7

PART ONE

1936

I

'—in declaring this bazaar open.'

With the cessation of that silver voice the Town Hall was stirred to action. The packed crowd, faces upturned to the brass-railed platform, shifted, some to the doors to watch the glamorous departure, others to their stalls guarded by a youthful policeman, grinning and consciously tolerant, amongst the thronging women. March sunlight entered in broad, dusty bars from the enormous french windows overlooking the High Street, and a further reminder of spring came from the cut flowers of the stallholders, brought overnight and that morning from their country gardens; daffodils massed in jam-jars, narcissi in pails on the floor, sturdy, chromatic polyanthus in basins.

The helpers, women with their daughters, the inevitable sprinkling of the earnest-unmarried, took up positions. They would make between thirteen and fifteen hundred pounds on the two days' market and sale. It used to be more, in former years. The charity was not a fashionable one: no money stuck by the way. Here, at least, were no society climbers, paying their thousand pounds for a place on a committee chair'd by a duchess; no gossip-writers' targets allotting themselves fifty pounds for 'expenses' in the shape of a gown for the afternoon's special matinée, no dummy patron whose giving ended at his name.

Aiming fairly, the organizers fairly and steadily achieved, with expenses cut to the bone by the secretary, who with humour, craft and reason, coped with income-tax officials and human beings in all moods.

PART ONE

The famous actress, passing with calculated absence of hurry through the crowd, bouquet of tulips in a suède-gloved hand, was wondering a little how to fill in the rest of the morning. It seemed that, here, you weren't expected to make a purchase and leave a smiling comment at every stall. Most considerate; but having got up and made an unearthly early toilet did leave you at sixes and sevens. And what a hideous hall. That Pompeian red, aligned with terrible statues of heroic size, the walls hung with oil paintings of bygone mayors and an occasional immortalized scene from the Borough's history. The King, when Prince of Wales — was it? — and the local Volunteer Battalion. . . .

At her side walked the current mayor in morning dress, and his lady, a pace behind that nice old secretary, Mr. Whatsisname, and the local honorary organizer, Mrs. ——, anyway, she seemed a really decent sort with quite a sense of humour.

The party passed out of the doors and were upon the circular landing, door'd on the right by its Artists' room where rested the visiting musicians at the monthly assemblies of the Music Club, and stair'd spirally on the left down to the chilly hall where various glass doors informed the residents of the Borough that Rates might be paid and General Enquiries made.

Above, on the landing, the actress paused.

On a semicircle of chairs and sofas of crimson plush sat quite thirty men and women. The actress's eye, trained to perceive effect and detail, saw that they were all elderly to old; those wearing clothes which fitted them were dowdy and a little shabby, even: the newer suits of some of the men, on the other hand, did not seem to have been made for them. They did not appear to be visitors to the sale, none carried a parcel, basket or string bag, but worn purses and in several instances white cards. A few talked together; occasionally one would catch a stall-holder's eye and smile, a look that the actress remembered from her own rare visits to her agent, and the sight of the eternal small fry of the stage in the outer waiting-room, eternally hoping against all reason and experience for a real chance, and registering that brand of vivacity at every opening door. She herself had never gone through that particular hell. As with so many of the present generation of actresses, well-born, well educated, of independent means and with far more brains than glamour, she had had no struggles.

The mayor said 'The Candidates and Annuitants'. The secretary deliberately quickened his pace and joined them. He feared that Miss Blanche Preston would begin to ask questions in a voice trained to carry to every hole and corner of large buildings. In any case, Mr. Hanson saw no reason why he himself should continue to mince behind like an all-fired bridesmaid. The mayor had only held office for three years while the G.P.s had been going since 1863, being incorporated by Royal Charter in 1911.

Miss Preston gave him a minute poke with the stems of her tulips.

'What are the cards?' she breathed.

'Combined luncheon and tea tickets very kindly given to us by our Life Governors and Subscribers to be distributed.'

'Oh.'

'This is quite an event for lots of the poor souls. See a bit of life, you know. And when you live in one room . . .'

'Oh-h.' The actress's face softened. He hoped she wasn't going to acquire a sheaf of tickets and broadcast them dramatically to the semicircle. The old dears needed careful handling, and poverty had by no means eliminated ingratitude or silenced caustic tongues any more .than the annuity had overcome the born complainers who took offence at everything and eagerly hunted for slights and patronizing ways. For years, now, the committee had had to admit those whose right to relief was only the partial one of dire necessity. Quite one-fourth of the candidature and annuitants were social semi-demis and yards removed from the top shelf. They were always difficult and tiresome, poor devils, ungracious and resentful receivers, queasily concealing from such private friends as they had left that they were in receipt of what the type calls 'assistance'. A further reason for admission of that class was the everlasting one of persuading — even of discovering — the old men and women of the upper classes to lay down a portion of their burden. They splendidly, rather enragingly, wasted away of various wants in their funkholes. Reticent in life, they preserved their privacy in death. There were exceptions, of course: the fine-drawn, aquiline-nosed old aristocrats who took their pension with philosophy and humour, writing their letters of heartfelt gratitude and appreciation in graceful handwriting upon cheap note-paper from addresses unthinkable . . . And the upper-middles; sensible women like Miss Scrimgeour and Mrs. Tatham, and men like old Professor Rattenbury . . . they made the whole shoot worth while.

Another rule which in the post-war years had had to be relaxed was that one which made pensions conditional upon the possession by the candidate of a maximum income of sixty-five pounds a year. It was soon realized by the committee that such a sum was neither here nor there. Roughly, people either still possessed far more than sixty-five pounds out of their particular wreck, or nothing at all. Now that Mr. Hanson came to think of it, the only rule which remained inviolate was the one relating to insanity. That ultimate infliction debarred everyone from candidature. One had to draw the line somewhere. Mental cases and senile decay were for the Institution and the specialist. They involved trained companionship. You can't go mad in furnished rooms. Old age commonly does not still possess private companionship because its friends are contemporary, and indigent old age cannot afford it. Mental cases were covered by the General Rate; the annuitants who subsequently became affected also became the charges of their parish and their pensions either permanently suspended, or, were the breakdown of a temporary nature, paid over to the local authorities to relieve the Rates.

11

Miss Preston swept an eye once more round the semi-circle. Their meals, at least for the day, were evidently arranged for, but one wished one could do something. Rapidly she reviewed the possibilities of paid service in her own roomy flat. But quite half the women gave the impression of never having seen a typewriter, let alone of knowing how to use one. And their general manner . . . probably quite impossible in coping with bores at door and telephone . . . and could one tolerate them in the drawing-room, or one's dressing-room? The next worse thing to being continually contradicted might easily be to be persistently agreed with. Yes-men of the stage were bad enough, but yes-women off it . . . !

She stubbed her toe on a trunk and remembered not to say 'damn'.

'The gift-box,' said Mr. Hanson. The thing, huge and with a domed lid, stood open by the door into the Artists' room. It was already partly filled with woollen bedjackets, dressing-gowns, pound packets of tea, even pairs of shoes. 'It goes back to H.Q. after the sale, and the annuitants apply for clothes as they need them to our Almoner.'

'What a *wonderful* idea!'

'We always ask for pretty things, too,' Mrs. Fernley, the local organizer, suddenly remarked. 'They're a pick-me-up in themselves, besides sometimes making all the difference if someone is going after a job.'

'But — how *very* wonderful!' Dispassionately, Blanche Preston was reflecting that it was quite odiously difficult not to sound insincere when you really, meant what you said. One must positively strive not to go on saying 'wonderful'. It sounded like a cocktail tea.

'Perhaps you would like to have one or two of them introduced to you?'

'Yes, please.' And one would like it, oddly enough. A nondescript woman flushing an unlovely brick-red, rising like a trooper. Miss Flagg. But Mrs. Tatham shook hands readily enough. A week ago, successful candidate of a week, she had applied for a pair of gloves. They had been warm and whole. But terribly difficult to talk to, both of them. The bazaar, what a jam ... (*Yes, Miss Preston*) and what lovely things to buy: no rubbish, but things you really wanted —

(*Oh yes, a wonderful little rubbish. Really objects to take home.*)

The Secretary rescued her. 'Miss Preston, Lady Mell,' and an old, small face, wrinkling with sardonic amusement into her own, a little claw put into hers, the other sketching a gesture of invitation to the actress to seat herself ...

'Ah, how good of you to come and enliven us poor old cats. I have heard such grand accounts of your new play, but unfortunately the pit hurts my ancient bones and the gallery gives me vertigo. The G.P.? Oh, it's badly needed, badly needed. And will be needed worse, unfortunately. I bless the day they picked *me* off the scrapheap . . . Death Duties . . . the most iniquitous and un-British thing we do. Making capital out of grief . . . not good.'

Blanche Preston bent yet lower to hear. This conversation, somehow, wasn't for the landing at large, but real stuff between the two of them. The worn old voice went on. 'We've got Sir William Harcourt and Lloyd George to thank for that. And the joke of it is that Death Duties, in their present oppressive form, like the income-tax, were never intended to be a permanent measure. Just four lines on the Statute Book that have been never repealed, and what they've done for our — ' the old woman checked herself — 'for rural England is beyond computation. Broken up estate after estate and so thrown thousands of agricultural labourers out of work. Lloyd George saved the situation in the munitions department, but destroyed with the other hand . . . Now, whom else can I introduce?'

But the mayor was civilly champing. These old people were terribly garrulous. Luckily a distraction presented itself. Some helper had come through the doors of the great hall and bent to the seated figure with whom Miss Preston had recently been in conversational labour.

'*I'm in!*' Miss Flagg half rose, glancing vaguely about the landing, and began to cry noisily with rasping gulps. Somebody mopped her up, led her away. Faithfully, reassuringly as a B.B.C. announcer during a national crisis, Mr. Hanson delivered intelligence to the actress. 'She's just got her quota of votes. Now she'll be an annuitant. Oh yes, I should like you to meet Miss Scrimgeour.'

The spare woman got up composedly; if her manner was diffident it was, Miss Preston sensed, rather of naturally nervous temperament than of social unease. She had glanced with a contempt that was almost dislike at the hysteric nominee; her gloves, of grey cotton, were much darned, noticeably so, yet her right hand was offered freely enough. The actress engaged her in talk, a cross between the caustic downrightness of the old Lady Mell and the painful acquiescences of the woman who had cried. They chatted with fluent sedateness. One noticed that Miss Scrimgeour didn't Miss-Preston one at every other sentence. And yet there was a hint in the whole interview that someone had once had the little woman in authority . . . a whip hand which hadn't always had its way, if those direct and still-clear grey eyes were any indication of character.

Already, many of the women in the semicircle were beginning to fidget and crane heads, suspicious, resentful, striving to overhear. That Miss Scrimgeour was no better than the rest of them and not so good as some. Lady Mell, impishly appreciative, ran her eye over the scene. The elderly professor sighed. He was hoping that Miss Preston might have time for him as well. A charming young woman was a wonderfully pleasant thing, and to chat with success a perfect tonic. It meant that there was still success in the world to be had.

His one comfort was his new boots, weathered a glossy chestnut and made by a craftsman of St. James's Street. The professor was an old personal friend of Mr. Hanson; the sartorial agony at least would never be his. And the procession was definitely moving downstairs.

Miss Preston went in silence, sped almost theatrically by the crowd-noise of the sale.

'— tempt you?'

'A shilling but — '
'No string at *all*.'
'Quite a good attendance.'
'Darling, not *that* — !'
'Seven and two — '
'But, naturally — '
'About one-thirty.'
'Simply arthritis. All the winter.'
'They're all sold, but — '

III

Miss Preston was feeling dazed. She had known, of course, in theory, what cause she was championing by her personal appearance that morning, and had said plenty of sympathetic things about the G.P. in her speech, that speech which, as usual, she had had to write out and memorize. A long course of producers and difficult authors didn't make for the extempore or flights of initiative where a misplaced 'but' or 'and' could bring down thunder on your head.

Her mind ran through inconsecutive bits of the speech: '*What could be more appealing than the needy gentlewoman who cannot work and will not beg? . . . but a voice, and no uncertain one, has been found to champion her: The Distressed Gentlefolks' Protective Association* (applause), *called by us, its friends, and so better known, as we are apt to be, by nicknames,* (laughter) *as "The G.P."*' (great subdued applause).

And one had even worked in a laboured joke about the healing brought by the General Practitioner and the mental healing conferred by 'the other G.P.', and 'the duty of ourselves — the G.P. — to support it.'

'Flatulent fool,' murmured Miss Preston.

'Pardon?' said the mayor.

They were in the hall. The steady noise of traffic came from the entrance. Drawn into the kerb, her (hired) saloon car waited. One wasn't yet, and probably would never be, financially up to owner form. She turned instinctively to the secretary. 'But — those two, Lady Mell and Miss Whatsername . . . Scrimgeour . . . they're *gentlewomen!* I mean, they're people of *our* class!'

The mayor found no irony or humour in the exclamation and turned away. Mrs. Fernley found plenty of both commodities, and laughed outright. Mr. Hanson smiled. 'I should hesitate to range myself socially with Lady Mell,' he said, 'but I know what you mean. I'm used to it, of course. When Lady Mell first joined us she had exactly forty pounds a year — '

'My God. But how do they *manage?*'

' — and Miss Scrimgeour had nothing.'

Blanche Preston gazed at him, bouquet crushed against her furs.

'But — *how* does it happen? How does it *happen?*'

PART TWO

1870—1888

I

WHEN Grace Scrimgeour gave her first wail, British house-holders were telling each other that the French were now living on rats (a change from frogs, don't y'know), while their womenfolk, sunk in the billows of exorbitant draper-ies, bustles pushing them inconveniently forward as they dispensed tea from stout silver pots, chimed in with faintish ejaculations.

Charles Dickens passed away that year.

Marie Lloyd was born.

All the Year Round was still a popular periodical, and one John Lawrence Beesley, Master Mariner, laid the first cable for the French from his ship, *The International*. In Paris itself, a haggard young woman of twenty-five, spare as a spindle, with haunted eyes under a snarled fluff of fringe, was recovering from the devoted nursing night and day of smashed soldiers in a converted playhouse, and from darting descents · upon her many men friends for their money, their help — the very overcoat off his back in one instance, and quick, quick, quick! And later, return to work and sanity. It was regrettable how stupid everybody was . . . simply forcing one to lose one's temper and throw up one's parts, and being offended when (in the right, of course) one told them what one thought of them. But she'd show 'em! Have her own theatre, one day. The Théâtre Sarah Bernhardt. Wasn't one's chosen motto *Quand Même*?

In London, the Alfred Hunts were entertaining the Hol-man Hunts to dinner at Tor Villa, Campden Hill, where a brilliant young man with a languid lock of hair, whose conversation silenced them all, was announced with wonderful regularity on Sunday evenings by the parlourmaid.

'Mr. Wilde, M'm.'

Artists' children were clad in the conventions of the pre-Raphaelite Brotherhood, and some extremist mothers even cut their hair, sending them out looking like Florentine pages. Horse omnibuses rumbled down Oxford Street, past the Princess's Theatre and the grey, pillar'd Pantheon, newly become a repository for the wines of Messrs. Gilbey, after its career as a place of refined assembly, and of Opera.

I I

In her bedroom on the second floor of the red-brick house in Brecknock Gardens, South Kensington, Charlotte Scrimgeour laboured with another baby. Between the usual bouts of pain that preceded the continuous final agony, she lay calmly, able to think of a dozen of odd, and somehow unsuitable, things, a phenomenon she remembered now, which she had observed before at these times, but always forgot when, descending the stair, delivered, to expect next time. Because, of course, one shouldn't be able to think of, let alone be interested in, dress at these times. The act of birth was holy, the vicar always assured her, while the doctor, these days, seldom had need to remind her that pain was not to be taken seriously — like colic, for instance — when it was caused by having babies, because birth was a natural function. And men were always right. They knew. Their verdict was more final always than that of a woman.

She remembered that when out shopping a locality sometimes eluded her memory, and that Gertie's memory would be called upon, and her eldest daughter gave the information, promptly, always; and Charlotte herself, though temporarily reassured, would make at once for the nearest policeman or even small tiger, rug over arm, waiting by the brougham at the kerb for his mistress's emergence, to have the information confirmed. It invariably tallied with her daughter's but put the matter upon a responsible basis at once. . . .

Dear Gertie . . . one missed the dear girl, but was thankful she had at last got herself settled. A daughter at home was perfectly delightful, but after a certain time a daughter in her own home was best. One wept at losing or keeping her, alike, and at the wedding. As it was, the match was a late one, with the girl turned twenty-two, but all had come right and she was now having a dear little baby of her own to bring on visits to her old granny. Old indeed. It was a great pity that one had had to be forty-one before becoming a grandparent.

Chloroform . . . it was supposed to save you a lot of all this. Cissie Hodley had had the stuff and was positively eating chicken ten days later, but Doctor Grant had phoo-phoo'd it. Dangerous to the baby he had told Mrs. Scrimgeour, and to her husband, speaking more frankly, it rendered the mother unable to labour properly. She had mentioned it to the vicar, making a little joke of it for the look of the thing, but actually anxious to secure the spiritual point of view, and Mr. Braby had been most kind and understanding and had said that there was Scriptural authority for suffering at these times. *In sorrow shalt thou bring forth children.* And the Prayer Book: *The great pain and danger of childbirth.* And in the most friendly, confidential way he had told her that without suffering the mother never loved her children so well. That which was hardest to secure was always more prized than the object easily obtained. The woman's highest duty and privilege (consulting his watch) . . . the Eternal Reward when the child was first placed in her arms . . . the purging by pain as by a fire (taking up his hat) . . . the stream of tenderness which filled the mother's breast at the first cry of the fruit of love . . . the innocent life (patting her hand and moving to the door) fetched by the mother from The Valley of The Shadow.

And at last, at overlong last it really seemed this time, Grace Scrimgeour was placed in her arms. Rather a hurried placing and an even more hasty removal therefrom owing to the debility of Mrs. Scrimgeour. But it was expected. A pretty idea. And the fruit of love gave her first wail and the valley of the shadow disgorged Charlotte Scrimgeour once more.

Beside her in the draped bassinet was her eighth great reward.

III

In the morning-room Captain Scrimgeour sat reading the *Pall Mall Gazette*. Of late years he remained at home from the time the knife-boy was dispatched for the doctor to that moment when the nurse, full stuff skirts enveloped in an apron, stood in the doorway and announced once more that it was a girl.

The Captain's presence in his home was not through anxiety; one soon got over that phase and refuged in the club. Men were best away at these times, he had told Charlotte, who agreed, for what could they do? Obviously nothing. (No, dear, nothing.) It was that, after giving him daughter upon daughter, Charlotte had once actually produced a son. That would be — what? — in 1861. The boy, named Charles for father and grandfather, though Charlotte had put in a plea for 'Harold', had lived two days, but ever since then the hope of another heir had kept Charles Scrimgeour at home on birthdays. Ever since then that hope had enlarged the family. But he sometimes wished that the fulfilling of her wifely purposes should not tend towards depriving her of practically every one of those qualities and attributes, lightfooted, slim-waisted and with a flow of pleasant conversation, arch and fetching, which had originally attracted him. A more or less chronic invalid wasn't quite what one had mentally bargained for. Yet, one supposed, all family men were in the same boat there. One had children. Besides, the country needed 'em. It was a fine thing to do your duty for England. Also, one was very fond of the girls when they grew older and past that infernal period of ailment which made the whole house uncomfortable, and of barking one's shins on concealed prams in the hall, and meeting strange female faces on the stairs which disappeared for ever just as one was becoming used to them. Luckily the house was fairly large and the assorted noises incident to extreme youth could be isolated. It was pretty, too, those stray glimpses one had of Charlotte surrounded by her children. Poor Charlotte had been known to make a great to-do — even with tears — about the prospect of a new baby, but when it came she, like all good mothers, adored it, and like all women she forgot the whole thing once it was over, and enjoyed — he smiled fondly — a perfect orgy of new clothes in which she looked wonderfully well, still.

Yet once more the Captain thought of the fundamental difference, the almost domestic revolution, that would come with the arrival of a boy baby. The lad would, one supposed, be liable as all the girls had been to the usual and quite inevitable complaints of childhood: to chicken-pox, measles, to mumps, whooping-cough and scarlatina, for all children had those however well the mother bundled them up when out at walks, however carefully the windows were shut at night . . . the doctor said so. But once over all that the eternally interesting part began, and the father came into his own.

There was the first pony (one must run to that) and perhaps the first gun, if country friends were kind; the entering the boy for one's own public school . . . taking him there — old boy and youngster — showing him the ropes . . . telling him what slang was *de rigueur* and what impossible . . . looking on desks in the hope of thirty-five-year-old initials and caricatures. Tuck-boxes, tips . . . then Sandhurst and the regiment, and telling him anecdotes of the Crimea — three years of it, and good 'uns, too. The boy in his first mess jacket, and The Queen, God Bless Her, a moment of which one never spoke, even to brother officers, save in the clipped language of facetious lament for the mess bills, but a thing you never forgot for all that, especially when among foreigners. Gad! it was after the Crimea that the army brought back the fashion for whiskers, and for the inside of a year had *flâned* up West as hairy as gorillas about the chops. And showing the boy a bit of life; Dolly's, in Panton Street (if she was still going eighteen years hence!), the Cider Cellar in Maiden Lane, and Ross, good old ghastly Ross with his famous grisly ditty . . . the murderer in the condemned cell on the night before the hanging. . . .

> And the parson he will come
> He will come:
> And the parson he will come
> He will come:
> And the parson he will come
> And he'll look so blasted glum
> And he'll talk of Kingdom Come
> *Damn his eyes.*

And the Brown Bear in Knightsbridge Passage where the privates and N.C.O.s from the barracks met and clinked pewter ... and letting the boy, because you probably wouldn't be able to help it, sow his wild oats before settling down with some nice girl of good family ... That, Captain Scrimgeour realized for the first time — since the birth of the son who died had been obscured in excitement and bitter disappointment and unlimited hope for another boy very soon — was the ultimate point of difference between daughters and sons. Daughters could never be companions; their softness, vulnerability and natural disablements together with the necessity to shelter and protect them always and fight for them when the need periodically arose, for ever precluded intimacy. And because in an idealistic sense they were the better half and the angels of life, beings to whom you aspired without at the same time intending to emulate, the ugly or sordid side must be kept from them, the doubtful story suppressed outright or watered down to pointless verge, the insult to tender, pitiful ears of even the most vague allusion to the bad lots of the town unspoken. Which was why three-fourths of the resorts of amusement were morally closed to the ladies. Take it all round, London was the most decent city in which to bring up one's family. . . .

The house was wonderfully quiet, a foretaste of the time when all the girls would be married and he and Charlotte left in sole possession to end their pleasant days together. Only at the times when she was being confined was there this stillness, for the children, even the elder girls, were sent on visits then, in case ...

Aggie, of course, was still being finished at a convent recommended by Lady Mell which took Protestant girls of good family, and Queenie at school in Brighton; but from the drawing-room above came none of those tinklings of china and conversation which normally indicated that Mary, Georgina and Arabella were dispensing tea to guests and each other. And one was beginning to wish that Charlotte would hurry up. Surely she was taking — counting the time from the dispatch of the boy for Doctor Grant — a longer time than usual? There were surely no so-called complications? Wasn't it a fact that the first baby was the difficult one and that, after, all became plain sailing? Nor was any charge of dilatoriness to be attached to the doctor, a capital fellow who often hurried from case to case without changing his frock-coat, stained and with lint and even hair adhering to it. The doc. was quite proud of the garment and said, truly, it was the sign of a flourishing practice. But one didn't go too near it, oneself, if possible. It emitted a faint odour of carbolic, and something else that the Captain occasionally wondered if he remembered from the Crimean trenches. . . .

IV

At that moment, in Brighton, Queenie Scrimgeour was hitting a classmate who had, backed by public opinion, derided her assertion that when she grew up she meant to have a career, like a man, and 'do' things.

Agatha was throwing a note over the convent wall to one of the young men from the crammer's, opposite, before turning to agree with Sister Aloysius that St. Francis would certainly have revelled in the garden 'in all its summer glory'.

In Surrey, Georgina, having pulled her full share in the skiff all the afternoon, was watching her rowing partner absorbing whiskies and sodas while she prettily accepted the lemonade more suited to the delicate female stomach.

She longed for a whisky and soda, too. It must be worth having or men wouldn't see that they got it, and if its effects were anything like the brandy that faintness or toothache automatically evoked . . . but she would have been sincerely upset if she had been offered whisky. It would mean that the man thought that something about her suggested that she was fast, or — much worse — horsey, that epithet which, having in this connection nothing to do with the turf, was understood by everyone to mean things which got you into social bad odour. Old Aunt Clara had once said that Gertie's new bonnet was a little horsey; and you had to remember a quantity of other things which tended to lose you men's respect and ultimate proposals. Being punctual to family prayers was, of course, essential, but on pleasure trips you must keep your escort waiting, always, or — Mamma once said — it looked eager, and even if you weren't feeling eager it made no difference, because the implication was that an eager appearance suggested a dearth of admirers and that 'put men off': put them in the position of seeking after the unwanted, who, because unwanted, was probably some-how to blame. And yet, valentines from once-met dance partners were allowable. That, Mamma said, smiling, wasn't the same thing at all. The Scrimgeour girls let it go at that. Some of them saw, too, that it wasn't.

Arabella, on the lawn, mallet in hand, was seeing through, exposing and rejecting her partner's chivalry in manœuvring to give her the game she was losing.

In the house of a London aunt, Mary was thinking of her mother and wondering for the hundredth time why she and the other two elders were eternally being banished their home during an event whose secrecy Mrs. Scrimgeour had more or less betrayed to them more than once in the past. Not directly, of course, Mamma was never that, but by innuendo and sentimental reference. Incapable of complete silence as she was of outspoken coherence, apparently oblivious entirely of the effect upon her daughters' minds, she paid confused tribute to some god of seemliness, was consistent only in insisting that the girls be all from home when the newcomer was imminent. Not *because* of the impending event, but — anyway, the visits were arranged, the girls packed and cabb'd and train'd to their various destinations. Mamma contrived to leave you wondering whether, officially, you were supposed to know anything at all. She had — Georgina had confided it — once complained to Georgina of the monotony of 'all this discomfort', then ('as though we'd always talked it over') 'it will be worse before it is better'; and a reference that rather horrified Georgie about 'one's body not being one's own for such a long time'. And yet, when Georgina, acting on this new, remarkable status of equality and confidence, had hung over her and alluded to her need of special attention 'just now', Mrs. Scrimgeour had briskly, and not quite pleased, retorted 'why just now?' 'It silenced one', Georgina told Mary, 'because one saw one had put her out. I don't know why, but one always knows when they're put out.'

One did. And one gave way, naturally, always, obeying the call to emotional harmony. 'But — it's *illogical*', muttered Mary to herself. Devoted to father, mother and home, it appalled her to find herself criticizing, because if once one started *that* . . .

v

In a smaller London house, Gertrude, convalescent of her own first baby, was biting her lips and looking out of the window. She avoided the much-draped bassinet in case, as she suspected, the glance she gave it was the kind a mother shouldn't shoot. She would at least do Fate out of causing her to commit that enormity, would have one sin less upon her conscience; because, of course, she was either that ultimate catastrophe, an unnatural mother, or — somebody else was. And the alternative was worse.

The toppling of an idol, the exposure of an oracle, is a thing unforgettable in its painfulness, and painful in proportion to the years one has reverenced it. One expected, Gertrude knew, little of oneself but error and faulty humanity. But that *Mamma* . . .

So *that* was childbirth? And you were let in for it and all that went before not only unprepared, but schooled from your cradle to consider all that kind of thing so shocking that it was never to be ever so faintly alluded to; that is, that it was entirely shocking before you were married and, quite suddenly, holy and natural and approved by everyone, headed by God, Himself, afterwards.

As a daughter living at home it was nasty to think about men and unwomanly to talk about marriage, unladylike to flirt, cheap to kiss men and not done to dance more than twice with the same one, ever. You didn't show your ankles or speak of legs. And then — *that*. Through Clarence becoming attracted to one (he confessed later it was one's shoulders and eyes), and a formal call upon father, and a time instantly setting in — a licence that left you inadequate — when one might kiss Clarence, and a whirl of new clothes and the increased respect of parents and staff, because one's shoulders had pleased Clarence, and the affectionate envy of one's girl friends, and a set of solemn I Wills made in public.

C   33

But — you didn't buy a hat without trying it on, or a new gown without seeing it. Clothes were too important to be left to chance. Marriage, apparently, wasn't. It was only woman's highest vocation, the crown of her life, not to be compared with a shopping transaction in which suitability, durability and the direct statement by label of the price to be paid was fully understood by buyer and seller before the purchase was made.

One was searching desperately for some fault in oneself that would explain everything, and by exonerating Mamma, save one the unthinkable grief of having to consider that she had been unfair or cruel and go through life with this against her. One had been unobservant, obtuse? That wouldn't do, for there had been nothing to observe, no hint, even, of one side of matrimony. Why — with a backwash of fury Gertrude remembered it — she and Clarence had very seldom been permitted to be alone together in the drawing-room during their engagement.

And then — *that*.

Then, Mamma was unkind? But that was untrue. She was at all times indulgent and the nursery could bring up no instance of excessive or unreasonable punishment or injustice such as obtained among sundry of the Scrimgeour's juvenile contemporaries. Then, if Mamma wasn't unkind, one was making a mountain out of a molehill?

And, sitting there, Gertrude knew that as far as she was concerned that wouldn't do, either, when one remembered the sick, outraged terror and dismay, the crucifixion of all decency, of her early days as a wife, logical outcome of the whole trend of her life's training. It had annoyed Clarence. Later, he was facetious about it.

Or, perhaps, Mamma had let drop some hint that one

had overlooked or not heard? But Gertrude knew she had not. And now one hated Clarence as well as the baby, though the nurse had been the earliest to join the procession by her assumption of one's maternal adoration, her demonstrably false extollings of it as 'a beautiful, pert baby' when all sane eyes could see was a nerve-racking infant the colour of salt silverside, all head and stomach. And the nurse, this bustling stranger who alone seemed to fill the bedroom, and who, when she wasn't wanting something to eat was heating something to drink, would be with one for what felt like all eternity, a stranger, yet licensed to the embarrassing intimacy of one's body and to watchful, gloating appreciation as one fed the baby; a brand-new personality in one's home who had, together with the baby, blown into some remote, scarcely-remembered past the life that Gertrude had planned and expected for, herself and her bridegroom. It was spoilt utterly. Had been from the very beginning. Just three months of married life and even most of that dismayed, and then the child on the way. And sometimes Clarence came to watch him being fed as well, displaying an alacrity which Gertrude, becoming fluent in unhappy, embittered suspicion, rather believed would be missing were the baby bottle-fed. Another stranger in the house. . . .

Pictures of Clarence during their engagement: winding wool for Mamma, hands ridiculously rigid and humorous asides to make them all laugh . . . discussing gravely with her the picture of the year at the Royal Academy . . . listening with languor to Arabella at the piano, a hand occasionally smoothing his hair . . . writing in all their albums selected lines from Tennyson . . . attentive always with scarves and wraps . . . gently feeding Mamma's canaries with sugar. And all the time he knew and

PART TWO

Mamma knew that he was soon going to show himself
as a totally different person.

Mamma had had children: eight, counting the one she
was having at the moment. She was over forty, though
even to speculate upon her age still seemed lacking in
daughterly respect. She had once told them all that she
was born in 1828, and Aggie cried 'then you're thirty-
nine', and Mamma had been hurt and a little offended,
and flushed and said, 'S'sh. You mustn't speak to Mother
like that'. Yet arithmetic was one of the subjects at
school. . . .

Over forty. And one was only twenty-three, oneself.
Years more ahead of this kind of thing. And Mamma had
married at seventeen and was still devoted to Father.
Then, she hadn't been pitchforked into the business
unprepared? Or she had, and typically had said nothing.
But whichever way it was, one would never forgive her.
For not only had she told one *nothing*, but had talked about
Gertrude's married life exactly as nurse Campion did.
Which made Mamma a liar as well. The comfort, the
strength a little plain fact would have been! Steeling one
to being as plucky as was in one, preserving some, at
least, of one's delicate illusions by exploding them *as*
illusions. And one had promised in church to undertake
all this kind of thing, and to break promises was dishonest.
But, if they were promises you hadn't understood? For
even on detail one had misinterpreted the matter. That
line, *with my body I thee worship*, that all these years one had
thought to be rather touching and chivalrous, and as
conveying a very proper state of obeisance — mental,
possibly, and certainly physical, for Clarence had proposed on his knee — to womanhood. And all the time it
only meant — *that*. But the Prayer Book said nothing
about mind-worship or appreciation of wit and brain;

36

it was all material concern about money and property and bodies and babies and the state of one's health and the kind of economy that made a wife an inexpensive 'remedy against sin'. And it was called a beautiful service by everyone. There seemed to be a wonderful lot of liars about. Or was it that people, women especially, were never taught to think clearly? Like Mamma, who, now one came to consider, was only really explicit in household concerns and perfectly helpless about everything outside her own front door. . . .

'It's time for His Majesty's little supper, M'm.'

Ugh.

'*Such* a pert young gentleman! He says "I want my 'ittle Mamma" as plain as plain.'

Faugh.

With the passing of the years, Gertrude was to have two more children with quiet philosophy; she even became quite fond of her husband in a semi-maternal and slightly contemptuous way. But all her life long she was never to feel the same to her mother. Something was killed in Gertrude Randolph in 1870 that there was no reviving, a general sense of betrayal that spread, insidiously tingeing her outlook upon everything. Self-sufficient, faintly caustic, coldly just, a little suspicious of affection, she hid her hurt and ordered her home.

CHAPTER II

I

THE doctor at last. No, of course, the nurse. One had, in thinking of the son-to-be, forgotten the routine of precedence.

'If you please, sir . . .'

'Ah, nurse?'

'It's a little girl.'

One didn't betray emotions to inferiors, or indeed to equals, if possible.

'Thank you.'

'And Doctor Grant is coming down in a minute.'

The woman vanished.

Ah well . . . it kept the nursery aired and old Nana and a nurserymaid in employment. In a very few years now, the Captain supposed, the pensioning of Nana would have to begin: either that, or a bed-sitting room permanently set aside for her. That would be pleasant, and kinder. He must speak to Charlotte about it.

The Captain enjoyed his visits to the nursery floor in the past, the flutter of the nursegirl at his appearance, the beam of welcome and the chair dusted with her apron, of Nana. He would look indulgently at the newest toys, at Queenie's peepshow, a long elaborate strip of cardboard delicately cut into tinted vistas and dotted with tiny figures of men and women, culminating in the fountain and the park; would humorously wind the tin handle of Aggie's panorama of the Great Exhibition and cause Queen Victoria to pass over one wooden roller and under the other while his children stood about and watched

38

him, affectionate, well-mannered and sensing accurately
that Father was very kindly putting it all on and talking
down to them. He must be, because once when Georgie —
entertaining her visitor — politely asked him if he had
met many members at the club that afternoon, he had
been at an almost total loss before refuging in 'And what
does Georgie know about clubs?' After that, there was
really nothing to do with the visit except to wait for the
usual distribution of pennies and father's departure.

Nana expected nothing of the Captain. He was a
gentleman and nursery affairs weren't his, but Mrs.
Scrimgeour's and her own, yet the Captain's visits were
an honour and the mistress's a commonplace, and could
be a worrit if you were keeping order or scolding, or
wanting to air the things on the fireguard. Nana was
devoted to him and grateful to him for his paternal feats;
the Brecknock Gardens place was an excellent one; you
knew where you were with big families; plenty to do, to
watch, to control, and without the misery of illness that
you had gone through as a younger woman where the
family was a small one and every death left a noticeable
gap. . . .

The nurserymaid only envied the pennies. Twelve
pounds a year was a good wage, but it must be lovely to
have something given you you hadn't earned by running
upstairs and down all day with trays and scuttles. But
the eating was lovely belowstairs — meat every day and
outings every other Sunday from two o'clock till seven.
There was nothing much to do, except listening to the
band in the park, but you were *out*, and there were
several suppers going in several areas where one had
struck up friendship with other girls in service; lovely
suppers, sprats and kippers sometimes, better than the
others had ever had, poor kids, so that although the

youngest but two of the family, one weighed ten pounds heavier than some of the eldest. But the Ragged School was wonderfully kind to the little ones.

II

'Ah, Doctor . . .' The Captain offered wine and whisky, hoping very much that his visitor wouldn't stay long (for what was there to stay for?) and above all that he wouldn't take the arm-chair nearest one's own. The frockcoat, to put it in plain English, was worse than ever in every way since the doctor's arrival some hours before. . . .

It struck the Captain that the doc. was being less at home than usual at these times and he turned to him bluntly. 'Everything all right, I suppose?'

'Well, not quite all we could wish, perhaps.'

'Eh?'

'Well, nothing, perhaps, that one can quite put one's finger on. . . .'

'Just a hard time and fatigue, what?' translated the Captain crisply. The child was born and Charlotte was alive and it was a girl and the details were merely tedious. One was sorry, always, for invalids, but that sort of thing was a woman's job, or Nature wouldn't have arranged it so, and one supposed Charlotte was accustomed to it by now.

'Well, the child is under weight: that always may be symptomatic . . .'

'What of?'

The doctor fidgeted his sherry glass. 'It may be, of several things.'

He welcomed the Captain's voice again. 'The wife's always had fine sturdy youngsters. Fed 'em all. No trouble there.'

'Yes, but I can't actually *advise* it this time, though of course that's for you to decide.'

The Captain was a little shocked. Even the genuine plea of inability to nurse children suggested something unwifely and unwomanly going on somewhere; also there was something which, if not precisely newfangled, about bottle-feeding infants, was almost in the new-fangled class. But he could still give sentiment pride of place.

'Well, of course, in that case . . .' A notion occurred to him. 'Look here, are you trying to convey something serious, don't you know?'

The doctor at no time liked being definite, but Captain Scrimgeour was an old hand and the case was urgent enough. 'As far as one can ever see, Captain, there is unusual debility and lassitude on the part of our dear patient. I —'

'Then we must send for Mr. Braby at once.' It burst from the Captain instinctively and the doctor agreed, readily, relievedly. What precise help the vicar was going to be in a matter requiring specialized bodily service neither considered for a moment; they only knew that, somewhy, the whole bungling business would be lifted with a churchman's entrance on to a higher plane where sordid personal and material responsibility ceased, and heaven, reverently, sincerely, but confusedly, it was believed, at last began to pay a few dividends in return for the churchgoing, family worship and almsgiving of regular custom.

During the interval between dispatch of the wide-eye'd nursemaid and the arrival of the vicar the time hung heavily. The doctor was upstairs again and the evening sunshine making its lingering effort — a highly successful one as far as the departed frockcoat was concerned, and Captain Scrimgeour pulled down an upper sash yet farther.

III

Doctor and vicar came downstairs at last: impossible to mistake a man's tread in that household of women. Their faces were professionally grave; the combined gloom of Church and Medicine shook the Captain, forced him to directness at the doctor's 'She's sleeping at last'.

'Look here, is m'wife — er — dying?'

The pause of embarrassment from the other two was easy to misinterpret and he put hands to face in a genuine emotion. The vicar was at his side instantly. 'My dear friend, if — the worst should happen, we must remember that God knows best.' They dumbly accepted the comforting doctrine. It occurred to nobody that by sending for aid human and divine they were tacitly querying the Almighty Omniscience. God was not questioned; His ways, it had long been decided by wiser heads, were past finding out. But the human sympathy was very good, something you could value and understand. The doctor spoke. 'I wouldn't go as far as to state that the case is quite hopeless, but from what I can *see* — '

'Oh, for Gad's sake, man, speak out!'

' — from what I can see it almost looks as though it would be — um — inadvisable to — don't you know — well — further enlarge the family.' *That* was over.

The Captain looked at him vaguely. 'But — '

'Oh, I quite appreciate . . . at the same time, this debility, you know . . . it *might* affect your future children.'

The man of family breathed more freely. This line of the doctor's wasn't, as one had feared sickeningly, a definite professional prohibition but only a general sort of caution. It would be all right, and they would all take special care of Charlotte and cosset her up a lot. He practically said as much but the doctor, most tiresomely, almost ungenerously, went on looking dubious. 'After all, Captain, you have a nice little quiverful,' he began.

This was abominable, forcing one to expose one's heart ... but if nothing else would turn the trick ...

'I — I want a son. Doesn't every man?'

'Oh, very natural, very, very natural. Well, of course, it's entirely for you to decide — '

'Then you think it wouldn't be actually *dangerous*?'

And then help came from an unexpected quarter; the vicar, listening with interest, here cut in with gentle authority. 'But, dangerous, Doctor? I do so feel that, as with us all, our dear patient is in the Lord's hands. This is no *personal* opinion, we have authority for knowing it true. *Take no thought for the morrow ... let not your heart be troubled ... ask and ye shall receive.* And that blessed assurance that we are, every one of us, under His care who will not suffer a sparrow to fall to the ground, Who has numbered the hairs of our heads.'

It was absolution for anything done, or to be done. It cleared the air at once, and by the time the house, that day, was back to normal, it was recognized that Captain Scrimgeour, once more, was entered for the paternal stakes.

EVERY morning at seven-thirty the housemaid would wait about in the kitchen while tea was measured, china arranged, bread and butter cut and the sugar-bowl replenished; then, balancing the tray carefully at the bend of the unlit kitchen stairs, would bear it two flights above to the bedroom of Captain and Mrs. Scrimgeour. Twenty minutes later the ascent was made twice more with two immense cans of red tin filled with hot water for the baths that, placed on a towel, were ready on the floor. The Captain hated it if the water was brought a minute earlier or later than the decreed twenty minutes. He enjoyed his tea. On the other hand the exact moment when pleasure merged into irritation at unpunctuality had to be watched, for if the cans arrived too soon the water would grow tepid. When all went well, the water was poured into his bath first, the curtains of heavy plush and of Nottingham lace drawn aside and the wooden blinds hauled up with a clatter.

On her way downstairs to repeat the process for the baths of those of the young ladies who were at home, Susan, the housemaid, would pass with daily, military precision the nurserymaid, Lotty, going up to the top floor but one with Nana's breakfast, a succulent one of kidneys, sausages, sometimes even a chop. The nursery landing possessed large, roomy cupboards designed for linen, and in one of them the children's crockery was stacked. This saved Lotty a certain amount of work except where hot food was required, and saved her nothing in the summer months when kettles could no longer be boiled on the nursery fire. There was no water laid on on the upper floors. But in spite of it all she enjoyed her early morning peeps at Miss Grace.

II

In the kitchen, the cook, flushed and hasty, would be trying once more to cook breakfast for up to twelve people in time for herself to be ready for prayers in the dining-room, and finding it once more practically impossible. You can't worship and fry bacon simultaneously and if you left the pans to that heavenly mercy daily promised by the master they caught and made a smother that came right up into the hall. She had tried it once. Never again. 'Oh, Almighty and Merciful Father,' prayed the Captain, 'Good Gad! what's that infernal stink?' and scarlèt she had had to rise from the domestic line by the sideboard and run downstairs, while Lotty and Susan giggled right out before the family. Therefore the breakfast was always a little late — the only hitch in the service of meals, or a little dry through waiting too long in the oven. But, prayers once over and her own good feed near, cook became herself again, and viewed with an odd, sadistic pride the mounds of hot eatables which entered the dining-room under their plated covers.

III

The unmarried Scrimgeour girls could only secure bedrooms to themselves when Queenie and Aggie were back at school, or by coaxing their mother: except

Georgina, who was not only now the eldest daughter at home and turned twenty-one, but the senior of an odd number to be accommodated. Her bedroom was therefore the smallest, but her own. It was only spasmodically that the girls raised or felt objections to the lack of personal privacy by night and day. They were used to dresses being 'passed on' and to what they facetiously termed 'doubling up'. It was often good fun and led to hairbrushing confidence determined more by the chance, original allocation of the bedrooms than by any fundamental affinity between the sisters. Quite often the confiding couple of overnight would, on descending to the common ground of the public rooms, discover dimly (and soon forget) that, after all, Mary or Arabella would have been more sympathetic. . . .

On the disorganized and fainthearted occasions when one of them hinted — to hint was more respectful than to ask outright — for a room to herself, Mrs. Scrimgeour would brush the remark aside if it suited her, in one of several ways.

'We'll think about it.'

'Not now, dear, I'm busy.'

'Mustn't be selfish, lovey,' or the humorous 'Why this exclusiveness?' or the most defeating of all, 'Mother thought you and Mary loved your pretty room'.

No definite answer, whichever type your request evoked; silencing, always, but not convincing. Not a clever woman, Charlotte Scrimgeour had for evasion a talent approaching genius. If the answer were 'We'll think about it', her daughters learnt in time to be sure of this much, that it meant a postponement of weeks before gratification. Mamma was like that about other things, they had all, separately, noticed, accepting it without pooling their findings, for one didn't criticize one's parents except (and that very rarely) to oneself. They had observed the manifestation on shopping expeditions: Mamma very authoritative and direct if household goods — dull things — were needed, and then the sight of the pretty draped lampshade or new cushion cover, equally needed even on Mamma's admission, or the silk-dress-length or curled plume for the hat, and at once procrastination set in; gentle agreement as to its desirability, a shy pressing on Mary's behalf, and the inevitable 'We'll remember that'; 'Let's think about it'; or, 'After all, it won't run away'.

It grew on her with the years, the tyranny of an ever over-indulged conscience, an acceptance of the worthy thing, logical outcome of a lifetime of unconsidered self-sacrifice to duty which, in its turn, would expect its toll of sacrifice, willing or otherwise, from the next generation.

Nor was she ever to admit that there was the slightest flaw in her logic. It is probable, her circle saw in time, that she did not even perceive it. Thus she felt no inconsistence in a system which faithfully, rigorously, kept empty bedroom and spare room aired, dusted and swept daily, beds made and warmed against the return of Queenie and Aggie, and denied their use to Mary or Arabella. Herded together her daughters continued, and daily the overworked maids 'did' the vacant rooms. About the inviolability of the spare room kept by Mrs. Scrimgeour against some vague, unspecified crisis there was the justification of the past, when the apartment, square, filled with its brass bed and enormous marble-topped washstand and smelling fustily, had housed the current monthly nurse, and the fact that she remained for at most five months out of the twelve before relinquishing the new baby to Nana, made no difference to

the inelastic mind of Mrs. Scrimgeour. For might not a
visitor come? It might, but seldom did. The Scrimgeours were hospitable but self-sufficing and one could
not, decreed Mrs. Scrimgeour triumphantly illogical, put
more work on the servants. Sometimes she would add
'the room may always come in'. Meanwhile her daughters
might always stop out.

IV

The trays and cans disposed of, Susan was free to
descend to the hall and to take the letters from the kindly
bearded old postman who would touch his peaked cap
with a smile and a pleasant word as he drew the packet
from the leather wallet slung over his shoulder. The letters
were then taken to the dining-room and distributed up and
down the table. Susan liked the dining-room. Not only
was it never entirely free from the odour of good food, but
on the dark red walls hung two oil-paintings in handsome
black frames whose subjects — a fruit piece and a bundle
of game — carried out the idea. The Captain's sword was
slung over the mantelpiece, forming an arch of honour
to the clock in Parian marble representing a lady with
nothing on and a large poodle dog. Why the young ladies
called it Una and the lion wanted telling, but it was
handsome and took the eye. When it ping'd the hour in a
high, clear mosquito-like tone which did not seem to go
with the heaviness of the group, Nellie hurried into the
hall and banged a small brass gong with a little drumstick.
The resulting middle-class racket was sometimes secretly
deplored by the Scrimgeour girls if they were newly
returned from the country house visit where the butler's
graduated performance upon his immense instrument was

a velvet demonstration of the art of crescendo and diminuendo.

Then Susan would pull out a little brass knob which rang a bell up in the nursery, and Nana, never best pleased and ch'king at all those things she was leaving undone that she ought to have done, would lumber slowly down to prayers, meeting on her way various members of the family as doors opened up and down the landings.

'Good morning, Nana.'

'Good morning, Miss 'Bella.'

'Good morning, Nana. Lovely day.'

Often Nana was too irritated and preoccupied to answer at all and the girls, arms entwined, made every allowance, for she was 'getting on' and they all loved her. You respected age. You had not only been taught to, but there came a time when you were unable to stop doing so, whether the age were respectable or not. It was like death and the *de mortuis* that rendered the sinner for ever beatified.

V

All over London among families of Scrimgeour standing public dining-room worship was at this hour being performed. Heads of households would tell you that it began the day well and, if pressed, that 'it was expected', the distaff side that it was 'nice' to have family prayers and, if pressed, that it 'looked odd to the servants' if omitted, and that every family they knew 'had them'. What nobody realized was that it was, literally, the only event which assembled and temporarily socialized the entire household, except its infant members. In houses larger still, the young ladies, from their more exclusive

D 49

places by leather sofa or dining-room window, would see, through the years, unknown faces in the sideboard line of seated domestics that the rare enquiry would place as 'the new vegetable maid', 'the second footman' or 'the third housemaid'. In the Scrimgeour's somewhat under-staffed *ménage* — for your family increases but the accom-modation never — the line of six was well known to the Scrimgeour girls, even if they accepted as natural that they never saw their own basement any more than it occurred to them to wonder where Tom, the knife-boy, slept, which was in a pantry on a camp-bed that had belonged to their father.

The Captain arriving first in the dining-room would glance with furtive hunger at *The Times* as he rang and greeted his entering family, then the staff filed in in order of precedence, cook, Nana, parlourmaid, housemaid, nurserymaid and knifeboy. And while he read from prayer-book and Bible, the staff (in order of precedence) thought of bacon, kedgeree and the boiler, of baby and the new towelling and milk-jug required, of a soldier seen from the area steps, of a piece the band had played in the park last Sunday and (Tom) of Lotty.

The Scrimgeour girls, their ears overlong attuned to the words of the service, did not even know that they had never known what they meant. It had been left to Gertrude in her awakened fury to read some human reason into the Book of Common Prayer. Captain and Mrs. Scrimgeour accepted, and taught, that the Bible was inspired. Between its covers was the record of every miracle, outside them the miracle was not and never could be. That, already, a message could be flashed under the sea from England to France was merely a modern invention not in the Bible and so no cause for marvel. Elijah was fed by ravens — large ebon fowls, and

David danced before the ark. On the other hand, in an epoch of literal interpretation and of sweeping ignorings of the trifling matter of mistranslation, the injunction to cast thy bread upon the waters was taken symbolically, as meaning that it was meet and right to give to the poor and so lay up reward in heaven.

VI

At all meals save tea the places of everyone were unchanged, a system by which Gertrude since promotion from the nursery and until her wedding day had sat on her mother's right hand for eight years, and Georgina next Mary and opposite Arabella for eleven. This again induced a tendency to arbitrary alliance that did much to cancel out those of the bedrooms. How and why the places had originally been so organized nobody remembered. It made it difficult on country house visits where breakfast was a leisured affair of come-when-you-like and sit where you please, and had on more than one occasion threatened to earn for Georgina and Arabella the fatal label of fastness, when, convention-ridden as a pair of cows, they turned instinctively to the men who had been their table landmark of the previous day.

Scrimgeour breakfasts were relatively silent affairs, the head of the house immersed in the newspaper, the women gathering their forces for the day's campaign of pleasure, mentally weaving social strategies, charting the fray from their maps of war, the morning letters. After the meal the Captain would withdraw to the morning-room and ultimately to the club.

'Are we alone for dinner to-night, Charlotte?'

'Er — yes dear,'

That meant that, lacking guests, they would sit down five to table.

The Scrimgeour girls then filed upstairs to the drawing-room from whence the housemaid would hastily vanish. There, notes of acceptance were written, fancy needle-work performed, the canaries fed, novels glanced at until midday, when walking or shopping took place. The girls having no personal maid went out in pairs. Mrs. Scrim-geour herself, still thrall to waning custom, was never seen outside her own front door until the afternoon. It was one of those taboos explained by nobody and under-stood by everyone of a certain social standing.

The girls, unless obviously about to purchase, did not linger outside shop windows, and if anybody had reason to believe that the eye of Man had been caught, she would turn with some earnest remark to a sister. The outings were conducted with ever a third eye upon that which might happen and that which the passer-by might mis-understand. Should a high wind spring up at turnings and blow summer garments into disarray — a contin-gency hardly to be feared, owing to their heaviness, in the winter — the only thing left to do was to laugh with great apparent amusement which was designed to deflect attention from personal immodesty to the sexless regions of natural law, a dilemma shared, it was hoped, by all. Even men's hats sometimes blew off. And although one could, as a woman, never be in the unassailable realm of clean fun of the hat-class, one registered by smiles a synthetic humanity and comradeship when ankles — and more — were revealed.

There were permissible contretemps; a loop of braid might become partially detached from the skirt, and this you could knot up or pin with absolute propriety, since it was to the public a loop already openly on view; hairpins, too, might tinkle into gutters as having come from a discussable part of your person, while the dropped bag, sunshade or glove mattered not at all. It must be quite terrible to be conspicuous, and the Scrimgeour girls were subconsciously grateful to the omnibus companies who had made the stair too narrow for feminine ascent. Georgina once said '*Nothing* can happen to a man, and if it did it wouldn't matter in the same way. Their hats blow off but their coats can't and their trousers don't'. Mary and Arabella had hurried home exploding with laughter. In common with nearly all other young women of the time, they were, without suspecting it, totally different people among themselves from what they were in the society of men. In those rare, sisterly minutes, they were, in short, human beings.

VII

Every morning in the dining-room Mrs. Scrimgeour rang and waited for cook. The tradesmen's books were paid once a quarter, and four times a year she scanned them superficially and unintelligently, Mary cast them up, while the Captain wrote the cheques. The system known as 'letting the books run on' was accepted by everyone, it had been an axiom of Mrs. Scrimgeour's mother: 'If you pay every week and miss a week they don't trust you. It injures your credit. But if you run large accounts and pay them regularly they know where they are with you.' And, oddly enough, they did. But the scheme also meant that the butcher's bill was often £60 for the quarter.

It was a slow and ample age; trade had been stimulated by the Great Exhibition, which opened up for ever hitherto unexplored avenues, and England profited, if her taste in decoration and furnishing became confused and bastardized.

It was a trustful epoch of large credits to large families committed to large houses from which escape from creditors must be a slow one ... The expensive product of the craftsman gave of the integrity of durable work whether in wood, leather or material, of solid well-joined tables, of smooth doors and chairs that knew no creak, of boots that lasted for years and silks that never wore out, and if the contrasts of poverty and wealth were sharp, the shivering barefoot newsboy, the wasted runner behind the luggage-laden growler were possibly happier than under the paternalistic regime that was to set in forty years later, and, by a foredoomed effort to be consistently unfair to one class alone, was to bring the country to the verge of bankruptcy; to inflict unemployment, that rose to figures unparalleled by crippling capital through taxation, upon the very class it was out to champion, and deal the charities a staggering blow by half ruining their patrons.

There was indifference but there was also freedom. Food might be scarce but it was good of its kind: the producers had not acquired the religion of the tin or fore-seen the possibilities of adulteration that a World War was to reveal. If wages were low so was the price of a room, and if education was disorganized and hard to come by, who shall say that it was missed? The masses knew their limitations, were trained to their jobs and oppor-tunities and seldom sought beyond them, and if they lacked the costly smatterings of largely useless, compulsory information to be dealt out by the coming century, at least they escaped the heartbreaks of disillusion, the alienation from their own families, that a slight social rise in occupation commonly brings, together with the uphill business of eternally straining to go one better than the person next door.

There were bad servants and those working in bad conditions, but whatever the conditions the average domestic was reasonably accomplished, and seldom reached the depths of dishonest incompetence that the twentieth-century mistresses were to plumb, bribe they, pamper they never so madly.

All considered, the government which promises nothing at least creates no strife or bitterness, and the coming century that was to witness a labour market ruled by trades unions and paid strike promoters, the arrival of Old Age Pensions, Insurance stamps, State schools and the rest of the paraphernalia for spoon-feeding three-fifths of the population of Great Britain, was to pay double in seeing at the same time a nation that was, despite the inevitable advance in hygiene and style of living, steadily becoming a second-rate power.

The diluted version of the feudal idea as represented by the Scrimgeours and their like had its petty abuses, but they were in the last resort petty, and the point of view set forth, for instance, in their method of household finance had the general effect of causing everyone to 'know where they were', a condition that the unhappy nineteen-hundreds were no longer able to claim. It was an error of judgment that misled the Captain Scrimgeours of the period into postulating permanence in their domestic arrangements. Perhaps understandably, they sowed lavishly.

But they died before the reaping.

VIII

The cook arrived in a clean apron over her print dress and carrying a slate and pencil which squeaked. Her memory — it annoyed Mrs. Scrimgeour — was not as good as that of her predecessors. One did not like being written at and it prolonged the lengthy process of ordering.

Luncheon: 'There's nearly half a leg of mutting left from Sunday, M'm.'

'You can finish it in the kitchen, or make a cottage pie or hash.'

'Very good, M'm.'

'We'll have cutlets, mashed potatoes and green peas. A little soup to begin with — gravy. You have plenty of stock?'

'Oh yes, M'm.'

'And one of your baroness puddings and stewed fruit and cream. And don't forget the radishes with the cheese. The master was vexed they were forgotten yesterday.'

Emma murmured suitably.

Dinner: 'Soles, I think, and a pigeon pie and a loin of veal, stuffed. Creamed spinach, fried potato balls, a wine jelly (have you cooking port?) . . . and you must think of some savoury.'

'Soft roes on toast, M'm?'

'Yes . . . yes, that will do.'

IX

Mrs. Scrimgeour was free to go upstairs. A chat with the daughters in the drawing-room, a glance at the fashion paper, correspondence, a sorting of wardrobe, needlework or crochet and the visit to the nursery brought the parlour-maid to the gong, just as the Captain punctually opened the front door with his private key. The spare key was in a drawer of his desk. If the girls or his wife were out at night it was either with himself, or, if with friends and admirers, they were sat up for by a maid, or Tom, sometimes even by himself if he were not too tired. It was pleasant, the sudden awakening in the dim-lit morning-room, to young voices, the clearing confusion of sleep that showed you a fine girl smiling in soft stuffs and colours in the doorway, the affectionate 'Caught you, Papa! Who's a lazy-bones?'

'Ah, my dear, and how was the play?'

'Simply wonderful! It must be — simply wonderful to be an actress.' He would laugh and stand waiting for her to leave that he might turn off the light in the gas-globe. Or they would elaborate the joke. 'Capital. And your wages shall keep the old soldier in his declining years.'

X

Once more in the kitchen, Emma would spend the next hour at the area door, while Susan and Nellie washed up, and Tom cleaned lamps, silver, and polished boots and shoes and knives in the pantry. Sometimes — rather often, Emma had noticed — Lotty would give him a hand if not wanted in the nursery. Often, too often, Emma could hear the children giggling and carrying on over their work. Then the sound of wheels outside, and the butcher's cart, and cook armed with a large flat dish. 'I shell want twelve cutlets, young man, and another three pounds of bones and a loin. Veal. Six pounds.' And a pause, and a clattering down the steps. The fish-

monger's boy. 'Eight soles if they're good sizable ones.'
Cook 'fancied' a sole sometimes for supper. Ten kippers
would do for the others. 'And a pound o' roes and five
pigeons — young birds, mind.'

Emma in common with all the cooks of all the areas
of all the squares and streets in London gave orders
deliberately rather in excess of requirements; it gave her
good standing with the shops and increased the Christmas
tip from the proprietors. It gave her a pleasant sense of
power at no personal cost, it increased the scale of living
belowstairs and it was seldom noticed in the household
books. Once a week she would send Tom out on two
journeys with two enormous bowls of dripping to sell to
the rag-and-bone man, and of every dozen of grocers'
port or sherry for sweets she abstracted a couple for herself. The empties stood in a corner of the large, rambling
area, upon an iron tree whose many branches supported
the bottles by their necks.

At half-past eleven the ordered hurly-burly slowed down
and the maids were punctually drawn by a sixth sense to
the kitchen, where they were joined by Nana. For half an
hour they drank strong cups of tea and ate as if their
middle-day dinner were six hours distant instead of two.
Etiquette ruled that you could eat as much as you liked,
only the snack must be of cook's choosing and dispensa-
tion, and no complaints. Sometimes it was great, cold
puddings in tins, sultana'd and brown-topped and known
as 'baked lights', sometimes cuts off this joint and that,
folded in buttered bread, or warmed-over bacon and
kidneys from breakfast — it was seldom they were reduced
to bread and cheese. Even Tom and Lotty had their
elevenses which they ate in the scullery.

The accompanying conversation began, led by nurse
and cook, with civil enquiry as to the doings of each other's

worlds. This paved the way for open gossip about the family and the progress of the young ladies' affairs, the numbers and names of those guests 'coming dinner' that night. If Nana considered that the discussion was becoming disrespectful, she would brush the crumbs from her stomach and leave saying 'Thank you I'm sure, cook'. It also served to remind the kitchen that rightly speaking her presence among them at table was a concession. Lotty would have brought her up everything, but in the empty nurseries Nana had learned to long for a little life and company in the years between the birth of Queenie and Grace, and the habit had come to stay. Given another baby, Nana would withdraw into her suite once again, and Lotty toil up and down with the elevenses and tea.

IT was after luncheon that the life of the house became significant. The test was the three o'clock caller and the visitor, who, entering the drawing-room, would deposit his silk hat upon the floor, gloves thrown across the brim, and remain to tea. In summer the double drawing-room was pleasantly cool, the parquet floor reflecting the fluttering movements of the women as they dispensed tea, the twitterings of the canaries vying with their talk and laughter.

From her place in the second room Mrs. Scrimgeour benevolently looked on. The distance from the centre of activity — tea-table and tier'd cake-stand which her girls called 'the curate's aid' — was designed to mark chaperonage without obtrusiveness, a fact perfectly understood by everyone; also, she sometimes remarked with arch ambiguity to some daughter, 'It will do you good to learn to manage'. It made Queenie and Aggie as nervous as cats when it was their turn to wield teapot, and blow out spirit-lamp; Georgie and Arabella always managed this gracefully, they lamented to each other, even Mary, grave and civilly bored, was adequate. Georgie and Arabella managed everything well, even conversation to men with Mamma listening.

'Just touch the bell, Mr. Elmslie.'

'Sandwiches, Major? I've remembered your favourites.' Remembered his favourites! That was Georgie's kind of luck, that cucumber sandwiches were on the stand the afternoon that Major Brailsford dropped in.

Often, Mrs. Scrimgeour would mime instructions, cautions and directions from her distant place . . . signals you could never follow and which sent you fuming, and gaily smiling, all across the floor to find out about, upon which she would lovingly breathe advice into your ear, tickling it abominably. Somehow, when Mamma whispered, everything seemed to begin with S's and end with P's, B's and T's that were draughty, and popped.

At a little before six o'clock, the men excused themselves. They had — of course — a wide choice of other engagements. It was as they slowly rose murmuring 'Well —' that Mrs. Scrimgeour definitely took charge, throwing over them delicate verbal nets of future appointment; Sunday supper . . . I believe we have some spare tickets for the Botanical Gardens fête. . . .

It always retained at least one of them for the time being. If, as often happened, the captive were an army man, Captain Scrimgeour would round off or do outright the work of his females, hospitably, bluffly and expeditiously. 'I want you to join us for the new piece at the Haymarket, Grahame. Plenty of room in the box.' 'Look in for dinner soon, my dear fellow. Shall we say Tuesday week?' And we said Tuesday week.

The men gone, the drawing-room settled down into flatness and the difficult hours before dinner set in.

11

It was Mary who first saw that they were difficult. For herself she expected little, having the Scrimgeour nose that came out ill on women. The nose, perhaps, might have passed along, but as time went on she was uneasily aware that her sisters were normally pursuing a line of

country that could never be her own. She had unhappily
wondered, and often, why she could find no satisfaction
in the social life of home: why she was the only sister who
read *The Times* and appreciated Dickens, Thackeray, the
Brontës, and Besant and Rice: why she was unable to be
amused by the facetiae of calling men. She perceived
their jokes weren't funny, and the test was that if a woman
said them nobody would laugh. You just weren't a
humorist if you were a woman.

Mary sometimes, in her dry and thoughtful way, had
given vent to some quite good things, and the men were
polite and Mamma signalled and it passed off like a bad
smell. Mamma, signalling, as she had done from the
nursery days, the look that meant 'you're showing off',
Nana's version of which was 'if you're so sharp you'll
cut yourself'. And yet if Charles in the nursery (in *the
nursery*) was really pert or 'forward', Mrs. Scrimgeour
would retail in the drawing-room, with slow appreciative
enjoyment, the answers-back of the four-year-old. It
began in the nursery, this privilege for men, just as when
the holder of the title dies the son steps into it as a baby.
And yet 'eldest first' was nursery law, obtained even over
adult matters, unless you married, when it suddenly
(through a man) gave you precedence over an unwed
senior. A woman, Mary saw, could never succeed to or
at anything in her own right. She wished she could
accept it wholeheartedly and of conviction, but always
there was a warring in her; an instinct that sadly knew
that, given a chance, she too could do something with
life. At school she had been the winner of prizes, the
girl who worked for the pleasure of it. She had a brain
and knew it, a brain that functioned clearly enough
to make home life unsatisfactory without suggesting a
solution.

But the difficult hours of six to eight p.m. perceived by Mary, at least, with her, stopped at perception, leaving her immune, lost in her books. With Arabella and Georgina — at times, even with Aggie and Queenie as well — the question of how to 'fill in' was as acute as unrealized, nor, if realized, would they have confessed it. There were, of course, South Kensington tea-parties, but you couldn't count on them to keep you going. In summer you could go for another walk, but didn't, much. A London walk should, like a good hunt, have a 'point'; the Row in the season was gay and pleasant and watching from the railings the stage and society beauties roll by in their victorias stimulating, but, Mrs. Scrimgeour had told them, it wasn't 'much good', or was 'a pity' to be seen there unescorted by a man friend, and if you sent a note round to his house in Rosary Gardens, carelessly, jollily suggesting his company, it was 'marked', and anyway he was always out or at his club. All you might do was hopefully to send for a brother-in-law, who, though no fun and no good wasn't a pity, and marked.

At the time of the coming-out of the elder Scrimgeour girls there was only Clarence, and for several months, and until Gertrude became openly restive, he enjoyed a demand that was by no means commensurate with the regard in which he was held by his sisters-in-law, and Gertrude had taken a firm line. She didn't want him herself — much, but would retain her own property.

In the winter, the six to eight p.m. problem solved itself through the fire. Round this you could assemble, waiting to dress for dinner, with the approbation of nature herself; sometimes even in September nature began to approve in this particular way. The Scrimgeour girls did not know it, but their dilemma was shared by thousands of daughters whose parents were neither rich nor actually in society. Even their aggravated dilemma of sheer weight of numbers was a commonplace.

III

Between the men the Scrimgeour girls married and the last ditch of brothers-in-law there were the fluctuating and more livening set, composed of those drawn sooner or later to the house through friends of the Captain's brother officers, sons of the girlhood friends of Mrs. Scrimgeour, an occasional relative of a schoolmate of the girls themselves, and, more rarely, a sprinkling of those whose initial attraction to a Miss Scrimgeour at some dance caused him to take a little trouble by following up the original encounter. This section, bringing a breath of novelty, the aching relief of fresh blood, into the household, was also apt to be the one of which in the language of chaperones 'least came'. For the young man, drilled in his turn by mother and sisters to regard every unrelated young woman as having an eye on him, 'marking him down', was cumbered in addition with the knowledge of the special and extra vulnerability which public opinion assigned to him. In brief, as a new friend owning no family or regimental bonds with the Scrimgeours, his intentions were assumed; the margin of tolerance allowed to youth and mere attraction was a small one. It made him, longing as he might be for fun with a jolly family of pleasant young women, stiff, cautious; the prospect of a finality of life together with one of them nipped many a sane friendship in the bud and often withered it altogether. It was entirely typical of Mrs. Scrimgeour no less than of the age itself that, upon one of these losses to her circle, she should gently, directly lament with tangibility for the loss of a tangibility, oblivious entirely of the natural results of a system which she herself spent her time in promoting and keeping alive. Sometimes their mother's regrets for the touch of a vanished hand were prolonged enough for Georgina or Arabella, pitifully, to take the law into her own hands and a note was written.

Dear Mr. Venner,

It seems quite a long time, as father said the other day, since we saw you. If you are free on the 20th, we should be so glad if —

Occasionally it answered: more often it did not. At this note the Venners would take fright, abundantly backed by their female relations.

But with river picnics, dances, dinners, teas, At Home days, theatre parties, backed always by a naturally hospitable father and a watchful, conscientious mother, the house was kept reasonably maled.

IV

When Aggie and Queenie left convent and school for good and became the younger Miss Scrimgeours they failed for some time to perceive the complicated machinery in motion on their sisters' behalf and — now — on their own. For months they revelled in what they called freedom. The first morning at home was never forgotten, nor the first shopping expedition with their mother, the first formal afternoon call in Palace Gate, the first wreath worn at a dance, nor the sensations aroused in becoming for the first time a part of the household pattern.

Fresh from establishments crowded with women dedicated to heaven, to teaching — to anything but men, the fact that the girls themselves were exchanging one woman-full house, for another was obscured by the tea-time men and the army friends dining, and the incredible lifting of a taboo which, from making men dangerous things to avoid and inaccessible in any case, suddenly became a condition in which you *had* to talk to them, or get left out. For weeks, shielding behind their youth and ex-schoolgirl status, they revelled, plungingly, gauchely, without system, and for weeks the men were 'fetched' and Mrs. Scrimgeour indulgent. . . .

It couldn't last. There were casualties: a moment when Arabella's fate with Captain Grahame hung in the balance through the attraction of a new face and ingenuous conversation which, quite obviously, sought no entangle-ments . . . a difficult time for Arabella, too proud, too essentially decent to admit or feel jealousy of a junior, realizing well that her own future establishment, children and standing were being jeopardized.

It was Mrs. Scrimgeour who wore down Queenie and Aggie and induced that self-consciousness that was called modesty, who imbued them both with 'a sense of responsibility' without giving them anything for which to become responsible, guiding them lovingly in the third person ('mother's girl'), and reducing them once more in their own estimation to the level of the classroom.

It took them three years to get the house's measure. The first year was vague hopes, daring experiments, the changing pleasures of the various months; the second year, faint, worried incredulity, healthy boredom unhealthily suppressed, and the third year an acceptance of every-thing.

It was in the second year that Agatha began to remem-ber wistfully her nuns and even to contemplate an altar in her bedroom: a best handkerchief draped over a book, a holy picture and a vase of flowers. She was still resilient enough to envisage that a set-to with her father over attending morning prayers would be interesting, still sufficiently of her world to shrink from becoming publicly *affichée* to the pious life. It happened, indeed, to be Agatha herself who had been instrumental in upsetting the largest Scrimgeour apple-cart. Over Mary, of all people.

Mary at one time had a young man — at least, if not quite that, one who looked as if, with nursing, he might be going to develop into one. Agatha in sheer high spirits pretended to admire him herself in that open way that was allowable because obviously a joke, and Arthur Malcolm switched over his discussion with Mary and for the next few visits allowed Agatha to monopolize him. Mrs. Scrimgeour signalled and sibilated in vain; it was not in her to expostulate explicitly to Agatha herself, that would have been putting ideas into the child's head, and the fact that she spent her life in insinuating that particular idea to her daughters made no difference at all to practical tactics. The signals, it was hoped, covered all the ground in conveying general disapproval. But she was open enough with her husband, and for the first time the Captain invited a man into the morning-room and asked him his intentions.

It was an undramatic session, and a baffling, for it appeared that Malcolm had not got to the point of even considering matrimony with anybody.

'Miss Mary? A very interesting mind. We often talk about books, sir.'

'*Aggie?* But — surely? A joke or two — '

Nor had the Captain even to forbid him the house. For Malcolm suggested it first, and they never saw him again.

It fidgeted the kindly Captain for days. Had someone,

perhaps, been mistaken? Charlotte, now . . . not a brainy
woman, he fancied, and none the worse for that. He was,
naturally, devoted to her even if he had long forgotten,
save in the most general way, the precise impetus that had
made him propose to her. But the interview with Malcolm
at least had passed off well. The fellow was a gentleman.
And there was plenty of precedent for the business . . .
old Blackadder, now, who had admitted to the most
infernal row with a young fellow over his own daughter's
affections. *He'd* got to threats . . . but they'd got the couple
married, though the divorce which followed had rather
put her on Queer Street and socially closed a lot of doors
to her . . . and Ossington of the ——th had boasted of
kicking another fellow downstairs. But that had apparently been a really nasty business . . . kissing and pawing
and not a word about marriage. But Arabella and
Georgie were about to be settled. That only left poor
Mary, Queenie and Aggie, for Grace one needn't begin
to think for in that way, yet. Their turns would all
come in time. Captain Scrimgeour sought calm in the
nursery.

The elimination of Arthur Malcolm left the first real
blank in Mary's life. He was her first glimpse at mental
affinity, which is to say that they joyously agreed about
All Sorts and Conditions of Men and, more joyously, differed
upon the character of Becky Sharp. The aftermath of his
disappearance she was not, most kindly, allowed to forget.
In those literary conversations she had lost sight of the
ultimate significance of Malcolm, was allowing herself
with daring, increasing confidence to believe in the possibility of friendship with a man, even if she could not
honestly admit that the possibility of marriage had never
occurred to her; the habit, if alien, was too deeply

engrained for that. But there was an inner strength in facing and voluntarily ruling it out.

But here the family stepped in, affectionately postulating a disappointment that was not her own. It was Aggie who, exuberantly, frankly penitent, was hard to bear or counter: her mother, evasive always, who provided the last straw, in unexplained outings, new gowns, a dead-weight of unintelligent condolence that was rather dreadful.

ONCE more the nursery was a place of call for those of the Scrimgeours who wished in that placid warmth and innocent atmosphere to forget their own difficulties.

Before the arrival of Grace and Charlie, the girls would mount the flights to sit with Nana. Even in 1869 it had occurred to none of them to put in for one of the rooms, as a boudoir, leaving Nana the other. The suite was the nursery, always had been, and none questioned the possibility of its purpose being at an end, or reflected that it was quite three years since that purpose could any longer be legitimately claimed when Queenie left it for school . . . and then, vindicating a situation that kept one more needed room at grass, came 1870, and Grace.

II

Grace, at six years old, preferred Lotty, the new nursery maid, to Nana. Lotty enjoyed a good game even if she was fifteen; Nana was just another grown-up among so many, and not only grown-up in the way the ladies downstairs were, but old. She said so herself even if one hadn't thought it for her. Grace for years called her sisters 'the ladies', unaware of them as sisters at all. One gradually called them Georgie and Arabella and Queenie and Aggie, but always with a faint sense of daring and unsuitability. With Mary, somehow, it wasn't so difficult. Mary was always more of a person with one, and the lady who gave one Mrs. Ewing, who skimmed *Anna Ross* and

The Fairchild Family and pronounced them 'great non-sense'. And yet Mary, such a person upstairs, talking *your* things to you and being interested, was not the same down below in the big room with the slippery wooden floor. She was easy to find — no peering round gentlemen's trousers as you often had to with the others, and always pleased to see you at the Children's Hour in a way the others may have been but showed so that you were shy at once, and bothered. Arabella and Georgie got up and made little rushes at you, and stooped over you and their ear-rings rapped you on the nose.

'Where's our Baby? Aren't we growing *rather* too-too, Captain Grahame?'

'Ra-ther, by Jove.'

'Give pandy to the great big gentleman, Gracie,' and Arabella, laughing up at Captain Grahame, creating little embarrassments for the little sister in order, charmingly, to disperse them, while the men stood about, delicate cups in large hands, and looked vaguely jocose and benign-at-a-venture.

Sometimes, watching the efforts of Arabella with Grahame and Georgie with Major Brailsford, Mary, pouring tea and conscious of the watchfulness of Mrs. Scrimgeour, would wonder if there were a genuine child-lover in the room. . . .

Grace, advancing carefully in many-buttoned plush frock, sash and best white boots, would occasionally see a face she had learned to memorize, a caller who was 'Gertrude' and your own sister. With her sometimes was a large, fair gentleman who was, they said, your sort-of-brother, and whom — it was so impossible! — you were encouraged with laughter and applause to call Clarence, and even to kiss. And then they weren't there any more and were forgotten until next time. Once, they brought a

horrid little boy with them, who stared, and had a
sausage curl and plaid knickers, and one was his aunt.
More laughter, in which even the gentlemen joined.
Once the lady had beckoned one to her and looked at
one, staring like the little boy, and had laughed too and
said something about 'Mamma really wonderful' — not
as though she were amused. Grace soon noticed, also,
that when the little boy came with sister Gertrude he had
more petting from her own father and mother than she
had herself. Because he was a visitor? It must be right,
of course, if they did it, but that didn't prevent your
being angry and hurt, and *that* made you what the ladies
called bold and forward, so that you called out for what
you wanted — a cake, anything — so that everybody sh'd
you, when all you wanted was petting. It was *your* father
and mother, *your* home, *your* Children's Hour, and the
minutes ticked away in the clock on the stone mantelpiece,
while the little boy stood at mother's knee or sat on her
lap having his curls smoothed.

And father: 'How's The Man? You must give him
riding lessons, Clarence, m'boy. Can't begin too young.'

'I should like a pony, Father, too.'

He hadn't even heard her.

Eldest first?

But they were the same age, sister Gertrude had once
told Grace so. Ladies first, then? But that didn't count,
it seemed, when there really was anything for ladies to be
first about.

Grace went to Mary about it. Mary, pitiful to any
grief, was, she discovered, at a loss. Why *did* men have
all the things? Fairly, dispassionately she considered the
question; she herself, surrounded by nothing but sisters,
had never had that particular grievance to cope with.
She hedged, rather cleverly.

'You see, lovie, father isn't a rich man.'

Clarence wasn't either, but the child wouldn't know that. It was Lotty who made the reason dramatic, her blue eyes shining.

'Why, Miss Gracie, my dear, it's because he's going to be a big man one day an' perhaps fight for you in foreign parts, like your Papa. Gentlemen must have a horse to charge on, like.'

'What's charging, Lotty?'

Lotty grew ecstatic. 'It's going forward in a rush to meet the enemy, like the picture in *Holly Leaves* las' Christmas.'

III

It was, despite constant visitors, a lonely nursery. The Captain, not so young as he used to be, had long exhausted the list of the possibilities of girl babies to charm him, as had Nana herself; the elder girls, training singleheartedly for a career of motherhood which they might or might not be suited to, were indulgent to the child by fits and starts, inevitably utilizing her on occasion as the photographer did his palm and plaster pillar. Georgina had even taken her to be 'done' at Elliott & Fry's, cabinets, Georgina's cheek against Grace's, and back in the drawing-room would often say to one of the men callers, 'I *must* show you the child's new photo', and more often than not the response would be 'It's charming, especially of you, Miss Scrimgeour'. Most of the men shared a nervous horror of photographs; they trenched perilously upon the borders of Art. You discussed the picture of the year at the Academy because that was part of social chit-chat, and anyway the things usually told a story you could understand, about gamblers' brides, and sailors' returns, and people going off by train.

With little Grace, Mrs. Scrimgeour herself had very little to do. Her memory had by this time forgotten all but the outstanding details of the routine of childhood — Children's Hours and hearing prayers said, and she felt she had earned her repose. Ever more adequate when a bodily rather than a mental effort was called for, she left Grace to Nana and the girls, mentally selecting Aggie and Queenie as little mothers, not only oblivious of the gulf which separated them from the youngest Scrimgeour, but of the fact that, for years the youngest themselves, they had had nobody to practise on. What would happen, if, the proxy mothering successful, Aggie and Queenie married as they probably would any day now, she comfortably failed to consider. Everything came right in the end.

CHAPTER VI

I

CHARLES SCRIMGEOUR was born in 1872, a pale, harassed-looking child with a head slightly too large, and weak legs that had to be put in irons until he was seven. He represented Mrs. Scrimgeour's final reproductive fling, the two years which separated him from Grace standing for the Captain's almost Tudor agony of impatience in conflict with the remnants of his consideration for his wife.

The birth had been a difficult one, and there came a point at which Doctor Grant had, out of his time, hurried into the morning-room to debate in haste as to tactics; which to save, mother or child? — a direct question calling for a direct and unsuitably prompt answer. For — the Captain perceived the trap — if he elected for his wife the child might be his son: if he chose the child it might well be a daughter ... and the doctor, he fancied, was looking at him accusingly. When both mother and boy happened — bless them — to survive, the Captain prided himself, eyes wet, on having supported the older claim. . . .

But even in fulfilment grief was centred. The fact of the little chap's legs, a personal mortification, a lowering of proven Scrimgeour standards ... a sense of someone having defrauded one. . . .

For years the sensitiveness of his father kept Charlie out of the drawing-room if visitors were still lingering during the Children's Hour. Gertie's confounded brat with his straight, sturdy legs might be there, or be brought in.

75

The girls, except Grace — of an age which slept soundly — were as usual sent packing during their mother's confinement, Georgina and Arabella to their riverside friends who accepted their belated reappearance with hospitality and humour, and Mary to the customary aunt who proved a little restive.

This time there was the additional problem of Aggie and Queenie. Mrs. Scrimgeour, always consistent to herself, showed them that they were a problem while withholding the reason of their problematical state. Of a very slightly more inquisitive and experimental generation than their three seniors, they dared to let the atmosphere become strained, but Mrs. Scrimgeour, impressive on her sofa, ruled them by mother-knows-bests, sentences punctuated with the closed eye. She looked, the girls thought, awful; she was feeling too ill to wonder or care what construction the latest batch of daughters put upon the whole matter. They were to go to Gertrude, who shrugged her handsome shoulders, thanked her stars the two were officially 'out', wrote that they must amuse themselves and for goodness sake to bring good evening dresses, and turned them loose in a spare bedroom with a large patterned wall-paper of what appeared to be sage-coloured pineapples and fir trees, and a vast framed engraving of the late Prince Consort with his favourite hound.

Queenie said tentatively to Aggie that even if it *had* upset what plans and engagements one had made, it *looked* like a round of visits.

Mary, in her aunt's drawing-room, cast up the Scrimgeour tradesmen's books; they had fallen due without

Mrs. Scrimgeour even having had an opportunity to see them, and Mary had, a little guiltily, taken them with her to Sloane Street without saying a word to anyone.

In the riverside house, Georgina watched the posts for an envelope having the crest of the Naval and Military Club upon its flap and Arabella wondered how much ground they would have lost through absence from South Kensington.

I I I

Every August the entire Scrimgeour family closed the house, put the servants on board wages, and left London for a month at the seaside. Captain and Mrs. Scrimgeour had often hoped that Gertrude, Clarence and their boy would join the party, but this, somehow, never happened.

'It would be delightful to have all the girls round one,' their parents said, and the aspiration came through Agatha to Gertrude, who laughed crisply. 'No, my dear. I've been a girl round Mamma too many years already, thank you.' Gertrude was privately convinced the arrangement wouldn't 'answer', and that her mother did not even mean it. She was simply sentimentalizing: visualizing a pretty, conventional picture, taking no account, so to speak, of the thirty-one days it would take to paint it. And Mamma didn't even know she didn't mean it, which had always made her so impossible to deal with. Even now, Gertrude's fingers twitched to slap the mild oval of that face which moo'd platitudes.

'Marriage has done so much for Gertie', was one of them. It had indeed. But not quite in the way Mrs. Scrimgeour meant.

77

The resort decided on, the London house hummed with preparation for quite a fortnight in advance.

Were the striped sunblinds ripe for the cleaner or would they weather another year? Mary, making notes of the utterances that fell from her mother's lips.

Drawing-room carpet and all stair carpets to be taken up and beaten. Special note to the maids to 'get at' the pelmets properly.

'The gas-globe in our bedroom wants renewing, Mamma.'

'Don't dear, I'm thinking . . . now you've put everything out of my head.' To the unbalanced mentality of Mrs. Scrimgeour any interruption was agony and anything broke the spell of her concentration. She could not, her daughters had learnt, even combine the writing of a note with a 'good morning, dear', but fluffed at once and waved one away, leaving them ungreeted and losing the thread of her sentence.

'The spare bedroom toilet set . . . now what did we say about that?' This required no answer at all: anything that might have been said had been said by their mother, and until she remembered the decision of to buy or not to buy all advice was wasted breath. Sometimes she allowed a daughter to write the labels, but, permission given, would hover over the scribe, urging her not to forget this or that, until all were written.

'Tell Susan to keep the blinds *well* down on sunny days. No. You may forget. I'll tell her myself.' Or she would send out two daughters to the trunk shop for straps and then remember when they returned that Mary's needed a new linen cover, upon which all three would sally out once more after waiting in the hall for twenty minutes while Mrs. Scrimgeour put on bonnet, mantle and searched for fringed parasol and tasselled gloves. Sometimes she would invite suggestions. Should she wear the light crash shawl in the train or the paisley, which, though of heavier weight, wouldn't catch the smuts from the tunnels? 'Oh, the light one, Mamma. It's sure to be hot in the train and it can always go straight to the laundry.' And Mrs. Scrimgeour would usually make the journey in the paisley. On shopping excursions she would speed the girls with reminders that seemed to have no end. New cream braid for Aggie's cape. One-inch. Yes, Mamma, we settled that. The drawing-room door closed to be re-opened immediately. *Cream*, mind, lovie.' 'Yes, Mamma dear.' 'And better get the one-inch. A broader trimming might look a little loud.' The door closed again and the girls achieved the head of the staircase. Once more it opened. 'Georgie! And tell the florist man about the palms. To be sponged every week.' The door closed, and the girls were in the hall. 'Oh, and girls, girls! Georgie have you gone?' '*No*, Mamma.' '. . . and while you're at John Barker's try and get me some more of my green embroidery silk: a skein.'

Out in the street, Georgina would sometimes say '. . . of course she has a lot on her mind'. It was the nearest approach to criticism that they allowed themselves.

The final afternoons were reserved for a round of farewell calls: in Rosary Gardens, Sloane Street, even as far afield as the stately West End squares whose inhabitants were quite often paying for their position by being unable to afford a summer holiday at all, and who solved the problem of keeping up appearances by closing all shutters and curtains in the front of the house and living in the vast apartments at the back. The Scrimgeour girls, card-case in hand, would regret that Lady Prinsemere and the old Misses Lebalmondier were out of town, and leave cards which had been inscribed P.P.C. The round completed, they would debate the next move on the hot pavement, their feet aching in their slim, high-heeled boots. If Mamma were with them one could go and eat ices at Gunter's, if she were not, a cab home was the only alternative, failing tea in some private house. There were no tea-shops. The coffee-house and the eating-house were impossible for gentlewomen to be seen in and were, in any case, concentrated farther west, and in the City. They had, of course, no club. Omnibuses relegated them to the inside places, and the hansom — that wheeled version of the most proper conveyance of a ceremonial age, the sedan chair — was taboo.

Back at home in the cool hall they would retire to their rooms where the larger trunks would have been taken from box-room and basement by the maids, then down to the drawing-room, and tea, vigorously fanning flushed faces, retailing to Mrs. Scrimgeour the experiences of the afternoon. Since the emancipation of Aggie and Queenie was still regarded by her as recent, she dispersed them among the elder three when dispatching them upon their social occasions.

'We *just* caught the Effingtons, Mamma. They're off to-morrow.'

'Eva Hargreaves took me up to her bedroom and showed me her travelling hat. It's awfully stylish. From Paris.'

IV

In the morning-room Captain Scrimgeour did the man's part: ordered plumber and sweep to clean drains and chimneys, wrote cheques, settled the gas-bill, ordered the winter's coal and the outside porter and cabs, scanned the wine-lists for replenishments of the cellar, key in hand checked what bottles remained in their wire cages, and wrote a cheque to cover holiday expenses, the girls' and his wife's allowances plus the board wages for the first week. It was Gertrude who had pointed out that a mass disbursement of the month's money to the servants led to givings of notice at the return of the family, to sudden departures without explanation. Clever of Gertie. He chuckled as he wrote.

On the day before the exodus he would take the silver in japanned boxes to the Bank, and returning, tip the constable, lounging top-hatted at the corner, to keep an eye on the house. He would also interview the foreman of any workmen who might have to be called in during the family absence.

On the morning itself he exacted a military punctuality from everyone but Mrs. Scrimgeour. Her family had long taken it for granted that she could never keep that eye on the clock which they did themselves. It became almost a symbol of her importance, the retarded entrance of the leading lady. As determined as was the Captain himself about punctuality in all household matters the rest of the year, the annual holiday degenerated, with her, into an orgy of last-minute rushes back, potterings round her bedroom, callings upon this maid or that, while in a patient line her daughters waited in the hall, gloved, veiled and ready, and the Captain almost fumed, watch in hand, upon the steps. At his wife's belated appearance he would permit himself to say '*There* you are', though chivalrously balking at the 'at last', and Mrs. Scrimgeour would respond 'I *think* we're all ready now. We must make haste. Come along, girls.' Then began a total redistribution of hand luggage. The girls had grown to expect it. They themselves preferred to 'travel light' and this reduced the articles that must be carried to a minimum. This was their mother's opportunity.

'You haven't much to carry, dear, you might take my work-bag, and Georgie can easily manage the parasols.'

The cabs were drawn up, trunks piled on the roof; then from the basement filed the staff to speed the family. Cook led, bringing more baskets bulging with luncheon. The farewells were said, the servants grouped and decorously waving in response to the friendly signals of the young ladies, while Tom grinned from the area. The outside porter was tipped and stood back, horses were touched up and the cabs turned the corner.

Back in the kitchen the cook went round the larder eating what she fancied. For almost a week feeding was sumptuous, off immense joints that had only appeared once in the dining-room; later, the depletion of the staple groceries would set in.

The drawing-room, left unsheeted for days, would be full of the servants' friends; for days, long after ten o'clock, the lights burnt all over the house, the piano was strummed by stiff red fingers, and at any hour Susan and Nellie might be found in the family bedrooms tilting scent over cotton handkerchiefs, trying on abandoned hats and trinkets, sometimes pilfering them.

Lotty mistrusted it. In spite of everything she had a natural aptitude for honesty.

v

Mrs. Scrimgeour's spiritual holiday set in from the moment she entered the cab to the day she re-entered her own front door. Abroad, she relapsed into a festival of dependence upon her husband, an attitude subscribed to in their degrees by her daughters. Nuns without final vows, they looked to the man of the party for everything,

creating him from being the giver of messages to becoming
the runner thereof. Milch-cow at all times, he became
travelling courier, ladies' maid, potential policeman, St.
George, amateur porter and Santa Claus. His to see that
his women were magazined, seated, protected from
draught or sun or smut, from jostling strangers, unfilled
purses, misunderstanding, loss of way or luggage and
inconsideration from everyone.

Quite often his actual station labours were lightened
by Captain Grahame and a trickle of other men friends
of the house who were paying Georgina and Arabella
attention, and circular posies in pinked paper would be
handed in at the window, one for each of the ladies,
and Mrs. Scrimgeour meticulously remembered.

'London will be a perfect desert for the next month,
Miss Georgina.'

'Oh — I know better than to believe that with *you*,
Captain!'

'Fact, I assure you. Won't it, Brailsford?'

'Yaas, yaas rather.'

'Now you two, try and be good while I'm not here to
keep an eye on you. I believe you're glad we're off.
There's a naughty look in his eye, isn't there, Father?'

'By Jove, I swear there ain't!'

Mary, revelling in her flowers, sat in her place. Why
did Georgina talk to the men as though they were babies?
Yet she did it very prettily, a thing beyond oneself. One
was too reasonable to be able to sound spontaneous over
that sort of thing ... better leave it alone. A little
saddened by an indifference to herself she guessed to be
symptomatic, sincerely deprecatory of the obvious nonsense, quietly contemptuous of mentalities which preferred tinkling badinage to exploration of a finer mind,
she sat there.

Aggie and Queenie, a little out of hand with the general atmosphere of attention and novelty, bolder than Mary, lacking the practice of the other two, were behaving shockingly.

'Cap-tain!'

'Hullo?'

'Are you going to drown your sorrows to-night?'

'*Aggie!*' Mrs. Scrimgeour was frowning, signalling.

'Ha, ha! You bet I am.'

'Are you going to get really tipsy and come home with the milk?'

'*S'sh!*'

The men were amused. 'I shouldn't be at all surprised, Madam.'

'I say, *what* fun!'

Queenie here joined in. 'Perhaps they'll cashier you — '

'Queenie, Queenie! Not so *loud*.' But Mrs. Scrimgeour became unexpectedly indulgent. She saw that the men were 'fetched' and instantly jettisoned her own convictions about bad form.

'Then I shan't be able to lay my heart at your feet, y'know.'

'Why not? We might take to the bottle together.'

The men exploded, but it was Mrs. Scrimgeour's last straw. Jokes of that kind from a young girl were going altogether too far, and she rather thought that, already, there was a different quality in the laughter of the men, of their eyes when they looked at Queenie . . . speculative . . . A girl's reputation was a thought more fragile than tissue paper at the best of times, and the mischief would not end at the men addressed, but get round and spread.

'Better come in and sit down, dear. The train will start

at *any moment*.' Queenie, satisfied and pink with laughter, obeyed. Mrs. Scrimgeour at the window remarked: 'You mustn't mind her nonsense. My girls are rather overdone after rushing about in town, you know.' The men civilly accepted the implication of the strains of an exhausting season. Queenie nudged Aggie with her boot and Aggie shrugged, eyes to heaven. Their mother knew, perforce, that in point of time they were all grown up, but seldom came anywhere near realizing the fact. It probably put men off . . . not that Aggie and Queenie minded. The army set rather bored them. They'd hook different fish when they felt like it.

CHAPTER VII

I

THE girls were usually glad when autumn stole on and they could return to South Kensington. Holidays were a pleasant change and excellent for the complexion, but unless they went back to a resort the following year, or to Cheltenham, or Hythe (near Shorncliffe) novelty wore off soon, and 'the time' as Arabella said 'depended terribly upon whom you knew, or father met at the local Conservative Club and could bring back to the rooms'. For not all the seaside places had libraries and assembly-rooms, where you met other families for tea and cards and dancing three times a week. Bath was impossible in the summer. A pity.

Sometimes when, five abreast, the girls swept along the esplanade they admitted ennui in the form of 'The evenings are getter much cooler. It's about time we went, the place is emptying'. Also, at home, there were things to do between those hours when callers or diners could arrive; Mary helping with the house-books, Arabella writing the menu cards, Georgina arranging flowers. If the three seniors also wondered what occupation Aggie and Queenie could find once these plums had been allotted elsewhere they loyally said nothing. Aggie perhaps might go in for reading, like Mary . . . Queenie would probably develop a hobby or a talent. A talent would be interesting. Arabella was a beautiful embroiderer but that wasn't much use, except in a pause in conversation, when you could point to what she had made. Georgina sang a little but preferred parties to practice.

Gertie had painted, on and off, until her engagement, when she had dropped it. Flower-pieces in water-colour, and tambourines for the wall.

With the approach of winter there would be the round of parties, and the delightful to-do of Christmas preparations would tide them all over for weeks.

II

The cabs turned into Brecknock Gardens, the runner stood sweating, the staff waiting in the hall. The outside porter leant on the railings waiting to heave trunks upstairs.

Friends had sent chrysanthemums: the brass tray was sprinkled with visiting cards, receipted bills were stacked on the hat-stand, mitigated by a few unmistakable notes of invitation. The canaries seemed well, the palms honestly sponged, the winter covers in the drawing-room 'had really come out again wonderfully well', a lifeless order hung over the bedrooms.

In the hall, Georgina and Arabella searched the correspondence for letters bearing the crest of the Naval and Military Club upon their flap. Warmer gowns reeking of sandalwood were assumed with a feeling of revitalization, and the family straggled down to tea at the sounding of the gong.

III

' — there's still half a cassroll left of the salmy of pheasant, M'm.' And soon after that, cook would leave for the basement, and her mistress proceed upstairs to

87

the visit to the nursery and the session with the girls in the drawing-room.

But cook wasn't leaving. She was, to the domestically-sensitive nerve-centres of Mrs. Scrimgeour, lingering.

'Well, is there anything else?'

Cook hesitated and plunged. 'It's about Lotty, M'm. Well, I don't hardly know what to think, but what I think I think I think Nurse thinks too.'

Creeping dismay invaded Mrs. Scrimgeour. House-wise, she guessed. In these cases it was either petty theft or — that. There had been a few experiences among the staffs of her own friends . . . But she remained mutely interrogative for the look of the thing. Cook sensed her employer's comprehension. 'It's that Tom, M'm. Mus' be.'

'But — this is incredible!'

It wasn't, and they both knew it. Cook looked chaste and respectfully pleased. 'Well, I didn't speak in the *summer*, M'm . . . not being altogether sure, like . . . but reely . . .' She sank her voice. 'The girl's bin *sick*, las' week before you came 'ome. I said to Susan, I said, "Whatever's upset Lotty?" I said, and there she was, retch, retch, retch — '

Mrs. Scrimgeour looked offended. It displeased her that presumptive virgins trespassed upon alien ground. Her voice to the woman who was her senior by five or six years was taut. 'I suppose I must see the girl.'

'Yes'm.' Cook departed in a glow of sadism, kind-heartedness, indignation, and pleasurable anticipation.

Mrs. Scrimgeour staring at the small figure — still decent — which replaced cook was slightly exasperated at her own failure in observation. It would look bad to the servants.

'What's all this, Lotty?'

'I — expect I'm in trouble, M'm.' The thin, immature voice was explicit. She wasn't, evidently, going to deny the miserable business which saved a lot of bother and difficulty. A regiment of admirable questions thronged Mrs. Scrimgeour's mind. The *embarrass de richesse* choked her and she heard herself saying something almost feeble. 'How did it happen?' Lotty's face crimsoned. In the overwhelming nature of the interview, the unreality of the entire morning, the sense of queerness that even one's regular jobs couldn't down, helped out by the girls in the kitchen who'd given up looking as though nothing was the matter, the feeling of finality, departure and heaven-knew-what to come, the question confused her and she thought that the mistress really wanted details . . . but she must *know*! The muddled silence passed for shame, with Mrs. Scrimgeour. Her voice, to Lotty, was an untold relief. 'What made you do it, Lotty?' asked the mother of nine.

Lotty knew thoroughly what was meant. Lotty wouldn't and couldn't plead that she didn't know what she was doing. She did. How otherwise? — living in two bedrooms with Dad and Mum. Three of the family had been conceived in public, like. She could, half honestly, admit she hadn't wanted it for herself . . . she hadn't liked it when she got it, even. Neither had Tom. They'd been scared, after, and Tom had come over all of a tremor and she had hated both of them. Everything had been spoilt, since: no more fun filling the lamps and giving a hand with the plate and knives . . . She couldn't even plead a bad sleeping-place. Hers, upstairs in the night nursery, was better than Tom's, come to that, and heaven after her own home. And she was old enough to know better. Old, she was sixteen on the night it happened, and Tom had prigged a bottle of Guinness and a bit of cold meat and pudding from the larder for a midnight beanfeast in the pantry. The beer? That wouldn't wash. She was no stranger to beer, from seven years old had filched nips from Dad's pot when he sent her out at night to the public. Sixteen ... and for years before that Mum had said to this sister or the other, 'You don't want to take too many funny looks from fellows or you'll find yourself in Queer Street'. And the fellow (fancy!) was Tom after all, Tom the pal, the playmate, who told you of the latest murder and lent you penny bloods, and did breakdowns you tried to imitate, and couldn't for laughing. They hadn't even meant to do wrong. Because it *was* wrong. Then, how?

They'd got dancing and fooling, like, and he'd missed his balance and fallen over the camp bed and pulled her with him. It was nastiness, that's what it was. They'd got nasty. Both of 'em. And it was that which'd spoilt everything. The next morning had been vile, and Tom had been crying his poor eyes out. They'd felt like a couple of strangers. She and *Tom*! And Lotty herself hadn't slept a wink for expecting the baby. Any second of that endless night the thing might've happened ... safe one minute, in Queer Street the next. It had kept one on the toss and turn, afraid to lie still because of an idea that moving all the time might prevent a baby. But you couldn't tell all that to a lady.

'Well, at least I'm glad to see that you're ashamed, Lotty. 'You know you have done a very bad and wrong thing.' Mrs. Scrimgeour was getting into her stride. 'And not only that, but don't you see, didn't you realize beforehand, that it is *wicked* to have a child you can't support?'

IV

The girl must go, of course; Tom, if the Captain approved, could remain. These things were nearly always the girl's fault. A man — let alone a boy of seventeen — doesn't do that kind of thing unless the girl has shown him unmistakably that she is willing. The risk alone was hers, and that argued, in all these cases, that she had premeditated the affair, which betrayed depravity. And at sixteen! You didn't court great danger without a very strong motive, and the only possible motive with the unmarried was — nastiness. The lower classes had no self control to speak of at the best of times, panicking at trifles, screaming with mirthless laughter at nothing, over-eating profusely and then getting bilious.

Mrs. Scrimgeour was a kind woman and meant very well. It discomfited her to send the girl packing and, inevitably, without a character. She had told Lotty that she must refer the matter to the master, and honestly wondered why that remark had been received with such emotion — the first Lotty had shown. Lotty herself could hardly have explained it except on the grounds that her modesty would thereby be taken from her. It wasn't nice to have gentlemen hear about you, when you'd done that sort of thing.

The Captain had listened to his wife and pulled his moustache and tutted unhappily, leaving, in the upshot, everything to her. It was all that was necessary. The head of the house had 'heard', had been officially consulted. But Mrs. Scrimgeour told her daughters that Lotty had done something wrong and was to go at once, adding, 'Don't talk to her *at all* between this and then'.

The girls reacted to the maternal veto in their various

ways; Georgina and Arabella shrugging and obeying, Mary saddened, guessing, demurring and acquiescing by a hair's breadth, Agatha and Queenie all tiresome protest and question. It was they who flouted the order, but out of sheer forgetfulness. Lotty, not knowing it, was humble with gratitude. It did not so much as occur to her that women of their age should not know all about that side of life. Why, Miss Aggie must be rising nineteen.

The Home for Fallen Women was not so much chosen by Mrs. Scrimgeour for her nurserymaid as fruit of a sub-consciously registered memory of an address mentioned to herself by old Lady Prinsemere, whose vegetable maid, overcome by the honour, had erred with the second foot-man. The Home, in a suburb of London, took in the un-wanted children as well as their mothers. It was a religiously run house in which the inmates were never left in doubt for long together as to their having offended a jealous God. Of whom God was able to be jealous in that place was, perhaps fortunately, never queried. The young women, Lady Prinsemere believed, were well but strictly supervised; the house was, she had seen in the brochure, detached, which was all to the good, and stood back from the road in its own grounds, which was better. What the brochure failed, humanely, to mention was that half the uniform'd inmates of a past but no future were what was known as 'daughters of joy'.

They had quite a lot to tell Lotty, the new kid. You couldn't fail to hear it, in the dormitory. And in apple and orange crates at the foot of each iron bedstead slept and wailed those females who, seventeen years later, would be the feature of the Empire Promenade, Leicester Square.

CHAPTER VIII

I

GRACE and Charlie leant out of the nursery window and watched for the arrival of the new governess. Nana's back was turned, as she called a temporary absence, or it would never have been allowed.

Charlie, at ten years old, had been out of his leg irons for three years, but was still anxiously considered by the Captain to be too delicate for the rough and tumble of school. The governess, Miss Banks, would tide him over until he could leave home, and she could stay on for Gracie — say about another five years. A governess would, Captain Scrimgeour had reckoned, come considerably cheaper than the finishing schools the others had had, and one must begin to look to the money-bags now that there was the boy's future to consider. . . .

Despite the six-year Calvary of the irons, the birth of a son had done for life much of what the Captain had hoped. The house, he thought, was transformed, quickened, rendered significant. Even in those early years there was much he could do, and if physical prowess must be retarded one had already laid mental foundations. The little chap must see others of his age. Pity Gertie's brat was two years older, two years was a bit of a gulf at that age. And poor Gertie's other two were both girls, and Arabella's and Georgie's would be far too young. Meanwhile, the irons had given him Charlie for just those few years longer.

II

The children, bunched together, drank in the street scene; the steep dark-red houses picked out with edgy

93

cream stone, people slowly going by — dots at that height. There was a yellowish look in the sky that they hoped portended a fog: London Special, father called it. When there was a fog, the house became a warm, safe fortress and Nana the last officer who hadn't been shot down, keeping it, and everybody who passed by was an enemy who couldn't get in, and lights were turned on at unnatural hours; and the whole house was kind and drawn together by a queer sense of almost-danger and emergency. The Guards need powder and by God! they shall have it! And the powder arrived, a fat pot of tea and a cake from the drawing-room for Charlie, warming signs that, bravely, the fort was being held elsewhere, too. Yet over father's principal present on every occasion, boxes of soldiers — and there were so many regiments to work through — ! Charlie cast a jaded eye. Tin soldiers, however splendid and elaborate, weren't, somehow, the same thing at all as holding the nursery against a London fog. Fog-days showed up the massed boxes of soldiers as just toys, like the whirling French pierrot who smiled and tinkled a tune under his pink and blue satin collar with bells on it that Auntie 'Bella had given Gracie on her birthday. Charles too had had his difficulties over the precise identity of those whom Grace used to call 'the ladies'. His own appearance at Arabella's wedding at St. Philip's, South Kensington, clad in a miniature edition of a cornet in his father's regiment, had done little to clear up the confusion. He had, Gracie said, missed Georgie's wedding altogether through being too delicate to come, a phrase culled from her mother. He hadn't cared. The Auntie 'Bella wedding was a big crowd, and feeling lost, and ladies bending over him and paying compliments right out loud. Always lots of ladies coming round him — even at home. The actual church episode had, as Arabella semi-humorously commented, really been far more her little brother's occasion than her own.

Always people . . . when the irons had come off his legs for good, they told him, there had been a family celebration and a dinner, and Charlie sent down to dessert two hours past his bedtime, and being made to drink a little glass of wine that tasted rotten and made you sleepy, and being told you must learn to carry your wine like a gentleman, and laughter, and father, red-faced and his eyes glittering, blowing his nose tremendously, like a trumpet sounding the charge, only not the same tune. One knew them all, had been taught them over and over by Father: Revally, Lights Out, Last Post. One knew them all.

Often the little boy was made to show off to visitors. 'Now then, Charlie, give us the Last Post,' and he would obey, without enthusiasm, as accurately as a parrot.

> Too — hoo?
> Too — hoo?
> Too — hoo-hoo-hoo!
> Too tittle-tottle too-too-too-too
> Too — hoo?
> Too-hoo . . .

Grace knew them all too and loved them with a deep, shy intensity. She sang them better than Charlie, clearer, with more vim, carried away by it; had learnt them sooner than he had, too, when listening to his drilling in them by the Captain, for her father had never brought them out for her, at Charlie's age. . . .

It had been one of the rare times he had shown impatience with Charlie and for days it had made Charlie so nervous that he went wrong on the notes and Grace had prompted, clearly, accurately giving him a lead, and Father hadn't been pleased about that, either.

'No, no! He must learn. Now, boy.'

Once, before visitors, Grace had been carried out of caution and manners, and begged 'Let me do the Revally, Father!' And nobody had taken it up, or even seemed to hear her. She accepted it, docile and wounded. It was the same over the toy soldiers. Grace had been found, deep in nursery-floor manœuvres, by Nana; by her side, Charlie, for once really interested in the straits and strategies she planned for them which had never occurred to himself, had forgotten the doll on his paternal arm. Dolls were good: they were people, and to the nursery pool Charlie contributed aspects of doll-life which had never occurred to Grace, whose education had stayed at the injunction to cuddle, dress and undress the things. Charlie made characters of them, and created the sheep and the goats, the just and the unjust doll. Fearsome wounds, overdressed parties which hung fire when the refreshments (ordered by Lady de la Pumfrey) went to the wrong address, and the Countess of Crimea had farcy-buds in the middle of the levee. Farcy-buds, beginning at an overheard remark to Captain Grahame by their father, started as being the trimming of an evening skirt, and for weeks the cream of the dolls wore nothing else, until Charlie turned them into a disorder, not fatal, but socially embarrassing. And then Nana had come in, stared, her face red with indignation as she twitched the doll out of Charlie's arms.

'Well, that's a nice thing, Charlie. Playing with a doll like a little girl. Whatever are you thinking of? I've half a mind to tell the Captain. As for you, Gracie, big girl like you taking your little brother's soldiers from him, you'll stand in the corner for that.' And the doll was dumped into Grace's arms. Thus the nurse encouraged recruiting for the Regular Army, and for maternity.

There was, of course, another occasion — that is, the one which was discovered, for Charlie and Grace, once over the non-comprehended feeling of shame with which Nana had successfully imbued them, continued to pool their amusements. This time (Grace never forgot it) it was the Captain himself who caught them red-handed, on one of his many and unheralded visits to the nursery, always more frequent since the birth of his son. To Grace, watching, her father seemed to pale. For herself he had little; he was thinking, if he thought of his youngest daughter at all, that the spectacle of a girl playing with soldiers was only another conventional attempt at imitation of the male, male knowledge which stopped short at complacence, recking nothing of a possible flaw in the social system perceived by feminine nature. Charles with dolls was another thing altogether. To Grace's dismay Charlie was marched downstairs to the morning-room. Man to man the Captain tackled him.

Had Charles snatched the doll from Gracie?

Not snatched, taken it.

Why?

He wanted to play with it (here followed an unintelligible sentence about a Lady de la Pumfrey which the Captain waved aside).

Why, then?

Because he *liked* dolls.

Liked *dolls*? The Captain grew purple. It was then that Charlie began to lose his head.

He had evidently made the wrong answer ... he was confusedly aware that his father expected something else; sociably, politely, the boy struggled to supply the man.

G

'Gracie didn't mind a bit, sir. She mostly likes playing soldiers best.'

'What?'

Charlie faltered and gave it up, stood there fatalistically waiting for whatever might happen. It chanced to be a voice he didn't recognize coming from a familiar face, and for the first time tears of fear stood in his eyes.

'And — you — mean — to — stand — there — sir — and tell — me that a boy, *my son*, prefers dolls, *dolls* to manly games?'

So that was the trouble? Better propitiate as soon as possible. Bad luck one had told Father the truth at the start, worse luck for oneself, because one hadn't remembered to say with equal truth that one quite liked soldiers, when Gracie was in command. But probably that wouldn't have been the right thing, either.

'It's — it's all right, sir. I don't *really* play with the dolls.' The lie was hasty improvisation and sounded rotten, even as good lies were. The Captain recognized the fact, and beat his son for the first time.

Probably from that day on, the boy — for surely grown-ups were always right however confusing? — set himself gamely to becoming all those people (and they were many) that his world seemed to expect. If he had ever had any illusions as to the existence of one, Charles Scrimgeour, his error was now made plain.

Roughly, there were some six Charleses that the family required. Charles the sturdy, fighting Scrimgeour, who must protect women always while not necessarily respecting them, be polite to girls always and at the same time despise them; Charles the child king of the nursery licensed to go pretty far in defiance, yet always liable to the ultimate victories of Nana; Charles the son from whom large, muscular things were to be expected; Charles the baby who, even at eight years old, mustn't indulge in the manly escape from the lap, if it were Mother's, and who must be at all times prepared for the swooping embraces, the suffocating kisses, of Mother; Charlie the star attraction of strangers, before whom the showing off that Nana everlastingly cautioned one against ceased, somehow, to be showing off and became instant obedience, and the semi-errand boy Charlie who obeyed Aggie and Queenie when he felt like it, a lowly person who, late king of nursery and *jongleur* of drawing-room, became suddenly 'a spoilt little beast' who could be hustled and even slapped.

Gradually, there were other Charleses to become: with the installation of the governess developed a tiresome and inky person, apologetic to Miss Banks for her elaborate patience; school, and an individual who was Hi, Scrim! a lowlier wretch than ever the roughly affectionate impulses of Aggie and Queenie could remotely imagine. Sandhurst: producing for one's nervous inspection an unknown youth among unknown youths, one Scrimgeour, the unfailing butt and jape for what seemed an eternity and was one term; then, recognizing this Scrimgeour, accepting the fellow willy-nilly, and the life and the codes and the horseplay, the polo and the debts.

It was a prolonged strain upon Charles that nobody in that house, from the jubilant, optimistic Captain downwards, recognized or allowed for. The child, knowing it, concealed and fought it. Surrounded by thronging women, he strove to win through to the standards of his father, over-taxing his ill-supplied reserves of physical strength in order to pass muster, suppressing taste and instinct, fatigue and boredom, that the shame of the irons be buried, scrapping in time (it took the longest) his natural feelings for Grace,

CHRISTMAS in South Kensington was to everybody but the servants an unacknowledged relief. It provided for the Captain an outlet for generosity and that expansiveness which measured joy in terms of the weight of the turkey and sirloin, hospitality in slight over-eating, and expressed the mentality of Victorian England by its list towards excess. It gave Mrs. Scrimgeour a legitimate outlet for sentiment and for that form of moral conscription known as 'drawing all the family together under one roof'. To Grace and Charlie it represented a measure of freedom from nurse and governess, to the governess a chance to write letters home plus the reasonable expectation of useful Scrimgeour gifts, which otherwise would have to 'come out of' her forty pounds a year salary. To Agatha and Queenie it meant parties and the possible turning-point of life, and to Mary definite jobs of work, all futile and leading to nothing save the blankness of another January, but employment of its kind. The post of mother's right hand was traditionally held by the eldest daughter at home, in any case. . . .

At Christmas it was no sinecure with reference to Mrs. Scrimgeour, whose custom it was to create all round her an atmosphere of explosive activity while the real work was done by others. You tied her parcels while she, keeping up appearances, made little effort-noises at your side; or she waited until you had begun to address envelopes before suggesting that you should address envelopes. When the jobs were all done, she would lovingly squeeze Mary's arm and say 'You shan't do another *thing*'. Yet Mary would be sorry when the jobs were over. They drugged thought.

She was over thirty.

II

Christmas in Brecknock Gardens.

The youngest eyes at the top of the house noted a van marked Cawthorne & Hutt stopping and delivering a book (that would doubtless be for Mary); a small red and cream van trotting up and disgorging a hamper for the Willis's opposite. Fortnum & Mason. The Willis's were very gay, Grace told her brother from the experience of her two-years' start of him; they always had a New Year dance and you could hear the music and see black figures against the blinds doing the lancers and polka. And at *that* house next to the corner there'd be a party we shall go to. Last year there'd been marionettes and a bran pie. Gracie would wear her new plaid velvet with the sash and cut-steel buttons. A converted lorry with a slip pasted over it printed V.R. would arrive at adventurous hours — there was a rumour it had once come at eleven o'clock at night.

'It's the tree,' translated Grace to Charlie, 'but we mustn't talk about it to Mamma because it's a surprise.' The tree was a yearly remembrance 'for the children' from the country estate of Lady Mell, a friend of Captain Scrimgeour's family. The children had never seen her, would have been subtly disillusioned if an actual encounter ever took place; the words as they stood were familiar and comfortable, interchangeable, like knife and fork or brush and comb.

Mell. Tree.

Other people, too, were not so much persons as things. Sister Gertie: a last-minute parcel sent round by a servant, the presents inside unmarked and a scribbled note to Mary, 'Up to my eyes with visitors and Xmas. *Do* distribute suitably!'

Toss-up. That was Sister Gertie. Might be treasure-trove but more often wasn't. Mamma: a dress for Grace, a drum or trumpet for Charlie — even on the tree a miniature drum rattling with tiny sweets, object coveted for years by Grace, fell to Charlie. Father: a money present, and once a rocking-horse for Charlie upon which 'you must give your sister rides'.

Christmas Eve, and a robust belief in Santa Claus, tempered by a sensible doubt as to the practicability of his method of arrival, for were not many of the Brecknock Gardens chimneys, including their own, twisted like barley-sugar, and fluted in imitation of those at Hampton Court?

Christmas dinner at one o'clock, beginning with soup and ending with crystallized knots and little fruits you drew off sticks with your teeth, and a big round box of Elvas plums studded with tinsel rosettes, attention from the wine merchant to Captain Scrimgeour, and competing with Sister Gertie's Albert, and pulling crackers with real Japanese vases in them or — oh triumph! — a slab of alicumpane. Then the moment when flatness fell and everyone seemed to go off somewhere else; the ladies — even Bertie — leaving in cabs or on foot into the unknown (it was Mary who said it was for Christmas teas with relatives, friends and in-laws), and the Captain, stretching and suppressing genial yawns, seeking the morning-room, and Mamma, Mary, Aggie and Queenie shutting themselves up into the drawing-room while

Gracie and Charlie were led upstairs, condemned to sleep — a life sentence of two hours — before the fun began again.

At tea-time, more people in the drawing-room (one could sometimes hear the knocker from the nursery), and more presents strewn about to look at, and tea with a monster cake made by Emma that you couldn't eat enough of, do what you might, and which two years running had made you sick. Then nursery again with Gracie, and another eternity mitigated by the morning toys, until eight o'clock when nail-scrubbing, face-washing, hair-brushing and tieing, buttoning and hooking set in. And another wait of over an hour. The children had no late dinner, but the logic of the period allowed them to be kept up for several hours past their normal bedtime in order to come down to eat the indigestibles of dessert.

This year, Miss Banks had had, with them, to undergo the process of absorption. The season made it easier, crushed her willy-nilly into the family pattern. . . .

She spent all permitted hours that would not be robbing her employer of her time in her bedroom, the smallest in the house, which, they said, had been Miss Georgina's. For that Christmas Miss Banks was, to Grace and Charles, a guest, a person you housed and fed.

Boxing Day brought Drury Lane, and a fleet of cabs to the door full of sisters, brothers-in-law and Bertie. They waited for the Captain and Mrs. Scrimgeour and the rest of the Brecknock Gardens family to gather in the hall, Grace and Charles cumbered in shawls against the night air. When Mrs. Scrimgeour slowly descended the stairs the procession started. At the theatre the stage box was sometimes taken; later, it was found inadequate and the whole of the third row of stalls was reserved.

Back in South Kensington, the governess was writing

letters home, and of thanks for gifts received, Nana would be stumping round the nursery and brewing hot drinks for the children. In the kitchen the servants helped themselves to the family store of oranges and mixed nuts, took surreptitious cuts at the family turkey and ham when their own goose gave out and distributed bottled beer to sundry relatives who popped down the area steps, while Emma cut sandwiches for the policeman and the footman from Number Sixteen.

III

With the New Year parties past, stillness fell upon Brecknock Gardens; even the streets and the weather were temperate of episode and effect.

Mary, reading by the spare-room window, caught herself listening for something to happen until her eye was once more in harmony with the printed word. It was too early by over an hour for the duty of tea-pouring: the household books would not be made up for another week. From the window, the intermittent glances out and down that she cast coincided with the protrusion of a thin wrist and a ringless hand which finically placed a nail-brush upon the ledge of the room below. Miss Banks.

On impulse, Mary shut her book and moved to the door. She would pay the governess a visit. Mary had, she supposed, hardly exchanged with her more than the bare civilities which the chances of the staircase and the table called forth in the seven weeks since the other's arrival. Miss Banks lunched and breakfasted with the family, which was, from Mary's observation of the routine prevailing in the homes of her married contemporaries, unusual. It had to be. Nana had objected, would rule the

nursery table while Grace ate upstairs and until Charlie
was old enough to join the family meals. Over the
question of the governess sharing the family late dinner
the Captain had put his foot down; the last meal, while
the most formal of the day, was yet the function dedicated
to the domestic circle alone: Mrs. Scrimgeour instantly
agreed, and Miss Banks was served with a supper tray in
her bedroom.

Half kind, half curious, Mary tapped at her door. You
never quite knew with these people . . . the children really
knew more about her than did their elder sister; they had,
Gracie said, seen her drive up in a cab. 'She had an old
trunk and a wicker basket and a funny hat.' Where she
had driven up from nobody seemed to know. It struck
Mary for the first time. Coolly, dispassionately, she blamed
herself for some vague lacking in duty, social, humane or
imaginative. Her sudden conversion to Miss Banks even
made her believe that behind the closed door was the
kindred spirit, the allusive discussion, the mute inglorious
Milton of the house. Mary's discovery. One of whom in
the years ahead she would cry: 'And I wasted seven weeks
of her!' . . . that, or the newcomer would be defensive,
even a little offended, at amateur intrusion, while she,
professional, read abstrusely, or secretly scribbled a book
that would live through the ages.

Miss Banks opened the door, said 'Oh — ' and stood
aside. Miss Scrimgeour said 'May I just come in for a
little chat?'

'The children are having their nap, Miss Scrimgeour — '
Miss Banks was explaining her own leisure, forestalling a
possible criticism, however light.

It was the tone of the whole interview. It was Mary who
led the creaking conversation, instigating topics while
the governess agreed and deferred. Mary, profoundly

disappointed, returned after twenty minutes to the spare room and her book. Of course, now one had really seen the governess, one realized that she wasn't a woman at all, but a girl of barely twenty. It was that manner, the way she had made the least of what good points she had and the way she dressed, which had misled. But she seemed to be a lady. On the mantelpiece there had been the credentials of family photographs: a moustached barrister, a plain young man in naval officer's uniform, an unmistakable mother in Court dress with an ostrich fan ... even Mamma had never been presented. And — even now Mary could not quite abandon hope — there were books strewn on the table. Miss Banks had evidently been deep in study.

I V

There were, and she had. Quite simply, Miss Banks had been privily trying to keep abreast with Grace and Charles and to learn something of the lesson she herself had set for to-morrow morning. Luckily — oh luckily! — the Scrimgeour children weren't specially intelligent or prone to quick-fire question which had already resulted in one's dismissal from one post. They, fortunately also, did not appear to take any interest to speak of in their lessons. Not that the temptation to make learning uninteresting and so safe would have, in any case, been an acute one to Florence Banks, who lacked not only the ability to englamour any subject, but regarded the position of mentor to the young in terms of food and shelter, clothes, and a shifting of herself for indeterminate periods as burden and problem to her own family. Yet sometimes, half sincerely, she thanked her gods that she had not married, when made increasingly aware of her own indifference to children, her inability to control all but the already tractable. And the fates had blessed her exceedingly in withholding the gift of imagination which, if it rendered the days colourless, at least saved her from that dark night of the soul which is Terror of The Future.

Thus when Miss Scrimgeour had left her she sought no looking-glass to picture what impression she might have made on the daughter of the house. She knew it all too well, from six alien mirrors in other bedrooms dotted over the provinces . . . fine, butter-coloured hair that only a net could save from straggly ends, slightly weak blue eyes, a prettyish mouth that life had offered no chance to be kissed.

Her story, such as it was, was just one of the dozen-odd permutations of the theme of parental incompetence. Her father, the Canon and Christian gentleman, letting charity outrun discretion, hoping all things, thinking no evil, believing all good, heading trustfully towards financial crisis that, perhaps, the sinner could have foreseen and averted, admitting too late to wife and daughter of grave difficulties over which he prayed most earnestly . . . luckily he would say, humble before them, the dear lads are pro-vided for; William in the Law, Arnold in the Navy. It had cost a bit, but was money well spent, well spent.

It had coincided with the period in her life when normally Florence would have 'come out' and even, perhaps, had a little fling in Town; deprived of that, there was the possibility of marriage with the first curate at St. Anselm's. Miss Banks, weighing a proposal which so far had not actually eventuated but was, as an emotion, more in the debt of honour class not recoverable by law, lost him to a girl friend whose hair curled naturally and needed no net. Inevitably, Florence saw it herself, the next and only step was to teach the children of gentlefolk. The absence of a choice of employment for women which might have some reference to ability and taste and inclination was recompensed by the retention, publicly acknowledged, of one's own caste in such an occupation. 'I never expected to teach' she would sometimes say to the scanning mothers and was too obtuse to wonder why the remark was received with chill. For the same reason she mentally waved aside a remembered remark of Miss Scrimgeour's: 'You know, I envy you, Miss Banks. It must be wonderful to be making the fullest use of your time.' Miss Banks, eyeing the good, solid afternoon silk of the speaker, had said nothing at all.

v

It was two days later that, between the depositing of the bath-can by Susan and the sounding by Nellie of the breakfast gong, the idea had come to Mary, simple, blinding, revelatory.

She would teach Gracie and Charlie herself.

The idea had evidently been working in her since the previous day when, faithfully pursuing Miss Banks lest she had unfairly misjudged her, Mary had actually cut through routine and instead of joining Aggie and Queenie in the drawing-room after breakfast, proceeded up the next flights to the nursery. What she had heard there had but served to stoke her private fires. It meant the end of a possible friendship, but had not that been foreshadowed already during the talk in Miss Banks's room? In any case the governess would no doubt find another place quite easily . . . one's own needs and the needs of the children, if it came to that, would spur one on to utilization of whatever influence one might prove to have with Mamma.

This morning Mary seethed through prayers and breakfast in an impatience new to herself; even the sheer discussion with Mamma would vitalize the day ... and Father must be there too. Mamma would decide nothing without him, nor he give formal assent without her. In the hall she stopped his progress to the morning-room.

'Father, could I speak to you?'

'At your service, my dear. Nothing the matter, I hope? Aha! it's the dress allowance, eh? Some killing bonnet you're going to die without having, what?'

She smiled with gentlest sarcasm. 'My bonnets never "killed", Father, they barely wounded. And we don't wear them any longer, you know. It's hats and toques now.'

'Eh? Ah ... well, if it won't take long, my dear — '

She answered conscientiously 'I think it needn't', and put her head round the dining-room door. Luck held, and she stopped by a split second the ringing of the bell by her mother which would bring cook from her basement. Mrs. Scrimgeour looked mildly harassed; with her any departure from the sequence of the day's programme spelt some upset.

'Mamma, I wanted to speak to you and Father.'

'Must it be now, dear?' Mary's need overrode her instant acceptance of the implied rebuke and she came right into the room.

'It's about Miss Banks. I — '

But Mrs. Scrimgeour, without waiting to hear what the subject might be, was already wasting the time which she herself had previously implied was precious in speculation as to the nature of Mary's communication.

'If she objects to the tray in her room, I don't see *what* we can do, with Nana feeling as she does.' It was at this point that her husband came in and she went off on another tack. 'You're looking for *The Times*, dear. But it went into the morning-room with you.'

'No, my dear . . .'

'I saw you take it.'

Her husband became the Captain. 'Tut, Charlotte, sit down, Mary. Now!' Mrs. Scrimgeour subsided, docile and relieved.

'Well, it's just this, Father. I — I want to teach Charlie and Gracie myself.'

'What?' Mrs. Scrimgeour said patiently. 'But we've got Miss *Banks* for that, Mary.'

'I know, I know! and she's no good, Mamma—oh, I've *seen* it. Indeed I have!'

'My *dear* girl!'

'Father, she's incompetent! She doesn't know any-thing — '

'S'sh . . . s'sh!'

'She's a *governess*, my dear . . .'

Mary actually interrupted the maternal-obvious. 'At *that* age! What should she know? Why, I didn't, myself — '

'She is quite twenty, my dear, I should judge. We don't look for a bluestocking for the nursery, you know.' Her parents laughed pleasantly.

'No, no, of course, but she doesn't *care*, Father — '

Mrs. Scrimgeour galvanized at once, thinking in terms of material well-being. 'You're not suggesting that she is *unkind* to the children?'

'Oh, she doesn't hit them . . .'

'T'tt . . .'

' — she *bores* them because she's bored herself. They aren't learning anything.'

'I think we're exaggerating, Mary my dear, and after all, Charlie will be off to school any day, now.'

'And Gracie? Doesn't she matter?'

The Captain smiled quite kindly. 'I can't imagine that any little girl is going to make a tragedy out of insufficient lessons.'

'It isn't the insufficiency of the lessons, Father, it's that they're dull and Miss Banks is just reading scraps out of the books. I can make them interesting, I know I can.'

'But why should you, dear? It's so unnecessary, with a governess in the house. If she had done something *wrong* perhaps we might consider your taking the little lessons until we found another woman.'

'Isn't it wrong, Mamma, to be dull and incompetent?'

'You mustn't argue with Mother, dear. Miss Banks knows her duties. It isn't her first post,' naïvely instructed Mrs. Scrimgeour. The Captain rounded off the interview, 'And we can't have you sacrificing your time, you know; while the old soldier has a penny he'll keep his girls from that sort of thing, what? Well . . . I'll be off, if that's all. I shall be home for luncheon, Charlotte.'

'Yes, dear, then we shall be just eight. Arabella and her husband are coming.'

It was hopeless. Out in the hall, Mary, lingering in thought, saw cook advance on the dining-room, heard her say: 'What about a nice saddle of mutting, M'm?' All the way up to the drawing-room Mary indulged in *esprits d'escalier*, arguments which could have been more telling, better expressed, a mien of greater determination — all those qualities which did not go to the make-up of Mary Scrimgeour. A display of authority which she had never had. . . .

CHAPTER X

I

SHE was in the drawing-room. Aggie was staring out of the window, Queenie working as if for a wager at a tapestry runner. She had all the time there was in which to complete the rather ugly thing and yet was driven on by something she could have put no name to. One year it had been transfers: delicate work that cockled and stuck and tore. You pressed it on to the flimsy material and then, with luck, tinted it 'by hand' and piped the edges with metallic paint. The bazaars and sales of work did not benefit much that year . . . and Mrs. Scrimgeour had veto'd the business on the grounds that it made a mess, which was true, and that the maids wouldn't like it. When some new form of handiwork was found that suited Queenie's strong, impatient fingers the finished product was sold at from half to three-quarters of the cost of the materials.

Mary said wearily, 'Don't tire your eyes out, they're the only eyes you've got'.

Queenie grunted, absorbed.

Mary drifted to the canaries. 'Arabella's coming to lunch, with Francis.'

Aggie turned from the window, a faint interest in her face. 'We're all going on to the Waifs and Strays bazaar.'

'Is that the charity that was started last year?'

'Yes.'

'Oh yes, I remember.' Mary sat down with a book. If she sat in the spare-room her mother would concernedly want to know where she was, and why; if she went to her bedroom the maid would still be doing it. It was traditionally too early for the morning walk.

After luncheon the Captain bore his son-in-law off to the club; prior to his departure Arabella had charmingly coaxed one pound from him to spend at the bazaar. Her parents smiled at the pretty gesture. Her husband gave her thirty shillings. They had only been married two years.

After the usual loitering in the hall for Mrs. Scrimgeour the feminine procession started, Arabella and her mother, Aggie and Queenie, Mary with Grace who was to peddle buttonholes.

'Why isn't father and Francis coming too, Mary?'

Mary was reasonably adequate over a question that had often idly presented itself to her, that system by which the almsgiving of the world is accomplished by the male by proxy, although his mere presence at the function would quicken the whole thing to animation, laughter and increased sales; while the funeral was invariably accomplished only by men, and their females were shut up in anonymous grief. It seemed an arbitrary allotment of activity. . . .

To Mrs. Scrimgeour the charitable appearances not only brought the family together but swept South Kensington friends for a couple of hours into a common sphere of activity. She was honestly glad to spend her husband's money and a portion of the allowance he made her . . . and those poor little children . . . public charges at that age, when a warm nursery. . . .

Her eyes fell on her own daughters, chatting, rustling about the hall; her thoughts flew to Gracie and Charlie, safe always with Nana and (of course) with Miss Banks, and, the four-piece amateur orchestra striking up a pretty air from some Italian opera, her pale eyes filled.

To Mary, these events were normal fixtures; you went

to them, your mind stimulated lest the kindred spirit
should lurk behind a muslin-draped stall, and in choosing
objects — own twin to Queenie's and made, Mary dare
swear, by a dozen of daughters of the house in a dozen
London drawing-rooms — you gradually forgot to expect
or even look for the kindred spirit. Back at home, you
remembered her with a little regret, but with no real surprise at disappointment. Mary had now had over twelve
years of bazaar-going.

Smart women fluttered round Grace in that eternal and
baffling state of enthusiasm and wonder with which the
co-operation of children is hailed. Shy but acquiescent,
no stranger to thronging ladies, Grace moved about the
hall while her mother signalled an embarrassing approval
or indicated moneyed prospects by much work with the
eyebrows. Agatha, having outrun her allowance already,
was spending ten shillings contributed by Mrs. Scrimgeour
together with a loving word of caution in respect of 'managing better', an injunction that her daughter, marking
time until the opening of the purse, hardly listened to.
You always got something. . . .

Un' bel di ve — dremo

'Ah, there's Mrs. Scrimgeour! She's always our prop
and stay.'

'Our stop and pray, you mean.' Laughter greeted the
old doctor's sally. He moved off, genially brushing aside
the clustering women.

Across the hall, Queenie, incredibly, recognized a man
her family knew. Resentfully, fatalistically she made her
way towards him. Men, somehow, never saw one in
crowds as one saw them. Pride got you nowhere, either,
so you were had both ways. 'Men like to do their own
hunting', Gertie had once remarked aloofly to Arabella

and Queenie. But if men didn't, after all, hunt? ... but Queenie would give fate and pride an honest chance. She compromised, lingered near Mr. West, looking animatedly in other directions if he seemed to be about to turn his head to her own. And he didn't see her.

She advanced on him. 'Hul*lo*, Mr. West!'

He looked faintly bewildered. 'Oh, how do you do? It's Miss ——' He had forgotten her name. And yet she had remembered his. She made her way back to family and safety. 'Sorry, Mamma. I was detained by Mr. West.' As she turned away, Queenie's eyes were suddenly, alarmingly, hot with tears; not her line, usually ... general, nameless exasperation at life, she supposed. One didn't even want Mr. West, though nobody would give one the credit for it. Yet it was enraging to be unable to annex even what you didn't want. Mr. West was plainish and rather a bore, his good points all negative, that he was presentable, a neat dresser and not old. Yet self-contempt-uously Queenie faced up to the fact that she would have been gratified to be seen making the rounds with him.

Thin, syrupy music and the smell of tea and hot scones.

'Can I tempt you, Miss Scrimgeour?'

'Hullo, Queenie.'

'*Queenie*, well, what a surprise!' Girl friends coming up to one; always girls and more girls. . . .

She bought half a pound of knobby home-made coco-nut ice in a sack of pink lampshade paper.

Back in Brecknock Gardens, Queenie for the first time thought steadily and in terms of reality.

I I I

No trifle is too minute to precipitate the mental crisis and the loss of a safety-pin can ultimately alienate families.

PART TWO

The episode of Mr. West of whom Queenie never thought, with whom she did not dream of reckoning when tallying her resources, had set her to staring, heedless of time, at the brass can swathed in its towel, reminder of the imminent dinner gong. Aggie — a mercy — had already changed, washed and left.

One was, incredibly, twenty-seven. In three years youth would be over and choice of any kind from life not only at an end, but no achievement would any longer be noteworthy; and, even granted achievement, it must for the same reason be first-rate. One had always been the member of the family who had asserted that she meant to 'have a career', even at school ... and there'd been a row about it and a tussle with Sybil Raikes, and the senior girls looking scornful and convicting one of bad form. One had come home for good nine years ago. Nine years. Then how had it happened? Even a proverb knew that time flies, but that was no real excuse, if one was honest. One had settled down into the routine of home and pleasure, told oneself that there was plenty of time 'later', and then later became now. One postulated a future of success, was a little scornful of the present, regarding it as a marking of time, so that one did not really enjoy it wholeheartedly. But the present *was* the future. If one was ever to choose, it must be now, now, now.

It frightened Queenie Scrimgeour. The time of illusion and childish things was past. One dreaded the pioneering business of selecting a life work as much as one longed for it. Oh, for a little more time to live that safe life that wasn't making one happy! Why, of all the sisters, should fate have picked oneself for unrest? Gertie, more a myth than a sister, whose life had seldom touched one's own, had fulfilled her destiny, and left. Georgie and Arabella had apparently got what they wanted. Nobody expected anything of married women ... even their looks could go without tacit public condolence because their life work was accomplished, and a full nursery was an eternal alibi against the empty engagement book. A family of your own, one saw, saved your face.

Aggie.

Always in love with the hopeless and unattainable person. She had now got down to an actor, Wilson Barrett, still, the obviously hopeless was better than the possible who didn't do what Mamma called 'come forward'. Queenie rather believed that Aggie had never had a proposal, and more than she had had, herself ... at least, that wasn't *really* true, for if one had really wanted anybody special, obviously one would have seen to it that something happened. One had been simply wanting fun, and there was all the rest of life in which to marry and settle down; still, the net result looked uncommonly like no actual offer. ....

One had usually got on with the men about the house, had had a lively sort of success with them unthinkable to, say, Mary ... dear Mary, to whom one was, now one faced things, far more attached than one had ever been to Arabella and certainly Gertie. But Mary had her books, enviable fastness that was rather fatal to your chances. What *fools* men were! And yet, it did tell in the drawing-room chaff and laughter and glances.

For the first time Queenie experienced a qualm. She was — how had it happened? — looking at herself in the swing-glass of the dressing-table. Not what, if not a Scrimgeour, one would have described as a pretty face, or a handsome one, or striking or telling, yet it must be all right because it was one's own ... nobody ever knew how one struck others.

Queenie gazed, striving to get a line on her own appearance and strike a balance between the intention of her

Creator as perceived by herself and His execution as stated in the mirror. One took after Mamma's side, the Cooper-Collis's. In common with most daughters. Queenie Scrimgeour, through living with her mother, could not see her at all, and would have been at a total loss to furnish a description which would be remotely intelligible of Mrs. Scrimgeour's type. It was one which pleased in early youth, penetrated the albums of English Beauty, with its oval face, round mouth and sloping shoulders, a face which wore badly and set into heaviness. The Cooper-Collis women at thirty were commonly lethargic and beginning to put on weight. Queenie's lean Scrimgeour body was to be spared that; she thanked her stars instead that fate had spared her the Scrimgeour nose that poor Mary had failed to escape; but it somehow didn't matter, for Mary. She had her books, and when you had your books it was subtly all of a piece that you should also have your nose. Queenie's self-scrutiny insensibly declined into a distribution of gratitude for blemishes unowned: that she had also escaped Gertie's height which was socially unpopular especially at dances, or Aggie's rather furry eyebrows and sallow skin which were like father's, Georgie's long waist and Arabella's straight hair. One's own at least was fuzzy. And if one was going to do things. . . .

What was there to do that wouldn't reflect on one's parents? Governessing she ruled out at once. It was a thing she would not only do badly, but dislike into the bargain. One would hate to look like Miss Banks . . . also it was a tame occupation, your position neither fish, flesh nor fowl. It was family life over again minus its opportunities and distractions. A headmistress-ship would be another matter, but one had left it all until too late. And there wasn't even any honest excuse for that, either.

Through Queenie's brain flashed a hitherto forgotten memory: of herself, Aggie, Georgie and Mary cutting out paper patterns in Georgina's room and of the big scissors flashing through a leader about a women's college called Newnham, at Cambridge. Something Hall. *Merton Hall*. And of how Georgie had paused to bend over it and laugh and comment about frumps with high foreheads, and Mary had suddenly put her hand on the paper and begged them to let her keep the cutting and they had chaffed her and made her read it out loud . . . phrases about 'intellectual young women', 'eagerly seeking learning and attending the lectures of eminent dons', and Aggie and Georgie punctuating the quiet, steady voice with laughs and 'My goodness *me's*'. Mary had looked out of the window, had forgotten the cutting-out and when next applied to for advice was found to have left the room.

That was eight years ago, in 1874. One was only nineteen then. There would have been plenty of time. . . .

Nursing. One would make a good nurse; blood didn't upset one, one had strength and could be interested in curing. At home there was nothing to practise on but cuts that Nana bound up, and nervous headaches and biliousness and palpitations, which, now one came to think of it, were probably not of romantic origin, but from tight lacing.

Cooking. Impossible, of course; naturally one never went into the kitchen except of late years to stir the Christmas puddings because Mamma said it pleased the servants. But serious cooking would annoy Emma and not be understood by the staff. Once, a cook had left without warning, and father had had to make an arrangement with Fortnum & Mason to deliver cooked meals. Nana only understood tea and barley water, and it wasn't her work, anyway. Suddenly, and rather desperately, Queenie

began rummaging for her engagement book; it was a sub-
conscious groping towards some excuse for postponing
action. If one was booked up for some days ahead . . .
but the book was nearly blank for almost a week to come.
Time to think and plan . . . and one didn't want to; one
winced from the preliminaries to action, dreading, as
much as one sympathized with, the upset involved to
father and Mamma by the introduction of eccentricity,
a departure from convention, to be brought into their
lives. And there seemed no plan in life.

Another idea occurred to her. If one could attract some
man, unmistakably this time, it would not only be a form
of justification for existence and flattering to the family, but
would for ever silence tongues on the subject of the work
one could take up later. Only thwarted women worked.
But if one hadn't been thwarted and still worked. . . .

The pert face of Nellie appeared at the door, part
alarm, part avid.

'Miss Queenie, the gong's gone this four minutes.'

CHAPTER XI

I

AGATHA SCRIMGEOUR stood in indecision in the hall, then turning, made her way to the nursery flight. Charlie was now at school but there was still Gracie. Agatha hoped that Nana would be out of the room. Nana was really becoming rather tiresome, making one's visits difficult, saying sharpish things possible only to the privileged servant. Miss Banks was in her bedroom, her white blouse bound with its belt of black petersham visible through the half-open door. In the drawing-room Mamma was receiving Gertie who had elected to fit in Brecknock Gardens between other afternoon calls. Agatha had joined them, glad of the distraction, only to be edged from the room by her mother's 'We shall see you at tea, then, dear'. That meant that somebody was going to be discussed. Queenie, no doubt. Agatha hoped her mother was making out a fairly good case for the family to Gertie. One wasn't — it was very wicked and wrong — very *fond* of Gertie but one wanted to stand well with her. Even Mamma seemed a little afraid of her. There was something about her eye, bright, black, mocking, which made you stammer, and above all about the quality of her silences that drove you to apologetic speech. It might have been her clothes, always rich and stylish, but Agatha guessed it wasn't. Mary wasn't intimidated by dress, but even Mary rather went to pieces when the ringing voice of Gertie, penetrating, and conveying a subtle enjoyment of the scene together with a number of implications, probably all damaging, yet which you couldn't bring home to her, challenged her in passing.

'Still the bookworm!'

It was a warm day of early summer. All over the house curtains were stirring in what breeze there was. Agatha, leaning against a landing window, let the enervating air play upon her sallow skin. The pause postponed a possible tilt with Nana and fractionally shortened the time until tea. She surveyed the rest of the day. After tea one might, perhaps, tidy one's chest of drawers, and then it would be almost time for Evensong at St. Matthew's.

To-morrow? Tea with the Willis's over the road.

Next day? Nothing at all. That would be a day that would tax one's entire resources of ingenuity to weather with cheerful assurance. And in another five weeks, oh God! the family upheaval of preparation for the seaside would begin, with the details unchanged and oneself just so much older as to be wellnigh unable to stand it.

The calamity of weeping at table had, once or twice of late, been horribly almost irresistible; one had fought it off because one knew that if once one gave way . . . also, one would be earmarked for life as 'the queer one'.

What *was* the matter? Agatha, of the generation which shrank from facing facts, did not admit even now that she was half dead with boredom and the flattening monotony of life which sometimes affected her like a physical sickness and made her averse from facing each fresh morning and long only to remain in bed. It was the dreadful accuracy with which events could be forecast that wore her down. Never, never the unexpected thing. It even sickened her, at times, to find in her room objects lying as she had left them.

It had driven her, one year, into what was universally known as 'good works', a visiting of the very poor under the aegis of a trusted church worker, that was in point of fact a frantic endeavour to find reassurance in the knowledge that in London hundreds of women were enduring a more miserable life than Agatha herself. The experience had not done much for her, had shown her little that, theoretically, she did not already know. The poor were the poor. Meanwhile her own problem remained as lusty as ever.

She had dropped the social work and found intermittent salvation in the nursery, drawn to it not so much through fondness for children of whom she knew and understood little, as for a very literal pastime. It was wary work and one at all times liable to trench upon the preserves of nurse and governess, but on the whole she snatched things, taking Gracie to Madame Tussaud's, to Kensington Gardens, a change of wardenship that Grace, trustful and docile, never queried.

Over the question of marriage for herself that her mother eternally prophesied by hint or look, and her father jovially, openly alluded to and no nonsense, Agatha's attitude was indifferent and surly. If it was true that, of course, she would marry, then why wasn't she married, or engaged? She was already twenty-nine. For years she had believed that her single state was a sign that a real love match — the first in the family? — was reserved for her. As far as she could see she felt things more keenly than any of the others, and, head in air, would take no stock of the drawing-room men and the army friends of her father.

She had been in love. There was an actor, a singer, and a bishop, glimpsed a year ago at Gracie's confirmation, beside all of whom the men friends of the family seemed stuffed dummies with but one voice of no inflexions. While the actor and singer lasted they had made her aware of unsuspected depths of feeling which had filled her every waking minute, until the curtain fell again and she could find no genuine emotion left, clutch at it as she might, and which left her to trudge life again, the Agatha of custom.

II

The nursery was smelling stuffy in spite of opened windows. It seemed, she thought, to be a concomitant of rooms used much by servants . . . even Miss Banks's room was sometimes fusty with a dreadful scent she would buy, called Opoponax. It seemed to be her one vice.

Gracie was reading, seated in a little pale blue chair at the table to which her elbows intermittently and surreptitiously strayed. 'No elbows on the table' was one of Nana's rules, Agatha remembered it well. There were many others, sensible, unreasonable, meaningless, that the little sister no doubt was going through. No talking at meals, no sweets before breakfast, bread and butter before cake, no butter with bacon; a grace peculiar to the nursery:

> This blest food which now we take
> Do us good, for Jesus' sake.

In the dining-room the etiquette of Divine approach was the better-known For These And All Other Mercies.

'You can't come in now, Aggie dearie,' Nana with her wiry eyebrows indicated Grace, 'we've not been quite a good girl and we're doing a lesson for our governess'. The well-known use by Nana of the first person plural rasped Agatha's nerves. 'I hope you two don't mean to keep the poor child in the whole afternoon, on a day like this.'

'She shall get down in ' — Nana glanced at the Swiss cuckoo clock — 'ten minutes. She was just a little pert with Nana. It's this weather's touched up her stomach,

124

poor mite. You look as though a good dose'd do you no harm either. You were always the first to go bileyfied in the heat.'

'Nana, I *will* not be spoken to as though I were a child. It may have escaped your notice, but I have been grown up for some time now.'

Nana chuckled comfortably. 'No fear I've forgotten, lovey. Why, we shall be having your birthday before we know where we are. Thirty candles on the cake. Why, you're getting quite an old lady. There there! It's only my fun. Thirty doesn't sound much to *me*, and there's time yet I *dare* say for Mr. Right to pop his head in.'

For the first time, Agatha, nearly weeping with fury, saw what an abiding curse the old retainer could become. Back in her bedroom she sat staring at an unfinished verse she had begun writing the day before, approximately rhyming lines that punctuated her progress through life, and which she believed to be poetry.

III

In the drawing-room Mrs. Scrimgeour was sitting on the sofa, too deep in the urgency of her intelligence to her eldest daughter to have time to be thrown off her balance by Gertrude's cool, amused rejoinders. Plump hands folded on comfortable stomach she was saying 'I'm so glad you've come, dear, I wish I saw you oftener — oh I know how full your days are . . . and Clarence, of course, and now the two dear little girls . . . but really, with Aggie and Queenie one hardly knows what to *think*.'

Gertrude composed her face. Now that she no longer had to live with them, the evasive ditherings of her mother sometimes entertained her. But Mamma could be much funnier than this and Gertrude began to bait her. 'You mean that you can't get the girls off?'

Mrs. Scrimgeour blinked pale eyes. She hated that kind of question. It was difficult to answer and not quite respectful. 'Not that, of course, but it seems so *strange*. Here's Aggie going on for *thirty* and of course now you and Arabella and Georgie are gone it does make a difference, and especially since father retired ... my dear, I assure you that some Sundays I have only counted three men at the tea-table ... dear Mary's not much *help* to me — except in the actual pouring. But it's Aggie and Queenie I'm anxious for. It seems so incredible even to say so ... one never even imagined — '

' — that they mightn't marry.' It was rather brutal, Mamma being Mamma, to put the business into plain English, but if that was what she meant she must expect to be occasionally taken up on her hints. She was looking helplessly dismayed. Gertrude, mother-of-pearl cardcase in hand, civilly waited. She meant to leave in another ten minutes.

'Of course I know some girls don't marry, but one never expected ... there are visits, of course.' Gertrude headed her off that line of thought. She saw that at any second her mother might throw herself upon her mercy and beg her to give the girls a chance, or even a season, and Gertrude couldn't conscientiously recommend either Agatha or Queenie; besides, she now had two girls of her own, and although they were still in the nursery, she did not mean to injure them by giving her house a name for harbouring sisterly deadweights. Aggie and Queenie — she had tested it in the emergency visit while Charlie was being born — had no fixed social manner or line, they were, one saw, but an enfeebled version of oneself, Arabella and Georgie, plus a harmful smattering of new ideas and general restlessness which led nowhere. Gertrude would not jeopardize the home she had built up in her own way. Aggie and Queenie, she remembered, alternated between stiffness and a kind of plunging gaiety which disconcerted visitors who, so to speak, liked to be able to put their hand on girls at any given moment if required! The race was, as ever, to the swift, but indubitably not to the fast. They were, of course, nice, decent girls, and thorough good sorts. Now one came to think of it one really hardly knew them; they had been at school when one was 'out' and only home for good when one had married. . . .

From the huge gilt cage by the window came the squeaking of Mrs. Scrimgeour's budgerigars. The canaries had all died off and the tiny green birds in their barred Egyptian headdresses, reminiscent of the ballet in *Aïda*, were minutely nudging, pecking and abundantly kissing. One of them could talk and now said '*I see you!*' in a voice like the wraith of a long-departed slate-pencil.

Gertrude was amused, but her mother was complaining. 'What more can one *do*? We are not, of course, *rich*, but it never used to make any difference . . . and soon, father's got Charlie to think of.'

'How is Charlie?' asked Gertrude firmly, but Mrs. Scrimgeour went on, 'And that brings me to what I wanted to say.' Her daughter suppressed a tapping shoe. 'Do you see a great change in Aggie?'

'Change? What change? She was always a bit sallow. I should think a good sulphur soap — '

'Gertie, she goes to *church* so. *Is* it natural? It seems so unwholesome. That very High church, St. Matthew's. Not even our own.'

'Well really, Mamma, if she feels like it — '

But Gertrude knew exactly what her mother meant, was for the first time remotely disturbed. When young women began to go to church at odd hours that looked like real trouble. She hoped that poor old Aggie wasn't unhappy, and above all that Mamma wasn't being tiresome and bungling everything.

'And then there's Queenie. Gertie, she's getting so *bold* with men, rather like the little trouble we had with her when she first came out; letting them see she's pleased when they come in, and actually getting up and walking right across the whole room while they're still at the door. Even your father noticed ... and asking Mr. West *herself* to supper — '

'Did he come?' This was being Mamma at very nearly her best and Gertrude's lean face was already deep pink with suppressed guffaws.

'Well — yes. But of course he didn't like it. Girls have no right to put men in awkward positions.' Mrs. Scrimgeour meant that. The awkward positions should be at all times parentally contrived. Gertrude rose. 'I really don't see what you can do. Queenie isn't a child — '

'A child! She's twenty-seven!'

'T'tt! What I was going to say was that, that. being the case, you can't pull her up except in the most general way, and as for Aggie, well, some people like religion, you know. My advice to you is: leave her alone. Wait and see.'

Mrs. Scrimgeour looked shriven. 'Yes, yes, and after all she's not thirty yet. There's still time ...' They left it at that. Gertrude said she would 'let herself out', closed the door and descended the stairs. The drawing-room door opened almost immediately.

'Oh, Gertie ... Gertie dear! There was one more thing — ' Her eldest daughter continued to descend. 'Can't hear!'

She waved a gloved hand and was out of sight.

CHAPTER XII

I

IN the warm, incense-permeated church, Agatha Scrimgeour was meditating her first adventure. Confession.
The need to speak to an outsider was nearly driving her
frantic. Counsel's opinion. Mr. O'Flynn had a strong,
sensible face; not, of course, as good as Wilson Barrett's,
but here one wasn't out for that kind of thing. . . .

The service was over. Already there was a sprinkling of
women lingering outside the carved Confessional box,
shielded by its red serge. Something one had never looked
behind, there, and available, but closed to one as life;
something that, like life, needed the moment's pluck to
penetrate, and then? The healing of discussion with
someone outside the family, or hot embarrassment which
would cling round one's pillow for nights ahead? And
the formula. There probably was one, something that
would disqualify and expose one at the start.

The women were, by turns (how know your turn?)
advancing and entering. When they had all left, she
rose, advanced too — and turned and left the church.
It was no good. When all was said, the vicar was a man,
a being at whom you could barely look, let alone engage
in conversation, without a self-consciousness that would
drive away all sincerity and coherence.

All the way home she congratulated and derided herself. She hoped on the doorstep that there was something
extra good for dinner. Lately, Agatha had relied more
and more on the many-coursed meals for their own
pleasure and for variety. Tested, she would have starved
by inches for a principle.

There was a heat-wave that summer. Grace enjoyed it, even if it did seem to make Nana extra cross. The paraphernalia for keeping cool was as interesting to the little girl as was the winter campaign for warmth. There was the nursery butter, propped in a dish on ice wrapped in flannel. Sometimes Nana allowed one a tiny piece, splintered off the block by jabbing with one of her blackheaded hatpins. There was the arrival of the ice itself, glittering and dripping in a wicker basket from the fishmonger's, to watch from the window. Sometimes strawberries and cream were sent up from the drawing-room. From six o'clock onwards, smells of hot bouillon ascended from the basement. There was the putting away in camphor of flannel petticoats and the finding and ironing of summer frocks; a man who came to the area with a stand of paper fans; choosing how few sheets to have over you at night, watching Nana make barley-water, going very slowly with mother and sisters, all under scarlet or pink or blue silk parasols, to Searcey or Gunter's to sit at little tables and eat wonderful ices; the change-over from bull's-eyes to pokes of sherbet when one spent pocket money, finding out what Miss Banks's summer hat would be like this year, being taken to Woolland's to have a new one chosen for oneself; lying down after midday dinner without a frock, the sun on one's bare arms and the way the sun could be blamed for indolence over morning lessons. The first glimpse of the drawing-room chairs, cool and jaunty in their slippery chintz covers. Then, the holidays to anticipate, and Nana rather sulkily allowing one to rummage in the housemaid's cupboard for dusty bucket and spade, and the moment when one found that a dab of sand still stuck to the bottom of the bucket. Above all, waiting for Charlie to come home from school.

But this year things weren't being so nice; even last year, one didn't seem to see Charlie much. He said the boys were 'all right' and then didn't play with one; he brought home things one was told not to touch, a bat, tennis balls, a stamp album. He was allowed to sit in the morning-room even when father was there; he and father went off together to Lords and the Oval, and — he had more pocket-money than she, Grace had found out by accident. It was a shock, saddening and puzzling. She hadn't been naughty? But if it was so, it must be all right. . . .

And this summer he wasn't even going to be with one at the sea. Father was taking him 'up north' to fish, had bought him a very special and important rod that one wasn't even shown, and hated, from a shop in Piccadilly. And a gun. A real one. Grace actually asked 'Why?' and Charlie said, offhand, 'For September, of course', which made one hate the gun even worse than the rod. They had cost pounds and pounds, he said so; and once, passing through the hall, Grace had seen the morning-room littered with exciting things, long rubber boots, and baskets with a slit in the lid, and caps and cases . . . so utterly different from the family baggage because owned by men. Men, even Charlie, managed to be very mysterious. Everything they did and had seemed to be more important than anything one did, or one's sisters did. Even on the rare occasions when one was given the same thing as Charlie he contrived to make his special and unapproachable sooner or later by doing something different and mannish with it, often a destructive something that, although it clashed with one's own sheltering and conservative instincts, made one feel that it was a better thing to do, and far more enterprising and effective.

Charlie never used to make one feel this way. It was ever since he went to school. One tried — so hard — in the holidays to be a companion to him in the new manner, and wasn't allowed to because it wasn't a girl's game or was 'rough' or 'not being like a little lady'. And even at twelve and a half years old, two years younger than oneself, he was allowed to go to lots of places quite alone. He had been on a bus, had once run to the rank for a cab for mother and returned inside it, like a grown-up, and once he had quite seriously been told to escort Aggie and Queenie to an evening party in the next street. Father would fetch them home. As high as their elbows he had trotted between them. . . .

His clothes . . . Grace soon saw that a boy's dress marked his life progress far more sharply than ever did a girl's. She remembered him in petticoats. Then came baggy knickerbocker suits of velvet. Now, he was in trousers indistinguishable from his father's save for the material and pattern. Yet she must wait nearly three years for a real evening dress with a train. And he had already begun to rebel against envelopes addressed to 'Master C. Scrimgeour', and even now received one or two marked 'Charles Scrimgeour, Esq'. But a girl remained eternally 'Miss' unless she got married; even Aggie and Queenie looked far too old for such a silly-sounding title as Miss; and dear Mary should surely have something more dignified that went with her clear, quiet voice?

It was over her brother, her only nurserymate, that Grace achieved thought, and the beginning of real imagination. The rest of life was acceptance of nearly every circumstance.

The August, then, would be as usual; Miss Banks sitting beside one on the beach and the sisters off walking together while mother lay down in the rooms. In the evenings round the lamp they would all play My Bird Sings and solitaire, and read perhaps *The Girl's Own Paper*, while Queenie did the fancy-work they had chosen at one of the many Art Needlework shops in the town, and which, as autumn drew on, were filled by grown-up ladies — residents — laying in stores of ammunition for the winter, Mary once said.

III

'Aggie can write the labels — oh, you're doing them. That's right. Better put the *exact* address and not just "Scrimgeour. Bexhill". ' Mrs. Scrimgeour oscillated at Agatha's elbow, peeping, reassuring herself. Agatha, her nerves twanging, could make no allowances for the fact that the absence of her husband from this year's family holiday was already unbalancing her mother to an unprecedented degree. He would of course see them out of house and off at station, and then, for Mrs. Scrimgeour, prophetically set in a series of unforeseen, inevitable hitches and catastrophes that the presence of three adult daughters so far from mitigating made infinitely worse. Nor could she be comforted or reassured. Only a non-member of the family, and one preferably male, could achieve that; and, so far, nobody seemed to have sent round word that he would speed them on their way. Her daughters, artificially flustered, preoccupied with personal problems, gave little of their mind or thought to that aspect of the holiday; in any case, daughterly apprehension of a voyage unescorted would be lost and swamped in their mother's. She was worrying for three, and they would get along, somehow . . . Mary hinted as much. 'You don't understand, dear. I'm afraid it will make a terrible difference without father, and I have all of you to think for.'

Agatha's damp hand clenched on her pen. She stood up. Her face was putty-coloured. 'Mamma, I'm sorry, but I don't want to come too.'

'My *dear* girl — '

Mary had gone to the window; her hands were trembling and she crushed them into her skirt. If one could only stand by Aggie . . . but, herself a stranger-audience as was Mamma, she could only listen. She had no real clue. Sympathy of generation and a hasty, childlike prayer was all the support she could offer. *Oh Lord, let her have her way. Let her be able to tell what she wants and stick to it, and get it.* Agatha's voice, roughened and cracking, was saying 'I'm sorry to be tiresome, but it's just that'. She had at least gained her mother's attention, if only by voice and looks.

'You're over-excited, dear, better go and lie down. We'll see to the labels.'

'Mamma, I am very sorry, but I really mean it.'

'But — *why*, Aggie? I never heard you like this before. And when we're all so *rushed* . . .'

Mary turned from her blind inspection of the street. 'Perhaps Aggie has some invitation, Mamma.'

'At this time! Surely not, Aggie? But why didn't you tell me before? With the tickets all bought . . .'

If her sister were grateful for the lifeline flung to her Mary could not be sure; it had been an unconsidered improvisation to relieve strain rather than a calculated suggestion. Agatha's next remark gave the impression that it had at least put an idea into her head, or given her impetus to advance one already there. 'I — I'd like to go off somewhere by myself.'

'By *yourself*?'

'Or perhaps with Mary . . . or Queenie.'

'But — it's impossible, dear! Nobody does it. And what would you two do with nobody to look after you? And think of the expense — even if it were possible, I don't think father would be willing to pay all that extra with this costly holiday he and Charlie are taking.'

It was defeat, the mention of money. Against that you could say and do nothing. To press for it was inconsiderate, unless one's need were of a grave urgency, and perhaps it wasn't . . . perhaps one could hold out. . . .

Mary was at her side. 'Couldn't she go to the convent for a bit? Didn't the Superior say she was always glad to see old girls, Aggie? And Cliffhaven has wonderful air.'

'But there's no *time* to arrange — '

'Oh yes, Mamma, it's really quite easy.'

'But, the ticket to Bexhill — ?'

'They'll take it back, and if they don't — '

'But, my dear — but I suppose if Aggie's really set on it — it would mean a first-class ticket, of course — a compartment for ladies only — one would have to tip the guard — and who would see her off?'

'Susan. She doesn't have her holiday for another week.'

Mrs. Scrimgeour looked pained. 'You seem to have planned it all, Mary.'

'No, no indeed. I had no idea — '

The implications of that statement suggested nothing to Mrs. Scrimgeour. 'But why do you want to be separated from mother and Mary and Queenie and Gracie, Aggie? I thought we were all so happy together.' As there was no answer, permissible or otherwise, to this, Agatha said stupidly, 'I don't know'. But it seemed to Mary that her expression was less taut.

IV

Her sister's action, the incredibility of which she would savour later in the days ahead, stimulated Queenie. Change and daring were in the air. Aggie's departure from routine would serve to pave her own way . . . also, it seemed to Queenie that the whole business had acted as an almost physical beautifier all round; even Mary looked quite handsome. Life was, suddenly, pleasant, as it used to be. There was the holiday which would — must be — enjoyable. And Gilbert Asherson was coming to luncheon.

v

He had begun by being Queenie Scrimgeour's fling at self-respect and justification for her existence in the eyes of the world, was to be her very own scalp. It had made her extra-careful, set her to delving her memories for cameos of the drawing-room tactics of Arabella and Georgina, to collecting the rarely-seen mannerisms of Gertrude. The result, necessarily a composite, had evidently been an improvement upon undiluted Queenie. Mamma for once signalled in vain. For he had come back, and was obviously, such as it was, hers, and not a family friend you pooled, or a misunderstanding, like Mr. Malcolm or anybody else's leftover. It gave her a little real confidence and poise. The fact of commanding attention as an individual made her in her own eyes of significance. The fact that in utilizing Asherson her own feelings might become seriously involved never occurred to her until too late. Magnifying everything, she brooded herself into love.

Thanks to Queenie herself the Scrimgeours did not go unescorted to the station, and Mrs. Scrimgeour's eyes lit with complacence at sight of Mr. Asherson lingering, laughing by the open carriage door. Oblivious of her almost-breakdown of faith to Gertrude, she began once more to hint and think in terms of sentimental speculation as to how long she still might look to keep a dear girl with her. It consoled her for the absence of her own husband, though reconciliation to the idea was only intermittent. There was a miserable scene at the terminus about trunks and porters which her two adult daughters could neither quell nor control and ended in their becoming infected by their mother's helpless alarms. They settled upon Miss Banks as proxy for the Captain. She was out in the world, a working woman ... Queenie, as cautioned, keeping near her party, did not allow the fracas to touch her. She was, with only a little effort, thanks to her mother and the luggage, in a world of her own with Gilbert Asherson.

They drove to the rooms from the station under a cloud of contempt. Mrs. Scrimgeour had never bestowed a tip in her life, it was the man's province. Her flurried notions had included twopence to the stationmaster whom she mistook for one of 'her' porters, threepence each to porter and cabman, and, losing the last inch of her head, half a crown to the shabby tout who opened the cab doors. Her daughters were equally ignorant. Their disbursements had been limited to the house servants of their country friends on a scale calculated by standing and length of visit and referee'd by Captain Scrimgeour. At her aunt's in Sloane Street Mary had not even this problem; the staff were such old servants that money offended them, and on leaving you had to buy them presents, which came to far more than tips.

It was Miss Banks and her pupil who led the most placid life at Bexhill; neither expected much, and the change, said the governess, was 'nice'. In a navy-blue serge tunic edged with white braid, and bloomers to below the knee, she bathed, bobbingly. The others had, for the first time, vital, concrete matters to think over; Mrs. Scrimgeour about Queenie's romance, late, but none the worse now it *had* come, and perhaps not white, exactly, but some pastel shade ... Charlie and the Captain ... she smiled fondly, thinking with pleasant calm of the child wading, thigh-deep, in chill torrents and rivers. People didn't catch chills when it was salmon ... She had never allowed the boy to paddle longer than half an hour at a time in a warm sea. And of course his father was with him. ...

Aggie ... she should be writing again. So far, only one postcard and a letter, though they had now been parted *three weeks*. There could be nothing the matter, surrounded by all those nuns, that was the only comfort.

Queenie thought steadily about Gilbert Asherson, Mary about Queenie and Agatha; Grace wrote to Charlie and tried to picture his superior life and amusements and Miss Banks wondered if her mother's news, half-thankful, half-regret, that she had succeeded in letting three rooms in their house to an elderly couple who wanted quiet and to be with gentlefolk, would make talk in the Cathedral set.

CHAPTER XIII

I

Mrs. Scrimgeour received her letter in the last week of their stay. Failing the presence of her husband, she referred the letter instantly to Mary. It arrived with a large, limp length of salmon from the Captain. 'The very *sight* of food,' said his wife, who had just eaten her usual capable breakfast, but her family made all sympathetic allowance.

The badly-written sheets seemed — which was clearly fantastic — to point to the fact that Aggie proposed to become a nun.

The Captain must be sent for at once, but how? A telegram — Clarence — or perhaps Georgie's husband — but one of them was in *Switzerland* . . . To her mother, Agatha, peas in her shoes, was already doing some frightful penance in full religious regalia, or was barefoot on 'the stones'.

'I don't think things happen as quickly as that, Mamma. Aggie will first have to be received into the Roman Church, then accepted as a postulant, then comes a long novitiate before — '

'My dear, what can you know about it?' Mary made allowance for the incivility. 'I — I read,' she answered, gently apologetic.

'Oh, books . . . I expect *everything* is different, now.'

'*Please*, Mamma . . . I want to see what she says . . .'

'Yes. You see? Here it all is. And she's been having instruction from a priest. "Instruction in the Faith", she calls it.'

'How *can* you be "instructed" in faith? You either believe or you don't.'

'It means in dogma, you know, not just believing,' Mary said, simply.

'Dogma, well, haven't we enough in our own Church? We *can't* allow it; it will be the end of her, socially.' Mary was too disturbed and bewildered to smile; she said more or less at random, 'Don't you think it might be the best thing?'

'How could it be? I suppose, after this, people will say we didn't make her happy at home.' The reality of the bitterness in her mother's remark dismayed Mary no less than the unusual appeal with which she turned to her. 'What more could we have done for Aggie?'

Mary didn't know. 'There's one thing: *father* will be against it.' It was a challenge to what initiative one had. 'Can't we wait, Mamma dear, and try and find out if it's only a whim of Aggie's, and if it isn't, let her have her way? Father will' — it was so unreasonably difficult to say — 'do what *you* suggest.' A faint complacency struggled through the worry and resentment of Mrs. Scrimgeour's expression. Mary, no schemer, failed to perceive her advantage and follow it up.

'It's the most amazing thing I've ever heard, but if you *think* it is safe to wait — ?'

'But, indeed I *know*, Mamma. I tell you, the Catholics don't make it as easy as all that — '

'Oh, they're cunning enough,' capped her mother with vague venom. The letter had ruined her already precarious holiday.

11

Owing to Charlie's school term and the statutory 'full week' of activity, of packing and general overhauling, sartorial and personal, prescribed by his mother, Captain

Scrimgeour was home a day before his family, resigning the boy — late a man of adult occupation in pastime and companionship — to the nurse. His son, but betweenwhiles, when the need arose, eternally a child, to be placed suitably, conveniently, without transition or explanation.

When the master of the house had glanced at accumulated letters and settled himself in the morning-room he would spend the rest of the day at the club. Charlotte and the girls would be back to-morrow. The domestic Captain hated the atmosphere of sheeted furniture and unfilled vases.

He bent to his desk, handling envelopes. Bills, mostly. Their total was a bit staggering. For the first time Charles Scrimgeour remembered that he was now on half-pay; still, one had one's private income. Three of the girls were off his hands; Queenie would, it seemed, marry any day now, and the others were bound to follow suit sooner or later. The weddings were always a bit of an item but a saving in the long run. One wouldn't be without 'em, wouldn't be without 'em. . . .

His holiday had cost a pretty penny one way and the other, but it was a good investment to consolidate friends for one's boy. Charlie looked like shaping into a fair rod. A poor shot, though. Still, plenty of time. All that would come, and if it didn't, Sandhurst would put that right.

Two letters from Charlotte on the pile. It was all of a piece that the dear good lady should bombard one with correspondence that in the very nature of things couldn't be answered; even in Scotland one hadn't been able to keep upsides with more than half of it.

He reached for his hat and left the house.

I I I

Agatha, accompanied by Nellie in the cab, came home a week later. Her family greeted her warily, with scrupulous justice. Yes, one of the Sisters had seen her off at the station . . .

Half dear invalid who had been starved in a nursing home, half family conundrum, problem and disgrace, she took her usual place at table. Quiet, defensive, uneasy, she ate under all those eyes. Mrs. Scrimgeour steadily tempted her with delicacies, acting upon a blind conviction that when pheasant came in at the door the Pope flew out of the window. The whole affair had been kept from Miss Banks and, of course, from Grace. Charlie, fortunately, was back at school. Grace wouldn't notice anything . . . and governesses hardly counted.

On the following day routine was disorganized, Emma kept fuming and speculating in the kitchen after breakfast, slate in hand, Mrs. Scrimgeour and Agatha crossing from dining- to morning-room to beard the Captain, who abandoned *The Times* and placed chairs. In the drawing-room, Mary and Queenie, silent and fidgeting, awaited the upshot.

I V

'Well . . . it's a most extraordinary idea, but I suppose if nothing else will satisfy you — '

'But it's for *life*, Charles!'

'Hum . . . but it's possible that Aggie may find she can't stand the life, eh Aggie? It seems a very morbid business to me . . . shutting yourself up — '

'It's not an enclosed Order, father.'

'Oh, well, that's something. What *do* they do?'

'It's a teaching Order; besides the girls of *our* kind who are educated there they have a separate house for the children of the poor.'

'Teaching, eh? I don't think you'd care about that. Can't see you as a schoolmarm!' the Captain chaffed her jovially. Agatha had shut her eyes to that side of the prospect; one had health, and a fair amount of intelligence, would force oneself to do well as price for solution and asylum. Besides, not all the Sisters taught. There were outside instructors for subjects beyond conventual scope . . . still, it *was* a pity that the Order was a teaching one. On the other hand the fact that she herself was an Old Girl whom Reverend Mother knew about had been in her favour.

Rather helpless before this daughter, pleasant to have about the house but whom he really hardly knew, who wished to enter a life of which he knew less, the Captain fell silent, uncomfortably tapping fingers, arranging and rearranging objects on his desk. He managed at last a 'Well, we shall hope — when do you want to — er — start, begin, leave us?'

'Reverend Mother would take me at once. It — it's *most* good of you and Mamma. I am *so* grateful.'

'Well, be as happy as you can, my dear.'

It seemed, wonderfully, to be settled, in spite of the agitated flutterings of Mrs. Scrimgeour, but there was just one more thing, and Agatha turned at the door. 'Father, I believe I haven't mentioned it, but — the convent would expect a — a dowry with me.'

'A what? Good heavens! I thought only brides got dowries.'

'We might have known they'd be up to something,' commented his wife.

143

'But, what's it *for*?'

'Well, my keep, you know; and my cell and my outfit.'

'Your keep? But, my good Lord, won't you be *earning* it?'

'Not for years, father, except of course in general work. The postulants are never given responsibility and the novitiate is three years.'

'Um . . . oh well . . . of course . . . seems waste of time, to me; still, I don't pretend to understand — pretty sharp ideas on a bargain these people have got, for "holy" women.'

'The Lay Sisters bring no dowry, father, unless they are able.'

'Oh, and why not?'

'They do the rough work — '

'Sounds like servants.'

'Yes, yes! That won't do, Charles, not at *all*. Aggie must be as good as the best.'

'Well, what's the damage?'

Agatha hesitated; accepting her quarterly allowance without question she had never thought of querying her father's resources, had not the faintest idea of his means. Money was, save in the most general way usually tinged with facetiousness, never discussed in that house. Reverend Mother, of course mentioning no name, had said that one Sister brought in £500 as her portion, but the Superior had also made it plain that the dowry varied with the home income.

'There's no *fixed* sum, father; people give what they can afford.' The Captain looked dubious. 'Pretty vague and unsatisfactory, a sort of moral blackmail, eh Charlotte?'

'Yes, Charles, a sort of moral blackmail.'

The Captain was displeased. The admixture of religion with finance, although he was a sidesman at St. Philip's, jarred upon his sentimentality. Nuns ought to be above that kind of thing ... that they were still women whose boots and veils wore out, who must eat and pay rates, rent and taxes did not occur to him. Foggily, he believed that convents were either 'supported by Rome' or by the begging-bowl tendered with the sweet, wan smile. His 'I must think it over, run along, now' was a shade ungracious.

In suspense for days, Agatha stalked the house. Mrs. Scrimgeour, losing no time, threw herself upon Gertrude who smoothly refused to become ultimately responsible for decision either way, and was not at home to her mother's second visit. It was Georgina (after all, a married woman) who turned the scale. 'Well, but Mamma, if money's all that's keeping father back, he would have given Aggie something if she *married*, as he did to Arabella and Gertie and me.'

'But, it's such *waste* ... going to a pack of women ... and if it's to pay for her board and lodging she can get that at home for nothing.'

'Yes, but after all, we didn't get our dowries, either, not to *keep*, you know. Of course they went to our husbands.'

'But — Aggie hasn't *got* a husband,' bleated Mrs. Scrimgeour triumphantly. Georgina looked embarrassed. 'They *think* they have, Mamma, nuns, you know; they wear wedding rings on taking their final vows and call themselves "Brides of Christ".'

'Disgusting. And ridiculous. Why, it's blasphemy.'

Her daughter rather thought so too. 'It just shows where *their* thoughts are ... and this Confession; always to a man, you observe.'

'A priest, it's not the same thing.'

'A man's a man, my dear, and human nature's human

nature. Still, as you say, Aggie's wedding would have meant a portion, to say nothing of the dress and reception and all that — .' Mrs. Scrimgeour looked with moony woe at Georgina. 'It's explaining it to the *servants* that is going to be so difficult.'

v

The girls, as their mother still called them, were up in Agatha's bedroom sorting clothes that would do for Queenie, trinkets that would 'come in' for anyone who coveted them, underwear which might now be given to the poor without extravagance. Gowns unsuitable for anybody, or that did not fit without alterations which would be hardly worth the trouble, were left hanging on their pegs. It seemed to Mary that there would be nothing left of her sister; the wholesale giving up of intimately personal property brought home to her for the first time what Aggie's future would be. This occupation of abandonment of all those things in which you were long familiar to family and friends was a little death; already Agatha was fading, half-way to heaven. . . . For days, since decision had been made, she was beyond one's reach.

'There's the blue foulard that you always liked, Queenie. There's only a tiny strawberry stain on it from the Lassiter's lawn party last summer.' It was amazingly painful. Half-remembered lines flowed into Mary's mind. *We brought nothing into this world and it is certain we can carry nothing out.*

Queenie, half saddened at the scene, half excited at the wholesale augmentation of her own wardrobe, was pondering the stupendous sum of £400 that her sister would bring to her convent. The fact that any of them was worth that amount augured hopefully. She did not know that, with her father, it had been pull devil pull baker, a gesture of personal pride and hearty contempt for the demand.

Agatha herself, having got her own way, was being consumed with remorse.

VI

The kitchen discussed it for weeks.

COOK: 'I always did think there wasn't something not hardly right about Miss Aggie.'

NELLIE: 'She didn't look what you could call reelly happy.'

SUSAN: 'They say nuns are brides of Christ.'

COOK: 'Don't talk so ignorant, my girl.'

SUSAN: 'It's *true*, Emma.   What I say is: it's bigamy. Talk about Solomon.   Hoo!'

COOK: 'You Solomon yourself into the scullery and peel them potatoes.'

In the nursery, Nana grieved indignantly.   The effort to pin the blame anywhere but upon Aggie, her nursling, made her ill-humoured even to Grace.

In the pantry, Tom, polishing silver, suddenly thought of Lotty, and in contrast with where she might have landed after all these years, the dust-up about a convent seemed small beer.   At least a convent gave a woman respectable shelter, by all accounts.

CHAPTER XIV

I

THE family, except Gertrude, saw Agatha off at the station. Unnaturally bright in talk as one humours an invalid or lunatic, and with awkward silences in which there seemed no suitable topic on earth. Tears sprang punctually to the eyes of Mrs. Scrimgeour as the train drew in, springing again as it steamed off. Hand in pocket, the Captain made his tipping gesture before remembering that this occasion was in a different category to the country house visit. Queenie and Grace waved to an Agatha heavy-faced and sallower than ever. If Queenie had tears, her mental confusion at losing a life-companion of bedroom, board and home arrested them. It was typical of life at present, this departure at an unscheduled time of year by Aggie quite alone, leaving the routine in Brecknock Gardens dislocated for the entire day. It was an event, sudden and real, which seemed to Queenie to be prophetic of general adventure. Even the fact that at last she would have a room to herself spurred on fate. She would miss Aggie painfully, yet she hurried along the street a little in advance of the others, avid to take possession.

II

Queenie, darting among her new possessions, trifled with the notion of having her room redecorated, until she remembered that any day now she might be leaving it for good.

All that autumn and winter she tasted fulfilment. At first incredulously, then cautiously, finally with confidence, she had tested Asherson as an asset. He was now at the point when even her family could, on the whole, rely upon him to fill a last-minute place at table, act escort to the play and even partner to dances; a little bit too much so, she had thought at first, when mentally organizing her attitude to this domestic annexation, until she remembered the debâcle of Mr. Malcolm and the episode of that session in the study, a news item tardily picked up from Gertie. That at least, if Queenie could help it, should never happen again. It made her acquiescent in the sharing of her admirer, seeing that there was safety and continuity for herself in numbers. It lulled him into a sense of security, for the same reason. Mrs. Scrimgeour purred at him hopefully, the Captain liked him and dined him at the club. Mary had been heard to say that she thought he seemed interesting, the married sisters approved; in the nursery, Nana, blandly flouting decorum, stated forthrightly that it seemed about time for another wedding and that Queenie's would 'go far to make up for the disappointment over Aggie'.

I I I

In all that house there was one who loved him.

Often running down two flights to get a sight of him over the banisters, Grace caught his eye. It was an eye, for some time, at a loss. She guessed and accepted the fact that he could not place her in the family scheme. Her urge to look at him, shedding Inverness cape in the hall, led her into forgetfulness, or thoughtful, deliberate snappings of the taboos of her short life. Charlie was not only at school but, she sensed, gone for ever out of her reach; Miss Banks was a governess, Nana very old: even the suspected, warm humanities of the kitchen were socially ruled out, she saw it herself. Too young for the drawing-room, outgrowing the solitary nursery, with Mary her only link between the two, Gilbert Asherson dawned upon her.

Neither by character nor upbringing an enterprising child, she was deprived of what chances there were of private encounter; fatalistically she took it for granted that she would be of no interest to him. He was of the drawing-room world and would take Queenie away from the dwindling crowd of familiar faces. She herself would be a bridesmaid once more, and stand behind him ... almost close enough to touch him. One might even whisper 'I will' at the proper time, and perhaps that might make one sort of married to him as well?

There came an afternoon when his eye, travelling up the staircase, had met the steady grey gaze of the little girl. She had been accounted for to him by Miss Mary with a warm, quiet affection which Asherson found attractive. He had smiled and waved. The next time (did the child *live* on the stairs?) he blew her a kiss, on the third occasion he spoke. 'Well, Miss Rapuntzel, shall I climb up into your bower by that hair?' Thanks to Mary, she could take up that allusion, but the answering smile, a tremulous one, he found a disappointment. The little lady wasn't pretty. And all that hair, though long enough, was thin and yardstick-straight and of a brown which was everybody's shade. It wasn't, he saw, even the kind of plain or ugly face that can be elfin or suggest possibilities, or be quaint, and the fact that he was ever so slightly going out of his way to court its notice was tribute to the circumstance of his own freedom of that house, a civility to an inmate; the continued salutes, easy to have evaded, to the little girl's manner on sighting himself. He didn't pretend to understand children, although of late he had grown a synthetic tenderness for them. . . .

He had come nearer to Grace by a flight and disappeared into the drawing-room. She almost welcomed the greater distance between them since it led to the view of him coming closer to her. The nearest point of all was vanishing point.

He had been the individual who first led her to the mirror, seeing, as against the looking, of the past. She gazed, trustfully, and almost happy; because he had waved, smiled, above all kissed a hand and spoken, this reflection was a right one. He had put her in the Rapuntzel class and by word of mouth.

She met him sometimes in the drawing-room during her 'Hour', and at the Sunday tea-table. It was almost disappointing, were she not aware of the secret link. A child among adults, of whom little but good behaviour was expected, but one could at least look one's fill. She did so, passionately making one sense compensate for the rest, using the feature that, Gertrude had once asserted to Arabella, was her only good one.

IV

The breakfast table was now made strange by letters from Agatha, whose correspondence imported an atmosphere of selfconsciousness that the Scrimgeours were never able entirely to shake off. The Captain for months turned scarlet with embarrassment at the conventual turn of phrase, while his wife hummed mosquito-like over the accounts of routine; Miss Banks looked civilly shocked and Queenie indulged in facetiae, unrebuked as coming from

Anglican lips. Mary, listening to, and between, the lines, sensed that Agatha was happy, if in a febrile way. She had work to do, there was at least no doubt about that. It was the temperament behind this activity which sometimes misgave Mary, that tendency to squeeze an experience for its final drops ere passing on to the next thing. There were the actor and the Bishop . . . Aggie had apparently forgotten both in six months, though during the infatuations she had, to her sisters, talked of nothing else, and a yearning look had made her impassive face a little repellent. Still, the actor and the Bishop had been beyond her reach from the start, which possibly made you fickle, having nothing to lose. The convent was her first real chance. Wanting some one thing she had, at last, secured it, and into the convent she was pouring her reserves of energy, loyalty, enthusiasm, and gratitude at an accepted self-sacrifice. The letters made that plain enough.

'. . . Last week, Sister St. Cecilia — she is our Novice Mistress — actually told me I was *doing too much*!'

And:

'To-morrow is a day of fasting. I cannot describe to you all the wonder, small and trivial though is its Expression, of this release from material *habits*. It seems to free one for Better Things . . . To us postulants, an even stricter régime would be welcome. The dear Sisters are allowed to observe a far more austere Abstention than are ourselves, which, tho' a disappointment, we are trying to bear obediently.'

v

Mary from the first refused to associate herself with the graveyard mentality that spoke of the nuns with the lowered voice of apology, or which implicitly referred to her sister as to a dear departed. Of them all she was the first to see the convent, and afterwards its most frequent visitor. The Captain tscha'd the suggestion that he accompany her. He dreaded he knew not what. 'It's no use, my dear, I don't care for the whole business, and I don't know the drill.' Mrs. Scrimgeour, unaccustomed for years now to any but an August exodus of the whole available family, was fretful at the idea. 'They'll try and get *hold* of one.' Queenie — Mary guessed it — now in another dimension of emotion, was inaccessible. It was natural. Mary bowed to the passing selfishness of the chosen ... sympathizing where she could not entirely condone.

Gracie, then? The prompt and almost-articulate veto did not altogether surprise Mary, long over-sensitized to family undertones. 'No thank you! At least I won't have a child interfered with.'

Arabella was at Aldershot, with Francis; Georgina, with lavish, Scrimgeour overplus of premature preparation, was already making what arrangements she could for her departure, three months hence, to India with her husband. From now on she would decree herself unavailable for any outing that did not appeal to her.

That left Gertrude, who, rather astonishingly to Mary, consented. Of very improbability, Mary had reckoned last with her eldest sister, yet they were actually in the train together, an intimacy which Mary had not enjoyed now for some fifteen years.

Gertrude put her feet up, arranged her clashing chatelaine, raised her veil of spotted net to nose-height, drew from her bag a bottle of lavender salts in a silver filigree case, denounced the smell of the station and stated 'The family wouldn't come, eh?'

'They will in time, I expect,' Mary apologized.

'Don't count on it. They're slow movers. Always better

to make one's own arrangements. My only wonder is that Aggie had the spunk to.'

Mary shifted. 'I think she was unhappy, Gertie.'

'Who *was* the man, by the way?' asked Gertrude, briskly.

'I — there wasn't one, I think.'

'Oh, *that* . . .' Gertrude's inflexion was a shrug. 'Yes, I remember Mamma in a state about it, now I come to think of it. She seemed actually *surprised*!' Gertrude Randolph appeared to be about to enlarge on the theme but glanced at Mary, paused and changed the subject, to her sister's relief. 'So poor old Aggie's happy, eh?'

'Very.'

'Good. No hankerings that way yourself, I suppose?'

Mary, flushing, shook her head with a decision that pleased Gertrude. 'I know one oughtn't to say it, Gertie, but Roman Catholicism always seems to me to be utterly incredible. It's like a solemn worship of Little Red Riding Hood, or reading Jack the Giant-Killer to grown-up people.' Gertrude's black bright eye snapped with amusement. 'But, my dear, that's what fairy stories are for, to keep children quiet.'

'It's wrong, Gertrude, when it's religion.'

'It gets results. Even granted that we knew it, how many people want the truth? How many can face facts unvarnished, or see things as they really are? To half the world so-called religion is an escape from reality, especially to women. The Church exists by their help. If religion were entrusted to men, there'd be nothing but St. Paul's and the Abbey left in London, and those only because they're historic. The most successful priest — or vicar, if it comes to that — is the one who makes improbability the most attractive and plausible.'

'Oh — '

'I'm sorry, my dear. I've upset you, and upset you because you're the only one of us with any brains — '

'Nonsense!'

' — and you think just far enough to disturb yourself and bring yourself to a dead end. I envy Aggie, personally. She swallows things whole. Much the best way.'

'But — you go to church, Gertie?'

'And pay calls and go to the summer exhibition at Burlington House. But I don't paint pictures and only call on tested persons. It's no good, dear Mary, I'm one of those damned souls who want proofs, and plenty of 'em. There isn't a religious denomination on earth whose promised rewards I covet, or whose threatened punishments I fear.'

'My dear . . . this is awful.'

'It's freedom, and it's honest.' Mrs. Randolph leant back and sniffed at her salts. 'If you had been robbed of your husband and your child at twenty-three, you might understand my point of view,' she said chattily.

'*Robbed?* But, Clarence . . . Bertie? . . .'

'Oh, in a perfectly respectable way, a most Godfearing way, that left one with just the husks of them. Not even in an unusual way, either. I suppose seventy per cent of young wives would have taken it all for granted, the hypocrisy and the lies . . . but there *is* the thirty per cent left, and they have to shift as best they can. Don't look so horrified! No, it's no good explaining, and in any case I doubt if it's proper food for the unmarried!' She broke off to laugh abruptly. 'And the tendency, as you see, is for us to withhold information and let the next lot enjoy the same disillusionments in the approved manner. Convention is very catching. I must see what I can do about it.' She put her feet down and craned out of the window. 'Is this us?'

PART TWO

In the passages and along the cloisters, smelling of
pipeclay and cold stone, Mary followed behind Gertrude,
who led with a Hospitality Sister detailed to show them
round. It seemed that even here the woman of God
deferred to the woman of the world ... There were fifty
questions of understanding that Mary was eager to ask but
it was, she saw, useless from the start; the Sister accepted
Gertrude as leader, who appeared in a superficial sort of
way to be being perfectly adequate. But then Gertie would
be ... cool, polite, subtly entertained.

Agatha, sallower than ever in her postulant's coif,
walked with Mary; her occupation, too, was gone. She
looked, Mary thought, thinner but happier. Half exuber-
ant schoolgirl eager to exhibit to visiting parents, tempered
by a submissiveness to the spectacle'd Sister, which Mary
found both pathetic and repellent in its servility.

'Ah, the dining-room', Gertrude indicated with her
neatly-rolled umbrella the long hall aligned with trestle
tables and deal chairs. 'The refectory', prompted Mary
sotto voce, and Agatha's correction was only a shade later.

'Of course, of course; what a pleasant, airy room.'
Mary's eyebrows rose. This would be Gertrude in civil,
social vein, meaning 'what an odiously draughty place'.
Agatha had accepted the comment, she hardly knew her
eldest sister. Gertrude, putting the nun at her ease, was
smoothly running on. 'And you have a pulpit, I see ...
but surely services are held in the chapel?' Agatha gasped
Godlily, but discipline held by a hair's breadth. Sister
Ursula took it in good part. 'Not a pulpit, that is where
the Sisters read to us during refection. The Lives of the
Saints.'

'Always?'

'Yes.'

'Then, do tell me, what happens when you come to the end of them? Do you start all over again?'

'Good books bear a second reading, haven't you found it so?' the sweet, flat, didactic voice, with its upward inflexion at the end of every comment, suggested in reply. '*Touché*' murmured Mrs. Randolph, ruefully waggish. It was then that Agatha burst bounds.

'Oh Gertie, on Friday — the week *before* last — we had the Life of St. Pancras. He was martyr'd *at fourteen*.'

'My dear! what could he have done in the time?'

Sister Ursula gently impelled them on. 'The readings are such a pleasure to us all', she intoned rapidly. Mary was thinking that the discovery of Agatha, fasting and scourged, would be better than the deliberate stultification of all this potential feminine intelligence. Why the higher life should demand the atrophy of the intellect she must think out, slowly, fairly, later. She supposed it was a literal interpretation of that injunction to become 'as little children', but even little children were supplied with literature graded to suit their mental development. The conventual life led merely to a crushing of all initiative; women who dared not think or reason, so dedicate to God that they shut their eyes to earthly needs and suffering and causes, leaving the salvation of sinners to the sinners. What would be the use of an army which sat about and prayed for the enemy? Were not cannon more effective? 'The Church Militant'. But the Church wasn't militant and the age of martyrdom was over.

She viewed the convent library with an incredulous horror that was greater far than ever had been the idea of her sister taking the final vows. St. Francis of Assisi . . . a few selected books of travel with those passages relating to the more intimate native customs carefully and neatly erased . . . a sprinkling of children's books . . . for grown women!

Classrooms and rows of bent heads, the nun on the rostrum exchanging brief bows with Sister Ursula; the chapel, pleasantly fusty with incense and redundant with brightly painted saints with staring eyes and haloes of tin stars, their feet ringed round with half-consumed tallow candles on iron spikes; Agatha crossing herself and genuflecting low; dim greyish bundles that were Sisters praying, or in meditation, or doing penance. It was here that the nun, making a sign to Agatha, left the sisters alone for the first time and hurried away, her bulky habit swinging. Outside, Gertrude said forthrightly, 'We'd like to see where you sleep, Aggie.'

'My cell,' corrected Agatha.

They clustered in the doorway. 'I am not allowed to ask you inside but you may peep from the door!' Her eldest sister thanked her dryly, her quick eyes taking in the narrow iron bedstead on castors, the pitchpine wardrobe, cane-seated chair, prie-Dieu and iron washstand with tin bowl and jug and thick tooth tumbler. On the wall, distempered sage-green to the dado, which was bice, hung a cheap coloured picture. Agatha followed, in preference, the eyes of Mary as they travelled round the little place. 'We all have a picture. I have Our Lady of Seven Dolours, and one of our postulants has St. James of Compostella —'

'Yes, I see,' Gertrude closed the pious inventory with decision, 'well, my dear, it's been nice to see you.'

VII

In the train Mary caught Gertrude's eye.

'Oh isn't it awful, Gertie! Somehow, in spite of all one has read, one hadn't really realized — '

'You're so deadly serious, Mary, you should cultivate a lighter hand with the pastry. Awful? Not at all. I expected to find Aggie's point of view, and I did.'

'But — the stifling of her brain!'

'Oh fiddle. She hadn't much to stifle, from all I've ever seen or heard. I tell you, it's *fun* for her, I quite see the idea. Roman Catholics are never really without something going on. If it isn't a feast day it's a fast, and if it's neither it's a Saint's day, each with its own little special ceremonies; plenty of drama, processions and so on, and endless pleasant trifles and knick-knacks like silver hearts and incense and rosaries and amulets and booklets and statues and candles, and enormously effective services — ever been to Tenebrae? Well, I did once, in Rome, no less. My dear, it's as good as *Hamlet*, and rather similar. *Lights, ho lights.* Perfect theatre.'

'Gertie, *dear!*'

'And when there's nothing special happening, there's a punishment to work off, or a medal for good conduct, or confession — an orgy of egotism. They all feel they are being taken care of by a sort of sublimated Waifs and Strays Society without the stigma of charity, and they are made to feel that each is a special case. Naturally it ropes in the lonely woman, and the woman who has been thwarted in one of the dozen ways women can be thwarted, or who wants colour and variety in her life, or who, without being a good organizer herself, enjoys regularity and system in her life, or who yearns to be 'mastered'. I respect that. It's a good idea, as far as it goes. Trouble is, it goes too far and the price is too dear. I'm not an intellectual woman or a clever one, but I agree with you that any religion that dares not let its followers think must have rather more than one rotten spot. Aggie's fallen in love with the trimmings. I suspect three-fifths of converts do. She calls it religion but with her it's really haber-dashery.'

Mary, overtired, worried, hurt, felt her eyes filling. She turned them away. 'Oh, Gertrude, if you would only leave one *some* illusions!'

'Certainly. You can have all mine!' But acute observation has its uses and Gertrude actually leant over and kissed Mary's cheek. 'Forget it. But hypocrisy and senti-mentality are the curses of the world. I tell you: don't fret for Aggie (that holy woman). She's enjoying herself enormously. It's *fun* for her.'

CHAPTER XV

I

QUEENIE SCRIMGEOUR was strolling in Kensington Gardens between tea and dinner with Gilbert Asherson. Enormous clumps of cloud broke the blue of the sky and the changing light made the new-foliaged trees stiff as profile models. The red façade of the Palace, enclosed in its lapping green turf, seemed lost in ageless thought, its long windows smitten to brilliance in the sunset.

Queenie moved with him slowly in the spring evening, she, stiff as her clothes and fashionable high-crowned hat, with expectation. What intuition she had was concentrated in those minutes when conversation dwindled, via small-talk, to silences. He was the first man with whom she had ever been nearly at ease, translating it as intimacy, affinity and profound mutual understanding.

He was looking at her shyly, eagerly, affectionately. In those minutes she was swung forward in time, without transition, saw herself and him as man and wife, of ten, twenty years' standing, companionably walking in the Gardens before a quiet family dinner at a home known but geographically uncharted. It was so real a sensation that the absolute blanks of memory, her inability to recollect the church, wedding day or honeymoon, seemed of small account. An elderly forgetfulness . . .

She drew a difficult breath of contentment in her constricting corsets.

'Queenie, there's something I'd like to say to you. I — as a matter of fact I've been wanting to for some days now.'

She murmured.

'Shall we sit here for a bit?' They moved off across the

grass. 'Queenie, I'm sure you'll agree with me that a friendship, however ideal, is not to be compared with marriage.' The murmur seemed to him this time to be one of entire acquiescence, but she hardly knew what she was saying; her eyes did not appear to be focusing properly and there was a singing in her ears. 'But a friendship like ours shouldn't be difficult to keep — ' That failed to register, with her. These were words, any preamble . . . she would probably remember them all later, calmly, and in smallest detail, like Mamma, who often told them all how she would never forget the morning when your dear father —

It had been at a Military Review at Chatham; Lieutenant Scrimgeour ('as he was then') very dashing in scarlet '. . . I wore a muslin gown sprigged with rosebuds and a pink sash and sandals and a chip bonnet with *more* roses, and a pink scarf.' Her daughters, secure in the modernity of the 1880's, sometimes smiled affectionately at that fantastic picture of vows and fancy dress. Queenie and Aggie, Queenie remembered, had once voted the army set dull, said they'd never marry into it, and now Aggie was in her convent and never would. It was left to Queenie to keep the flag flying, for Gilbert was not in the army, but on the Stock Exchange.

'And so, I want you' — her mind clicked back suddenly into the old, acute awareness of him — 'to be the very first to congratulate me.' He was smiling trustfully into her eyes.

Congratulate him? She was to be spared the prompt response which she would have been unable to make, for he had slipped a hand into his breast pocket and with-drawn it holding a photograph. Even then she was incredulous. 'Who *is* this?'

'Ah, I didn't mention the name. It's Maud Waring.'

'And — ?' Queenie heard her voice crack.

'Our engagement will be in *The Times* on Saturday.'

Queenie bent over the photograph, her hand shook so
that she was ashamed. 'She's very charming,' she
stammered. '*Very* pretty.' She did not really think so,
but you said that, even at dances, when a partner indicated another girl. One wasn't exactly a beauty oneself
but — one *could* look well — besides, wasn't sterling worth
to count at all, ever? And one was *such* a good sort. . . .
And here was Gilbert, one's own Gilbert, committed to this
six-a-penny chit. . . . How, when and where had one
failed? Was the whole thing mere chance — a question
of which young woman was on the spot at the right
moment — or was there a definite point in time when the
man's regard for you peak'd and then descended, so that
you saw it, and accepted it as you must?

'I'm sure I trust you'll be very happy, Gilbert.' She began
to laugh a little shrilly. 'D'you know, there was a fearful
moment when I thought it was *me* you had your eye on!'

He joined his laughter to hers. 'Oh, my dear, you're
far too brainy for my likes! and you know me too well.
No illusions, what?'

'Brainy?' Her voice sharpened. Nobody had ever
called her that before, except now at the impossible
moment, but he was solemnly thrashing it out. 'I always
understood that you wanted to have a career and that
matrimony came very second with you.'

It had been true. Once. She had even tossed it off like
a slogan in drawing-rooms to interest men in herself. It
would be true again, too late. The envenomed perversity
of life filled her with despair. '. . . And then there's Miss
Mary. Quite a bookworm, I'm terrified of her erudition!
And Aggie giving up the pomps and vanities, y'know.
Oh, I always think of the Scrimgeours as very brainy.
That's why I was so enormously touched and flattered at

your all taking me in as you did. I've no sisters of my own, you know, and it's my dearest hope that you and Maud — '

Queenie got him and herself home in some unremembered way.

11

There was no concealing it, Queenie, wandering her bedroom, calculated. This was Thursday night, one clear day before father pounced on the news in *The Times*, twenty-four hours in which to make her face and prepare her version. The lifeline Gilbert had flung to her of her own alleged 'braininess' she rejected instantly. The intellectual, even the clever, was a rôle for which the family had never cast her, it had probably been an insincerity at that, invented to get Gilbert out of a tight corner. She cringed with shame at the new idea and then grew hot with rage that she should be saddled with a shame she had done nothing to deserve. And the dickens of it was that in these cases by behaving with dignity you did the man's work for him, played his game, made it easy for him, just as you did in the ballroom where all neglect and breaches of faith must be met smilingly. Pride — something you must feign even if it went against your every instinct. Why? Because, as Mamma said, it never 'did' to show that you were hurt. Why? Nobody knew. And so the man was free to go away and you were left to the mercy of everyone, to become an object of derision, pity or contempt. And Gilbert had taken her employment from her. Over the months she had known him Queenie had gradually built her life, the very hours of her spending, round him. He was there, or just gone, or about to arrive, a condition which made the recurrent hiatus in activity negligible.

The fear of to-morrow and all the to-morrows filled her. The *time* there was! Yet men filled it to the brim, in work which brought them in money or fame and in social engagements which never failed, or there was the club; even little Charlie was having a future built for him already that would put him beyond the reach of ennui. Whereas a woman's life was one of eternal waiting, to be taken out, called on, danced with or proposed to. How had it originated, this division of opportunity?

The only possible confidante was Mary. If books made you brainy then Mary must be brainy over this situation. Meanwhile there was dinner to be got through and a rather recent reputation for vivacity to maintain. Even in the bosom of one's family one continued to shield Gilbert from criticism, it seemed.

III

There were two chances of unloading it all on to Mary, one during the time spent in the drawing-room after breakfast, the other during the morning walk. Queenie selected the former. You can't have a heart-to-heart discussion while dodging pedestrians and hansom cabs.

In the drawing-room Queenie automatically drew out some fancy-work from the Indian cabinet where she was allowed to keep it. Until Grace 'came out' they would be two, herself and Mary, in these morning sittings. Queenie did not altogether regret the shrinkage, rather agreed with Georgie who had once complained, humorously, 'Sitting here all five of us does *look* so unmarried.'

In — what? — three years, Grace would join them. Queenie, choosing skeins of silk, wondered what the child's occupation would be. Fancy-work, too? A solid book, like Mary? Fidgeting about the room (Aggie), or chatter, laughter, note-writing and fashion-papers (Georgie and Arabella)? The sittings had, long years ago, begun with two, now one came to think of it, with just Gertie and Georgina. Queenie wondered for the first time what form Gertie's occupation had taken. Any opening would serve, and she spoke.

'Mary, what did Gertie do before she married — here, after breakfast, I mean?'

'She cleaned out the canaries' cage until Mamma stopped it and said it would spoil her hands, so Susan did it after that and spoilt hers.'

'And then?'

'She used to paint flower-pieces, and net purses and wrote out menu cards and answered the notes.' A full programme that Gertie *would* contrive to corner for herself. When the drawing-room filled up with adults the jobs had had to be shared out—and by that time Gertie was gone. She was probably brainy, Queenie thought, forlornly.

Mary at the unexpected mention of her eldest sister was back again at a fixed point in their railway conversation. Gertie, secure and aloof, hinting at something amiss in her own life . . . Clarence, Mary sadly guessed, being unfaithful. Some rift one read of . . . But the allusion to Gertrude had acted with Queenie merely as an unsealing of tongue and she plunged without finesse into her matter.

'Mary, Gilbert is engaged to be married, to a Maud Waring.'

'My *dear!*' Mary flung the book aside.

'He told me quite as a matter of course.'

'But why didn't he tell us before?' That, for a flurried improvisation, would do, Mary thought, until one got some sort of a line upon how this was affecting Queenie. The brittle, artificial voice was continuing, 'I thought I'd

let you know before it's in *The Times*, as you probably all
thought it was *me* —'

That was a facer. Did Queenie need any lying denials,
or the rich, warm, surging indignation, helpless and pitiful,
that filled one's heart? Mary saw that Queenie, unlike
herself at one period, had never even remotely conceived
the possibility of friendship between a man and a woman
that should be liking and trust and incentive, and nothing
else at all. She had not to wait long, for her sister's face
suddenly screwed grotesquely and her voice thickened
with tears.

'It's the rotten unfairness of it! . . . and he said he hoped
I should be friends with *her* . . . no woman would have
been such a cad.'

'You must have behaved uncommonly well, Queenie
darling. It's lack of imagination, I suppose, that makes
men so unlike women.'

It might be that, but it was an eternal something else
upon which one couldn't put one's finger: the inevitability
with which the woman was reduced, even in fiction, to
tears or meekness, the way in which it was the man who
dictated terms, delivered ultimata. 'Don't make me
scenes or you will lose me' (when the cause of her tears,
his version of 'scene', was his own callousness). 'You will
not see that man any more' (and she gladly recognized a
jealousy which, if exhibited by herself, would call down
another sermon upon her head). Men, of course, expected
not only to have things their own way, but all ways at once,
as Nana said. And they got it. In Queenie's case, Mary,
anxious not to be biased unfairly to her cause and by that
sentimentality against which Gertrude had waxed so
vitriolic, perceived the dilemma. Girls like Queenie were
being brought up tacitly for marriage, but the business
faltered and stopped at assumption, was neither honest

nor sensible enough, having postulated her destiny, to fit her for it in any way whatsoever. Whether she won depended then upon side-issues, matters of looks, dash, charm, brains or personality with which nature, always unreliable, might or might not have equipped her. And here was Queenie in tears.

'Did — did you care for him such a lot, dear?'

'Yes, yes I did. I do. And he must have seen it.'

Mary bit her lip. Here was Queenie up against it again. If she had shown in advance that she cared — that was a breach of the etiquette of modesty they had all had insinuated into them from their childhood, and if she had respected that etiquette and left Asherson uncertain of her feelings, then he was without blame. Another score. Really, men! . . .

'He — he said that I was too clever for him and that he thought I wanted a career and not to marry.'

'Well, you did *say* so, Queenie.'

Queenie checked. It was intolerable to have your words used against you and by Mary, when what you needed was sympathy and indignation and plenty of both.

'Oh, *don't* be so unkind, Mary!'

'Sh, *please* dear! Mamma will be up any moment now.'

'I don't know what to *do*!'

'I can't begin to tell you how sorry I am. To be honest, I'd no idea he meant so much to you.'

'I'd like to hit his face till it bled,' almost shouted her sister.

'Oh come, nonsense.'

'Would a man take it meekly and say "thank you for kicking me away after making use of me"?' Queenie, in satire, was not pretty and Mary flinched. 'I tell you, I'm going to write him a letter he'll remember till he's dead. I'm going to do it *now*. I'm going to say, "Dear Mr. Asherson — " '

'Queenie, you can't.'

'How do *you* know?'

'One doesn't, I'm sure I'm right about that, it would be undignified and not being like a lady.'

'Where does being dignified and a lady get one? No-where!'

'Well then, have more pride.'

'He won't feel that.'

'No, but *you* will.'

'I shan't. I want to hit back and hurt him.'

'Queenie, you *shall* speak more quietly!'

'Well . . . what am I to do?'

'First of all, take the announcement calmly, and tell Mamma and father that you knew about the engagement. If he brings Miss—?'

'Waring.'

' — Waring to the house, as he's bound to, you'll have to see her and be pleasant.'

'It's too much to expect. A man wouldn't stand it.'

'It's not the same for them, but it's the only thing possible for you. If you feel you really can't go through with it just yet, get away for a bit, and *then* you can really begin to find some work. Oh Queenie, *do!* I should miss you terribly, but you mustn't think of me. You don't know how I've longed for — for one of us to do something, to learn something that wasn't just smatterings between engagements, and if you can make a little pocket-money at it, all the better. What fun it would be! One's earnings!'

Of sheer exasperation Queenie disparaged the scheme. It was the last straw, this urging of Mary's that she take a line she had long promised herself she would take . . . it robbed her of her final possession, the gesture; yet she *had* got in first, said she would have a career.

'I couldn't do anything *yet*, Mary. It would — you know — look as if it was because I'd been jilted.'

'Well, my dear, who cares, in the last resort? People would soon forget if you made a success. Why spoil your chances for public opinion?'

'They'd *always* remember; people do.' Her sister was obstinate in misery, and Mary hesitated with the scrap of newspaper she had taken out of an inner compartment of her purse.

'Queenie, you won't remember this, but it's a possible opening for you. It would combine a change and new surroundings with work and a career.' Queenie listlessly took the paper, its print blurred, the paper faintly yellowed, softly falling into its accurate folds with much handling . . .

'Oh . . . that women's college at Cambridge. I've just heard of it.'

'Yet it's been going for thirteen years!'

'But I don't want to teach, Mary.'

'Oh Queenie, just think, you might get a high position, or become a lecturer or a specialist in some art or science, meeting interesting people, hearing what people are really thinking, and you could tell it all to *me*. How I should look for your letters!'

'I don't suppose they'd accept me. I'm twenty-nine — and a half,' Queenie added with surly honesty.

'We could find out. Father would help you. He's so generous and kind, and don't you see? now that Aggie has made a break it makes it easier for you to. He settled money on the others when they married — I don't know how much, of course — but he gave the convent £400, because Aggie told us. He'd do something for you. Oh, *don't* give up. Go and ask him!' But even Mary burned to slap her sister when she turned to her, the heavy oval face sullen with indignation.

'It's monstrous that one should have to think of things like that at a time like this.'

Yet later, luncheon was, Mary thought, passing off fairly well, with Queenie in a passable imitation of indifference, giving out the news of Mr. Asherson's engagement to mother, father, governess and Gracie, newly emancipated from nursery midday dinner. One backed Queenie up with casual sentences about Miss Waring, stifling at birth the incredulous ejaculations of Mamma which at any second might give the show away. It was Mary's ears that caught the alien sound first.

Somebody sobbing. Her eyes turned amazedly to Grace. The hazards of the table had allotted the child a place opposite her own, a position which would be hers for the years ahead . . . one could only try to catch her eye . . .

It had to be Mrs. Scrimgeour who gave voice to the situation.

'Gracie, what ails you?' Even the Captain was looking at her over his glasses; Miss Banks had already turned pink at the implied reflection upon her own powers of keeping a child, if not happy, at least in order. Grace, crimson, her eyes brilliant with tears, revealed that she was no liar: the face which had disappointed her staircase love was incapable of the whimsical improvisation that would bring adult laughter.

'It's Mr. Asherson!'

'Eh, what?' chipped the Captain, carvers arrested.

'If he's not marrying Queenie I shall never see him again!' She could not know how absolutely the lament displeased everybody at table.

'I think you'd better go upstairs, Grace. Miss Banks — won't you? — will bring you up your pudding when she has had her own.' It was Mary who shepherded the little sister to the door.

CHAPTER XVI

I

Of all the emotions aroused by the loss of Gilbert Asherson
those of the Captain were not the least powerful. For the
first time since the birth of Charlie he experienced a
personal apprehension that all might not be well with his
life or family. One never used to worry . . . but things had
been rather cumulative, somehow . . . that business of
Aggie and the convent and four hundred of the best gone
glimmering. It had been an unexpected call upon his
purse, and he'd had to sell out of a good, safe investment.
Canadian Fours. And once you began that racket you
never got straight. He wished it could have been for a
marriage portion but supposed that, financially, it came
to the same thing in the end, as the girl was provided for,
for life. But this fiasco about Queenie was disturbing and
continued to be so in spite of the fluttering, alarmist outcries of Charlotte, who rather tended to diminish a man's
anxieties by crying wolf as loudly about trifles as she did
about matters of possible real importance. A broken
heart or a mislaid trunk-strap bulked about equal with
Charlotte. Queenie's affair had set her father to the first
curious thought about his family that he had so far experienced. It was not the circumstance itself, for girls, he
supposed, were mistaken in a man's feelings for them, and
even jilted, and Mary had not found a husband, which
had surprised nobody, now one came to think of it . . . it
was the appalling way in which life was passing and time
getting on. Queenie must be nearly thirty. Queenie,
thirty! and at that age women didn't marry. In his young

days all girls married and married early, and here one was
with three spinsters on one's record . . . and Gracie rising
fifteen . . . and even she hadn't managed to be pretty.
Daughters, confound 'em, were a problem, God bless 'em,
and bad investments, too, because you couldn't plan for
them. With loving exasperation he pondered his offspring.
Girls who were girls no longer and who didn't marry upset the order of things; one was irked by system breaking
down, always had been. The old days were best, in spite
of having a woman on the throne. But old Kent's daughter,
of course, was an exception.

Queenie . . . what was beginning to be the matter with
the girls that one left home and the other couldn't get
married?

With a flash of insight that led him nowhere and was
extinguished on the second, Charles Scrimgeour thought
that what was beginning to be the matter might well continue to be the matter. Also, it might have financial re-
percussions. To put it in plain English, one had paid off
the initial debts which were Gertie, Georgie and Arabella,
but if the other three were going to sit about to all eternity,
piling up the bills? For an instant he saw them, lines of
them, exaggerated to meet his bewildered irritation,
sitting, long-waisted, futile grenadiers pouring out fathom-
less gallons of tea. . . .

And Charlie was coming along, would very soon now
be at that point in his life which one had dreamed of, a
delightful expense, but an expense, and one that would
also be cumulative.

Money.

Half complacently, half disturbed, the Captain considered and dismissed retrenchment. One was committed
to a certain standard of living against which nothing
effective could be done. The house was a bit large, of

course, but contrived to be in some ways inadequate.

The girls had never possessed a sitting-room, there was no bathroom; if one wanted a game of billiards one had to get it at the club. For the first few years of his marriage they had had a billiard-room; with the multiplying of the family it had had to go. He had given the table to a friend. Better than selling it at a loss. In a very few years now the nursery must be converted into a den for Charlie where the boy could receive his friends, but even when Miss Banks could be sent packing for good they wouldn't get the good of her space, as a room must be reserved for old Nana. As for the servants, the house always gave an effect of being understaffed, so one couldn't charge oneself with extravagance there. In all their years he and Charlotte had never run to a valet or personal maid.

In reviewing the luxuries he had involuntarily foregone, the confidence of the Captain was restored.

11

It sagged a week later when the totals of the housebooks were put on his desk by Mary; as cash totals he scanned them with an unbelief which was only partly humorous. They represented a tribute to social security and standing, but — £40 for meat alone! Still, one always had had it, always must. The roast beef of old England. Nothing so nourishing or patriotic, or a song wouldn't have been made about it. The very word brought warming associations that were not merely physical: pleasant Sunday luncheons, the family aligned about one, winter and summer alike ... one's friends and neighbours all over London's streets and squares similarly carving and eating at a fixed hour ... the longing for Sunday and its som-

nolence and its joints when in the Russian trenches . . .
the bond that a standard dish could be, in a foreign land!
Good God, in the last resort it was a symbol of Britain for
which, incidentally, one fought. The integrity of an under-
cut, the solidity of a family. Why not? No symbol was too
humble to help you do your duty to Queen and country.
It was often the lowlier associations which meant the most
to you in conviction, when patriotic abstractions failed.

Over forty pounds . . . and yet Lady Mell in Hampshire
gave a sirloin to every last one of her tenants at Christmas.
But old Mell, of course, bred his own cattle. The butcher's
account had roused the Captain to a grimmish curiosity in
the other totals. For the first time his mind noted them,
up to now they had stopped at his eyeballs. And all
because a hitch had occurred over poor Queenie's affair
. . . like a twig cracking that started a bombardment.
One took it for granted the servants were wasteful because
they all were, as a class; there again you couldn't economize because the menial character represented inevitable
wear and tear to the householder.

Grocer, £54 10s. The girls' allowances were due.
Gracie would be wanting one, any day now, the way time
sped by; another £50 a year to find, plus travelling expenses and endless extras. How one resented the everlasting forking-out, yet giving to the pack of them as small
children had been charming enough. Then why did it
become a bore when they grew up? Why was one already
simmering with spleen at the thought of Gracie's fifty
pounds? She cost nothing now, and seemed to be suitably
clad. If it hadn't been for all these claims one might have
kept a hack and got one's riding every morning, and a
carriage. This eternal four-wheeler business for parties
probably came dearer than owning your own turn-out.

He ferreted for pass- and deposit account-books.

Current account only slightly overdrawn and the September dividends would right that, as usual. Deposit was earmarked for Charlie. A pity one couldn't have a flutter now and again, but a family man has a duty . . . in any case it takes your Jew to make a success of speculation. Writing cheques was reassuring. One had been through all this before, and would again and again. The standing luck of the British army . . . it must be all right or one couldn't have done it, or be doing it. Touch of the Spring going to the liver, all this worrying. But the rap on the door was like an electric shock to his nerves. He looked up in abstracted annoyance. Another woman wanting something. Queenie, of all people.

He registered a lightning and entirely objective view of his younger daughter and for the first time his sight refused to take her appearance for granted.

Held herself awkwardly . . . no manner in entering a room. He was a little puzzled to discover that she was plain. Gertie had good, clean lines and Georgie and Arabella good bone. Mary (he must have another look at Mary) was a pleasant-looking woman . . .

'Father, I wanted to speak to you.'

Yes, she certainly was growing distressingly like the elder Cooper-Collis's . . . his assent was not genial.

'Father, I want to *do* something. There's nothing for me to do here, at home. . . .'

This was being intolerable. He had a vision of the morning-room door being rapped on for the rest of life to admit a female file of malcontents with heavy Cooper-Collis faces and porous skins. Even Mary had once had a go at him, he remembered, with a whim of teaching Gracie, but that had soon blown over. . . .

His sarcasm was leaden. 'And so you want to go posting off to a convent and take out four hundred pounds worth of nun, I suppose?' Even her eagerness, he thought, was ungainly.

'No no, oh no, I should simply hate that — '

'Well, that's something, at any rate. You know, I don't understand you young people. In my young days girls were contented at home with their hobbies and amusements and friends until they — anyway, there was none of this dissatisfaction.'

'Are you sure, father?' At his look of astounded displeasure at the interruption no less than at the challenge she buckled ever so slightly. 'I mean, you can't *know*. They probably only didn't *say* anything, Mary says — '

'I don't know what Mary means, and I don't know what you mean, either. Really, Queenie, this is very disheartening, a little ungrateful, eh? after all we've done for you.' It was hitting below the belt, of course, this appeal to your feelings, she knew, but like a foul it winded you, you lost sight of the thread of your argument, you even for the moment went over to the enemy, and became spuriously grateful for roof, clothes and food. But those things couldn't be enough or you wouldn't want anything else, and you did want something else, with violence. Helplessly she cut the knot of all her rehearsed arguments. 'I'm dreadful sorry, father — oh, I'm *awfully* sorry, but I'm bored at home.'

'This is a pretty rotten reward for your mother and me, Queenie.'

'I know how you must feel, but indeed I can't help it. I wish I could. There's nothing to *do*. I mean, Mary could do the menus and flowers and housebooks and notes, you know, singlehanded, and if we share them they're over in an hour, and there won't be anything left over for Gracie when she joins us.' It was, she saw, a conclusion preposterous but true none the less.

'Let's hope Gracie will have a bit of sense when she grows up. Why didn't I have all this hullabaloo with Gertie? or Georgie? or Arabella?' She didn't know, even privately, to herself. The others had been part of a pattern. She and Aggie hadn't.

'You see? You can't give me a single reason why you can't settle down . . . well, let's have it. What is the idea?'

'There is a college at Cambridge, for women,' she faltered.

'Oh, good Gad! My dear girl, haven't you had enough lessons that you want to learn more, at your age! You've had a good education and finishing school . . . don't tell me you want to teach children!'

'I don't. I should hate it — '

'I couldn't allow it, it would be unsuitable and unnecessary. Besides, you'd hardly make the price of your dress allowance.'

'I — could lecture, or specialize in some interesting subject.'

'But what for? My good girl, do you really suppose the academic world would listen to a woman lecturer, let alone give her jobs? I suppose that was Mary's idea, too?'

'Yes.'

'She's as full of theories as a balloon is of gas and just as liable to get lost in the clouds.'

Queenie was stung. 'I'm sure she's right.'

'Oh, then your idea is to lecture or specialize.' He leant forward, elbows on desk. 'What's your subject?' he shot at her.

'I — I don't know. I haven't thought.'

'That's splendid, isn't it? She wants to take an unwomanly job at which she wouldn't even earn anything and then doesn't know what to speak on.'

'That's not fair — I'm sorry, father, you confuse one so, but men at the universities don't always know what they are going to take up for ages — '

' — they usually have a pretty shrewd idea based on a general trend of taste or ability, and if not that, an inherited business or profession awaiting them.'

'And we have nothing, and because of it we've got to go on having nothing — '

'Queenie, this strong-minded stuff isn't your line a bit. Better drop it. *Do you want to go to this women's college?*'

It was the weakness of her case and she knew it. Mary had put it forward as an escape at a time when one would have snatched at anything, but that didn't affect the principle of her demands. The Scrimgeours at least seldom lacked courage, and she looked at him squarely. 'No, but — '

'Ah! I thought not!' At once he was magnanimous and playful. 'It'll be something else to-morrow, I'll bet.'

'But the fact that I don't want Cambridge doesn't mean that I want to go on as I am, father. It's that I don't feel clever enough for Newnham . . . but one might be clever in other ways.'

'Such as?' Oh Lord, if only he'd stop smiling. Even anger was better than this roguish tolerance!

'I don't know, yet.'

'Oh women, women! You'd make a wonderful business man, wouldn't you, child? Two and two not making five, so unkindly, and all that. Oh, good Gad!'

For his daughter was in tears at last.

It hadn't even ended in compromise or the usual last ditch of a reconciliation of sensibility, which, though it got you nowhere, was traditionally comforting. Aggie, Queenie suspected, had won because choosing to love God wasn't exactly advanced or unladylike and religion silenced people always. Even parents. Because there was a misleading sort of suggestion of unselfishness about it. Being a nun 'showed' rather to one's world, but not as badly as being a bluestocking. She wept out the sorry tale to Mary.

PART THREE

1888 — 1936

DUKE: And what's her history?
VIOLA: A blank, my lord . . .
Twelfth Night

I

GRACE SCRIMGEOUR would never forget the day she entered the world, at eighteen. She lay awake — still seventeen — until past midnight with intense inward excitement. Tomorrow one came downstairs, found out what happened, everywhere. People to meet as a real person yourself. It was funny that one had felt so sorry at parting with Miss Banks when one was so swellingly, triumphantly glad. She had left Brecknock Gardens in a cab, as she came, for a destination unknown, only in clothes and a hat one did know, which somehow gave one a pang . . . Grace, mysteriously urged, had gone into her little bedroom when the cab had rattled out of sight, and stood there, drinking in equal measure of lifegiving freedom and a sense of sick dismay for a departed soul, so acute it had driven her out of the room. It wasn't, always honest she reasoned with herself, that one had been devoted to the governess, or even more than tepidly fond of her. But there it was. A nameless feeling of suffocation, loss, and bewildered heartache. The trifles that, pack they never so carefully, visitors left behind . . . an empty bottle of Opoponax scent in the wastepaper basket . . . picking it out and sniffing, and a stab of remembrance for all the yesterdays . . . and yet it was an awful scent and one was glad that life, free of Miss Banks, had begun. On the mantelpiece was a triangular chip of repoussé silver from a photograph frame. The barrister man . . . Grace would post it on to Miss Banks and re-establish a brief contact with her . . .

The mantelpiece, filmed with a day's dust, showed oblongs of cleanliness where the frames had stood.

It was going to be a hot day. It increased Grace's sense
of invincibility as she lay in bed under one sheet. Fate had
allotted her a summer birthday, that meant hot-weather
treats. Autumn and spring people must have a very dull,
betwixt-and-between time. Mary was an autumn person.
Winter and summer were the important seasons, definite
and clear. Snow or sun, muffins or ices, gaiters or parasols. Being born in July meant that you had got used to
being a year older before going to the seaside instead of
waiting to be older in the rooms, like Mary, and then
coming home and suddenly being a year older all through
the winter parties. It was only because one loved Mary
that one didn't pity her for being old. Getting on for
thirty-eight, she had told one. It was hard that Charlie
would be away at school, missing the day by only a week,
but boys, even young men it seemed, didn't attach the
same importance to things that girls did. She doubted if
she would have seen much of her brother if he had been at
home; he was always out at school friends' — even staying
away with families which were only names, whereas Mary
and Queenie were even now only allowed to visit among
people upon whom Mamma had called. Or Charlie would
be out with father; he was hardly ever in the drawing-
room even on Sundays in the holidays. One snatched at
Charlie still, doggedly and hopefully, but it was no real
good. He was sixteen, and for some time now had been a
boy only in name and a man in privilege. At the Christmas dances for young people his name was always included under Grace's, though hers was far from always
bracketed with his in the envelopes addressed to Charles
Scrimgeour, Esq. . . .

'Mind you give Gracie a dance,' father or Mamma would say as they waited in the hall for the cab to arrive. He had only forgotten her twice. But one had enjoyed the dances and the elderly gentlemen were kind — and one had had a good many partners, the lady of the house saw to that, with brothers of other sisters who had been adjured in other halls not to neglect them. Unconscious of hair, looks or clothes, Grace at sixteen and seventeen had gratefully enjoyed herself.

III

In half an hour the can of hot water would be brought in, and Nana stirring. Grace threw aside the sheet and ran to the window, tilting the slats of the blind for a view of the warming street. Already figures were assembling; the old man who appeared every June with a basket of gilt paper shavings for fire-places was trudging by, a milk-float stopped at number five. Mary said the floats were survivals of the Roman chariots, as the hansom was of the sedan chair. Miss Banks had never told one tit-bits of that kind. They would pass on, the hawker and the milkman, not knowing that from a top window they were watched by a young lady of eighteen who in an hour and a half would be coming downstairs into life.

Confidently she dressed and did her hair in haste, barely glancing at the swing-glass. It did not even occur to her buoyant mood that the whole room, its very corners seeming rounded with use, was now an unsuitable setting. It had been the day nursery, Nana occupying the adjoining room, Charlie in the holidays the spare bedroom below. Always in a state of flux, the domestic arrangements in the Scrimgeour household were still provisional, and would remain so until the majority of its son and heir.

The bulky white cupboard whose paint was now yellowed had been cleared to accommodate Grace's coats and frocks, but if the lower flap were pulled out a cascade of toys spread over the floor; the paintwork round every handle and keyhole was indelibly smudged by the hands of bygone nurserymaids, the débutante's dressing-table was a chest of drawers, the bottom drawer still stuffed with cot blankets, the brush and comb nudged by seaside souvenirs, a watch-stand with a view of the Brighton Pavilion and a tree-trunk on which finger-rings could be hung. Sooner or later all unwanted bazaar purchases found their way upstairs to be suspended from knobs, handles and nails, or draped incongruously across chair-backs. The pictures in the nursery were festive or religious; Christmas supplements of grandparents being greeted by descendants with packages, a Hunt breakfast of beef, beer and gallantry to the serving wench and a photogravure entitled 'Her Maiden Speech' in which a bride in a bustle leant upon the arm of her groom by a laden table and a four-tier'd cake, and seemed about to swoon at the boldness of her action in thanking the smiling guests for their good wishes.

In the adjoining room the morality of the age was upheld by a caustic chromolithograph of hell labelled 'When The Wicked Man', a Bavarian oleograph representing The Last Supper which appeared to consist of one ewer and three dinner-rolls, round which the disciples sat looking forgivably depressed, a Nativity with a star and beam half the size of the roof, two Crucifixions, and the martyrdom of a young gentleman in a portion of a leopardskin studded with arrows, which appeared to afford him a mild but comely surprise.

And even to-day the youngest daughter of the house

must perform her toilet by the light of an oil lamp which hung in an elaborate wrought-iron bowl from the ceiling by three chains. It cast fantastic shadows, but in the winter evenings was cosy enough. Her writing-desk was the old nursery table, solid and ovoid, veteran of a thousand meals, lessons and ink-splashes. With affection she viewed it all, then slowly, reining impatience to enjoy her every step, she went downstairs.

I V

They greeted her indulgently, as ever, with perhaps the little extra of facetious outcry because it was her birthday, a warm, family-manner in which little of tribute to her womanhood could be detected. If she was the centre of interest it was in the anniversary way of custom. It was Mary, in the drawing-room after breakfast, who stooped to her, squeezing her hand, and said 'Welcome!'

Grace would never forget that morning. Even the cage of budgerigars was exciting because one was seeing the birds at an unusual hour, while the very room itself looked different in the summer morning light, with the faded sunblind already protecting the stone balcony; objects hitherto glimpsed through the open door on the way upstairs to lessons took on an entirely different aspect. Like a visitor politely extolling her hostess's bric-à-brac, Grace wandered the room. Mary watched her tenderly, the book ready at any second to be discarded at her little sister's need.

Even Queenie, Mary thought, seemed more cheerful, less apathetic. Birthdays supplied a small routine of employment . . . together, the three would go out at 11.30, Grace under the mauve parasol presented by her mother, to Gunter's to eat ices by the window just over that barred basement which, all through the London season, wafted warm delicious odours to the pavement for the tantalization of errand-boys' nostrils.

But it was to be her second descent of the staircase in the afternoon, having changed to a more formal gown, which was the great moment of the day. All her life, Grace remembered the texture and the colour she wore, of the new material called Louisine Silk in the fashionable shade of brown known as La Vallière, standing away from the figure, with, at the back, its modified 'dress improver'. The shade, Mamma had told Mary, was not 'hers', but it was stylish. Grace's hair had given her trouble. Chignons had moved from the nape of the neck to the back of the crown, and it was difficult to believe (since it was the fashion) that a fringe actually did not suit one. Perhaps if one's hair was thicker, like Mary's ... but Mary wasn't very interested in the styles though she always looked nice in her own way. She, too, had donned her best, a handsome Victoria ribbed silk. Mrs. Scrimgeour, always in the fashion, offered no specially festive note, the hot weather had made her abstracted, a little peevish; already for her the festivities were over. She had seen six daughters through their emancipation ... at fifty-nine she had put on weight, pale and lymphatic yet clinging to the murderous waistline, she had for some years been a problem to her dressmaker. Accustomed to her mother from the Sundays and Children's Hours of the past, Grace accepted the presence; she had never had much of her mother, her own birth had coincided with a decline in maternal vitality, and when the years which should have been mother-filled arrived, the little brother had appeared and diverted the remnants of emotion.

Grace drew as much of breath as her dress allowed and opened the drawing-room door.

V

It was wonderful. For Grace, Mary was at the tea-table, for Grace the laden 'curate's aid', for Grace Queenie and her smart mother entertaining. To Grace's blurred and uplifted vision the very silver took on a brighter glitter, the ladies postured more elegantly, the men bent more solicitous. For there were men — three of them. True, one of them was Clarence, her own brother-in-law, but the gardenia in his buttonhole was festal as the cake that old Emma — dear and wonderful old Emma — had made. To Grace, the room was full. The day itself bore her along, and in secret flashes of memory of all her presents stacked on the nursery table, in awareness of her new gown, her freedom, the late dinner to come, she achieved animation. Birthdays spelt licence and her mother forgot to signal or sibilate, Mary observed.

The men, roused at a new female face in that drawing-room, were attentive. Gertrude herself actually came over for afternoon tea, a figure whose garnitures were guarantee'd to quell only the most sartorially knowledgeable, and subsided with a nod to the men and a peck to the maternal cheek upon a crimson sociable in a distant corner. Mary, her duties suspended with guests cupped and sandwich'd, rustled over and joined her. This was to be Gracie's day, and you never quite knew, with Gertie . . .

'It was good of you to look in,' she murmured.

'Oh well . . . poor child . . . really Mary, she looks wonderfully well, considering.' Mary refrained from asking what implied allowance was to be made for Grace. Affection, she guessed, hooded your eyes, whereas the vision of Gertie had ever been acute, and might well represent the majority-opinion of the world at large. 'Of course she's in the wrong colour, with her pale skin and that mousy hair. When she's a bit older she'll find out that it pays to suit yourself whatever the fashionable shade may be.'

Mary turned the subject. 'The Indian mail was in yesterday. Georgie wrote' — Mary lowered her voice — 'she is expecting a baby.'

'What shocking things you do say, my dear,' Gertrude, entertained, accepted a wine biscuit.

'One feels so sorry for her in a strange country, and the awful heat.'

'You can't kill women. They're practically indestructible. And I've already written her what to expect, poor wretch.'

'Oh, Gertie!'

'If I don't, nobody will.'

'To frighten the poor darling for nothing! . . .'

'Rubbish, Mary. Have you ever waited for a gun to go off, knowing it would and expecting it? You know as well as I do that one is tensed, prepared, but you know equally well that one nearly has heart failure on the 5th of November when ragamuffins let off a squib at one's back. Dear old Georgie was most amusing about it all. She just could *not* bring herself to the point, but did the Lancers all round it: kept on calling it "this coming change in our lives", and, if you'll credit me, began her letter, "Before you get this, our *ménage* may be three instead of two". I had to laugh. And talking of babies, I'm sending a man along to you all, with my love. Most presentable, and I know one more is always welcome, in this house, at any rate. Roy Pomfret. He says it's a good old English name. I always tell him it's probably *Pommes frites* and means that his ancestor was one of the Conqueror's cooks. He'll be along presently, has the usual dozen of tea-fights to

look in at first. I suppose I shall have to stay to introduce
him, or mamma will consider herself assaulted.'

V I

'Oh, Mr. Pomfret, I couldn't eat any more cake.
Really. Honestly, *I've had enough already.*'
'Oh, never say die, Miss Scrimgeour. At your age I
could clear the dish.'
'Oh, did you?'
'Fact. Don't I look it?'
'Oh ... I — well, I never thought about *that.*'
'Please think about me or I shall be hurt, and cry.
Boo hoo hoo!'
'You are funny! But won't *you* have some more? Cook
— her name is Emma — made it. She — '
'Mes compliments to cook Emma.'
'She's been with us a *long* while.'
'Who wouldn't?'
'Oh, I didn't mean it like that — '
'But I did.'
Grace gave a wriggle of delighted embarrassment. She
was getting on! though sometimes men did say things
which left you tongue-tied. He was thinking the youngest
Miss Scrimgeour was an uncommonly juvenile eighteen
and thanking his stars the eye of Mrs. Randolph was not
upon him. Perhaps it was Miss Grace's physique ... she
couldn't be more than five-foot odd. A pleasant little
goblin reeking of the schoolroom.
Grace herself regarded him with trust and interest,
tending him through instinct no less than upbringing
Because of Asherson she would always have a tender heart
for men: because of him they would ever stand for a
personal kindness, a smile and a kissed hand. . . .

On her sociable, Gertrude, putting up her chased lorgnette, remarked pleasantly 'Did we ever talk like that at eighteen, Mary? It's a humiliating thought ... six o'clock already. I must rescue poor Roy.'

VII

A day to be remembered. Grace handled the brown silk which now hung in its cupboard. Her nervous system still tingled with achievement.

Who wouldn't?

What had one said then? Something all right, or one would become deflated at this point in the remembered dialogue. Ah! *I didn't mean it like that*, and then the triumphant *But I did*. In bed one would reconstruct it all in sequence, but first to the glass to see how one's hair had looked, because he had seen it so.

Was one going to be in love with Roy Pomfret?

And Miss Banks was gone and there were no more lessons and nothing to do for ever!

CHAPTER II

I

For the first time in all her years Grace walked the seaside promenade with her sisters one on either side, an equal. It was Grace, that August, who contributed the majority of the conversation. Mrs. Scrimgeour took her rests in increasing doses, feet up on the sofa in the lodgings, Mary, never a small-talker, looking upon the after-tea walks merely as health-giving, swept along thinking her thoughts while Queenie trudged in blank depression of spirit. Queenie had now sighted that stage in life when it could not only offer nothing, but in which she would soon admit as much. She filled her time with trivia in an effort at postponement of that admission. She had, she believed, disappointed Mary in accepting the set-back over the Cambridge affair. Well, so be it. Who cares? But she did care, and what else could she or anyone have done? Round and round the old, old thoughts, getting one no-where, defiance, and self-justification as monotonous as the ring of their boots on the asphalt. And one had dis-appointed Mamma as well, in the ancient and obvious way, because no man had proposed to one. Quite soon, any year, any month, week, even while one was drawing the next breath, one might be passing, in the eyes of Mamma and one's circle, into the musty ranks of those who 'would never marry now'. Perhaps one had passed, already in the minds of one or two? Mentally, exhaustedly stale with thought, one fought with time for the privilege of being rated as still in the running with life.

PART THREE

II

To Grace, her own lengthened skirts and the adult companionship transfigured the holiday; joyously she paid the
price by restriction of wind and limb, for young ladies no
longer built sand castles or paddled — ever, that was now
left to factory girls, shrieking in feathers, down for the day
on an annual outing by brake, taking donkey rides and
showing leg up to the knee where their skirt of red and
purple face-cloth rucked and strained. It kept the
Scrimgeours to the rarer air of the esplanade, tiring to the
feet but still select. Young ladies did not do this or that,
above all, the other. Delighted to be joining in the bustle,
Grace had addressed labels, done all that they allowed her
under Mary's direction, for Queenie cleared right out of
the way thankfully (she said so), and Mary seemed relieved
to have one's shoulders to place the jobs upon. Mamma
saw to everything, of course, although it was a little difficult
to find out exactly what she did except talk and issue
orders and cancel them. But there were, no doubt, big
things that she controlled, not the trifles allotted to oneself . . . it was all good fun and would have been perfect
if one could have owned a new trunk of one's very own
with initials on the lid, instead of the old black American
cloth which had belonged to Georgie and Arabella. And
Charlie. He was paying a country house visit and would
join father in Scotland in September. It had left father
free to come with them to Brighton. They did not see
much of him; he was at the Conservative club most of the
day, but Mary said his presence certainly improved the
standard of cooking in the rooms.

It was Mrs. Scrimgeour who noticed and commented
upon the unusual absence of any of their men friends to

speed them at the station. Grace had alluded to her mother's remark later, and Mary said that in the old days men friends did come, with flowers, to say good-bye. Grace was impressed. It set her to visualizing Mr. Pomfret, bloom-laden, against the sooty pillars of the terminus.

He would say —

And she would say —

For several miles the easy dialogue, warm, personal, affection-ringed, flowed through her brain, a duet she could sub-edit, embellishing, deleting, creating the perfect, satisfying thing. In those conversations, one was the person of one's hopes, and shed the tongue-tied maladroit Grace of everyday.

Sometimes in their walks or in the town, his daughters would come upon the Captain. Occasionally he joined them, more often passed on with a flourished stick of greeting. He was, Grace guessed, disappointed at losing Charlie for August. Hopefully, diffidently she tried to make good her brother's careless defection, but it was, naturally, no real use. She did not know his subjects, the language of his sports. But he was kind and indulgent always to the small figure hurrying at his side, endeavouring with shy incompetence to keep him entertained.

III

They discovered the wool shop up a side street in the old part of the town off the Steyne. Two worn steps led up to it, the glazing of its bow windows was uneven, offering a wavering view of the coloured stock within. Overhead beetled a brick roof like a lych-gate, patched with stonecrop.

It was Grace who cried, 'What a darling shop! It's simply Miss Matty's, Mary! How I'd love it!'

They entered on Queenie's business of choosing fancy-work for the winter ahead. The tinkling bell brought them a fair, fadedly pretty woman, anxiously polite. Mary at one glance and hearing astoundedly realized that Mrs. Cator was a lady. Queenie chose canvas and silks in a dream; it was her sisters who talked of the shop all the way home.

In the days which followed they noticed that Queenie seemed to be in an altogether unusual set of difficulties concerning exact matches of skeins and textures of canvas. She would go off alone as many as three times in a week to the wool shop.

She had made a self-discovery, had found a thing she wanted of life, a thing which subconsciously she had always, as it were, accepted and filed as a dead letter. She wanted a little business of her own to create, to be active for, to audit and buy for and sell goods at a profit because that imponderable asset, imagination, had gone to their purchase and display. In a similar back parlour to Mrs. Cator's she would sit and watch the profits grow. She might in time even own a Bank balance! Father would show her the ins and outs of that. Thoroughly, with thought swept clean of pettiness, Queenie examined and tested her desire, found it fool-proof. When you utterly wanted a thing perhaps you found words that convinced in which to ask for it?

I V

The unnecessary purchase completed, Queenie had got into conversation with Mrs. Cator, leading the talk, drawing her gradually out as became the independent woman ... extra-courteous as you were to inferiors, until the day came when her growing interest betrayed her into naturalness and Mrs. Cator, simply, and flushed a little, had invited her eager customer into the back parlour.

'If you are seriously interested in the idea of having a shop too — '

'I am, I am, Mrs. Cator!'

'I see. By the way, I have to tell you that my name isn't Cator — and it's Miss, not Mrs. Miss Wardour.'

Queenie was blank. Her hostess picked at the ball-fringe of the mantelpiece. 'You see, my mother and some of her relations still live in Brighton, and you can under-stand — '

'The name over a shop? Yes, I understand,' answered Queenie downrightly.

'*I* shouldn't have minded, but one must make allow-ances ... and I called myself "Mrs." because it gives a kind of *solidity*, you know, not I suppose that it matters, in my case (I'm forty-five), but I should recommend it to any young woman.'

'I see. Please go on. I want to know how you started, and everything.'

'It was losing our money, of course. We had always understood, my mother and I, that we should be provided for when my father went. We had a very comfortable home — well, you know all about that, Miss Scrimgeour, and when my father died, it was found that he had left nearly all his money to another woman. She — he — they lived together ...'

'But — your mother? She was his wife! She came first!'

Mrs. Cator shook her head and stared into the paper fan outspread in the fireplace. 'They can do it, it seems.' She roused herself and turned to her visitor. 'In Scotland a man is compelled by law to leave a proportion of his estate to the widow. In England, no.'

'It's incredible.' Queenie spoke slowly.

'It's true. So then I thought things over and decided on the shop. Relatives helped me and with a part of what we had in the bank and from the sale of our unwanted furniture I laid in stock. I had always been fond of needlework and you would be surprised how many of my women friends made things for me — '

'I shouldn't!' shot Queenie with venom. 'I'm sure it was the unmarried ones.' The other thought, then laughed. 'As a matter of fact I believe it was, bless them! I had thought the hardest part was going to be in persuading my mother to allow me to set up in trade, but when she knew about Papa, she seemed to change all her ideas. I sometimes think she let me have my way because he would have hated it so.'

'I don't blame her. What beasts men are!'

'Ah, don't say that. Some of them are so splendid and fine, and really, you know, it's all the more to their credit, as things are made so easy for them to be bad lots.'

v

Within another week Queenie had a good working idea of the practical side of the business. She went to her father armed to the fingertips with prices, discounts, wholesalers, upheld with the power of direct purpose.

He refused her point-blank. To his financial exasperation was added the rage of unsuitability. Trade ... a daughter of his ... She had blurted out the story of Mrs. Cator's father and it added fuel to his fires; to put Captain Scrimgeour into the same category as a blackguard and a wife-deserter . . . listening to sordid tales from a complete stranger in a back street . . . even if they were true . . . He hoped the day was long distant when Queenie or any other of his family would have to open a shop. What next, he would like to know?

Nothing. Nothing next, ever. She was defeated, and knew it; up against prejudice and lack of capital.

Her stillborn love affair, her spinsterhood she might forget if they would let her, the loss of her shop never. It was her real broken romance. 'I could have made a success in business but they wouldn't let me.'

That would be her story in all the years to come.

CHAPTER III

I

THAT winter, Grace Scrimgeour dressed for her first dance. They had secured her an invitation with only a little difficulty — a matter of determined allusion by Mrs. Scrimgeour and Mary to friends who entertained of the début of yet another Scrimgeour daughter, plus the hint that it was the Christmas holidays, so (luckily) Charlie would be at home to take the child about. . . .

Helplessly the hostesses wrote upon their engraved cards

Miss Scrimgeour
Miss Queenie Scrimgeour
Miss Grace Scrimgeour
Mr. Charles Scrimgeour

A roomful already! And only one family polished off!

In the years to come, many of the London dance-givers crossed off the name of Scrimgeour entirely. In the fear of giving temporary offence by selection from the clan they maimed the chances of Grace all through her young womanhood. Heaven knew, the mothers-in-council would agree, they had done their duty by the Scrimgeour girls in the past for what seemed like an eternity, and the present lot were rather deadweights, weren't they? And men were so difficult to pin down that you had to bait the line with pretty faces and young faces, or they never came again.

II

It was Mary who saw the peril ahead for her little sister, she who opened such campaign as there was by the counter-move of letting it be known that she herself did not go to dances. Refutation of the statement was unlikely, her own contemporaries had long passed out of the ball-room to marriage and chaperonage of its own daughters. That left the problem of Queenie. It would be a sacrifice none the less that it could not be described as a premature one to hint to Queenie that she give up dancing too, and for this season at any rate must not be mooted in face of the blow about the wool shop. Yet Queenie in her present mood of savage unhappiness might well be a factor badly damaging to Gracie on the dance floor. She was indifferent to her appearance and had lost, for the present, any interest she had ever had in dress, and — she could not afford that particular kind of carelessness. . . .

With puzzled concentration Mary traced the cause of the dilemma which might well be Gracie's. In the old days there didn't seem to have been this difficulty and skirmishing. Gertie, Georgie and Arabella — even Mary herself — had had quite a gay time. She supposed that the tremendous gulf in age which isolated Gracie from the rest of them had done it . . . that, and being governess-reared. Gracie had never been to a finishing school, as had the others. Why not? Thinking back, Mary found that she had missed that particular decision in the family politics. Finishing school, of course, was a farce, but it built for the future, and *anything* which did that . . . The rest of her sisters, Mary supposed, had drawn self-confidence from each other, had been able at a pinch to do a lot of mutual spade-work . . . Even father and Mamma contributed. But now, father was wrapped up in Charlie and Mamma was turning into an old-age which wasn't being much use to any young girl, a time of life that still combined the demanding of a full measure of authority and interference, a clinging to the fashions and a share of public attention, with a tricksy habit of evasion on the score of age of any duty that promised to bore or fatigue. Thus, over Grace's dance, she had decided that chaperon-age, these days, meant draughts, uncomfortable chair and 'one of my heads' next day, and then became offended when her name did not appear on the invitation. And because of all this, of the possibility of their having scamped Grace among the lot of them, Mary vowed that, if by any sacrifice of her own, compensation could be paid, she would pay it.

Over Queenie she need not, after all, have worried. All through 1889 Queenie doggedly withdrew into herself, farouchely refusing invitations 'right and left' as her mother optimistically put it. She hoped she did not actually dislike Queenie. . . .

Queenie's choice of line, that year, would have been all very well had she stuck to it, but from 1890 onwards, she abandoned it, desperately, hectically, awkwardly thrusting herself back into that society which believed it had seen the last of her, sitting among the wallflowers and the daughters of her friends, removed from the sweet nothing by a generation, ever a bar behind the rhythm of the latest joke and catchword.

It did not improve the chances of her sister Grace.

III

But in the winter of 1888 Grace dressed for her first ball. She was heedless of that popular delusion of fiction (had she not read it, often?) in which the débutante, starry-eyed, heart beating 'high' with expectation, clad her slim body in swathes of fresh tulle and wondered when He would appear to claim her, holding the flowers

He had sent her by messenger with the card (scribbled with a few words in his writing that she alone would understand) tucked into the roses — white roses, for innocence. She was innocent enough, in that way, raw, preposterous and rather endearing, which was to prevail with young womanhood up to, and even into, the early twenties for the next quarter of a century, and by which they half believed that, man-kissed, they ran grave risk of having a baby, a terror real and parentally unsuspected, and which waited to pounce too late to save the illogical creatures who were to discover they were warm human beings and not calculating machines. She would enter the ballroom with curiosity rather than that expectation which derives from assurance, and if her heart was thumping already, it was not through thought of amorous adventure ahead, but from that nervousness, an over-emphasis of the event, that was to accompany her all through life. It took the humiliating form of making the palms of her hands moist and cold. Already her twenty-four-button-length gloves looked limp, she despaired to Mary, who told her she looked very sweet. It was Mary who had made Mrs. Scrimgeour engage a man from Truefitt's for Grace's hair. Mary was quietly helping, had been dressed and ready an hour before her sister, to give her all her attention.

Circumstances had compelled Mary, after all, to attend the ball. The child must have a chaperon — that insurance-policy against the appearance of neglect which was still popularly deemed to be the shield and buffer against undesirable attentions and familiarities . . . Grace was thankful for her support. Longing to take her place, a woman of the world, to enjoy the company of men, all the circumstances of her life had worked to make her at her best with women. She half suspected it herself, knew that it must be fought, that, and her natural shyness and unreadiness of repartee. The ball, she was ready to believe, was the turning-point in her life, the source of all future adventure; yet as Mary draped the cape over her chilly little shoulders Grace cast a glance of maternal affection and regret round the warm, disordered nursery. On the floor was a discarded stocking, the lower drawer of the white cupboard had been accidentally loosened in the bustle of preparation, and a box of lead soldiers lay scattered over the carpet.

IV

Charlie philosophically awaited them in the hall, gibus under his arm. He barely glanced at his sisters as they moved to the front door. Already, at not yet seventeen, he had met and danced with some of the prettiest girls in London, who would, in a year or so, become the beauties of the current season, those rumour-garlanded glamoured ones whose photographs adorned the show-cases of Elliott and Fry and at sight of whom, on summer evenings, people would surge forward as they drove in the Row.

Grace was proud of him, this well-dressed, tall, pale young man who was her brother. To-night at least she missed the strained look upon his face, the fatigue under his eyes, the very fact that his admired height was sign of outgrown strength.

'Buck up, Mary.' He shovelled them into the cab and lay back, his scarlet-lined cloak thrown open.

They were a little early; it was better, Mary said, at first dances. It had annoyed Charlie to whom exact timing with an eye to partners meant nothing. Grace calculated her chances. Clarence would possibly be there

and her nephew, Albert, and there was, of course, Charlie
. . . say three dances. Mary might know some of the men
though it was unlikely, and for the rest Grace must count
upon her hostess.

v

Before the stream of guests had steadily set in, Grace
had booked four extra-family dances.

'Will you give me a dance?'

'With pleasure.'

'Have the pleasure?'

'With pleasure.'

Even to Grace's ears that exchange had sounded
ridiculous and for the rest of the night she varied it to
'Certainly'. She accepted from the first that the men
your eye took a fancy to were never the ones with whom
you danced. That was no doubt the common lot of girls.
As it was, you took every man that came up with mingled
distaste and gratitude. About the programme problem,
Grace, later, was to listen to girl friends in their dens and
boudoirs debating the various advantages of booking
partners 'all in a lump' so that you looked in demand
(this was implicit, never spoken), or spacing out names on
the card so that you kept the evening going that way
instead of starting off with a bang and then fizzling out.
It was a question never finally solved. She thought herself
that giving up your programme for men to initial was
horrid; it showed them at a glance how you were
doing. . . .

When the blank spaces came round she hurried to Mary,
sitting by her side, watching the dancers with a naïvely
genuine interest that the chaperons thought pathetic and

likeable, but green. She had yet to learn the technique of wallflowerism: the vivacious smile that masked neglect, the earnest conversation about nothing accompanied by emphasis and gesture, the brow knitted over the programme to convey the error being traced, or some private absorption which, dreaming, had let the dance go by. Some girls, she learnt, plunged boldly, and lost a dance sooner than admit availability, if at the last moment a man was led up after the music had begun ('Too simply done, so sorry') or, 'I've just done the *stupidest* thing and turned my foot a little, shall be all right soon'. Or there was, it seemed, The Signal, which partly occupied you and conveyed high spirits and absence of rancour. This consisted in calling out and waving hands during the dance to friends, real or imaginary, who had secured partners. 'Is ours the next?' or, 'Hul*lo*!', being type-ejaculations. They kept you in touch . . . put you in the swim . . . were practically undetectable (except at very small dances) because every girl and young man took it for granted you were hilariously greeting somebody else . . . It was an intricate course in applied dramatics that would have taxed and disheartened the experienced professional actor. Being sheltered young women of the period, they took it in their stride.

VI

Three of Grace's four dances had passed before her sister Gertrude entered the ballroom attended by a daughter and some men. The girl turned to one of them and without a by-your-leave put the flowers she carried into his hand. He turned and laid them on a chair. The trivial incident rooted Grace's attention. *That* was the way things should be done . . . and Paula was a year and a half younger than herself. . . .

Grace fell to examining her dress. She could not honestly admit that her own gown failed to survive comparison, but, somehow, the clothes of other people, however simple, always contrived to suggest a spontaneous rightness that confounded one into wondering why one hadn't thought of just that effect, too. But perhaps other girls were thinking the same about one's own dress? Yet Grace expected that they weren't, and never would.

Paula was talking to two men at once, another thing one had never thought of. Grace must try to . . . Paula was looking up, impudently amused, she even tapped one of the men under his chin with her fan. Then she saw Grace.

'Hullo Auntie!'

Even the fact that the greeting was one of affection and accentuated humour could hardly save the situation. Grace had known her niece was to be present, but it took the surroundings of the ballroom to bring home to her that you oughtn't to be an aunt at your first dance. . . .

She glanced round in apprehension. It seemed to her that the near-by men had heard, and were amused, and alienated. She hastily forestalled mockery, said to her partner vivaciously 'I am, as you see, an aunt. She's only eighteen months younger than I am.'

'I beg your pardon?' He hadn't heard. Grace, dismayed, found herself committed to a full explanation which could have remained her secret. And it didn't even interest him, she saw with despair. And some devil flogged her on to telling every subsequent partner in a determination not to admit an initial mistake. 'Have you come for The Aunt?' 'The Old Woman can still hobble round'.

She bored herself to frenzy, and even repeated the memorized catchwords to the same man twice on the one occasion that she had been asked for two dances.

'It seems to be on your mind.' The look he gave her, bantering, humorous, made her lose her head. 'Oh ... of course, I've said that to you before. But really it's too awful ... and rather killing too, you know ...' For a frightful second Grace believed that she was going to relate the story all over again, but he took her arm and said 'Shall we come if we're coming?' and like a flustered passenger achieving her reserved compartment, Grace began to dance. It was a poor beginning to the small-talk of the interval which loomed ahead. Grace, revolving, rehearsed what she might say.

Do you know many people here? But perhaps she had already said that, too?

What plays do you like best? But how could one lead up to that? With luck he might give her an opening, but how it could happen she couldn't imagine. (*'Will you have some cup?' 'Please. By the way, have you seen Ellen Terry in "The Cup"?' 'These palms look like a forest.' 'Talking of which, have you seen Irving in "Macbeth"?'*) Or, *'Have you been to Drury Lane pantomime yet?'* But men didn't go to the pantomime, even Charlie voted them 'slow'. Or there were books ...

Gertrude Randolph had looked her over with an upward glance that undressed her, a downward glance that put her clothes back, and said unexpectedly that she looked 'very well', and got three dances more for her. In shy gratitude Grace hammered the subject. 'But are you *sure* they oughtn't to be dancing with Paula, Gertie?'

'Oh, have done, my child! Paula can look after herself.' Paula herself confirmed it. 'Help yourself, auntie! Heaven help you with Crocker, though. He dances well but is a bit too Macassar for me about the hair. I've had to give

him two hops, though, as he came to Mum's dinner first.'
She looked smilingly at Grace. 'And how are we enjoying
our first ball?' It was intolerable to have that said by a
junior. Grace flushed, but could not put the chit in her
place. People had a demoniac habit of saying things you
couldn't openly resent and yet which left you helplessly
annoyed.

She answered 'Oh quite well, very well. I hope you — '
but Paula had ceased to listen and was already talking to
somebody else. That, it seemed to Grace, was going to be
another thing: the difficulty of getting your remarks heard.
It must, she thought, disappointed and dashed, be something temperamentally wrong, a lack of personality?
Then it was no use fighting it. Even one's gloves had
already gone grey at every fingertip through nervousness,
whereas Paula's continued to look like new. It was all of a
piece with having a mother like Gertie, a diamond,
brilliant but hard. But Paula hadn't got a Mary ...
Paula was pretty, no doubt about that, with Clarence's
fair hair and Gertie's marked features and dark eyes.
Quite soon the younger girl, Caroline, would be coming
out too, and Grace would probably have to fall back on
the aunt joke for years ahead at all the balls they would
all be asked to.

VII

The band wailed softly to a close and Grace turned to
discover with warm pleasure a girl she knew at her side.
Sometimes, governess-escorted, they had been to tea in
each other's homes.

'Fanny!' Her companion turned and said absently,
'Hullo, Grace'.

'I *am* glad to see you, I haven't seen you since — '

o   209

But Fanny's eyes were roving round the room as Grace worked at her.

'Do you remember Miss Banks?'

'Miss who?' Grace had her attention.

'Banks. Miss *Banks*. My governess. *You* remember her. Her name was Banks — '

'Oh, yes, Banks. Have you seen my partner?'

Grace hurriedly denied. 'Look here, Fanny, if you're disengaged for supper let's sit together and talk.'

Fanny looked at her. 'Oh . . . that would be rather a pity, wouldn't it.'

In one evening the alliance, the secrets and the shared youth had been swept away. Grace, obtusely unable to draw a parallel between Fanny's social difficulties and her own, was saddened and wounded. She was to meet it often, the public desertion of old playmates, the roving eye and the vague smile, the apparent blank of memory concerning the mutual past. To Grace Scrimgeour the dance-floor was a place where you danced. She would not admit that it was a battle-ground. Life was a joyful thing, and any other view of it couldn't be a true one.

CHAPTER IV

I

ALL the rest of the night, lying in the quiet of the nursery, Grace re-lived the evening. Sometimes for a minute sleep caught her, stilled her brain, then stranded her. The bed was gently revolving in a waltz, into her drugged mind came electric crashes of subconsciously registered dance music. Then she drowsed, to be shocked awake once more by voices of the ballroom, faint but clear, repeating scraps of conversation. At half-past five, satisfaction and unease blurred into heavy sleep. Two hours of it. The can of hot water would appear as usual, and Grace had gathered overnight that she would, as usual, appear at family breakfast. Paula had said 'I mean to sleep till ten, to-morrow, and breakfast in bed'. But other homes, other customs . . . the Brecknock Gardens one couldn't put the maids out. Even Charlie was expected to be in his place, and he was, but twenty minutes late and very cross and silent. It seemed to affect the whole family and Grace succumbed to the atmosphere.

II

Upstairs in the drawing-room even her attentions to the budgerigars were desultory. Over her book Mary watched her. Queenie asked a few grudging questions that Grace eagerly answered and then withdrew into herself. She was loitering about the big room, her hands unoccupied. Mary hoped that the little sister wouldn't comment upon it,

knew that the abandonment of Queenie's fancywork was
an admission of its meaninglessness. Sitting there ob-
servant, Mary hoped quite desperately that Grace might
steer a clear course, that life might not be too much (too
little?) for her as it had been for Agatha, that if, like
Queenie, she should desire a trade, the way would be
made easy.

What Mary did not know was that Grace, quite simply,
wanted home and love, romance and frivolity, and plenty
of it.

III

Mary gave Grace a year in which to test the house and
local possibilities. Afterwards, she suggested that she take
up some occupation, social work, hobby. Or there were
classes . . .

Grace fell in with all the suggestions, to please Mary.
She regarded them as only slightly time-wasting affairs
between herself and the real business of living. For another
year she took lessons on the guitar but displayed small
aptitude, although it was amusing enough to sit in a semicircle of young girls, watched by maids and chaperons,
instruments bunched with ribbons and twanging Italian-
ate sentiment. Paula was actually learning the banjo and
already played with spirit, as well, her mother humorously
complained, as any beach nigger. Some of Grace's contemporaries even attended cookery classes, but the mothers,
including Mrs. Scrimgeour, on the whole veto'd this
particular form of time-filler. It was not an accomplish-
ment. It was quite superfluous, for when the girls went
to homes of their own there would, of course, be a qualified
staff, and in their maidenhood homes the servants naturally
knew their duties already. Above all, learning to cook 'led

nowhere', and it might spoil the hands and even the complexion. The guitar and mandoline were another matter.

Some of the girls affected to rave over Signor Mengozzi,
others were amused at his foreignness and tittered at his
accent when correcting them in English instead of the
Italian they did not understand a word of. All foreigners
were a sort of fancy-dress attempt at being English, just as
England was the only country that didn't speak with any
accent, but in the one, pure language. Midway between
insular contempt and eternal woman, Grace watched the
Signor. Could one fall in love with him?

There was roller-skating at Prince's. Grace occasionally
went, but lacking regular male escort her attendances were
few. Sometimes, if with a party, she could share in the
men her young hostesses had brought. She soon saw that
you couldn't settle down to a career of social piracy, and
this was a trouble one couldn't take to anyone. The only
thing left was to say you didn't care for it . . . it tired your
ankles, or you were engaged that afternoon.

Queenie accepted whatever came her way, with bitter,
fervid determination, seeking she knew no longer what
from life eagerly. At thirty-six, her voice and laughter
were too loud, her clothes a thought too juvenile, her whole
effect *démodée*. Once, on the sole occasion that Grace and
her sister had gone together to the rink ('Will Grace — and
one of her sisters if she cares to, of course — join us?')
Grace had intercepted glances between the two men of
the party: a wry grimace, a slightly tilted head, the scraps
of an undertoned dialogue.

'Your turn, Bob.'

'Oh lor!'

' — 'blowed if — '

and one rolled off with another girl while the second took
Grace round. She had adored him for it. Poor, poor

Queenie! To be thirty-six must be terrible. She revelled, as they rattled round the huge floor, in being twenty-one, with all of life before her. It was only when at home that her heart ached for her sister.

It was the rink affair over again at dances, only worse. Grace felt a traitor at her own relief that Queenie's name so seldom appeared these days upon the invitation cards. Mary didn't care for dances, and now the cards were, as often as not, addressed to Grace alone. She had, by now, a tiny and precarious circle of acquaintance in those ball-rooms to which she had the *entrée*. Queenie would arrive knowing nobody but her hostess; it was terribly difficult to get even half her programme filled, and the boys and young men committed to a turn with her supposed that she was somebody's mother, or the companion.

IV

Grace had had a twenty-first birthday party, of a sort; dinner and a small reception afterwards. It was not, of course, so big an affair as the Captain was already planning for Charlie if he could get leave from Sandhurst. This celebration was to include a dance at the Wharncliffe Rooms with supper and breakfast to follow.

Queenie, surveying the drawing-room in Brecknock Gardens, suggested a family dance for Grace, and the sisters bent over lists. It was Grace herself who, wistful and a little amazed, discovered that the plan was impossible.

Literally, they didn't seem to know any eligible men. If eligible they were unavailable and the merest acquaintances; the friends of the Captain were old and sometimes infirm as well. There was Grace's godfather, of course . . . he still danced, but also had a wife and daughters who could not be omitted and whose combined numbers would take away all the advantage of one man. All the young married men had wives, Grace confusedly murmured to herself. There were, perhaps, four possibles to be recruited from among Charlie's friends, and those whom Grace herself had met sufficiently often at other dances to invite without its looking 'marked', but men were always booked three-deep in the summer. Even if the quartet were secured to form a nucleus she had no such guarantee with regard to anybody else. That left Gertrude and her big circle. But you can't fill your ballroom with men to whom you yourself have to be introduced . . . and one shrank from being further beholden to Paula and Caroline. . . .

That left one man who 'never went out in the evenings', the family doctor, the vicar, a brother and a nephew not to be counted on, at Sandhurst and Oxford respectively.

To judge by their faces, Mary and Queenie had also arrived at the doleful conclusion. They helped each other out loyally.

'Don't you think a dance is rather *hot* for summer?'

'It isn't as though we had a garden. . . .'

'You might miss a good ball yourself, Gracie, through giving this one — '

'Of course it would need a tremendous lot of *organization*,' Grace assented. There would be no dance. The sisters were rather careful to avoid each other's eyes.

V

Once, at a regimental ball at Aldershot, Grace experienced a rapidly filled programme, a compliment on her dancing and some flirtation which she took with grave intensity. Arabella and her husband chaperoned her.

'The poor lambs are so maddened with boredom down here, hanging about before manœuvres, that they'd kiss my shoes for sight of a new face and a young one,' Arabella wrote to Mary.

Grace, flushed with happiness, stood in the middle of the group of big, good-natured men, leaning down to hear what she was saying. The whole wonderful world seemed full of scarlet mess jackets and gleaming hair, and Majors being gallant. She thought, 'Which shall I marry?' and the next minute was laughing aloud at the fusillade of witticism and genial insult carried on above her head.

'Dammit, Lassiter, this is my dance with Miss —'

'Scrimgeour.'

'All right, but you can't hog her the whole evening.'

'Don't take on Scarsdale, Miss Scrimgeour, he's a nasty bit of work, aren't you, Scar?'

'Oh, I'm *sure* he isn't, Mr. Fleming!'

'What yah mean, you're sure he isn't?'

'One on the chin for you, Fleming. Miss Scrimgeour knows a good, Godfearing, well-spoken man when she sees him.'

'When *does* she see him?'

'*Now*, you fool.'

Andrews, one of the subalterns, discovered her interest in his profession about which she spoke with the sure directness of knowledge. They argued, chatted and harangued with the freedom and ease of a shared enthusiasm. He asked for her address in London. She gave it, eagerly. The boy said, 'It's been a real refresher to meet you, Miss Scrimgeour. Most girls can't talk about anything but the floor and the band.'

But the epoch-making semi-assignation of the confided address was to pale before the dance with his superior officer, and, the Lancers over, Captain Lassiter took her elbow, scooped her into a curtain'd alcove, gleamed at her through his monocle and said, 'Why haven't we seen yah before? Sit back and tell me the whole lurid story.'

'Well — I — there's nothing to *tell*, you know.'

'No. I don't know.'

'I was invited by my brother-in-law, Captain Grahame. He — he's a dear. I love him.' And for the moment, she did, for all that he had done for her.

'Nonsense. Nobody loves their brother-in-law. Why not have a whack at me?'

Her ideas whirled; her tongue seemed to be saying, 'Well, of course, I *am*, you know.'

' "Am" what?'

It confounded her. 'I — you're all so *kind*.'

'Oh my God, you know! That sounds like a spreading waistline. If I'm kind I'd better put the shutters up.'

'But, don't you want to? — be kind, I mean . . .?'

'Certainly not. I want to sit here and tell a certain tiny young lady that she's got a pair of uncommonly decent eyes.'

Grace Lassiter. . . .

A memory flashed into her brain. She raised her fan and mockingly tapped him under the chin. It was a faulty aim, directed by a trembling hand, but he took the cue, and leaning forward kissed her with a laugh and a murmur.

She came back to Brecknock Gardens in a daze.

VI

For the first time her thoughts were rich. She was in love! With varying degrees of emotion they swept from Fleming to Scarsdale and Andrews, before homing to Captain Lassiter. He occupied her with hot, tingling memory, for months. In her room she talked to him aloud, the discourse of imagination and of fact, rehearsing again the gesture of the tapped fan.

All through the rest of that summer she would change after luncheon and flit to the spare room where, until the gong sounded for tea, she watched the street. He would come in a cab? Or on horseback? No, he would dash up in a hansom and toss silver to the driver.

And the trickling procession of nursemaids and children bound for the Gardens was all there was to see — that, and the man selling paper fans. Fans. . . . He would be in the drawing-room?

The summer holiday was a fret of anxiety lest he should have called during their absence. Once back in the hall she flew to the card-tray, dealing the cards like a whist-player.

Then — had she dreamed that kiss? Was memory playing one a trick? Impossible. One would not have dared so far. Her elation in the discovery of young Andrews's card in the little heap was all but swamped in disappointment over Lassiter. Over this she would grieve at leisure. But she abstracted the boy's card and put it in her writing desk. Fighting step by step she gradually accepted what she thought of as her loss, then, after many hesitations and qualms, wrote to Andrews. It was a letter stilted, carefully facetious and italicized, the circumstances of their meeting cleverly slipped in as bona fides. . . .

His reply came in three weeks, headed from an address in a Hampshire village. 'How nice of you to remember me! We're on manœuvres . . . hope one day we may meet and dance again and pull the British Army to pieces! . . .' The nice friendly letter of a nice friendly young man, but — he *had* called, and if she had been at home, who knows? . . . Parted through family affairs . . . that was one way of looking at it.

IF love can be a beautifier its withholding can work reverse effects. The huntswoman in Grace Scrimgeour had tasted blood; it sped her to future dances with the beginnings of expectation and demand from life of her womanly rights; it made sets-back and failure more hard to bear, and in the watching for the lover to come striding through the door, the eyes that were her only feature grew strained and lost their childlike appeal. The belated growth of her self-esteem withered prematurely and she would sit on gilt chairs, the dance eddying round her, searching in all those men's faces for the sudden look of awakened interest, the arrested gesture of admiration. Too proud to use what slender stock of wiles she possessed, she was quiet and withdrawn. The ideal person would see below all that . . . would divine one . . . dig down for one, letting nothing fool or deter him. The forced attention was worthless; it must all come from him, spontaneously, with no assistance, vulgar and dishonest, of glance or challenging word, from herself, in spite of what the world said about 'helping things along'. Real love needed none of that pinchbeck.

Life went on and on. Gertrude's younger daughter, Caroline, was engaged in her first season. Her mother gave a Trousseau Tea for her to which all the Scrimgeours were asked; coffee and sandwiches in the drawing-room, the dresses and underclothes laid out in a bedroom upstairs over chairs, bed, screens and even the gas-bracket. Grace, generously pleased and interested, carefully handled the pale pink and blue satins, shyly congratulating her young niece, contrasting Caroline's pleasant, offhand composure with her own hot confusions were she in the other's shoes. Already Caroline, at eighteen, seemed set apart, a married woman; Grace wondered if poor Paula must not be suffering at the success of her junior; one could gather nothing by her manner as she joked and played showman. It was from Gertrude herself that Grace with a sinking heart learnt that Paula had already had two offers, and refused them both, to her mother's tolerant, amused annoyance. The incredible creature, it appeared, had actually declared that she would rather wait and chance marrying someone she really cared for and with whom she had mutual interests.

Grace was humble before these immensities, they sent her, subdued, into the drawing-room. It seemed to be full of men drinking sherry. 'I discovered that the wretches liked something at about six', Gertrude said. She addressed the nearest couple downrightly. 'I expect you've given my house a bad name among the lot of you, so you'd better have another drink before I decide to turn respectable. No, go away, Victor, I want to talk to my little sister.'

Grace's eyes travelled from face to face. The glances of the men slid past her or met her own with smiling, general geniality.

III

Back home, it drove her to her looking-glass. She gazed long, peering, turning, in the hope of discovering what all her years she had assumed because she was still young and adventurous. She summed up, and the pause before the delivered sentence was a long and unbelievably painful one.

That was it. She wasn't pretty. Never had been? Never would be. Her rejected face swarmed with tears of self-contempt and pity for this mirrored person. Yet — there were so many men in the world!

IV

That winter of 1893 Mary, Queenie and Grace had, at least, no grievance on the score of lack of occupation. The nursery and night nursery were at last to be reconditioned for his casual occupation by Charlie when home from regimental duties, and that meant the long-foreshadowed reaccommodation of Grace and Nana. The campaign — it lasted for weeks — originally instigated for the benefit of the son of the house developed into a battle fought and won by the nurse.

Nana at seventy-five knew exactly what she wanted and meant to get it.

The Scrimgeours, with the consent of their mother, had furnished the old bedroom of Arabella and Georgina. Busy, interested, they hung new, cheerful pictures, hemmed curtains, even spent a portion of their allowances on new ornaments, warmed at the thought of the old woman's pleasure and the tea-parties she would invite them to while snow whirled outside the window, or yellow fogs enveloped the street; the toast and muffins she would hold to the flame on the battered nursery fork. As a final touch (Grace's suggestion) they stealthily and by degrees filched from her old quarters certain small household gods to welcome her. And then they led her downstairs, her feet in their roomy felt boots slow to their impatience.

'There, Nana!' Arms round the bulky old woman they stood, smilingly scanning her face.

'Well, whatever's the matter with the room? You've got it in a fine pickle among the lot of you.'

'It's *yours*, Nana.'

'That it's not, Gracie, and never will be.'

'It's your new room.' Queenie's voice had an edge to it. Mary put in, hastily, 'Look, dearie, new curtains and pictures, and a pin-tray — that's from Gracie. They've been working for a surprise for you all this time.'

Nana looked like a hunted mule, distressed but obstinate to the last.

'You ought to've asked *me*, girls. It's *my* room in question.' Her eye fell upon sundry of her treasures. 'And my Things gone, too! You hadn't ought to have touched my Things.' With almost a whimper she toddled round the room, collecting in her apron every personal possession in sight.

It was defeat; even Mrs. Scrimgeour recognized it. Quite simply, Nana coveted the room now allotted to Grace, the ex-chamber of Miss Banks, and the smallest room in the house. She liked to have her Things within reach . . . the fire-place was where she was accustomed to seeing it . . . it had the outlook she was used to . . . she would keep her bones warm here, perhaps. The other place was well enough, but large . . . she wouldn't know where to lay hands on anything . . . one here, one there. . . .

With work that seemed endless they reinstalled her. She missed the old paper and plastered the walls with every knick-knack from a lifetime of service, fans, tambourines, shells on plaques of plush, family photographs. Grace's pin-tray was exchanged for the one Nana knew all about, a large, bumpy heart made of red velvet on the upper side and blue on the under that a young man who 'went for a sailor' had made her in some dim past and which spelt 'Bless Our Home' in pins. By the time she had finished, placed the bright tea canister (originally presented by a crony in 1860) on the right of the mantelpiece, and the tea-cosy in the shape of a black cat on the left of the fire-irons, put the sewing-machine she would never use again in its niche by the window so that fresh air was a problem, you could not get round the room save by sidling. The very under-side of the bed was so wedged with hatboxes filled with nobody knew what that the maids would never-more be able to sweep underneath it. Wheezing with triumph, half stifled, Nana settled down. She was to do light mending in return for her board and lodging. The fact that already her eyes had nearly given out even with steel spectacles loyally occurred to nobody.

Grace, relegated to the rejected bedroom, looked patiently at the furnishings designed to the taste of the old servant and with which she must, in future, live.

Unless . . .?

V

There were always the Sunday afternoons. But it was a truth admitted by nobody that the tea-hour was becoming rather terrible, quite how forlorn a hope, Grace, in years of the younger generation, could not know. The men of their original circle had long skimmed the Scrimgeour cream of that house, married and passed, while its women waited on because they must. They weathered it variously, Grace with a lit face smitten to apathy and daughterly attendances upon Mrs. Scrimgeour, Mary with a swift glance round the room and at her little sister, and a bitten lip, Queenie, lowering, with a shrug. Aloud they were saying:

'Nobody turned up yet?'

'*Such* a day, one wouldn't turn out, oneself.'

'Did I really forget to ask Mr. Pomfret and whatshis-name to look in?' And:

'A quiet Sunday at last!'

Drawing-rooms no less than trenches possess their candidates for the Victoria Cross.

Always now, after the tea had been slowly drunk, the spirit-lamp blown, Mrs. Scrimgeour would get up pon-derously and leave them as though, at last, she washed her hands of the whole business. At the door she usually said, 'If I am wanted I shall be upstairs,' or 'If people should drop in ring the landing bell.'

VI

It had once driven Grace to the side of that unknown legend, her sister Agatha. She felt confusedly that in the stern sureness of convent walls she herself might find, if not a similar certainty of solution if need unbelievably arose, the relief of contrast that would bring content with home.

Down the polished stairs, aromatic with beeswax, her sister came to her, took her hand and kissed her with a vehemence which embarrassed and alienated Grace. Nobody at home kissed you like that . . . not even Mary, ever.

'We will go into the grounds.'

Soon, they were sitting together on a semicircular stone seat ringed with clipped privet, this sallow woman of forty-three who was her sister plying Grace with eager questions, her hands twisting in her habit.

'. . . and father, how is he?'

Grace had to think back. Old people, unless ill, were

'all right'. She could at no time see her family as it actually was, being blinded by loyalties and custom, but impressions were unknowingly stored and she brought one out now. 'I think he doesn't look very well, perhaps. He is out a lot when Charlie is at home.' It was while Grace was embarked upon the establishment of their nurse in the new room that Sister Teresa, suddenly and terribly, burst into tears.

'Aggie! Dear!'

'Don't notice me.' The black figure was pressing to her sodden eyes a coarse cotton handkerchief. She put it away but spoke with averted head, her voice thickened so that it was difficult to catch the awkward sentences. 'It was hearing of it all, again . . . it made one want it all — '

'But, Aggie, you knew you were going to leave us, you chose to?'

'I knew, theoretically, but I didn't *realize*.'

'Are you so unhappy?'

The pause was a long one. 'If I am, it's my own fault, I suppose. Oh child, how I envy you!'

'Envy *me*?'

'For being at home among them all . . . and yet, if one had stayed there . . . oh, I don't know, I *don't* know.'

'But, Aggie, there's something to *do* here — '

The nun looked at her for the first time, sharply, anxiously.

'What? You, too . . .?' It escaped Grace.

'You have a position here, Aggie.'

Her sister shook her head. 'Never. I know that, now. I am a bad religious and Reverend Mother knows it. Oh, I don't disobey orders, but — I'll tell you. There was a time when I was very nearly dismissed as having no real vocation. I was almost happy as a postulant and a novice, it had all deceived even me. It's in the second or third

year of novitiate that the life tells, that's why they make
the period so long. It was in the third year with me. Up
to then I'd been borne up, carried away, glorifying every
hardship and deprivation, fancying myself peculiarly
called, a modern saint. They do, you know, the novices.
. . . But in the third year all that exaltation went completely. One doesn't see that it is the true test, one only
feels deflated and undervalued by everyone. Pegasus
harnessed to the plough. And it's then that all the old sins
of indulgence seem so wonderfully good.' She stopped,
abruptly, her heavy face flushed. Even to Grace she could
not, after all, confess the tragi-comedy of that time. For
she had gone to pieces over the question of the convent
food; victim of the fleshpots of home, her system had
suddenly and dreadfully revolted from wholesome, un-
garnished monotony, crying for its roasts, its comfortable,
leisurely meals of many courses. The Superior, herself a
woman of the world, by no means above a twinkling eye
and a brain swept bare of illusion on the subject of the
crowd of young females about her, had been quite funny
about it. . . . It was the humour no less than its cause which
had demoralized Agatha; committed to a way of life of
which she was already doubtful, and marked, as it seemed
to herself, with a brand there was no erasing. That smooth
voice emitting sarcasms which etiquette forbade you to
counter . . . that small, bright eye fixed on you at refection.

'Then why don't you leave?'

'And be excommunicated?'

'Well, it's only a *word*.' But Grace knew what Agatha
meant, was no less shocked in anticipation than her sister.
The valiance of Grace was of affection rather than con-
viction. She brought the other what comfort there was.
'You — you mightn't care for it if you *did* come home,
Aggie.' She swallowed and blurted 'There's nothing very

much to *do*'. The nun once more gave her a glancing look
of anxiety, but she let the statement go.

'No? Well — don't tell them, at home.'

'Never!'

They parted in mutual distress.

CHAPTER VI

I

THE man's voice, gruff and blusterous, the thinner, clearer voice of his son, could sometimes be heard from the morning-room by passing maids who would exchange grimaces (Those two! At it agen!), and by Grace herself as she stole upstairs or down. Worshipping, furious, the Captain was in no mood able entirely to let his son alone. To him the man of twenty-five was boon companion, crony, god of sacrifice, and failing all else, eternally child to be hectored and controlled. It made for confusion. They clashed primarily about money. The boy must have what was suitable to his position and if possible what he wanted as well; yet, the allowance outrun, Jove thundered, booming, round the subject of that self-denial and the management of funds which he himself had never taught, while Charlie shifted and looked bored.

II

Sometimes, if exasperated sufficiently, if they met about the house, and perhaps in remembrance of old alliance, Charlie would let himself go to Grace, wide-eyed, pitiful, torn between duty to the old and what of understanding of a contemporary her brother allowed her.

'You never know where you are, with the Guv'nor. One day he'll hand you over an extra tenner without winking and the next you get a sermon a mile long.' Before it all she was helpless, out of touch as were all the women with the dealings of their menfolk. 'It's enough to drive one right away from home.'

'Oh, Charlie, *please* dear don't go! I think it would kill father. He's never so happy as when he's with you.'

'Well, that's another thing. . . . I know he's been awfully decent to me, and all that, but he does rather hang on to one. One does sometimes want to be out alone, or with the fellows, but Dad wants to come along too, all the time. It makes one look such a damfool. Once or twice, I don't say, but *all* the time. . . .'

(The joy if father wanted one's own society! It was incredible, the richness of the things that Charlie was throwing away.) 'And if one does sometimes contrive to give the dear old buffer the slip, he comes down on one to know where one's gone, and it isn't always — oh well, I needn't go into that.'

Grace flushed scarlet. Once, when they had first fitted up the old nurseries for Charlie, she had run upstairs with a watchstand that she had embroidered, hoping to give him pleasure. She had opened the old white cupboard to hide the gift in a drawer, and in the drawer, under a pile of her brother's shirts, she had found a garter. A woman of more humour might well have laughed aloud at the plodding calculation that it could not be her own, or one of Nana's, but where humour failed her, instinct filled the gap. The thing was of a raucous pink satin with a horse-shoe buckle made of glass, clasping a spray of thickly-scented artificial flowers. Upon the horse-shoe the wit of Burlington Arcade had engraved 'Good Luck'. The actual sight, touch and smell of it brought home for the first time to Grace as a certainty what before had been but furtive, ignorant guesswork. Faithful to tradition, she blamed the owner of the object that on conventional impulse she had tossed into the fire. It nagged at her for days until thought replaced prejudice. Men dishonoured love, the most wonderful thing in life, and yet love that could be shown forth to all the world was theirs for the asking, waiting in its drawing-rooms. . . .

III

Charlie Scrimgeour, railing handsomely, missed the pathos of his father. But none in that house realized that the pace, self-set, doggedly maintained, was telling upon the Captain. He had, and knew it, failed, in his anxiety to be a companion to his son, to adhere to that programme laid down at the boy's birth, a schedule which should include a right and proper sowing of wild oats while the father sat at home. In practice, the business had on the whole broken down at the start. Literally, the Captain could not resist his son's company. Years were so brief. Oh time, stand still! One was over seventy. Slowly he would shrug into his topcoat and wait in the hall for Charlie's casual descent of the stairs; together they would sally forth at night, the Captain gamely striving not to pant and flag, Charlie resigned and a little embarrassed. When you'd seen the town and gone the rounds, why go on? He thought the halting doggishness of his father rather awful. Surely a book and early hours were more his mark now? If it came to that, one wouldn't mind it oneself a bit oftener. . . . 'That cub of old Scrim's' . . . one curdled at what the fellows might be saying at the club, thanks to this everlasting companionship. And they neither of them had very good heads, father, of course, owing to his age, oneself because one never had been able to stand an over-plus of booze, for some reason . . . like the accursed way one got so quickly pumped, so that even polo and riding weren't the pleasure they should be.

Civilly, valiantly, father and son worked at conviviality by ordeal of bar and lounge and beer and devilled bone and music-hall. It was a singularly costly way of acquiring a headache plus biliousness and dyspepsia, but the ailments certainly gave the Captain good value for cash.

I V

It was a foredoomed effort, the incompatibility which can prevail between one generation and another never better exemplified than in Charlie's attitude to age's memoirs and anecdotes and the failure of the elder to recognize that youth prefers to create its own reminiscences, and above all make its own discoveries. It sometimes seemed to his son that he could not see London at all for the thumbmarks of his father which smeared every turned-back page.

'Ah, you should have seen the Haymarket in the old days . . . nights, rather. The flower-women sold buttonholes up to midnight, then. Tipsy as Lords they got, too. We youngsters used to dance with 'em . . . ten years before you were born, but not unthought of, my boy. And Kate Hamilton's, and Sall — what was her name? Ah! Sutherland. Sutherland. Sally Sutherland! You could drink to the dawn, at Sally's.'

'Really, Sir?' (*But what imported this Sally woman, anyhow? She had her modern prototypes, so why harp on names?*) What was the old man on now? Had one missed anything and run the risk of making the wrong response?

'. . . but London's so jolly respectable now . . . an excellent thing, no doubt.' (*But was it? It was still, apparently, impossible to walk home from the West End without being ogled by some trollop.*)

'I tell you, *we* used to carry life-preservers under our coats.'

'I say! Really?'

'Yes, and not only in outer London, Ratcliff Highway,

and so on (you'd have opened your eyes at 'Paddy's Goose').
It had a pretty bad name even in those days. But on the
whole we had spiffing fun.' (*'Spiffing'! God!*)

'It sounds like it.'

'Yes. Many a sailor was murdered there after having his
pockets rifled of his pay.'

Charlie would glance curiously at his father, this frail
old family man contentedly smothered in South Kensington by wife and children, and ponder the odd streak in him
which in retrospect dwelt with affection upon the more
lustful and violent side of London's social night life of a
bygone quarter century.

' — and the women: nothing like 'em, to-day.'

(*Bosh!*)

'I often wish you'd seen Zazel at the Aquarium. Fired
from a cannon ... 'strordinarily effective. A lot of the
lads thought she *was a boy*, ha ha! Some of us used to wear
a "Zazel ring" on our finger engraved with her name.'

(*Lord, Lord!*)

'And the Menken, the beautiful Adah — '

(*Would the old chap never stop? How one hated the blasted
Adah! She couldn't be a patch on the Gaiety team.*)

They would sit in the Oxford, blue sheets of tobacco
smoke undulating between their eyes and the stage, and all
round them waiters took orders for food and drink to the
clashing of glasses from the numerous bars. The Captain
frequently slept through the turns, though his lips would
move to the chorus numbers. Then supper, and home a
little unsteadily, the dues of convention paid, and a muttered parting on the stairs. The ladies of the house, paying
dues to the same convention, had long been abed and
asleep, or, if awakened by a missed footing and a fallen
stick, made no reference to it then or thereafter.

CHAPTER VII

I

IF to Charlie Scrimgeour it was not easy through paternal garrulity to see London as it had been, it was almost equally difficult to view modern life as it actually was, and above all to discover his own opinion. An only son is not a person. He is a symbol, an idea, the victim of the thoughts, assumptions, aspirations and apprehensions of his family. He must conform to a certain standard of wassail to satisfy his father that he is not a milksop, but if he oversteps the mark mentally laid down he is a waster; he must spend, and complicate his life with a mass of largely useless gear, but if he spends the pound too much he is improvident and a disappointment; he must at all times steer a course that shall impossibly satisfy the paternal boast of female conquest conveyed by the wink and the dropped hint, while trimming his sails to the maternal desire to have had a son who never gave her a moment's anxiety.

It was over his association with the owner of the pink garter, the plucky, town sparrow little syphilitic, that Charles came nearest to finding himself: with her sharing a bottle of rotgut red wine labelled 'of Port type' that for the first time he did not feel his very thoughts overhandled, with her in her 'combined' in a Soho street that speech was original and not dictated by the taboos of home or the herd-utterance and thought of the regiment.

Expecting nothing of her but her sex function he was amazed at the smallest evidence of shrewdness which — a wavering dip — sometimes lit for him his own path, fitfully illumining his destined track, and, as a candle, could cast shadows. One, it was inevitable, was that with his discovery of the essential ease and freedom of the half-world came a temporary but very real contempt for all women, a cheapness of outlook that covered his own sisters. Odd that Ruby was so much better company than they ... when all was said, poor old Mary and Queenie and even Grace had only bred profiles and voices with which to rise superior. It didn't seem to be only a matter of the professional slickness of the daughter of joy with men, either; down under all the tawdry, mechanical assurance was the perfect woman, the woman of friend-ship and laughter, of grief and of the world who exercised mind and body fearlessly, as they should be, and as ap-parently they never could or would be, in South Kensing-ton. .Yet, if he incredibly met a sister while in Ruby's company, he would cut her, or leave Ruby humbly stranded, while he kept in play the bore that was the woman the world considered it could still respect.

II

One night, the girl had said to him, 'You look tired out, dearie. Why you letting 'em work you so hard? M'm? White as a sheet, and chance it. I tell you: you pop on to the bed an' take a bit of bye-byes. I'll fill you the hot water bottle, shan't be a sec. No extra charge. I know a sick kid when I see one. *Come* on.'

Unromantic as a landlady she worked at him.

It touched him profoundly. In all that worshipping house in Brecknock Gardens nobody had ever noticed that one was tired.

His proposal and refusal was the first and only intima-
tion that the world was not entirely his for the taking. In
self-esteem it set him half-way back to his ridden childhood.
It was a puzzle and a shock for which nothing so far had
prepared him.

The girl, sister of a brother officer, was pretty, the
popular and only daughter of a houseful of men. He was
in love. It should have been simple. . . . He was not the
only claimant, which was confusing: he was not the most
highly regarded, which was unbelievable, for underneath
his feeling for her was a streak of awareness of the favour
he was also conferring. . . .

He remembered how, in his childhood, he had visualized the power to confer pleasure that was going to be his,
seeing the proposal to any girl objectively, as children do,
as a toy in the pocket, something you withheld if it suited
you and then magnificently bestowed. And Gladys, the
known, the loved, had waved it away.

For years he lost all interest even in the Rubys of
London while Captain Scrimgeour fretted unendurably
for his grandchildren, the offspring of his son, while there
was still time. Father and son wore each other down,
gaining nothing in tolerance as each grew older. Charles
had told the family nothing of his proposal or its reception,
dreading the flutter, the fuss, the endless discussions and
general thumbing of his emotion to which an announced
engagement would give rise in that household that had
not had a wedding for over twenty years. In a vacuum,
he even began to observe his family.

He hoped he was fair, but it didn't seem to him that
they were keeping very up-to-date; they dressed all right,

of course, but hadn't any go ... contrived to miss the points so admirably and variously stressed by Ruby and Gladys ... and poor old Queenie was frankly rather awful. To judge by her photographs Aggie must have been a bit of a stumer as well. Sensible of her to have hidden it in a convent. Gertie was hard as nails and treated one like an inky nephew but contrived to keep you at once entertained and minus rancour. Other people's sisters got about on bicycles, why on earth didn't his lot? Mary said it made Mamma nervous, but surely there were limits to fear for your skin? Muscle-bound, that's what they were ... mentally and physically. And never would he forget the day he told them that he might bring two or three of the chaps in after, or for, tea — he couldn't say — on the following day.

He had dropped into the drawing-room first, the others would follow on after polo at Hurlingham. His sisters were grouped round an extra table spread with a white cloth and supporting a bottle of sherry and glasses. From his arm-chair the confabulation reached him.

'Well, girls, I think to offer wine is entirely unnecessary. It's too soon after tea, and they won't be staying for dinner.'

'But, Mamma, Gertie does it.'

'Is one bottle enough, Mary?'

'Don't ask me, my dear!'

'Well, I think it's a ripping idea: gets the conversation started.' (That was Queenie.)

'But — does one offer them tea *first* and then, if they don't take it, offer sherry, or just say "which will you have, tea or sherry"? after we've all got introduced?'

(*Oh God!*)

'Perhaps if they see it's there they'll just help themselves?'

'But suppose they don't see? Does one hand it *round*?'

'You can't wait on men like a barmaid, Queenie.'

'My *dear* Mamma —'

'Handing tea at the table when you're pouring out is a different thing.'

'Then can't we put a chair by the sherry table?'

(*How long, oh Lord?*)

'Oh, settle it yourselves. You've voted for wine in the drawing-room, which sounds odd to me (brandy with the coffee after dinner of course isn't the same), and what your young men are going to think I can't imagine.' Grace looked stricken, and suddenly all the pleasure and mild excitement went out of her face. It was Queenie who, with a lot of high-pitched facetiousness and laughter, kept the project alive.

They had arrived, three hot, large, healthy men, receiving introductions by Charlie. They drank enormously — of tea — until Mary had to ring for more hot water. Mrs. Scrimgeour, watchful and smiling, took up her old place in the back drawing-room.

Conversation creaked like an unoiled dray-wheel. Grace, her eyes passing from face to face, forgot the sherry business altogether.

It was Queenie who first began the furtive signals to Mary, who didn't see them. Quite simply, she was interested in what the men were saying.

'Well, old Bronckhorst thinks there's going to be a scrap in South Africa. He says that Lord Roberts —'

'Oh, Roberts! . . .'

'My dear Langley, Roberts is always putting the fear of God into us about something.'

'Well, he can't be wrong *all* the time.'

'Why not? It keeps you up to the mark, Scrim, and does nobody a ha'porth of harm.'

'But, I say! A row in South Africa! Pretty good lark, eh?'

'Too good to be true, Jimmy. Knightsbridge Barracks-cum-Tidworth, etc., is *our* permanent address.'

Queenie continued to make sherry-signals. They penetrated Mary's brooding eyes and thoughts. Queenie hesitated and rose. The men rose with her and she gave a disconcerted gasp and a confused exclamation. Her 'Wouldn't you all like some sherry?' was drowned in the polite rumble-speeches of that departure which, relieved, they thought her action had hinted. Courteous chaos descended. One man had actually made the door and Queenie's despairing 'Oh, *fetch* him back, somebody!' did not assist matters.

I V

In her room, Grace was thinking: 'Oh, bring them back again — especially that Mr. Langley! . . . but if it can't be he, then anyone of them you can. He looked at me so nicely — well, kindly — as large men do, so that one felt sort of taken care of.'

It was a form of inner, conversational prayer that filled much of her life.

In the morning-room, her brother, finishing the sherry and skimming the evening paper, thought 'never again'.

v

She was thirty. A despairing knowledge that only frantic absorption in house and friends could temporarily stifle. She was, as a comic pendant to tragedy, a great-aunt. Not that anything more could hurt you, at thirty. . . .

Gertie's younger daughter, Caroline, had had a baby, years ago. A lovely baby. Holding it for the first time

Grace had felt the shameful beginning of tears, had had to pretend that baby had poked a finger in her eye. Once, forgetful, she had told her mother of the baby's charms and cried 'I wish she was mine!' and Mrs. Scrimgeour had been shocked. 'You had better not go about *saying* that, Grace.'

You were a failure if you didn't have a baby, but a disgrace if you wanted one, and said so.

CHAPTER VIII

I

THE young men of the sherry episode had barely been given up as hopeless by the Scrimgeour women when England, with semi-incredulity and delight, found herself at loggerheads with what the man in the street soon learnt with a valiant spit to call The Baws. The Baws it seemed owned as leader an improbable figure in Guy Fawkes clothes, called Krewjer. The remoteness of the arena brought illogical confidence to the public and they soon settled down into a period of wearing celluloid buttons on lapels featuring favourite military faces: White, Buller, French, Kitchener and Baden Powell. Also, confided the fathers to fellow club members, it was all only pea-shooting and would be over in three weeks. Six *months?* My *dear* fella! —

I I

In village halls, parish rooms and on the London concert platform *The Absent-minded Beggar* by young Mr. Kipling became a National Anthem rendered in costume, rural odds and ends or 'full' evening dress, recited, with gesture, by young ladies, marched to by the Church Lads' Brigade in forage caps, bandoliers, and cornets not always more than a semitone off the note. In the suburbs, enter-prising hostesses gave dinners to the City Imperial Volunteers of the district, and wreathed their damask tablecloths with natural ivy inscribed in gold paint with the letter C. The young men, stetson hats jauntily turned up at one side, enjoyed it all, departed roaring choruses in the troopships. The thoughtful civilians bought large-scale maps of South Africa into which, as the bàttle fluctuated, they stuck paper flags on pins.

The country drew together, bound man to man in a common realization of trust in the Throne which time brought to them when the theories of the pea-shooting brigade were set at naught, and the celluloid buttons became family portraits as the men they pictured grew into friends and heroes whose fortunes, with a sense of personal discovery, the wearers actually shared. Pretoria, Ladysmith and Bloemfontein were not places on the map but the abodes of Our George, Young Ernie and Mrs. Pettitt's Harold.

The women of England formed small work-parties among their personal friends, and at Christmas, the First Lady In The Land despatched to every fighting Tommy Atkins a small tin box containing chocolate, its lid embossed with a medallion of the old Royal widow.

There were some who swore those boxes won the war.

III

On Mafeking Night, the interested foreigner, intending to proceed down Piccadilly to view the decorations and admire the cut-crystal shields, crowns and Garter stars sported by the great shops, found himself borne irresistibly down the Haymarket, a sailor's arm tucked in his, the arm of a factory girl with matter-of-fact affection round his neck. Half-way up a lamp-post trolling a comic song was an intoxicated loafer singing to whoever would listen. Only he was not intoxicated or a loafer, but a famous judge of the Queen's Bench. At Trafalgar Square an impromptu set of Lancers was in progress, with two grinning and helpless policemen willy-nilly accomplishing the Grand Chain.

These English! No dignity at all ... what hope of maintaining respect for law and order? The question is promptly answered as a Peeress tweaks his coat. 'Come on, come on! You *must* join Freddie's party. Savoy.' They are nearly run down by a brougham run amok in which, bowing to the enchanted crowd, sit a crossing-sweeper and a last year's débutante, who on slender evidence addresses him as 'Uncle Jo'.

'Cheero, 'Arry!'

' 'Arry? Whadyer mean? Mike way for the Baron de Nocash. Three cheers for 'is Grice! and 'is lady!

What's the matter with Buller?
'E's all right.
'Oo's all right?
BULLER!
What's the matter with Bobs?
'E's all right.
'*Oo's* all right?
BOBS!
What's the matter with Krewjer?
Good ole Krewjer! ...'

The respectable foreigner, outraged, advances to rescue the young girl. It is disconcerting that she instantly throws herself upon the protection of her battered escort. A scene? A massacre? The Consul ... an International Situation?

' 'Ere, you bung orf, Alfonzo.' The sweeper vanishes under the seat of the brougham to emerge with a bottle of Guinness. ' 'Ave a drink, cock? an' leave the girls alone, you bad ole man!

What's the matter with Powell?
'E's all right! ...'

The foreigner, stranded in a side street, walks pensively home to his hotel. These English . . . but something likeable about them in spite of their lack of dignity.

Upon his coat tail is pinned a lady's feather boa.

IV

The private houses in the squares and streets of London also do well with flags and fairy lights. There are few exceptions.

One is in Brecknock Gardens, South Kensington. It shows no gilt trophy or lantern, and the colours of the solitary Union Jack are black against the night sky.

In the great drawing-room five women in mourning sit avoiding each other's eyes. In a far corner, a nun mechanically tells her beads. Their clicking is the only sound in the room.

V

The Scrimgeour women had been shocked at the idea of even lashing one flag to the balcony. It was the old master of that house who slowly overruled them.

'I know what you feel. But it was the country's war, and we won it. Most of the boys came home. I — should like to give them a hand.'

CHAPTER IX

I

THE cracking of a heart and the smashing of a life-work
was accomplished. The son he had bred to war had
perished in war, and the logic of it comforted him not
at all.

In the following year, Captain Scrimgeour pulled himself together and set out on a solitary tour of remembrance
no less reverent that its surroundings were unconven-
tional. Alone, he would haunt the bars and lounges of
all those music-halls where he and his son had taken their
pleasure, his body slumped in red plush divans, the object
of maternal concern from peroxided barmaids who liked
the old gentleman. They were singing new songs, now,
with words he didn't always catch, and tunes that
offended by not being the old ones. They diverted the
flow of memory and worried him . . . so that sometimes
he had to put hand to head to control the blood which
pounded there. If one walked out carefully, and cun-
ningly refrained from any sudden turning, one prevented
giddiness . . . never do to have it thought one was tipsy.

Sometimes, memory stilled, he would be entirely aware
of the places themselves, seen through a mist of recollection. The music-halls seemed to be getting damned
tame . . . there were actually ladies present, and once or
twice one had seen a family party in a box, and once two
obvious gentlewomen, unattended. That would mean the
decline of everything . . . humour, prosperity, the closing
of bars, the scattering of the Pink Bonnets and barmaids to
God alone knew where of dingy, pillar'd lodging in

Pimlico and the backwashes of Victoria. When ladies got their foot in, the world would become soft . . . soppy, hermaphroditic.

Cheer, boys, cheer . . .

That was a good, rousing tune . . . and *Soldiers of the Queen.*

Spion Kop. . . .

II

The women had retired for the night when the knocker and bell roused the staid road. It was the old nurse who heard it first; Nana, a little dotty now, who entertained such fantastic alarms that she had much ado to persuade 'the girls' that this clamour was no figment of a clouded brain. She put her head round Mary's door.

'It's the Angel Gabriel, come for *me*,' she confided. But soon they all heard it, gathered on the landing, frightened figures in dressing-gowns. Mary took the lead.

'Don't tell Mamma. I'll go.'

Outside the house, a man in mulberry uniform waited; on his peaked cap was inscribed in gold braid the name of a famous music-hall.

'Name of Scrimgeour?'

'Yes.'

'Sorry to upset you ladies, but I'm afraid we've got some bad news for you. The old gentleman. We found a card in his pocket.'

'*Father?*'

'There was a doctor in the audience, luckily, *and* it happened during the interval so there was no disturbance, like. The — he's in the manager's room, and will you ladies come at once? I've a cab here.'

Mary asked quietly, 'He's dead?'

'I'm sorry, Madam. . . .'

It was Queenie who started the hysterical outcry which brought Mrs. Scrimgeour from her bedroom. 'Queenie, if you don't stop I'll hit you,' Mary announced. Queenie continued, and Mary, with only a fractional hesitation, slapped her face. It was a half-hearted blow in the very nature of things and had the effect of magnifying the noise.

'Girls, girls! What are you thinking of?' The ridiculous figure, bulky in its bedgown and outmoded nightcap, peered fearfully over the banisters.

'It's all *right*, Mamma (Oh *Queenie!*).'

Grace to the surprise of them all quavered, 'I'll go, Mary, you stay with them.'

'You? You can't, dear, to a place like that!'

Grace wavered, bowing to public opinion; it was 'a place like that' for her, whatever sort of place it might really prove to be . . . but at the same time this was a huge event which had happened; that explained everything to onlookers. Death, surely, was a respectable errand? And the messenger looked very kind and large. . . .

'I *think* this gentleman will take care of me, Mary.'

'That'll be all right, Miss. You comealongerme and I'll see you safe.'

'But *who?* — '

'Oh *please*, Mamma, one moment! . . . Very well, dear, and call Tom, he'll help you.' Mary rang the dining-room bell; it tinkled in the kitchen but was audible in the pantry where the elderly handyman still slept.

They drove in self-conscious silence to the West End.

Under the glass canopy of the music-hall the audience was dispersing: coloured placards of the famous comedians Grace had never seen were being taken inside the foyer. Her nervousness no less than the unfamiliarity of the whole episode combined to make her purblind and deaf. For whom did one ask? Perhaps if they saw that a man-servant was in attendance? . . . All the way she had been rehearsing sentences. 'My father died here a little while ago' (which sounded absurd). 'Can I see Captain Scrimgeour?' (but that suggested he was still alive). 'Can you take me to my father? . . . I've come about the death of my father' (too flippant).

The management took all initiative from her, people (two men) seemed to be waiting for her in watchful yet casual abeyance by the red-carpeted stairs. Treating them as guests of the drawing-room she advanced at once. A pity one's voice was so out of hand.

'I am Miss Scrimgeour.'

'Ah, will you just — '

She was in an office, past a cubby-hole scrawled in gold paint with places and prices. She had never seen death, or any reality. With conventional sentiment they kept the sight from her. It was Tom, the lamp, knife and boot-cleaner, who went submissively forward to a sofa.

'Yes, that's the Captain, all right.' They seemed, to Grace's deafened ears, to confer. She would have liked to do something helpful, but men managed everything, always.

'Now then!' a tall man was saying (to her?), with mechanical kindliness. 'Will you sit down — no, over there, please.' The authority piqued her but she scrambled to obey. 'Now then, Miss Scrimgeour, did your father have regular attendance from your own doctor?'

'Well, when he was *ill*, you know.'

'Yes, quite, but the point is: would you say that Captain — er — Scrimgeour was more or less in touch with his doctor in the sense that he either had attendance from him fairly regularly, or that your doctor understood his constitution in a general manner?'

'Yes, I should say so.'

'Well, that's easily confirmed, I shall want his name and address — '

'It's Doctor — '

' — now, tell me . . .'

' — he lives in Astley Gar — '

'How often did your father go out? What were his habits?'

'He went out a lot.'

'Always?'

'No. I don't remember that he *used* to much, except with my mother and some of us.'

'And then he began to go out more?'

'Yes, with my brother.'

'Ah . . . yes, I see. Now, just one more thing; what were your father's — um — ideas about wines and spirits, and so on?'

'Ideas?'

'Well, was he a heavy consumer of intoxicants?'

Grace flamed, sensing an attack from a stranger. '*Certainly* not.'

He almost smiled. 'You mustn't mind my asking, it all bears on the case, you know.'

'What?'

'When people alter their routine late in life it's apt to be rather dangerous to them, get hardening of the arteries, and so on.' He swerved upon her. 'Didn't you yourself notice a change in him of recent years?' She was at a loss. One's father one took for granted and the old grew older in their mysterious ways. He must have been *all right* or he wouldn't have gone on, or looked even as he did. At the doctor's 'T'chk!' she was filled with a sense of complete inadequacy; she had pined and thought enough, but when it came to rendering an account of her mental stewardship, she failed.

248

III

The Scrimgeour women assembled in the drawing-room to hear the Will explained by the solicitor. It was, he thought, simple even to feminine intelligence. The invested capital would bring in some sixteen hundred pounds a year, considerably less than he had expected, but there had, over the years, been a tendency upon the part of his client to sell out of sound securities . . . luckily the widow seemed placid as the voice of her lawyer continued.

Captain Scrimgeour with the customary habit of the men of his generation, that was half chivalry, half contempt, had never discussed finance with his womenfolk. As popular opinion goes he was a good man.

He left his entire estate unconditionally to his wife.

CHAPTER X

I

AFTER her full period of decent mourning, Mrs. Scrimgeour emerged, interested in a personal state that she took
for granted to be wealthy widowhood. She was abetted
in this belief by sentiment, conventional and characteristic. 'Things must go on exactly as they were in dear
father's time.' And they did. Even to a refusal to consider
the reopening 'now that things are so changed' of any
sort of scheme that would keep Queenie and Grace in
congenial and profitable employment.

Infinitesimal variety fell to the lot of her daughters.
Mary could now go through the household books and her
own reading in the quiet, unfamiliar morning-room, and
their brother's quarters at the top of the house were used,
at first furtively with a sense of daring, as a sitting-room
by all three. The old nursery gradually became a curious
hotchpotch, still housing stray toys upon which were
superimposed pipes, a gun and salmon rods in their cases,
and, finally, refeminized with work-baskets, photographs
and the table-game of the moment. The discredited bag-
atelle board stood against a farther wall. The table held a
ping-pong outfit now. Friends with gardens, Queenie
complained, were playing clock golf and Bumble-puppy,
that active, monotonous and fashionable pursuit which
sometimes ended with the captive tennis ball in your eye,
she admitted, but which brought people together . . . and
the so-and-so's had a Polyphon, that made things lively.
We'd better have one too. Heaps of room to stand it.
Where? Well, the drawing-room, don't you think?

The musical instrument, a magnified grandfather clock with a. glass window through which could be seen the large perforated discs of metal that played a dozen tunes, including *The Belle of New York*, with precise, luscious clickings, and Sousa's *Under The Double Eagle* with 'effects', was strongly advocated by Queenie. It cost £60. None of them, even by clubbing together, could afford it. The Scrimgeours had no Bank account. Mrs. Scrimgeour must be approached, she would surely see that a phonograph wasn't the same thing ... most people had a phonograph.

To their mild surprise, she baulked, jibbing at an unfamiliar expense ... yet the housebooks seemed to remain as high as ever.

It was at an autumn At Home — Progressive Games — that the booby table, still laughingly chasing the marbles with pencils held like chopsticks, asked for some music, and a daughter of the house started the family Polyphon. It played a medley of songs and marches of the Boer war. Down the cheeks of the entering Mrs. Scrimgeour tears, like that small shot which had killed her son, rolled.

The Polyphon was in the drawing-room of Brecknock Gardens by Christmas. The family grew sick of it in two months and the maids complained that it 'caught' the dust.

II

On the subject of their furtively annexed sitting-room, Queenie sometimes ventured that they were not doing with it all that they might. The atmosphere of piracy still hung over it. Continuing to occupy it, ignorant of whether Mrs. Scrimgeour was even aware of their action, they were at the same time evasively unwilling to tackle her on the subject of installing gas-ring and tea-service so that they might informally receive their friends. They all hankered for the taste of such dilute bohemianism yet found themselves still inarticulate, filing punctually down to drawing-room tea at four-thirty. They even made excuses among themselves for their failure to take independent action. Milk: the maids would make a fuss at taking up a fresh jug every day on the chance of guests, and if it spotted the stair-carpet ... And would Mamma allow extra bread and cakes? Individually they all knew that the catering problem was capable of instant solution, given team-work and foresight.

It was Queenie, after months of procrastination, who put the idea to Mrs. Scrimgeour in what she hoped was a light and extempore manner. She remembered all the arguments in favour of the scheme, and her mother rendered it utterly null.

She was hurt. That was obvious to them all.

There was a silence while her face became bleached and the pale eyes blinked.

'That sounds a little unsociable, doesn't it?'

It was as though the practical details did not exist for her, that she had fluked clean through to the actual reason motivating her daughters which was not for picnics and sociability so much, in the case of the two elders, as an old sick desire for liberty, and, in the heart of Grace, a hope never quite quenched of some place where her personality might find elbow-room. People might come if they knew they could see one alone ... that was her self-told story. In the past, she had watched from the window for the arrival of Captain Lassiter. Now, when she had the spirit to, she watched for anybody.

Mary guessed. 'One misses father's and Charlie's friends' was the translation she made to Grace in tacit apology for the manless household, and after the last of the *habitués*, their condolences paid, had faded away. The idea that she had once planned the giving of a dance for her twenty-first birthday was, to-day, incredible.

Over the sitting-room teas affair, Mrs. Scrimgeour once more tricksily capitulated; it was a concession rendered ultimately void by their own fervent gratitude which took the form of playful indications that their mother should often 'come and have a peep at them all'. The peep stretched into a gaze . . . the gaze to a 'just five minutes, then' which expanded by degrees into half an hour and ultimately into the rest of the visitors' stay. The conversation ceased to possess its epoch and merged into that courtesy to age which is of all time. On the occasions when Mrs. Scrimgeour did not join them all, or some woman friend slipped through without her knowledge, the incautiously raised voices on the stairs as she took her departure brought Mrs. Scrimgeour to the drawing-room door, where she stood watching them with a washed-out air of accusation.

Her daughters could not see her inevitable pathos, she closed her eyes to their need of escape. The episodes would end with sentimental scenes of assurance, protest, exclamation, disclaimer that re-established peace and got nobody anywhere.

III

But the days were not entirely empty. If there was no change within the house, young gentlewomen had at last the freedom of the streets, could take tea and even luncheon at restaurants. The first Lyons shop for the tired surburban housewife up for the sales had been open for some years in Oxford street, the Tuppeny Tube arrived to effect domestic revolution; women took to the tops of omnibuses as though no ban had ever existed; the bicycle was outmoded and the motor car was slipping into public life to change the quiet face of England and its slow clear thought for ever. On the principle that what Manchester thinks to-day London will think to-morrow, a Northern Registrar and his wife were talking about votes for women. He was to die during the stage of discussion, but the widowed Emmeline Pankhurst came south. . . .

The Scrimgeours of England were unmoved; they did not want rights but privileges and bitterly resented the imperilment by logic of their sole weapon of coaxing. Their men would speak for them at the polling-booths and the fact that the Scrimgeours themselves now had no male representative at all save their manservant who possessed the right denied to themselves occurred to nobody but Mary. But then Mary was rather like that. . . . 'When men were agitating for their vote they burnt down half Bristol' she would say thoughtfully in the militant years to come. The others could see no connection at all between demand and action, and why Bristol, anyway? But even Mary never dreamed of taking any part in securing the franchise for her sister women, it was unthinkable, in South Kensington. Her family quite kindly dismissed it as one of Mary's notions. Grace, when she thought of it at all, echoed Katharine:

> *I am ashamed that women are so simple*
> *To offer war when they should kneel for peace.*

What was a vote to a husband and a baby? Yet they said that plenty of these women were married . . . but then some women, of course, got things, and others never did; like the girls of her own circle whose drawing-rooms still managed to keep a list of men visitors, and those who,

like Paula, had had not one offer but two, and had refused them both and contrived to be still fresh and in that
demand she herself would not supply; girls who sometimes even forgot which of two men was to fetch her for
theatre or luncheon, race meeting or river party; girls who
received presents from men that were not of birthday or
Christmas, saw the sudden arrival of messenger boys with
flowers, as Gertie's daughters used to, and that Gladys
who Charlie himself had once taken out in the evening. . . .

IV

Grace by now knew a number of nurseries, was sadly
and diffidently familiar with the routine of babyhood,
had stood without occupation making her little comments
on the bathing babies to efficient nurses who took no
notice, touched them and was sometimes deterred by the
young mothers, casually, facetiously or with authority.

'Oh, let him yell, Gracie, it's all in the day's work, isn't
it, Bobo?'

'She says "don't do that, please, Auntie Grace, I don't
yike it".'

'You'd better not take him, Grace, he rather hates
strangers.'

From girls younger than oneself . . . and women, even
at that . . . one must remember that one was thirty-four
. . . oh God, thirty-four! But women had children at
forty and over. . . . Grace's mental life was in constant
conflict with time. Each birthday was a pang. She got
through life by shutting her eyes to facts, and once a year
— at the seaside — by running away from them.

There was still a handful of unmarried contemporaries.

They met each other in drawing-rooms and ballrooms and the compromise of the 'subscription dance' — that hint of social decline which crept into Edwardian life — with eager enthusiasm and a deep, unspecified relief ... the sight of each other, still level in the race, restoring a flayed self-respect. It affected even dance-floor behaviour so that co-operation was abroad and warm, generous pleasure or inverted self-esteem was achieved at any minor success scored by the girlhood friend. Old friends, they discovered, were best, because they instinctively remembered you as you used to be and look; it was fatal not to see them for too long a period or changes were instantly noted with an effect of shock.

The annual holiday held out hopes of adventure and change even now, yet of course if one should link up with — well, interesting new people, the price one paid was that unlike the old friends, they saw you exactly as you were, sharply and suddenly. But it might cut both ways? At least they would approach your appearance with open mind and make their own discoveries; they could not say 'She has changed', 'She is ageing', or 'She isn't wearing well'.

v

They danced, when and where they could, slightly wilted flowers of a Victorian bouquet, competing gamely with the ruched chiffons, circular skirts and cartwheel hats of Edwardianism.

Grace recognized it as not the least of their sickness that about their common trouble there was a conspiracy of silence. One suspected that these girlhood friends had had no chance of marriage but the healing of discussion was denied them; that, and the stupendous relief which would have been the pooling of a flaming resentment and the open expression of a frightened, mounting grief. Appearances must be kept up, even among confidantes, in private. Sometimes their whaleboned reticence very nearly broke down. But never quite. Pauses in the conversation would be filled by the quick, furtive glance in which revelation and confession hung in the balance. Then the danger passed. Relieved, unshriven, profoundly regretful, they talked of other things.

They contrived to meet and live with a smile, martyrs sustained by no principle, dying by inches for no cause at all.

V I

Intermittent occupation was tossed to Grace by married sisters and nieces. She had learnt over the years the routine of spinster aunt and great-aunthood, met trains and schoolgirls — always herself the one who was fearful of a missed connection, uncertain of the bus to take, so that it was her charge who took over the transport; always conscientiously at the barrier twenty minutes too early, shopping tunics, socks and hockey sticks at Harrod's and Woolland's with even the freedom of choice closed to her by the clear, uncompromising directions sent with the request; chaperoning nieces to the roller-skating rink at Olympia, wistfully grateful at being of use, hoping with each child to establish love and understanding, glowing at sight of the curved cheek of laughter or wonder in the stalls at Maskelyne and Cook's, the bright eye goggling at her over buns and ices in tea-shops, hoping always for confidence or statement of school difficulty; paying for it all in the twanged nerves of terror at each crossing and at the responsibility that was hers for the guardianship of the children of other women.

Queenie saw the whole thing in another light. 'They're simply fagging you, Gracie. I wouldn't take it on. Catch *me!*'

So she expressed a snarling resentment at the patronizing assumption that because a woman has failed to acquire a husband she has nothing on earth to do but make herself of use to the married.

VII

The children told their mothers that Aunt Grace was 'all right'. Even she herself could not, against all hope, admit that with the young she was a conspicuous success, though the possible reason evaded her. The mothers could have told her that children instinctively mistrust an over-anxiety to please, and are swift to scent inexperience and any type of inefficiency, and that eager agreement and a too-hasty falling in with their wishes and whims rouses their contempt at once. Also, Auntie Grace wasn't pretty.

You could, Grace found, win a friendship that did not outlast the afternoon by tips and presents. It outraged her decent heart and after overlong hesitation she stopped supplies. Sometimes she was robbed by the mothers of even that gesture of negation.

'Don't give 'em anything, Gracie, they know they're not allowed it.'

Was one too old for the children — at thirty-four?

CHAPTER XI

I

EVERY Christmas, Mrs. Scrimgeour, scanning the little stack of charitable appeals, was wet-eyed at the final paragraph, and writing cheques three minutes later. It was sweet to be Lady Bountiful to the dear little mites: they came from *bad* homes . . . and so many of them . . . to think of a baby crippled, or diseased. . . .

She had, since the Captain's death, even opened a bazaar on the strength of stocking a stall and of contribution to the funds, and that meant a pleasant chat with the Bishop, and a bouquet. But it also meant, Mary noted, a purchase at every stall and a new fur coat to appear in. Giving bred spending. The coat was fifty guineas; 'such a bargain' said Mrs. Scrimgeour, 'and these good skins wear for ever'. They might have, thanks to the then integrity of material and workmanship, but she loved a change and the sealskin was replaced two years later by a mink at seventy-five guineas.

In common with thousands of women who without training or experience are, by death, suddenly put into sole control of the family budget, custodian alike of invested capital, current and deposit account, her disbursements were dictated by mood and temperament, her knowledge of finance confined to the drawing of cheques. She was far from ungenerous to her daughters, but her dolings out of Bank notes were at no time to be depended upon. It made them of necessity bad business women. They would confidently run bills at milliners and tailors, relying upon the last-but-one maternal mood of indulgence, to discover

when the accounts were rendered that scoldings and re-
proaches were their portion. But, as Queenie said, at least
Mamma wasn't as bad as Fanny's, who, on losing her
father, had had the choice of her allowance being cut in
half or clearing out to fend for herself, or poor Amy Willis
whose widowed mother lost half her income at the
Bridge table.

Mary said to her sisters, outright, 'We ought to have
some money of our own.' But they were not unreasonable,
and nobody else had — not even Gertie's daughters.

11

The money question did not exist for Grace, who took
no part in the discussions between her sisters. She was
concluding a little amorous practice upon Gertrude's son,
Albert, who at thirty-six was incredibly and wonderfully
still a bachelor. He was her own nephew — but he was a
man, and attentions knew no kinship. And strangers
wouldn't know. . . .

They had achieved one or two outings together, Grace
tingling with self-consciousness; she worked perseveringly
at old, shared memories. It was a pity they had been so
few. She did not allow for the fact that it was their relationship combined with those very memories which wiped out
all possibility of his being able to regard her as a young
woman at all.

Once, returning at night from Earl's Court Exhibition,
she had kissed him, closing her eyes and imagining that he
was somebody else, trusting, with a forlorn remnant of
caution, in their relationship to escape censure. He was
twisting about in pockets for change to pay the cabby.
'That's all right, old girl, it's been quite a good evening,

hasn't it?' She assumed a repulse that was more final than he had probably intended, though he was certainly a little surprised at the demonstration.

She started from him as though stung, gave a forced little laugh and hurriedly explained that the cab had thrown her against him. It sounded to her own ears so thin a story that with nervous vivacity she flung herself against him once more to confirm it.

'There! It's done it again!'

She never repeated that experiment, but, unable to make a clean break, compromised upon acceptance of such invitations as he intermittently suggested.

III

'Mamma, I should like to speak to you about the house-books.'

Mary stood in the drawing-room with a pile of the tradesmen's books under her arm. Mrs. Scrimgeour as usual looked up with an instant alarm that was not so much tribute to a matter of which she as yet knew nothing as to the tone of a speaker's voice. 'Has cook — ?'

Mary sat down. 'It seems to me that they are far too high. Mamma, I assure you that there's hardly any real difference between the books to-day and what they were when Aggie and Arabella and Georgie and father and Charlie were with us.'

'It *must* have made a difference!'

'A certain difference, but not all it should. It's — the *scale* of the whole thing . . . to take less quantities of goods counts of course, but what I feel is that a great number of items could well come right out.'

'Oh?'

'Yes. There are our own meals, to begin with; is it really necessary to have three courses at lunch and four at dinner just for the four of us?'

'My dear, we must live *properly*. Besides: if cook doesn't get enough to do she'll lose heart —'

'But —'

' — as there's nothing so discouraging as dishes which don't give them *scope*. Besides: people might drop in.'

Mary's smile was ironic at that valiant, die-hard slogan. 'And you can't set them down to a dish of mince.'

'Mamma, there's a slight difference between one dish of mince and two ten-pound joints every week.'

Mrs. Scrimgeour mused. 'Do we really eat twenty pounds of meat a week?' she asked with a remote suggestion of complacency.

'I should think probably not! But the point is that we *buy* it, and that's not counting kidneys and sausages and things. And that's another thing . . . don't you think one breakfast dish for us ought to be enough? If sausages come up on Sundays we never take more than one each and they go down and are never seen again, and it's the same with potatoes and lots of things. Cook always sends up too much. And kidneys. I don't like them and Queenie doesn't eat them at all, but the number is the same as ever. I vote for one dish in future.'

'But, Mary, we've always *had* two . . . we ought to be saving — I hate to say it — now that so many of us are gone.'

'But we *aren't* saving, Mamma —'

' — and we must keep the servants contented and well fed.'

'I think you can trust them for *that*.'

'And if we cut down our orders it will give such offence to the tradesmen. There's Meares, now . . . he's always been most civil and satisfactory . . . and his big family . . .'

'His family isn't *our* concern.'

'Now, now! Don't get scratchy, dear. I suppose I've dealt with Meares now for — what? — forty-five years.'

Mary took another plunge and battled with the current. 'And there are no end of items for everything — fish, butter, cream — which I can't even *trace*.'

'They must be correct or they wouldn't be entered.'

'As I never do the shopping I don't keep track of what comes *in*. Wouldn't it be a better plan if, in future, either you or I went down daily and looked at the larder? It would help one to know where one *was*.'

'My dear child, cook would be cut to the heart! It would look as though we didn't trust her, and she's been with us now for — what? — nearly — '

'Mamma *dear*, I don't suggest she's dishonest for a moment, but there's no getting over the fact that at present you've only her word for what's needed. Or we might give out the stores once a week, as Gertie does — '

'Well, we've all got our own methods and that doesn't happen to be mine. I don't think I need any lessons from Gertie at this stage — '

Mamma was offended. The session closed with apologies, explanation, disclaimers and reassurances from daughter to mother.

Mary, customarily battered after any serious passage with Mrs. Scrimgeour, retired to the nursery. The soft obstructionism of her parent was not, she saw, entirely of ignorant obstinacy so much as a conservative mistrust and dread of any change which would, for instance, if Mary's reorganization was carried out, have the effect of depriving her mother of her after-breakfast parleys, bumbling, pleasant and familiar, with her old servant the cook. Rob Mrs. Scrimgeour of that alone and you left a blank in her morning which would put her at a total loss and with no occupation.

But it was not entire defeat. Mrs. Scrimgeour recognized a fragment of method in Mary's madness, and ever afterwards kidneys were deleted from the breakfast menu and the luncheon courses reduced by one. The latter deprivation incidentally presented the Scrimgeour women with nearly twenty extra minutes of vacant time. . . .

IV

Every night at nine-thirty punctually Mary and Grace left the drawing-room and filed upstairs to put Nana to bed.

The business, at no time a sinecure when dealing with garrulous, finical and habit-ridden age, had now for some years become an ordeal. Nana, they all at last admitted quite openly since it was impossible to conceal it, was definitely not 'all there'. She was over eighty and still had, as old people so commonly do whose decline has been a prolonged and natural process in easy circumstances, a fund of incalculable lucidity which made her far more difficult to deal with than if she had been consistently insane. It was, they discovered, never safe to count upon either deafness or loss of memory; if you did, Nana would suddenly confound you and make a scene, or distract you by a dismally clear recollection of an object passionately desired for no ascertainable reason which you had burnt or put into the waste paper basket the day before. It had led on one occasion to the upset of routine below-stairs for the whole morning while a housemaid, scarlet with rage, was set to searching the dustbins. 'But at least she doesn't out with Juliet's-nurse remarks', Mary once said with a last glimmer of humour as she sank, pale with nervous exhaustion, into an arm-chair.

Queenie who once had been thankful for those visits to the nursery that saved her face and filled the hours had now long recognized that there was no social appearance to keep up, and declined to officiate at the nightly ordeal of nurse-bedding. She trusted neither her talents nor her temper. Agatha would have been the ideal solution, but Aggie's Order, worse luck! was not a nursing one.

The old woman was a terrible problem in August when they wanted to get away and the staff were, turn by turn, taking their own holidays. For years the older of the servants under the spell of tradition had looked after her, but as the elder maids were weeded out or left, the fresh incomers refused even to consider the proposition. They tried it once. It was awful, with Nana weeping and clinging to her nurslings, crying that 'she' and 'they' had 'starved' her, and you couldn't bring it home to anyone belowstairs because they were armed with the riposte that nurse 'wasn't responsible', which was partly true. In time the self-imposed duties of Mary and Grace spread to the actual carrying up of her meals, filling the tray which was brought into the dining-room and bearing it in turn upstairs. It was, Queenie thought, a pity Nana wasn't put into an institution and be done with it, but even Gertie agreed that one just couldn't. Nana had given up her life to the family, they dubiously explained to each other, and an institution in plain English meant the workhouse, Mrs. Scrimgeour, shocked at heartlessness, said, adding 'It's nice to think we can keep her here in comfort', and, 'She must always feel she has a home with us'.

She did, if her chidings of 'the girls' for a tardiness, real or imagined, was anything to go by. At times she ate enormously, at others there was no suiting her with food.

'I want to be Tempted' she would murmur, regardless of
the effect of the remark upon complete strangers, coming
often without context from her antique lips. With Nana
so trying, it really began to look, Mary said, as though she
would have to have an attendant, a suggestion that was
negatived by Mrs. Scrimgeour. The woman would cost
goodness knew what a week . . . *and* her keep . . . besides:
could one endure her living with the family? And the
servants would make difficulties.

'Mamma, she needn't live with us, she could have the
night nursery or one of the empty bedrooms. If the worst
came to the worst Gracie and I would take up her trays,
but I think we could stand her just for meal times. And
the saving to us I couldn't *describe* to you.'

'Ah, poor old Nana, how she'd hate a stranger! She
loves to be petted by you and Gracie, dear. And really,
Mary, it isn't as though you were being all *that* much tied.
It isn't as if you and Gracie went out a lot in the
evenings — '

After that there was nothing more to be said. Her
mother would never realize that a duty, light in itself as a
spider's web, can be as effectively binding as a steel cable,
so that you must learn to live the more important part of
your life with reference to its claims, and one eye on the
clock.

v

Nana one night advanced upon them with welcoming
mystery and led them to one of the holy chromolithographs
upon her wall, and pointing to the kneeling figure of St.
Joseph announced 'That's Fred'.

They concurred amiably. Her mind had gone back to

266

the misty donor of the heart-shaped plush pin-cushion. The old woman with this exception was perfectly aware of the other figures in the group and talked affectionately of 'the dear little Jesus', while Mary and Grace, chafing to begin, shifted and made the suitable rejoinders. It was an endless business, involving first of all a sheeting up of every picture on the wall to satisfy Nana's fixed belief that 'the glass might be struck by lightning'. There were twenty-three pictures, and to each its special square of muslin or gingham. Then her piece-bag must be hung on the brass knob of the bedrail, and in winter the black-cat tea cosy taken from the fire-place into a position of safety, and photographs of the family propped by the bedside where she could see them; the night-light prepared and lit and placed beyond the reach of dangerous, fumbling old hands, and a search made beneath the bed for the kitchen cat who was never there, and could not have squeezed in among all those boxes if he had wanted to. Sometimes Nana suffered a disastrous last-moment conviction that the boxes themselves had been 'tampered with', and every one had to be hauled out and counted under her eyes. In another corner was a browned heap of newspapers which, their type almost unreadable now, gave ghostly news of the Crimea, the death of Charlotte Brontë, the Diamond Jubilee and the opening of the Great Exhibition. They were never read and must never be thrown away.

Even after Nana was at length between the sheets she would sometimes want to talk about the family photographs, about which she was in a chronic state of confusion. 'That's Gertie's youngest', and she would point to a portrait of Grace, and 'Here's Georgie's husband', producing a cabinet of Captain Scrimgeour.

The final item was the hot milk drink. She liked them to stay while she absorbed it. With luck it made her drowsy, leaving Mary free to pull down the chain of the incandescent, and dusty, heated, fatigued, with nerves on edge, go upstairs with Grace to wash. That was putting Nána to bed at its best and easiest.

That summer of 1905 Mary had to remain in town for August to look after her, leaving Queenie and Grace to accompany Mrs. Scrimgeour to the sea. At the unaccustomed event Mrs. Scrimgeour meditated protest, but hoist with her own petard was forced to acquiescence. But not to silence. Mary must remember *not* to 'sit on all the chairs' but only unsheet one if she was alone . . . and not the best china out if she had a friend to tea . . . remember that cook goes on the tenth and Emily on the twenty-fourth when cook returns, and if *any* difficulty arose to write to her mother at once — oh, and the electricians were expected, but Tom would keep an eye on them.

Leaving her daughter the spadework of full responsibility, she robbed her in advance of all credit and initiative.

CHAPTER XII

I

MARY was not entirely without company during those hot, quiet days, a little unnatural in their shuttered half-lights, their semi-picnic meals of half-laid cloth still served as tribute to seemliness in the dining-room, their freedom of time and life and limb, so that almost fearfully she seemed to breathe full breaths for the first time.

This was London in August, its secrets, formerly shut off by the departing luggage-laden cab, laid bare for one's slow, casual, interested inspection, leaving one to watch the two months merge imperceptibly, as against that abrupt contrast of hot summer morning road and lit lamp-post and blue night-sky of the past. If the unfamiliarity of it all and the quiet freedom became too much for her there was ever the steadying sight of Nana's door, the knowledge of the old, rooted woman in her room. . . .

With diminishing guilt Mary Scrimgeour faced her happiness.

One missed Gracie, of course.

II

It was the first week which brought, and cleared off, her visitors. London, as the gossip writers continued to remark, was now empty, meaning that only four and a half million people were left in the city as against the seven million of custom. There had been some doubt as to whether the King would pay his usual visit to Marienbad.

His general health of late had given rise to some anxiety. The police force, on the contrary, drew a breath of relief at the emptying of London, as did Mr. Asquith and Lloyd George. The suffragettes had recently been rather too much for all concerned and it was hoped that in the dog days they'd go back to their kennel in Clement's Inn and express their social venom by nothing more lethal than the printing of vast blocks of purple, white, and green pamphlets, and what was known in the Movement as 'literature'.

But if nominal Edwardianism hung upon a thread, upon the life of a man, old before his time, on whose shoulders the heavy mantle of responsibility had fallen in late middle-age after over half a century of semi-cipher-dom, the eternal spirit of Edwardianism lived on.

Come Queen, King or Premier, the country houses filled up. Already upon a thousand lawns whose turf lapped the mansion like a carpet guests under chiffon parasols were moving, were drifting off to inspect the stables, while courtyards below their vaned clock-towers drowsed in the warmth of a timeless afternoon. In the servants' halls of England politics were gravely discussed in an atmosphere of rigid etiquette seldom observed in the duke's dining-room. For quite nine years a vague catch-word called 'The German Menace' had got into the air; after a while it was retained as a sort of stray dog to whom you find yourself committed through some forgotten, initial act of kindness. Nobody, except possibly Blatchford, Roberts, Belloc and Kipling, knew exactly what it meant, but it kept conversation alive over coffee.

In the long, cool galleries, faintly musty of old oak and of stiffened folds of Stuart work, the Companions of England — those spare, devoted friends of the family — hurried gaping trippers past historic treasures. In the grounds, head gardeners still refused 'my' peaches, grapes and sweet peas to assured young ladies of title who, débutantes of that season, had weathered the ordeal by dinner-party and presentation and Star and Garter, but who buckled before Scottish obstinacy in a worn alpaca jacket, while in the distance hawk-nosed dowagers with shady hats tied under the chin did a little gardening where Macpherson considered they would achieve the least harm.

Flower-shows were driven to and My Man awarded the Challenge Cup for gladioli for the second year.

Society mothers sank exhausted in the Mauve room in the west wing and regarded from the window an avenue of fir trees and rhododendrons, while in the old school-room the girls discussed conquests and tweeds for September, and the governesses of England were driven to the station in the pony-trap for a month of what might still be left of home life.

III

Mary Scrimgeour read it all with appreciation and pleasurable envy. If there were a menace, German or otherwise, she saw it pictorially as a child does, not as an affair of military efficiency out of a job and spoiling for any showy action that would get called desire for expansion by the Press, but quite simply as a mailed fist smiting down a Queen Anne mansion. Just as, sometimes, she visualized with a faint grin of self derision, the Socialist as, in the last resort, tilting quixotically at a glossy top-hat. It was these social annals daily recorded which roused their ire, apparently. But she also saw that an account of a house-party at Knole was in its degree no less a paragraph of history than the battle of Flodden, and that while

an oak tree grew in an English park and the pursy butler
served tea under the cedars, England would endure with
all her faults and fineness ... these things were stability,
assurance to the panicky public and the nervy townsman.

The greatness of any country is the greatness of its
families. And when families broke up —

IV

Upstairs, the hammering was beginning again and the
front door bell rang. Mary's niece, Paula, ran in from the
hot street. She was fond of her quiet, elderly, humorous
aunt, and kissed her affectionately, pulled the pins from
her flower-massed hat on its tilting bandeau and sank into
a leather arm-chair.

'I had to see you before the annual trek. Mother ought
to have come too, as I told her, but you know what
mother is. She sent her love instead.'

Mary smiled. Outspokenness had evidently passed from
Gertie to Gertie's elder daughter, yet Paula's had a
disarming quality. 'Why the morning-room, Auntie M?'

'We're having electric light installed all over the house.'

'Ah. I can't imagine how you managed, before, but
then I suppose that everybody said that when gas came in
and lamps went out, until you get back to rushlights and
tinderboxes.'

Mary liked the fairness of that. If *this* was the maligned
rising generation ... still, Paula must (incredibly) be over
thirty by now, although she contrived not to look it. She
answered 'I must admit I'm looking forward to it. Those
mantels were always flaking away and my eyes aren't
quite what they were, and when you read a lot —'

'It must cost a fortune to install. We've been on electric

light for three years now, but of course, our box of a house
... well, how is everybody?'

'Well, Auntie Georgie may be home from India in a
few weeks —'

'Auntie M, isn't "Georgina" an astounding name? It's
so utterly dating. "Caroline's" bad enough and always
reminds me of heavy German meals in Kensington Palace.
Can't you *hear* all the Carolines and Charlottes saying
"Undt, will you not some more rrrroast goose bekomm?"
Still, thank heaven I escaped the Gladys and Dorothy
epoch that Hayden Coffin started. All the babies I know
are Dorothy, now. By the way, oughtn't you to be getting
a holiday?'

'It's old Nana, somebody's got to be with her.'

'Oh Lord, oh Lord ... you know, Auntie M, I have
my moments of wondering whether the lethal chamber
isn't the coming solution for the unwanted.'

Mary looked at her hands. 'One can be unwanted at
any age, Pauly.'

'Your score. I'll think that over. I'm sure there's an
effective answer but I can't lay m'hands on·it. But on the
face of it — oh well, it's a great problem. We had a nurse
too, you know, who threatened us with the same thing,
only mother saw it first and sent us to boarding-school.'
Gertie would, Mary thought, and would, moreover,
always contrive to keep within her rights while failing to
satisfy entirely the sentimentalists.

'There were nine of us, Pauly; your mother was twenty-
three before even Auntie Gracie was born, and *she* wasn't
the last.'

'Oh well ... of course Nana had you that way.'

'Would you run up and see her before you go? She
loves visitors, it makes her feel of importance.'

'Of course I will.'

'She'll probably think you're your mother, but you won't mind that.'

'Anything to oblige. There's something awfully uncanny about being dotty, isn't there? I sometimes wonder who there'll be to look after *us* when we all get like that. I mean, well for instance, I've not married and you and Auntie Grace and Aunt Queenie haven't, so we're not putting ourselves in the *way* of assistance . . . if and when I go off my head, I do hope I do it in the grand manner — no half measures, but "Out, damnèd spot", and all that, with scream at end of effective speech.'

'You silly one! You haven't told me yet where you're going.'

'My very dear Auntie, we're all going off on our own, this year. Much better. We've agreed quite dispassionately that we all see enough of each other for the rest of the year, so Dad's gone yachting and mother's paying a round of visits and I'm going to Lyme Regis with a friend. Why doesn't every family do it?'

Why indeed? Mary was thinking. Why did it not lead to scenes and bad feeling when Gertie's family separated, as it had with one's own? Why hadn't one taken a firm line, casual, matter-of-fact, with the parents? Yet Mary knew that, given her life again, she would inevitably have once more submitted to the system. One was as one was and conditions as they were. Yet it all sounded so tantalizingly simple as stated by Paula.

'Well, it can be a matter of cash,' she murmured.

'Yes, I see that. Which reminds me: I've got a job.'

'My dear, how good!'

'What a one you are, Auntie M. You ought to be throwing your mittens to the ceiling and asking what the world's coming to. Ah! you know I don't really mean that or I shouldn't be saying it. But there's still a good bit of moral

mitten going on in our family. Well, anyway, mother didn't
want me hanging round the house all day, and nor did I,
so I put in a bit of time in the East End in a club for
factory girls. I used to play the piano and dance with 'em.
I can't say I liked it much — it smacked a little of Good
Works, and they're apt to smell. If it was a variety of
smells I might have weathered it better, but it was always the same smell. Sour. Ugh. I suppose I've a snob-
bish nose . . . but the girls did occasionally tell me I danced
well, and that gave me an idea. Oh Auntie, my love, have
you ever seen The Valeta? It's the most bourgeois dance
I know. It's 'walking out' made flesh! You take hands
barn-dance wise and mince forward and dip, to begin
with, and then turn and do it again. It's the kitchen-
maid's dream! And so's the music. Like a genteel
conversation at a dustman's funeral tea.

> La *tah* ta ti ti
> Teedle-eedle-dee?
> Rump a *tum*-tum tum ta *tay!*'

Paula, raising her skirt and silk petticoat, Valeta'd
round the room while Mary looked on with a tear of
laughter in her eye.

'Then I chucked it and began to teach girls of our set,
and so it spread. I thought I'd spent years enough in the
ballroom, so why not market the well-known charm?'

'What a *very* capital idea. I do feel so glad.'

'You're a pet.'

'And — do you ever give special attention to the shy
ones? Those who — aren't very pretty?'

Her niece stared at her and Mary's heart sank, then
leapt.

'My hat! That's an idea! I haven't, but I will. You
mean the kind who've got rather hopeless prospects . . .
give 'em poise, and so on?'

'Exactly.'

'Well, I could, I believe. It'll depend on how much imagination I find I've got. You see, if one may say so, I've never had that type of ballroom trouble, myself.'

Mary's voice was carefully dispassionate. 'They mind so . . . one's seen them. . . . And Gertie, how does she like your work?'

'Oh, she was very reasonable about it, just as she was over my refusing those two men because I didn't feel drawn to 'em. Mother has her points, you know,' said Gertrude's daughter to Gertrude's sister.

'You'll have a glass of sherry before you go up to Nana?'

'Won't I!' They sipped, and a memory returned to Mary.

'Pauly, you're a modern young thing. Would you say that when men drop in, they expect sherry at six o'clock?'

Paula sensed a trouble, glanced without seeming to at the strong-featured, gentle woman with the fine crows-feet of age and private laughter round her eyes and answered with chivalrous directness, 'I don't think there's any hard and fast rule about it, m'dear, and I'm pretty sure that your men wouldn't look for it when the men of the house aren't there any longer. But I'll make quite certain, and ask my flames as a hypothetical case; you don't want 'em queueing up for your good drink! I do know sherry when I get it. Yours is better than ours. Grandpa's, I suppose?'

v

The visit to Nana developed into a tour of the house itself, their feet rattling on the uncarpeted floors. Paula peeped into the drawing-room where white-coated electricians moved about whistling softly and throwing remarks to each other which boomed and echoed. On the staircase she turned to her aunt. 'I never realized the size of this house, one's taken it for granted all these years. Don't you find it's too big for you, now?'

The hammering began again.

CHAPTER XIII

I

THE electric light was an immediate and rather unexpected success with Mrs. Scrimgeour. But if it relieved her eyes it also, she complained, showed up the furnishings in a manner which threw into relief the less pleasing aspects of those souvenirs. It made the rooms 'look soiled'.

It was true. Wall-papers of half a century, durable, patterned and flocculent, now were shielded by no kindly wavering shadow, and the rooms stood out gauntly, displaying in a cheerful uniform radiance every scratch and stain. . . .

They must refurnish. These new chintzes and cretonnes were really very light and effective, and gilt frames certainly showed off pictures better than that dark wood.

Mary, shaken at Paula's comment, was moved to moot the question of expense. Her remarks, as she guessed in advance, had no effect at all. 'Gertie on her own admission had the electric three years ago and her furniture is all modern stuff.'

'But, Mamma, think of the difference in the size of the houses! I mean, do you think we *ought* to spend quite so much — ?'

' "We"?'

Her daughter flinched at that; the fact that it was humorously intonated mollified it not at all.

'You see, there are only four of us now, and if — well, Gracie might marry and leave us.'

Her mother, side-tracked, looked henlike. 'Is there a likelihood? Have you noticed anything?'

Mary avoided her eyes. 'No, but she might.'

'Oh! . . .' That objection was dismissed; the other, that Mrs. Scrimgeour herself could hardly hope to be with them many years longer, one could not advance. Indisputable and telling at least though that fact was, it was also one of the things you did not allude to. People of well over seventy must know they had to die ere long but it led to scenes if you even hinted as much. . . .

The refurnishing and redecorating was put in hand. Once more, Mary, Queenie and this time Grace as well, were farmed out with friends and relations.

Mary, once more at her aunt's, looked out of her Sloane Street window. The well-remembered view at least was unchanged and unchanging, unlike herself . . . and her aunt who, at ninety, was now invisible for great tracts of the time and in the grip of old and faithful maids. And Mamma was only in the seventies, so perhaps one had saved on a little bad feeling in not bringing forward the age question with reference to the house, even had one been able to get it said. Mamma, Georgie had once declared, had a lot of luck; without being intrinsically right she often was justified in the event. . . .

Writing-case on knees, Mary re-read her correspondence from Arabella and Georgina. Remote by way of life no less than by distance, their comments upon the Brecknock Gardens upheaval were clear and definite, unlike one's own confused opinions:

'I think it's a mistake and so does Francis . . . why didn't Mamma do it before if she meant to do it at all? Then you girls would at least have had the extra benefit of the refurnishing, etc. But I agree with you: it's no good talking. If they mean to do a thing they'll do it.'

And:

'So Mamma remains at home to supervise? God help the workmen!'

Husbands, Mary thought, seemed to make sisters very outspoken. In the old days not even Georgie would have said God help anyone ... it was probably a good thing. Better late than never. But it jarred, a little. . . .

Before Mary and her aunt had time to tire of each other a letter came from Mrs. Scrimgeour. Mary and Gracie must, after all, return ... Nana ... *very* difficult and unmanageable about the workmen and the maids were being tiresome about looking after her.

Nana was being all that and more; fighting every innovation to the death. They had to give in, leaving her room the one Victorian oasis in an Edwardian desert. Her case won, she sat bodefully in the midst of her treasures. The workmen who liked directness grew quite fond of her. Occasionally when the battle was at its height the men would report progress to each other, and news of their mascot.

'She 'it me, "smornin'.'

'Go on!'

'She *did*. With 'er own little fist.'

'I never!'

'Straight she did. I come in to start strippin' the walls and "no you don't come in 'ere," she says. "Come on, ole lady," I says, "we're goin' t' fix you up pretty. You won't know the ole place not after I done with it", I says. Then she starts off alarming. Says she wantster go on knowin' it and that was jes' what she wuz afraid of *all* along, and with that she 'its me. Right on the jore. Straight. Stunger bit, too.'

'Go *on!*'

'Well . . . not *arf* she ain't a fair ole cup o' tea!'

The men blissfully mused on Nana over their lunches. When they clattered downstairs for the last time Nana stood watching them go. The one she had hit had brought her a bunch of flowers from his back garden in Islington. She put a trembling hand on the arm of another, quite at random.

'You're a *good* boy, a good boy.'

The good boy, a plasterer of sixty-five, gave her a kiss.

11

The bill mildly astonished even Mrs. Scrimgeour. But she supposed it must be all right if house decoration *did* cost all that, and the items were explicit enough. Besides: it was for the dear girls' sake as much as for appearances . . . people liked an attractive house to drop in to. If it came to that, it was ridiculous to go on paying rent and would be a positive saving to buy the house. They must have spent thousands of pounds all these years on rent, and the house wasn't theirs yet. Being a business woman one would talk it over with the Bank manager and with the solicitor.

She sat down and wrote to the latter, but Mr. Mowbray intensely disliked mixing business with friendship and regretted that a press of work . . . Sunday, then? Three o'clock, and they could have a quiet talk before tea at which it would be pleasant for Mr. Mowbray and 'the daughters' to meet each other. Mr. Mowbray was extremely sorry that at the week-ends he was usually out of town, and suggested a conference at his office. Mrs. Scrimgeour was offended and cancelled the meeting altogether. But Mr. Harrowe would do.

Before the interview at the Bank she spent her time wondering if one of the girls had put Mr. Mowbray off? But surely they hadn't seen enough of him for that? . . . Occasional dinners in the old days, when the Captain brought out his second best port. . . .

One wished the girls *helped* one more with people. And it would have been nice to show Mr. Mowbray the house and all the improvements.

Dinner, now? But his elderly wife would have to be asked too and nothing serious would get done. Besides: he had really behaved most cavalierly. No. Mr. Harrowe, decidedly. Such a kind face, and always gentlemanly.

III

Two days later, Mr. Harrowe and his kind face joined Mrs. Scrimgeour in the manager's room at the Bank. He disliked doing business with women; half angels and half imbeciles, as some writer had once remarked, and whichever side came uppermost a Bank was not the place for it. He installed her and politely cut the threads of her opening sociabilities.

'So you want to buy the house, Mrs. Scrimgeour? It's a big step to take.'

'Yes? But it would *settle* everything, and then, of course, the associations . . .' He steered her away from all that. 'And what do your daughters think?'

'I haven't mentioned it to them. It is really hardly their province, is it? Such a purely *business* matter.'

He raised his eyebrows, then bent to some pencilled notes on a sheet of paper. 'I've been in touch with the house agent and I see that you have three more years of your present lease to run.'

'Splendid,' murmured Mrs. Scrimgeour vaguely.

'Captain Scrimgeour renewed the lease three times — '

'Did he? Ah, he was devoted to the house.'

Mr. Harrowe gazed hopelessly at her through his glasses.

'The point against buying is that if you do so now, you lose three years of what has already been paid for.'

That had to be explained again, twice, until Mrs. Scrimgeour said she 'saw'.

'Now, I'm not going to pretend that if, at the conclusion of this period, you still want to purchase you might not be able to do so on favourable terms; there is not quite the demand for these large houses that there was.'

'Really? I should have thought everybody liked them.'

'Quite so, but "everybody" isn't always able to afford them. It's not only the purchase money, but the upkeep that tells.'

She blinked trustfully. He mentally strangled her, leant back and shot at her: 'Your best move would have been to have given the house up years ago when you might have hoped to dispose of the remainder of the lease. As things are — '

' — you're in favour of my buying it?' she assented rapidly.

'I am *not*.'

She was hurt, dismayed and disappointed as a child.

'Oh!' Another woe struck her. 'And I've just spent fourteen hundred on redecorating. Through*out*.'

He bit his lip and spoke as casually as might be. 'Before you ascertained how long the lease had to run?'

She scented male censure and began to go to pieces. 'Well, you see, I expected to *buy* it.'

He turned again to the pencilled sheet. 'They would ask three thousand five hundred for the house.'

'Couldn't I manage that?'

'I suppose you *could*, but it would mean a big hole in your capital and would reduce your income by nearly one hundred and fifty pounds a year.'

She looked acute and critical. 'Well, that isn't *much*.'

He slew her with a hammer, this time. The corpse was not an appetizing sight. 'You know, of course, that your husband sold out of a rather unfortunately large number of good investments during the latter years of his life? . . . If you buy your house you must make a further encroachment upon capital. In *any* case you will have to sell out once more to meet the redecorating of the house.'

'Not *really?*' It meant little to her but a phrase: less, in that her husband had done it before her. But she sensed that in some way she was in disgrace and was confounded by the injustice, when she had only spent the money on an impersonality . . . for all four of them.

'Then, what do you want me to do?'

'It is entirely for you to decide, Mrs. Scrimgeour.' He was too contemptuous to discover any merit in her serene acceptance of the imperilment of her and her daughters' future by the incurrence of a son's debts and a father's indulgence. The more obvious disaster was before his eyes: the imperilment of the future of three women through a mother's financial imbecility, and a law which made it possible.

IV

She left quietly enough. But he had stampeded her mind. The safety of three more years in the familiar house was no comfort to irrational panic. It was difficult to think clearly, or at all . . . and she must plan for all of them. The idea of taking her daughters into partnership of confidence did not occur to her. The young must have their pleasures. . . .

Visions of 'a crust' and 'the House' flitted through a mind which leapt from one extreme to another, often a feature of a lifetime of security which has received a preliminary warning.

In her bedroom, she wept tears of self- and vicarious- and world-pity, sitting there, a portly, confused old woman to whom life was, incredibly and incomprehensibly, not being kind.

CHAPTER XIV

I

THAT winter brought with it a fine crop of bills. Mrs. Scrimgeour, impervious to illness through all the years of childbearing, went down before unaccustomed mental effort and succumbed to a bad bout of influenza. Nana, from whom the news had been unable to be kept, thanks to a sulky housemaid, toddled determinedly from her own room to take charge, and was only routed when she caught the complaint herself, and much more seriously.

While Mary nursed her mother, a trained nurse at two guineas a week was installed for Nana, who made a sad grievance of it.

During the upset, Mrs. Scrimgeour's consolation lay in the Christmas preparations executed by her daughters from her bedside orders. At this time, at least, no blame could lie in spending. Was not the Season of Goodwill a sweet, traditional obligation? Money spent for the good and pleasure of others was justified of itself and the cash consideration a vulgarity; even the bills which followed hard upon were not as ordinary bills. . . .

There were, happily, so many dear ones to remember; the list lay on her bedside table. Georgie, husband and two children, Arabella, husband and daughter, Gertie, Clarence, Albert, Caroline, husband and girls, Paula, Mary, Queenie, Gracie, Nana, the servants, Aunt Susan, friends, a box of good fare for Aggie's convent (though one disliked the encouragement by nourishment of Popery) and Nurse Franklyn. She would be offended if omitted. With tentative guilt Charlotte Scrimgeour drew cheques as a child steals cake.

And there were the appeals.

Propped with pillows, soft and weak with convalescence, she read them through.

Every year we have to turn away hundreds of urgent cases. Delay may mean death or permanent disablement to these Little Ones. Immediate treatment and care would save them. We cannot build without YOUR help.

NO ENDOWMENT.   NO FUNDS

Already warm tears were stealing down her cheeks. Mary had placed the glass of champagne by the bedside and she took another sip. It was — actually — doctor's orders. Doctor Ripley was nephew to old Doctor Grant, dead these fifteen years, a young man, not yet fifty. He made Mrs. Scrimgeour shy. Young enough to be your son . . . but very managing. 'I'm not going to drench you with medicines, Mrs. Scrimgeour, they only upset the liver and the liver always goes back on you after a spell in bed. Get 'em to give you a glass of good fizz — medium dry — when you fancy it and you'll be feeling quite different about life after a bit. I always recommend it.'

Guiltily she enjoyed it, as she did all luxury that was not like such things as dress and a good table, a matter of custom and necessity.

FIVE HUNDRED POUNDS WOULD NAME A COT IN PERPETUITY

That was cheap. Usually it took at least one thousand pounds to name a cot; the hospital was making a desperate drive for patrons in offering the personal touch. And how right they were. No feeling woman — no mother, above all — could fail to respond to it.

So took up another brochure.

287

PART THREE

THE EGLINGTON HOME FOR DISTRESSED GENTLEFOLK
We appeal to you for coals for empty grates, for warm clothes and for parcels of Christmas cheer for a number of most distressing cases. We are annually helping four hundred gentlewomen who, through no fault of their own, are brought in old age to actual want.
Their need is Desperate
WE PLEAD FOR THOSE WHO CANNOT PLEAD FOR THEMSELVES

Mrs. Scrimgeour's interest flagged; still holding the Eglington Home leaflet, she had already seen with the practised eye of a one-track sympathy the glossy illustration of another appeal. The Blind Babies, having a tea-party on a lawn, and she laid the pamphlet aside. These needy women (if genuine) were evidently shiftless. It was almost irritating that in face of all the sadness in the children's hospitals they should push their claims and steal badly wanted sympathy at the Festival of the Children, and 'gentlewomen' was no doubt an elastic phrase like the 'five minutes from sea' of the holiday lodging-houses . . . or 'liberal table' when the food was a disgrace. Most reputable women had reputable friends to help them and people of our class just did not lend themselves as subjects for a public appeal to charity.

The hand which wrote the cheque that would name a cot was not entirely Charlotte Scrimgeour's; it was at least guided by the Christmas spirit only slightly disordered by Veuve Clicquot.

II

There was a fair muster round the dinner-table with its symmetrical piles of crackers at every corner. The crystallized fruits and dishes of sweets and salted almonds

288

glowed in the electric light under its circular red silk
shade and upon the alternation of black sleeve and bare
arms of the men and women down the table's length.

It was, Grace thought, wonderfully like a real dinner-
party. . . . Queenie had tried hard not to be there, but
hadn't seemed to be able to get herself asked to the house
of anyone else. 'People always expect one to be deep
in the bosom of one's own family, so nobody invites
anybody,' she explained to her sisters as time went on
and it became evident that she was sealed unto the
Brecknock Gardens table again, for that year at any
rate. For herself Grace asked nothing better. At
Christmas the private, creeping dismays of the rest of
the year were discarded, and one gathered closer to those
whom one loved best . . . and a gap in the table would
grieve Mamma so . . . one was always armed with that
reflection when brooding the invitation, should it ever
come for oneself, that existed so far in one's brain: of a
large, log-fire'd mansion, snow and a flight of steps, and
light and a chorus of welcome . . . and new eyes that
would see the new dress and its wearer. There must be
such places and such people, and when the call to them
came, one would somehow be able to respond without
Mamma minding. Meanwhile, the fact that she did mind
defections was used very freely, and had probably (as
Queenie said) held people off who really wanted one. . . .
It was a version of their affairs that the sisters clung to
still. They annually hung mistletoe and referred mainly
to the holly. Yes . . . it was genuinely sweet to be all
together and probably the joys of the dream house would
be rendered null anyway by one's own shyness, or one's
face. With a rush of warm gratitude to her family for a
disillusion escaped, Grace helped herself to almonds and
raisins. Her brother-in-law, Clarence, was on her left,

T   289

at the right of his hostess, for Mrs. Scrimgeour was 'down'
against the advice of everyone. Dressing her had been
rather a business, and made Mary and Grace a little late
in the drawing-room where Gertrude loitered in barely
suppressed impatience with her husband, son, daughters,
son-in-law and Queenie. It was a feat recognized by
Mrs. Scrimgeour to 'get' the Randolphs and had increased
her determination to take her own place at table.

Gertrude had written Mary:

'I really think I will say "Yes" this year to the family
dinner business. The present lot of maids are being
tiresome and I refuse to eat cold turkey at night to save
them trouble. Clarence and Bertie don't mind, so I
suppose eight o'clock as usual? PS. — I take it this
includes Paula? We shall be seven females to three men,
with Carry's husband, but it is "family", so will pass along.'

That stung a little: Gertie's assumption that the women
would outnumber the men — as they always did. There
were times, and this was one of them, when almost Mary
could have paid some stranger to enter their hall — anyone within reason, so it was clean, sober and in trousers.
Why not? There were employment agencies for every
other type of hand, but the hostess's acutest social dilemma
went uncatered for. She smiled inwardly, picturing her
own appearance — elderly, greying, placid — versus the
thoughts aboil in her brain. It must be quite an experience
to be kissed under the mistletoe . . . but it would be equally
an experience to travel to China. Yet Grace made one
vicariously vulnerable in the way of lamentation.

Electric light was really regrettably unbecoming; it
left faces no illusions to stand up in, any more than it had
the wall-papers they'd had stripped and replaced. How
Mamma was revelling in it all! Maternally Mary regarded

her mother. Thank heaven Nana's supper had been disposed of earlier. She was now in the grip of Nurse Franklyn, poker-backed, youngish and weakened by no sentiments. As it was, Nana had as usual contrived to exceed on sweets and oranges, and as usual would be prostrated with biliousness on Boxing Day. She had begged one for them so hard . . . But Nurse would have to come downstairs for dessert, they had all wanly agreed that ('at this time') to leave her to pace between her own room and Nana's would be scarcely humane, and it was hoped that in the no-man's-land of cracker pulling she would be submerged, together with her embarrassing hospital reminiscences. Retrospective grievance and unvarnished horror appeared to comprise her anecdotal repertoire, and apropos the midwifery saga Queenie had remarked with a loud laugh that it made her 'thankful she had escaped motherhood'.

Paula was talking to Queenie now; Mary heard the clear, confident voice.

'My dear Auntie Q., I assure you that men seem to think that because you teach them to get round a ballroom without looking like lynxes with lumbago you can be embraced with impunity. It's curious, and quite interesting.'

Grace was listening now. 'I can't see the connection,' said Queenie primly.

'I couldn't either for a long time, and then it came over me that it was because they were paying me for the lessons. You see? A woman who will take money from men deserves all she gets. And the fact that they'd be paying double in any other dancing school for far less personal attention makes no difference at all. Hurrah for male chivalry!'

'Well, what do they *do*?' Queenie's voice was ungracious.

For some reason unknown to herself she mistrusted Paula. It made things difficult for — well — ladies when girls of one's own set went into business involving association with men. . . . Paula was being cheap and rather disgusting, and the attentions she received from men didn't *count*. It was enraging that Paula realized that, as well . . . but was probably an assumed manner to cover elation.

Her niece answered with bald directness. 'If you take them as private pupils you sometimes bearlead them to subscription dances as a preliminary canter for private ones. And then they kiss you in taxis.'

Queenie's voice was stony. 'That's a great drawback to such an employment. I wonder you don't take up something else, don't you, Grace?' Grace didn't, and was privately fascinated at the incredible chronicle, but she replied gravely that it did seem a pity when Paula was trying so hard to succeed, 'but of course, men *are* like that'. She flushed scarlet and looked round rapidly lest she had been overheard. Her niece eyed her. 'They aren't, Gracie, except when you try and strike out for yourself. My opinion of men is nothing if not low, bless them, but you only get down to brass tacks when you're ostensibly earning your own living. It's the theme of all the novelettes, now I come to think of it. The virtuous and lovely factory girl (that's me, Aunt Queenie) and the villain in an eternal astrachan collar, eternally symbolizing labour and capital respectively.'

'You mean that men don't respect women they aren't called upon to protect and support?' suggested Mary.

'What a nice woman you are, Auntie M.! Yes, that's what it boils down to. What you've paid for you value most.'

'But — how terrible to be — er — flirted with in a taxi,' Grace laughed affectedly. She seemed unable to let that aspect of the subject alone. 'I can't bear to *think* of it for you. What do you say?'

Paula was already finished with the theme and answered absently, 'Oh, there's plenty to say. Chaff 'em. It's our only weapon, these days. Ripping good dinner, Auntie M.'

At the head of the table Mrs. Scrimgeour was beaming and shifting in her chair. This usually meant that she wanted something procurable by some daughter and Mary caught her eye and half rose with a look of enquiry, but her mother shook her head, frowning a little and signalling and lifting her glass of wine. She was, oh God, going to make a speech, reflected Clarence Randolph wearily.

To affectionately mocking applause the large old lady rose.

'Before we drink Absent Friends and my dear Georgie and Arabella and *their* families — and Aggie, of course — I give you "The Charles and Charlotte Scrimgeour Cot".'

'The what, Mamma?' asked Queenie loudly.

Explanation followed, with Mrs. Scrimgeour very incoherent and excited. She hadn't meant to say anything, but where philanthropy was concerned to let her right hand remain in ignorance of the doings of her left, but the time, the place and the company had proved too much for her. Queenie with a slight shrug subsided; Mary, lips compressed, thought it regrettable that her mother hadn't told them all before; Grace was delighted and said so; Clarence, a nut between his fingers, raised his eyebrows and the others looked civilly interested.

It was Gertrude who asked briskly, 'And how much did *that* stand you in, Mamma?' It deeply annoyed her mother as she had foreseen.

'Well, my child, we don't want to drag in that side of things, on Christmas Night.'

Gertrude looked at her. 'Oh, you mean that you just lent your name?' she suggested smoothly.

'Nothing of the kind.' Between sentiment triumphant and exasperation at Gertrude Mrs. Scrimgeour to the slightly harassed eyes of her guests fairly wabbled. 'Five hundred pounds was the sum required and which one was so glad to be able to give them.'

Gertrude was thinking that her mother had come out of the questionnaire rather adroitly, for her. Her husband opened his mouth, then closed it and cracked his walnut with a loud report. He was a son-in-law, true, but to-night he was also a guest.

It relieved Mrs. Scrimgeour when Nurse Franklyn put her head round the door, primed for bromidic facetiousness, a relief out of all proportion to her feelings for the stranger in their midst, and from which fact Charlotte Scrimgeour drew no conclusions whatsoever.

III

Clarence Randolph arranged his women in his car, started her, and remarked, 'Your mother, you know . . . she's going it a bit, isn't she?'

His wife maintained an acrid silence. 'I suppose she can afford it?'

'Why suppose so, my dear?'

'She can't go on like this, y'know. . . .' He turned the corner into Gloucester road. 'Why didn't Mary put her foot down?'

'*Mary?* My dear man!'

'One of the others, then.'

He subsided before his wife's continued silence. 'Well, I suppose she knows her own business best or she wouldn't have done it.'

Caroline and her young husband walked to South Kensington station. Under the coldly brilliant sky the stars seemed to suggest something to him and he said: 'Somebody ought to tell old Queenie-piece not to wear sequins. She looked like the Madam of a disorderly house.'

Gertrude's younger daughter laughed aloud. 'You ought to know, Bob.'

'No, but honestly, Caro, it's very rum. I don't understand her. To talk to she's as tightlip as bedamned, and yet the way she *looks*! . . .'

CHAPTER XV

I

THE subject of the hospital cot was allowed to drop in the immediate Scrimgeour circle. Mrs. Scrimgeour, oscillating between self-justification and guilt, was touched and grateful at the loyalty of her daughters as evidenced by their silence . . . so unlike Gertie.

Once convalescent, it took the form of driving her out into the highways and byways of London, secretly, and shorn of the companionship she longed for, in effort after effort to find another house — a new home for the girls. House-agents within a five-mile radius grew almost to remember her name, and cab-ranks profited exceedingly. There were limits, and if one overtired oneself walking it might cloud one's judgment, render one's bargaining less acute. . . . One minded leaving the old house so badly that to seek a new one without allowing oneself the chance of being weakened by discussion must be the right thing to do. Duty was seldom pleasant.

The house agents' clerks, unlocking front doors in Terraces, 'Places' and Kensington side streets, found that Mrs. Scrimgeour wavered between impossible, grandiose demands and sudden cedings of every point and capitulations over every glossed defect. At one stage she was dangerously near closing with the offer of a house because the young man looked tired and ill. The house, which combined a break-leg basement with small windows and cramped rooms, had beetles in the kitchen and cockroaches in the larder; it was never to become the home of her daughters because next day her eye had been drawn to another address in Brennon Gardens which sounded so dearly like Brecknock. . . . Also it had a turret room where the Captain's sword would look in its right place and silverfish in the fire-places about which the clerk was silent.

The fascination of house-hunting grew upon her, if she gained little by it of experience. She had come direct from her own parents' comfortable Kentish home to her husband, and the interval between honeymoon and the Brecknock Gardens house which was staffed and furnished by her own mother was filled by stops with relatives in London. A home and staff as going concern Charlotte Scrimgeour could run and control. Before a home in embryo she was at sea. Subconsciously she was expecting a dwelling differing only in address from the one she was abandoning and for long her remark 'We can do without a morning-room' was to be the sole expression of her awareness of altered circumstances.

11

In five years the Scrimgeours had moved house three times. It was a combination of bad luck, bad management and hopeless effort to mollify the individual and made them the joke, bane and apprehension of the married branches.

'How's Mamma?'

'Well — she's rather worried, just now. We are having to get out of the house.'

'It has dipped me a lot,' Mrs. Scrimgeour would tell relatives wistfully.

Every fresh move left behind it a trail of wasted capital. In the first house, reasonably comfortable and of a medium size upon which Mrs. Scrimgeour prided her acumen, the Brecknock Gardens carpets, stair-carpets and curtains proved to be far too large and had to be scrapped and replaced, a geyser installed to counter tepid baths and waste of coal, and most of the rooms repapered. The pieces selected by the landlord the Scrimgeours united in considering impossible. The second house developed dry rot in the scullery. When that had been attended to, their first winter revealed the fact that falls of snow collecting on the roof would, when the thaw set in, thunder down upon the glassed-in area and smash the panes until the servants gave notice and a *cheval de frise* was constructed against the gutters. But the real cause of the move was Nana's hatred of the house. Mary and Grace — even Queenie — had offered her in turn their bedrooms but she was determined in prejudice. Her bed-sitting-room overlooked a garage and she said the chauffeurs worried her. 'I don't *know* them, Mary. They're after my Things . . . aren't they?'

Sometimes the abandoned houses found tenants quickly; sometimes the Scrimgeours were paying double rent. Mrs. Scrimgeour herself, resigned to the break-up of her life, alternated between a doglike craving for her old, ordered home and a sense of fulfilment at the constant changes. Of every house they occupied she thought, fearfully, 'So this is where I shall die', and the upheaval and departure seemed to assure her of an extension of life . . . each fresh furniture van in the road was a reprieve.

III

Mrs. Scrimgeour now had her fill of servant troubles. She considered that by reducing her staff to cook, house-parlourmaid and daily charwoman she had cut her expenses to the bone, reached social bedrock and silenced possible criticism for ever. She found instead that the rise in wage-scales all over England resulted in an expenditure which, in the old days, would have purchased one maid more and a girl for the kitchen. And there was Tom. The old handyman had been in their service for over fifty years and could not follow the family to their new houses where there was no room for him. He was now too old to get a place anywhere, with only semi-skilled and out-dated labour to offer. They had had to pension him off. Thirty pounds a year. Even Gertie had agreed that it was the right thing to do. It seemed hopeless to attempt economy. . . . Mrs. Scrimgeour also believed that in cutting the staff to the size of her house she had purchased peace and found that in point of fact she had merely taken on two more discordant female malcontents, tied by no loyalties and out for all they could get. By the time adjustments and concessions which ensured a reasonably smooth-running programme had been made they had usually given notice.

These smaller houses were very sounding-boards; from their dining-room the family could follow the salient bouts of kitchen quarrel and when, often past their time, the servants went up to bed, they frequently woke up Nana, who took an hour's quieting and soothing.

Mrs. Scrimgeour struggled to keep the domestic reins in her own hands; relinquishment, to her, was defeat and the shadow of death. She did not see that at eighty-two a healthy retirement was unremarkable; she had immense powers of resistance and her sight was only just beginning to give her trouble and cause her to wear glasses, but then Mary and Queenie were now wearing them, too. . . .

It was Arabella and Georgina who persuaded her at

last by affectionate flatteries to 'let Mary take some of this strain off you'. Gradually, watchfully, grudgingly, she allowed Mary to control the house, bestowing the authority as an honour.

It was an honour that had come too late; it was a wrenching of a contemplative personality into the lime-light of often sordid domestic strife, and Mary made plenty of blunders which equally gratified and exasperated her mother. Her daughter was extra-handicapped by that knowledge. Perhaps if one had an entirely free hand . . . but this led to a train of thought which must be stifled at once. One was of course devoted to Mamma. But — it was all amazingly difficult. You never knew what servants were going to complain about next, and having listened to them, were never sure as to the extent of their rights. All that emerged as guidance from the domestic proces-sion was that they all shared a love of pork, a hatred of game, a habit of leaving soap to melt in the pail and a detestation of bedrooms which didn't face the street.

One reform Mary had instituted: no longer should the tradesmen call for orders and place the family purse at the mercy of the cook. Grace, glad to be of use, undertook the shopping and made plenty of errors in the under-and-over-estimation of supplies on her own account. The morning walks were now no leisured strolls but waiting your turn in shop after shop with an eye on cook's requirements for luncheon.

It at once gave life a little purpose while limiting freedom to an extent she had not anticipated. Grace hardly knew what she felt about the moves; the strange-ness of the new houses was for her lessened by the prompt way in which an inexorable routine was run up out of chaos: morning shopping, taking the afternoons off turn about with Mary in being at hand for Nana, the evenings devoted to talk or cards with her mother. Sooner or later any house they occupied looked the same, a diminished and sometimes looking-glass version of the Brecknock Gardens home, with all the old remaining pictures and ornaments in their same relative positions.

Often, lapped in fancied security against repining and steeled at last as she believed to life as it presented itself, Grace in some shop mirror would see herself and was shocked into painful realization. This, then, was oneself, this staid-looking person? It couldn't be. It was an effect of light. All glasses lied, and top-lights were notorious. She forgot the pangs, they came and passed and routine once more sheathed her warmly. She could look at such men as were socially available with the steady eye of spiritual atrophy that sought and expected nothing, and was apparently justified by finding and receiving nothing.

IV

She was sustained by an inner conviction that in time all would come right; this life they all seemed to be living was only a phase, a rather prolonged one, but nothing went on for ever. It was a pity that it had to come when one was still — well — fairly young, one would have chosen rather the comfortable monotony for the closing years of life.

She had now almost taken it for granted that no man would ever look at her. It gave her a kind of confidence in facing conditions, it was the last capitulation to fate that would be exacted, a long, weary battle which was over at last. But the implications of defeat were stupendous. She saw that the fact that the hopes of youth had failed altered the whole, long rest of life. It set her to going over and over the stages of her girlhood which had led to this aridity, wondering and weighing, puzzled to know wherein the mistake had occurred. They were gropings which led nowhere.

Sometimes, the thought that her own familiar body could any time and even now create children for her drove her even from the society of Mary. One went on saying 'No' to it because you may not have a baby without a husband as well. And soon, perhaps, it would be too late. The idea that the world might, after all, never know a child of Grace Scrimgeour's was unbelievable. Yet the subject of illegitimate babies was so painful that she was distressed at allusion to them. It shocked Grace profoundly if mention of such things were made in general conversation by Caroline, or even Paula.

v

They clung to such old friends as were still available and faithful with redoubled warmth, but even Mrs. Scrimgeour could not blink the fact that the cessation of the large house amenities tended to lose them a handsome proportion of their visiting-list. She strove in her first years of small-house life to recreate a version in miniature of the Brecknock Gardens hospitality, but even heavy expenditure was no guarantee of success when pitted against a cook's temperament, undependability, lack of finish and of pride in her work. The departing servants sometimes threw at Mary that they disliked the place — plenty of work and no life. It was their translation of the lack of stray tips going in hotels and private houses where men were frequent callers.

More and more Mrs. Scrimgeour missed old Emma, past service now and gone to end her days with a married niece in Lambeth. It was a regret not wholly selfish, and the old, comfortable half-hour succeeding breakfast was now a blank keenly felt. The speed of life within and without the house distressed and confused Charlotte Scrimgeour; meals hastily dished up with plates twitched away took but a third of the time to consume that they used to, and the rooms were done with a flick and a bounce, with good mahogany and walnut furniture scrubbed as though with sandpaper instead of having their surface patiently humoured back to condition. And in the midst of all the apparent hustle, the days were very long.

Never a great reader, the modern novel to her was no solace and certainly no substitute for the tried and reliable works of Mrs. Henry Wood, Mrs. Alfred Hunt and Rhoda Broughton. Quite three times a week one of her daughters would return the current batch to the circulating library. 'Mrs. Scrimgeour doesn't care for this type of thing.' 'We can't read that.' In the literary world t's were beginning to be crossed and i's inexorably dotted, and the Scrimgeours were not good at facing facts. Sometimes a book slipped through their guard, creating secret havocs, never between Queenie and Grace mutually admitted. They solved the problem by instant elimination of the book, half regretful, half relieved, fighting their thoughts as revealed to them by this author and that, a mental contest between prudery, sanity, frustration and funk.

V I

With time heavy on her hands Mrs. Scrimgeour appreciated keenly the visits paid her by the younger branches of her family and let it be seen that she was wounded at neglect. Surely in these days when everybody seemed to possess a car it should be easier than ever? There were numerous small outbursts that her daughters must quell by soothing explanation and extempore excuse for the absentees.

She had decided that Caroline's young husband, Robert Bridgewood, was her favourite, and looked upon him as a grandson, gradually finding in his face that which affection urged, a resemblance to her dead son. She made him a number of money presents. He was not a bad type but would not have been human had he failed to take passive advantage of the situation which, to do him justice, he had genuinely misunderstood. That business of the hospital cot that the old lady had let out on Christmas night looked as though there were plenty more where that five hundred came from, and Caroline thought so too, not that she saw much of Gran, who bored her.

Mrs. Scrimgeour bought him a car and left him a thousand pounds in her Will. It was her oblation to present prudence and fairness to Mary, Queenie and Grace.

VII

The evenings improved at once. It was very sweet to Charlotte Scrimgeour to have once more a young, attentive male at her elbow, delighting her with stray kisses and jokes. Even her daughters were pleased ... her nephew-in-law's presence relieved Mary of much of the task of finding employment and entertainment for her mother, while Queenie and Grace privately regarded him as possible magnet for other men.

CHAPTER XVI

I

In 1910 Agatha had died. Queenie and Grace went down for the funeral, Mary remaining at home. Somebody must be at hand to look after her mother, Nana and the servants.

To Grace, save for that one hour together many years ago, her sister had been but an interlude in life; now, the incidents of that day came back to her, reawakening all her pity. She travelled down in a mood of mounting indignation but her resentments were partially stifled by the experienced handling she and Queenie received inside the convent. The nuns were not unused to Protestant relatives. They consented to every request, gave gentle sympathy, anticipated desires and even broke a rule in allowing the sisters inside the dead woman's cell, and still Grace would not let herself be disarmed. It was irritating to her conventional Anglicanism that the nuns were giving no loophole for criticism. It was Queenie who disgraced them, at the solemn Mass itself through whose windings ameliorated by no music she struggled to find her way. Queenie had begun by fidgeting and yawning which Grace mistook for bad manners, and ended by turning greenish-white and having to leave the chapel. The nuns, bowed in rows, took no notice at all. Queenie looking frightened said later that it must have been the incense and 'all this about poor old Aggie', but it seemed to Grace that, back in her study, the Superior eyed her sister rather oddly ... a look of awareness and reminiscence, like a doctor recognising a symptom ... yet the Reverend

Mother was a stranger, her predecessor, they said, had died five years ago.

Queenie was already in the passage chafing to be off; Grace and the Superior stood for a few seconds together. The elderly woman put her hand on Grace's arm. 'Try not to grieve, my child. Your dear sister died very peacefully.'

Grace gave look for look. 'But she was miserable here while she lived,' she answered with the extreme bluntness of the habitually unready when it does speak its thought. But the assurance of the statement failed to daunt trained diplomacy, proofed in its plating of authority. 'I am very happy to say that in this matter you cannot know the true facts . . .'

II

It was not until the June of 1911 that 'people' as represented by the bank manager began in Mrs. Scrimgeour's idiom to be 'tiresome'. She was by now accustomed to the condition of being overdrawn, but the tone of the letters from the manager had, even to her perception, gradually acquired an edge there was no mistaking, and she sent Mary at random to cope with whatever ire needed soothing. Mary returned home disturbed; the conference had made plain several unimagined matters. The actual overdrawing, it seemed, was not the worst of the business — 'everybody' did it sooner or later, said Mr. Harrowe in a loose effort at politeness — but it also appeared that in order to meet this call and that the old game of selling out had been resorted to. Mrs. Scrimgeour had learned it, he thought, as a child learns a trick. He named for her daughter the lost investments which *faute de mieux* he had himself recommended relinquishing.

'I sent the necessary papers authorizing us to act in the matter to your mother, as you know.'

Mary flushed. She did not know, except that her mother sometimes tutted from her desk at uninteresting correspondence. Knowing her, Mary guessed that she had signed the papers in honest belief that she was pleasing Mr. Harrowe and probably putting 'a little something' in his way into the bargain, like the price of the cheque-books which, Robert had once told her, were 'managers' perks'.

Mr. Harrowe leaned forward, hands folded on the table.

'. . . and quite frankly I was very much opposed to it, but your mother is — ' he stopped and surveyed his nails.

'Yes. I know,' said Mary.

'She is getting on in years, of course, and the judgment doesn't tend to become clearer. . . . I sometimes wonder if in these cases the children should not be invested with power of attorney. But that might lead to abuses, too. It's a difficult point.'

Mary's fingers tightened upon her umbrella. 'Yes, I can see that. Meanwhile — I suppose one ought to know — can you give me *some* idea — to what extent — ' she did not know the phraseology and stopped.

'Miss Scrimgeour, since your father died, your mother has reduced your income by roughly five hundred pounds a year.'

She looked enquiry.

'That means that your income has now dropped to one thousand a year, and if I may suggest it I think the time has come to put pressure upon her . . . fortunately the remaining investments are as sound as one can ever foresee.'

'And they are?'

'London Midland and Scottish Limited, Prussian Consols and Trans-Siberian Rails.'

III

They would have to move house again, Mary saw; it would be a last drive of expense as a permanent stand for economy. They must consider reduction of staff, she and her sisters be content with smaller allowances — further retrenchments would no doubt occur to them all gradually. It was, she guessed, easy to cut down expenses on paper, but she dreaded the temperamental issue, the response of her mother before whose dismays and coming discomforts Mary was already apologetic. Mary had been thoughtless, they had all been thoughtless, taking everything for granted, actually indulging in dissatisfaction . . . they must keep as much as possible from Mamma for it was not right that age should suffer. They would cut down expenses — if she would consent.

A small house . . . not only a relatively smaller one.

IV

She waited her chance and put the facts to her mother at the best moment, between the postprandial nap and tea, and Mrs. Scrimgeour looked startled and complacent and a little offended by turns. She would have taken the news from no one but Mary, who had never sprung false alarms upon her.

'And I've been thinking things over, Mamma, and I don't *believe* that perhaps we ought to have a summer holiday, this year — except you, of course. We should save on the rooms and fares, you know,' faltered Mary.

Mother and daughter stared at each other, mutually staggered. Nothing she had so far revealed could have as effectually brought home to Charlotte Scrimgeour that all was not well. The practical suggestion that they give up a tried and familiar thing — going away in August, something everybody did — succeeded where days of appeal to reason and imagination would have failed.

'But — what will the servants think?'

'We can't afford to consider that, Mamma.'

In the rambling discussion which followed, enfeebled by explanation, concession, reassurance and Mary's 'It's only for this year', 'later we shall all know better where we are', it seemed that each foregone luxury, so admirable as a theory, was the very one they could not possibly do without.

But on the whole Mary was agreeably surprised. Her mother, she thought, was being very good. No complaints ... and her outcries only the understandable ones of bewilderment. She had the qualities of her defects and in this instance her life tendency to give way under pressure stood her in good stead in the eyes of the world, her habit of irrational panic causing her to meet Mary more than half-way.

v

Grace took the news quietly with a murmured 'oh dear!' and a frown of distress for Mary's anxiety. It was Queenie who exploded, running the rounds of the relations to air grievance and gather sympathy, returning to fling their findings at Mary.

'Clarence thinks — '

'Even Caroline said — '

Mary looked at her sister, this thrawn, badly-painted person of fifty-six in her over-emphasized dress.

'Queenie, can't you work *with* us and help us round

this corner? It's hardly fair, is it? to wash all our dirty linen in public.'

Queenie began to cry. Guiltily, Mary was more exasperated by her in that mood than in vituperation. She seemed for some years rather to have lost touch with this particular sister, in spite of the inevitably closer communal life they were leading in these small houses.

VI

Upstairs in her overcrowded room Queenie sat repairing the ravages of her outburst. The restricted space was littered with half-empty bottles and jars on which a large proportion of her allowance was spent and whose labels gave unanswerable guarantee of rejuvenation of hair and skin. But it came to this: in youth your face worked for you against all neglect, in late middle age it responded to no cossetings. Then why go on trying? But one did.

Mary had misunderstood her, luckily perhaps. Mary — nobody — would ever know that the scene one had just made wasn't simply of temper or selfishness or even indignation, but from a brain-sick dread of the small house — the smaller house — which was threatened. Constriction of privacy . . . walls closing in on one. . . .

That day in the chapel at poor Aggie's funeral . . . again one had publicly been credited with a respectable alibi in assumed grief for a departed sister, whereas actually the small-house feeling had come over one, suddenly, in a hot wave, leaving one nauseated and shaking. And yet, one had always shared rooms in Brecknock Gardens. But logic was no buckler against nerves, and even there one had wanted to get away from it all, its space and high ceilings and big windows. Also, that was a different urge, the clean directness of ambition. This craving was for sheer room to move freely, unwatched, and about that one would be as dumb as self control lasted, for how explain to one's family that they are — quite terribly — on one's nerves? Gertie could convey it, but oneself was weakened by lingering sentiment. It was Gertie of all the family who had given one the only real scrap of hope in a sentence that, again, one must try to forget.

'After all, Queenie, all this can't go on for ever. Mamma is over eighty.'

Unsurely Queenie Scrimgeour rouged her thin cheeks. Her nephew-in-law was expected to dinner, and Caroline too, for once.

CHAPTER XVII

I

Young Mrs. Bridgewood accepted the family dinner resignedly, an acknowledgment, she told Robert, of Gran's undoubted decency to him. Money was not exactly tight, but didn't go as far as it used to, with another child to educate. Molly was a dear kid and thank God one appeared to be fond of her, but she had been of course an accident — what Gertrude with a commiserating smile for her new grandchild no less than for its mother had termed the result of '*cinque minutes de paresse*'.

The Scrimgeour dinners were pretty awful — bad food and worse conversation, and the wine was beginning to be horrible since they had exhausted Grandpa's cellar and were now offering what Bob called 'linen-draper's burgundy', but that was the worst of all living in London. It wasn't that one minded offending bores by refusing their invitations but that one simply ran out of excuses. Aunt Mary was a thumping good sort, and Grace might have had possibilities if she had ever been thoroughly seduced or made tipsy, but Queenie! And here they all were round the table with 'Old Q.', as she and Bob privately called her aunt, looking like a frequenter of the Empire promenade found drowned after three days.

The new ballet there? No, that wouldn't do. The Aunts would be bound not to have seen it as it still rather meant being taken there by a man. . . . The Shakespeare Festival at His Majesty's? But that led to a dead end, as old Tree usually put on the same revivals every summer and there wasn't anything to say about Shakespeare except the unmentionable: that one couldn't understand how he had ever won a reputation as a dramatist save on the grounds of negligible competition.

Gran was bumbling on about 'the move', but she was always moving and at this rate would soon have slept in as many beds as Queen Elizabeth. Pity mother wasn't here; she would just have thrown a stick of dynamite into the middle of the British salad and got them all going in no time. Explosions might not be pleasant but they left no company as they found them. Gran's salads probably didn't actually have caterpillars in them but were surrounded by an aura of cocoon. No onion, either. Gran probably thought it 'perfumed the breath'.

'Will you take a little more shape, Carry?'

Shape . . . oh God.

Mary said in one of the silences, 'How's Molly?'

'Oh, she's all right, Aunt Mary, thanks. Getting to an age when I've got to decide the education question, I suppose. Matter of fact, I can't decide between boarding school, which would get her off our hands but probably turn her into a female Hearty with legs like magnums of champagne, or a gov' for a bit who'll say "pardon?" and drive me into a nursing home at ten guineas a week.'

'Auntie Grace had a governess,' said Mrs. Scrimgeour.

'Oh? And did it answer?'

'She was quite a pleasant woman.'

'Grace?'

Grace said she didn't know.

'Mother went to a finishing school,' went on Caroline, 'but she doesn't seem to have learnt anything except how to cope with men.' That didn't go down well. The speaker suddenly remembered that the pulpy old woman at the head of the table was her own mother's mother, turned pink and said rapidly that it was probably the fault of her mother and not of the school at *all*, and felt her argument fading as she realized that this too was a *gaffe*. Mary rescued her with the glimmer of a smile. 'I quite agree about finishing schools, except for the social opportunities they can give.'

'Ah, but social opportunities are apt to mean getting into a set you can't afford to keep up afterwards, Aunt Mary. I'm not going to have that to contend with if I can help it.'

The unmarried women listened respectfully as the girl aired her views. Mrs. Scrimgeour said: 'I think if we have all finished — ' and slowly struggled from her chair. It was, she saw, ridiculous to leave Robert solo with the decanter, also the maid would be fuming in the kitchen to clear, and she wanted Robert's arm up the stairs.

The crocodile gravitated dispiritedly to the drawing-room.

11

For the first time in her life Mary Scrimgeour, at sixty, knew the meaning of responsibility.

They had all left to her the business of finding them a new home.

To her mother the deputing of authority was but another bewilderment in life as it was now being lived, and though she was thankful at the physical relief, a corner of her mind was soothed by knowledge that henceforth blame for all mistakes could be placed elsewhere. . . .

Full of misgivings Mary started out each morning — Queenie must really pull her weight with Nana while Gracie did the catering.

Mary had scrapped all scruple at the outset and more or less frankly canvassed her family for hints, but Georgina, in India again, could only write of a long procession of bungalows ameliorated by a cheapness of native domestic labour that sounded enviable and feudal but which was no good when applied to conditions in England: Arabella, bumped from one English military station to another, had changed house twelve times in twenty years but ever in the easy, patterned routine of known and reported ground, with hints passed on from officers' wives who were themselves pickled campaigners, knowing to one inch the best and the worst of every town, village, and available servant, and assisted into the bargain by their husbands' batmen. Gertrude had not changed her address in Victoria Road, Kensington, since her marriage, and Caroline and Robert had a flat.

Mary investigated flats. She disliked the idea of such compressed and soulless living, but the rent came first, and it soon became apparent that rents within their means offered accommodation that was entirely inadequate. Later, perhaps. But even now she hardly believed that her mother realized that being overdrawn at the Bank meant repayment to the Bank and a lowering of spending-power. She had built her life on the affections and the personal touch and reverses were to her a personal unkindness, abstractions, almost a disrespect to age.

III

Instinctively Mary clung to the old locality, that square mile in South Kensington which had seen them through their lives. It was her first personal discovery that smaller income meant a less exclusive neighbourhood — the things one didn't realize until one began to put practice before theory!

She turned regretfully in the direction of Gloucester Road Underground. How many times had she and her sisters plunged into it for the Wednesday *matinée*, returning to discuss Waller, Ainley, Tree and Alexander over the tea-cups of home!

She had found the new house in a turning off the High Street, one of a short row of three storeys and semi-basement, with minute front garden. Ramillies Terrace. It faced a similar row called Oudenarde Terrace and had been built some fifty years ago, the agent said.

Standing in the bareness of the unaired rooms, Mary, confused by the absence of atmosphere and the way in which the little house was waiting for her decision, consulted her private notes.

Maids' bedroom and five for the family. And there were only four bedrooms and an attic. The agent said that more bedrooms in houses 'of this type' were unusual and uncalled for. Then somebody must share a room. It would probably be herself and Grace, Queenie she felt pretty sure would never consent. It was, of course, Nana who threw out all one's calculations; wherever the family moved to they must budget for her.

She brought her sisters to see the house, but their attitudes to it, of antagonistic indifference and ready agreement with her own opinions, did not help matters forward. Gertrude, joining Mary after her morning shopping at Barker's, obviously thought it a regrettable example of a regrettable architectural epoch, but said 'it might do', it was in good repair and there was a tiny garden at the back. Her verdict was more favourable than her thoughts which were to get the family settled once and for all and end the eternal seeping away of funds. She offered her car to Mary for her mother and Nana at the moving in and was a little touched at the gratitude shown for the trifling consideration.

But first the fortnight at Bexhill must be arranged for and a daughter chosen to travel with Mrs. Scrimgeour. She was too old to holiday alone, which diminished a little Mary's economical plans. They offered the change to Queenie, who said, 'Certainly, if you want me to throw myself off the end of the pier,' and the alternative was Grace. Mary must be at hand to deal with furniture packing and the removal squad. Mrs. Scrimgeour saw herself that no other combination was possible and acquiesced, only a little put out at the choice.

All their now surplus furniture was put into a sale-room for auction, but English taste had veered and was not to return to Victorianism real or pseudo for another twenty years. The good, heavy stuff was knocked down at purely nominal prices and the cheque for the lighter Edwardian pieces unexpectedly small. The vogue for genuine antiques had begun and all over the country attics were being ransacked for discarded period furniture, for outraged Sheraton and manhandled Adams.

Often when Mary looked up from some dusty job she would see from the window the sale pieces being loaded into the pantechnicon: objects kept out of sentiment through all chance and change, the big white nursery cupboard, the brass double bedstead from the room Mamma and Father slept in, the red plush *causeuse*. . . . Grace always turned away, the sight saddened her, roused her longing for her old home. But they would still be all together, and home was where Mary was — and Queenie and Mamma too, of course.

IV

Grace brought back her mother at the end of the fortnight. It had been a sober and responsible little holiday in which Grace had sometimes seen herself through the eyes of the public, not as the girl whom God had intended to create, but as the woman, drawing no man's eyes, walking beside a hired bath-chair. . . .

They moved into Ramillies Terrace two days later: procession of Gertrude's car containing Mrs. Scrimgeour, Nana, and endless baskets and parcels mainly consisting of the old nurse's Things, a taxi containing two Scrimgeour daughters with trunks, and another with Mary, more luggage and the house-parlourmaid. Mary's last action on leaving had been to cram the grate with Nana's historic newspapers, and the guilty fear of detection worried her ridiculously throughout the short drive.

It was an afternoon of early autumn, of soft light and a film of rust over the trees in Kensington Gardens. In the shops, the clothes were already hinting of warmth and winter. Normally, Grace thought, they would be coming in for tea and drawing the curtains, yet here they were, once more, in taxis, driving away from what had become familiarity to set up familiarity in another road. One always hated the first tea in the new place. Cook sent up the wrong cups and the whole thing was slapdash and provisional for days.

This time, there was not even tea laid when they assembled in the little drawing-room slightly overshadowed by its plane-tree, but a ringing of the bell by Mary and a deliberate, heavy tread on the stairs.

'Florence, we're quite ready for tea.'

'I was wanting to speak to you, Miss.'

Why couldn't one say 'Another time', or 'We'll have tea first'? Mary tiredly wondered as she heard herself replying 'Yes?' The woman's face was a dark red and she was speaking too loudly.

'I can't sleep in that bedroom, never saw such a place — '

'Oh, Florence, *don't* make difficulties. I've done the best I can — '

' "Two in that 'ole?" I said to Daisy, an' she fully agreed.'

'What — '

'And that ol' dotty thing with one to 'erself, well it ain't right or fair.'

'What do you expect me to do? Miss Grace and I are sharing a room — '

'I can't stop if that's the arrangement and if I'd known Ider never've consented to come 'ere.'

Mrs. Scrimgeour said feebly, 'Don't speak *in that way.*'

'I shall speak as necessary. Miss Mary done this . . . going be'ind my back an' putting me an' Daisy in a place not fit for a dog.'

Mary discovered that she had a temper. 'Florence, if you're going to behave like this you'll have to go. I didn't build this house — '

'You *took* it, didn'tcher?'

'I think you're overtired. We'll talk it over to-morrow.'

'I don't sleep in that room unless I get a place to meself,' raged the woman confusedly. Unexpectedly to her sisters, Queenie took a hand. 'I think you'd better take your notice. I don't know if Miss Mary can stand this impertinence, but I can't and won't.' There was a spot of scarlet in each of Queenie's cheeks and it seemed to Mary that at any minute she herself might have two competent fishwives on her hands. . . .

'One minute, Queenie dear — '

'*Very* shocking,' murmured Mrs. Scrimgeour.

'I'm not taking anything from you, 'sQueenie, and never have. Go? Yes, I'll go and I'm going now, and next maid you get per'aps you'll 'ave the manners to say to 'er I'm putting you in a cat's bung 'ole that I wouldn't shut the dog up in.'

The door banged.

Fatigue, nervous strain and Cook's zoological simile were too much for Mary and the suppressed laughter of years came bursting forth. Nothing stopped it, not Queenie's envenomed pallor, Grace's fluttering indignation or the tear of mortification that rolled down her mother's cheek.

Ten minutes later the Cook left, looking up at the windows and shouting all down the street. The Scrimgeours, apologetic to a purse-lipped house-parlourmaid, dined on boiled eggs and sardines.

'Some day,' said Mary, 'we really *must* take some cookery lessons.'

CHAPTER XVIII

I

THE weeks that followed were difficult, and Mary's hilarity at the Cook soon quenched in the thankless task of combing the agencies for a substitute who should be clean, honest, capable and contented. Queenie seemed to hate the house worse than usual and dragged about looking really ill but shied at any suggestion of a doctor, and Mrs. Scrimgeour would often gently commiserate the scheme of things when callers were present.

'My dear Mary is trying so hard, but of course . . . this house . . . but one doesn't like to discourage her.'

'It's not exactly what I should have chosen, myself — '

Nana was always upset by moves and it was becoming almost a full-time job to look after her. She was now in a few ways, all unlovely, entirely helpless, and Mary and Grace discovered that affection, punctuality and conscientiousness were no substitute for a certificate in even elementary nursing. Candidly, she needed a trained attendant, they realized. But the domestic problem was perhaps the more insoluble. Four cook-generals in three months was their preliminary record. Servants warned of the accommodation either refused the place, or came, and left it after creating discontents and dissensions one would have thought impossible in the time.

Affairs came to a climax in the winter when Nana fell ill, partly of the non-resistance of age, partly of the diagnosis-defying suffering from transplantation that can be a psychic thing. On the face of it it called for a night nurse and the question of where to put her overshadowed even Mrs. Scrimgeour's lively pleas for 'a family Christmas'.

It was Charlotte Scrimgeour herself, heady at the pleasures in store, who solved and dismissed the problem when it was discussed before her.

'Couldn't one of you go and pay a little visit for a bit until poor Nana is well again?'

Her daughters fell silent: Mary was mentally selecting the absentee, Queenie, her interest faintly stirred, considering the possibles among friends and relations; Grace conservatively beginning to cling already to the new home. Mary said: 'We couldn't ask such a favour of friends, at Christmas.' That, broadly speaking, left Gertrude, Caroline and Arabella now that Aunt Jane was dead and the house in Sloane Street given up. Caroline lived in London — *much* more convenient and no railway fare as there would be for Arabella (therefore, Mary thought, Carry would be the one to refuse). But Caroline, hinted to, proved unexpectedly easy.

'Well, I don't know that I shan't be quite glad, Gran. It'll be nice for Molly to have someone to go out with and it'll free me a lot. We've got a spare bedroom at present and perhaps sometimes Grace will read to her and try and get her to. I can't. Is it usual for them to be tiresome about books, at seven? Anyway ... we'll try and put up as jolly a time as funds permit. ...'

Queenie said jauntily: 'Or I may come along myself, Carry.' Grace brightened at the reprieve but her niece answered swiftly: 'You'd better leave it to Gracie, Aunt Queenie, Molly would worry you to pieces — '

Queenie's face clouded. Luckily Mrs. Scrimgeour cut in: 'There's one thing, Carry dear: you'll spare Gracie to us for Christmas Day?' and her granddaughter's reassurance was fervent. 'And Boxing Day as well if you like, Gran. As a matter of fact (though of course we should love to have her) it might be rather a squeeze as there are people for dinner and no end of Bob's friends are sure to drop in afterwards, and of course next day we all go to the pantomime — '

It was settled, then, and all that remained was the various consolation of her sisters. Grace, upset, was reasonable as always, but Queenie seemed unable to get over the disappointment. It took the trivial outer form of resentment and heavy silences, and Mary would never know that she regarded it morbidly as the writing on the wall. The shelving of age by youth was an indication that Queenie Scrimgeour must now stand aside and be content to settle down for the rest of life to — to what? They didn't realize that there was sometimes nothing for you ahead.

To the trickle of Christmas callers with parcels who were willing to spare a minute to see old Mrs. Scrimgeour she would say: 'I've arranged for Gracie to stay with Carry while the house is a little upset.'

11

'A Happy Christmas, Miss,' and Mary hurrying home from early service must spare time to give coppers to the sweeper who would now be dumb until Boxing Day and the New Year and after that until another December was upon them. Dickens has much to answer for. One had to hurry a lot, these days: to sit with Nana and Mamma, to shop personal gifts and all Mamma's, provision the house, keep the servants up to the mark, be ready with plenty of conversation for the nurse at meal times and after dinner, and keep an eye on the cheques Mamma drew. She still tried to put her signature to sums they couldn't or shouldn't afford and that meant time-wasting arguments which must be kept at affection-level, very, very reasonable and one's voice low — an excellent thing in women. She meant so well, poor dear Mamma, and it was hateful to have even to scrutinize envelopes for telltale addresses which pointed to remittances. . . . There had been a note addressed to Robert, left for somebody to take round with the presents for Caroline and the girls, but about that Mary could not bring herself to enquire. There was a decency . . . at the same time, you don't send men Christmas cards — much, and there was no parcel for him on the pile. Mary was evidently becoming an unpleasant character: one of those narrow, soured spinsters one read of . . . she had for the time being certainly become one of those fabulous persons who 'had no time for reading'. She had disbelieved in their claim all these years, but it could be true, it seemed. One couldn't even read in bed, now. One could weather the days better if one had privacy at night, but she had had to give up the room she shared with Grace to the nurse and sleep with Mamma. The question had been, who was going to mind Mary most, Queenie or her mother? But Queenie had looked so sick with dismay at the sheer idea, and luckily Mrs. Scrimgeour took a fancy to the arrangement — she even said she found it rather pleasant. She probably missed father still. But Mary could not persuade her to open windows more than a crack at night.

That note to Robert. But perhaps Mamma owed it to the Bridgewoods who had, after all, relieved the Scrimgeour accommodation of Gracie? That cot Mamma had named. She was now rated on the hospital books as a wealthy woman and they had made special appeals to her ever since. Luckily their correspondence was recognizable and could be abstracted and destroyed, making Mary feel like a forger or a thief. But any time an appeal might slip through her guard. With others, one had to take a chance that Mamma's emotions might not be sufficiently stimulated to cause her to sign away another fraction of the family resources.

Family dinner. A pity that they could dig up nobody to share it with them, since the expense of it was being undertaken. It would be dull for Mamma and Queenie, but the available were the bores and unwanted ... heavens be praised the nurse was a pleasant one, but of course she upset the servants who really seemed to seize any pretext ...

Queenie was so unhappy, but what to do for her? One couldn't really blame Caroline ... besides, Queenie would be no earthly good with children whereas Gracie probably might suit them very well. She adored babies, always had. ...

'Heavens, what a frump!' thought Mary, amused by her own reflection in a shop mirror.

I I I

In the kitchen the Cook was saying to charwoman and house-parlourmaid: 'I shall stay till the New Year and get my presents, and then go.'

The house-parlourmaid, impressed by the simplicity of the scheme, pondered her own move.

I V

Grace surprised herself at the way she settled down in the Bridgewood flat. There was something about Caroline which shoo'd shyness into a corner; it wasn't so much that she tried to put you at ease, but more as though she hadn't time for other people's exhibitions of temperament, that, it was conveyed, must 'amuse itself', as busy hostesses said to guests. And then of course one was a relation ... could in the last resort always go home. Nana's illness — poor Nana! — couldn't go on for ever.

To Grace Scrimgeour Molly seemed a very nice little girl, not talkative, and open to tentative suggestions which were Grace's rendering of the crisp directions tossed off by the child's mother. In growing confidence, Grace did not allow for the mechanical awes created by her own relationship; to herself she was a visitor making friends with the child of a niece: to the child she loomed as the great-aunt that she was, and great-aunts, whatever their appearance, were of an immense age and probable power. . . .

Sometimes when Grace's letter-writing or personal mending was done she would amuse herself by taking a story-book and going through it with Molly. Incurious, attentively uninterested, Molly strove with her portion, reading neither better nor worse for the session. Grace could not remember the corresponding phase in her own childhood, it seemed to her that she had always been able to read, and anyway it would come — only a matter of time.

They would put on their hats and go out for walks, companionably. Grace would often choose her own favourite route.

'Not down B'ecknock Gardens *again*, Auntie Grace, we went there the day before yestiddy.'

'Sh, dear! You know you like that way, Molly,' Grace would answer at random, gently determined to have her own way.

The old house was an hotel now. Through swing-doors

one could see a lift going up and down in the hall and a baize board for letters where the hat-stand used to be. Heads of strange men and women at the drawing-room window, reading, knitting.

The Brecknock Hotel.

She longed and dreaded to be shown over it, and shyness won.

Perhaps it was better so.

v

Christmas was over, January half-way gone and Caroline's elder daughter Sylvia off to spend a year with a German family in Heidelburg. At seventeen, she was to Grace unrecognizable as the 'lovely baby' of whom she had rhapsodized to Mrs. Scrimgeour. But one had a tenderness for her because of the baby she had been.

Well-grown, mannerly, neat and assured, she left surrounded with tennis rackets and hockey sticks.

Perhaps you noticed the change more when they weren't your own? But — to send her abroad . . .

Grace said tentatively: 'Won't it rather spoil her *chances?*'

Caroline looked blank. 'Oh, you mean about men. Let 'em be free as long as they can. Plenty of time for complications later. She's very keen on going and languages help you to better secretarial posts, which is what she's after. I'm only so thankful that I'm not called upon to go through any of the transitional ballroom stage that poor mother had to with Paula and me.'

'But, Carry, it gives a girl a *start* — '

'It can, of course, but what happened in our case? Paula wouldn't marry and I met Bob somewhere else, so mother sat the bottoms out of about fifty gilt chairs and sneezed some eighty-five times for nothing.'

Grace looked unconvinced. They were so sure, these girls ... they had plans and carried them out. Fine, possibly, and enviable, certainly, but it jarred a little. Youth was for pleasure and — well, yes, attentions, and not just a preparation for wage-earning. Surely?

VI

Every morning Grace was able to telephone to Mary. Nana was 'much as usual', 'had had a fair night'. Grace would hang up the receiver wondering how, if they had had the instrument in her own girlhood, the face of her life and of her sisters' lives would have been changed. Messages, notes left by hand, delays in which a man could change his mind and refuse your invitations in peace and leisure against a telephone call. ... Captain Lassiter ... you're through to Aldershot ... conversations which faded off the air and were not so 'marked' as paper and ink. Yet if they had had the thing, might not the future have worked out precisely as it was doing? Leaving one merely tantalized by a vocal accessibility?

VII

'Oh, I've been perfectly glad to have her, but I never expected *quite* such a visitation.'

'That's the worst of relations, they're so damned difficult to shift. Fact is, Carry, it's quite true, that one about not mixing business with friendship.'

'Luckily, Molly seems to like her, but I'm not sure that

328

a good nursemaid ... one does want one's home to one-self sometimes, and then one comes in fagged and there's Grace all over the drawing-room or at the phone when I want it.'

'Yes, it's a bore. And having people to dinner. ... I always forget she'll be there when I'm inviting people —'

'I know. Poor old Bob! Well ... it can't go on for ever. Old Nana *must* get better soon or cash right in. Dammy how these old women do last!'

'They certainly do. Still, your respected Grandma was very decent to me at Christmas, blowing me to £25. I never expected it.'

'Sh! Grace. ...'

CHAPTER XIX

I

IT was not until March that Grace and Mary found themselves alone for tea, with Queenie and the nurse out and Mrs. Scrimgeour upstairs with a slight cold. Her tray arranged and taken up by Grace, they could with luck count upon an hour together. Yet Mary did not seem as pleased as one expected. But Nana was better? Nurse possibly only an affair of a week or so, now?

Grace took cake and began: 'Nana is really on the mend?'

'I think so. And you're still making out at Carry's?'

'Oh, it's really quite pleasant — a little noisy sometimes, perhaps; people coming in after dinner and disturbing one if one wants to go to bed early. One doesn't quite like to *say* anything.'

'No.'

'Mary dear, there's nothing wrong? The servants — '

'Cook left me early in January but we've got an excellent woman now, elderly, capable, helpful, you know. I'm praying we keep her.'

'So glad. Well, when do you expect me home?'

Mary had got up for no apparent reason and, hands on the mantelpiece, was looking into the fire.

'Gracie, it's like this: do you think you could possibly stick it out at Carry's a bit longer?'

'I — suppose so, but why?'

Mary had found her tongue. 'It's this *cursèd* domestic problem. It's true that nurse'll be going for good any day now, but it seems that we shall have to face giving up one more bedroom to the servants if we're to have any peace. At present there's nothing but friction and if one goes it infects the other, and all these changes in cooking are so bad for Mamma and Nana ... oh Grace, it's been awful! ... and poor Queenie is such a drag. Oh I suppose it's all my fault and due to bad management and bad everything — '

Mary's voice broke. It moved Grace profoundly. *Mary* giving way!

'Of course. Anything you like, dear. I'd no notion — '

'Bless you, Gracie, and whenever you want to come home we'll have to get Queenie away on a visit, if anyone will have her. She *must* help us out, somehow. And of course all this can't go on for ever — '

The sisters agreed upon that, but refrained from explaining exactly what they meant by it.

11

'This morning, I want you to go to Woolland's about Molly's hat, Gracie. It's half a size too small. And there's the list of things Cook wants at Barker's. Provision department.'

'Gracie dear, I know you'll be an angel and stay in this afternoon. I must go out to that Bridge party and there's that phone call I'm expecting and it's Cook's day out and I've had to let Ella out too as her confounded mother's ill in Bermondsey.'

'If you've *really* nothing to do, there are Molly's socks needing attention. I do do it so badly — oh, and be a lamb and wash my brushes and comb, will you, when you do your own?'

'Look here, Gracie, I'm frightfully sorry but could you *possibly* manage dinner out to-night? Bob's got a business friend in. Gran'll give you a meal . . . oh, I see. Well — damn. Ella could *easily* bring a tray into your room. I wouldn't ask you, but —'

Half cajolery, half assumption.

It was, Mrs. Bridgewood confided to intimates, a difficult situation all round. 'One doesn't like to give her definite orders, but after all we're standing her her room and grub. Salary? She'd be offended. You can't. My dear Barbara, she's my *aunt*. Besides, if one wanted to make a change . . . paying people seems to make 'em so *final*. Oh, I know, I know! But the Scrimmies are really becoming rather a problem.'

Grace herself wavered between anxiety to be the perfect guest, the indispensable inmate, and resentments at the growing claims made upon her by her niece. Willing, occasional service, yes, but wasn't Carry rather imposing on one?

It all came to a head one morning after breakfast — about taking Molly to her dancing lesson with Paula. 'Paula gives me very special terms, of course, but when Molly's more advanced I shall send her to a really good teacher,' Caroline had told Grace, taking the line prevalent in most families that an intimate (especially a relation) can for that reason never rise to crack professional rank.

Grace, for once, had her own morning fully planned: a little shopping, a fitting at what Caroline called a 'tame' dressmaker in Earl's Court Road ending in a call at Ramillies Terrace.

'No, I can't take Molly to-day,' Grace explained, for the first time omitting regret.

Caroline paused and looked slightly astonished. It irritated Grace.

'One can't *always* be available, can one?'

Caroline murmured agreement, half civil, half annoyed. Her own compunction and exasperation drove Grace to further speech. 'I'm sorry, but I don't think you quite realize, Caroline, that although I do all I can for you with Molly and in other ways, it isn't exactly right, is it? that I should have to be — well — at the beck and call of someone younger than myself — '

She hadn't meant to say that, but in a dispute you never knew what argument was coming from you next, and she had chafed more than once at going in to dinner behind juniors, because they happened to be married. Because, quite absurdly, of Robert.

'Really, Grace, I — '

The telephone bell began to shrill and Caroline snatched it with a glance at Grace which swept her out of the room, but her aunt wasn't moving. Damn the woman. Damn all women. And the call was, after all, for Grace, a thing that didn't happen nine times out of ten but which had, to-day, to make one look a fool. Caroline went ostentatiously to the door, but Grace wasn't taking that hint either, it seemed. She had listened, given a little exclamation and was in tears. Caroline hesitated, disarmed.

'Oh Carry, Nana's gone!'

Three loud cheers, thought her hostess, looking alarmed and sympathetic. 'Oh, poor old — '

'Just a minute ... yes, Mary? In her sleep? Oh *why* wasn't I there? ... she wouldn't have? You're *sure?* ... I'll be round at once.' She hung up the receiver.

PART THREE

III

Clearing out the room, burning the rubbish of a life-time (the little garden was put to its first use), a van from the Church Army to take the usable of Nana's Things and a souvenir of the old woman to be chosen by each of the family, even the younger branches, whether they would or no. Nana would have loved to think of them owning it, Mrs. Scrimgeour, flaccid with grief, had said. Grace, her mind elsewhere, took the heart-shaped red and blue plush pin-cushion, Mary the black cat kettle-holder.

The whole family contributed to the funeral expenses, but the headstone? Mrs. Scrimgeour knew Nana's tastes, and deaf to opposition thumbed stone-masons' catalogues. Something simple and symbolic: this angel pointing upwards . . . or those cherubs crouched at the open book whose pages were inscribed R.I.P. . . . or —

The family flatly refused to club for this item; a plain stone cross or a marble border was enough. 'Then we must give it her ourselves,' said Mrs. Scrimgeour simply, and her eyes filled again.

Nana would have hated a modern motor hearse, so quick and undignified — almost as though the mourners didn't care . . . the adagio of horses and plumes was respect, a long thought for the dead.

The marble angel was £140, and not what Mrs. Scrimgeour thought 'the most important' in the catalogue at that, but one must consider the dear daughters. . . .

Charlotte Scrimgeour dressed for the funeral that day of late March. Remonstrations — remember your attack of influenza — went unheard. Nana would miss her:

hadn't one always sped and welcomed the traveller?
Yes, they could hire a closed car for her as Gertie's would
be full, and Clarence, Bertie and Robert would give her
an arm and the dear girls be by with restoratives. . . .

IV

Less than a week later, Grace, packing her trunk at
Caroline's for her return home, heard the telephone bell
and Caroline's call.

'It's you, Grace.'

Caroline had for the past five days been the perfect
hostess . . . kind, considerate, but Grace saw it clearly as
manifestation of the irrepressible relief that it was. High
spirits . . . she went to the telephone.

'Gracie dear . . . Mary speaking. Oh Gracie, it's
Mamma. I'm afraid it's pneumonia.'

'Age, shock and exposure,' the doctor had told this
capable looking Miss Scrimgeour. Then how came she
to be such a damfool as to let a woman of her mother's
age go gallivanting off to windy gravesides in March, of
all months?

V

Grace hurried to Ramillies Terrace to discuss the situation with Mary, white and harassed. The nurse had been
recalled, the Cook was being unexpectedly loyal and
human, circumstances that Mary described as 'great good
luck'; Queenie, subdued, was rambling about offering help.
All but Grace seemed to have work to do. It appeared
that her share was to be a return to the Bridgewood flat
for what the sisters realized to be an indefinite period.

335

Grace faced Mary. 'Mary, I don't believe I *can*.'

'Oh, *Gracie!*'

'Carry doesn't want me. I've outstayed my welcome already. One can *see* it.'

'It's *too* bad of Caroline . . .' Mary thought, distractedly, trying to be fair. 'Gertie then? Or Arabella? They *must* help us out. Or Queenie? Would *you* like to stay with one of them for a bit?'

Queenie's smile was sarcastic. 'My dear Mary, don't you see that whoever either of us planked herself on would be bound to get restive too, sooner or later? You can't blame them.'

'They are sure to *offer*,' Mary murmured.

'Well, I shall decline with thanks if they do. Honestly, Mary, I think I've done all that's to be expected in sharing my room with you since Mamma was taken ill in order to truckle to our servants. At my age it isn't very pleasant to have no privacy —'

' — or at mine,' flashed Mary.

' — and I cannot see that we need go making poor relations of ourselves —'

'No, you don't see, Queenie. That's the whole trouble. I tell you, it's more than likely that Mamma may have to have *two* nurses, and I can't cut down staff with illness in the house and all the extra work. And as for the expense, it's awful. Doctor's bill, medicine, oxygen, and nurse alone is three guineas a week not counting her food. Then there's the extra laundry and wages and Nana's funeral expenses we've only just paid off, and that headstone. I didn't like to countermand the order. . . .'

Mary had come into full authority, at last: possessed the dubious honour of drawing the cheques.

CHAPTER XX

I

GERTRUDE RANDOLPH took in Grace. Once more she found herself in the small spare room, repapered now, and minus the engraving of Prince Albert with his favourite hound. Modernized, lighter, pleasanter, yet the room was unchanged, to Grace's mood of unwilling, temporary dependence. 'It can't be for very long — *anyhow*', Mrs. Randolph said to her husband in reconciliatory vein.

But the days and weeks went by and the reports were 'about the same', 'a slight improvement', 'no change'.

From the first, Gertrude, warned by Caroline, had put the arrangement on what seemed to her to be the best and only possible footing, briskly, sanely, directly. She offered her sister ten shillings a week, board and room with the rider that she might make herself useful. Grace, unused to being blown upon by practical breezes, chafed but tried to respond. The salary outraged her sense of social service and family feeling. Also, as a sum, it by no means compensated for what once had been her allowance, taken for granted. And Gertie's manner . . . nothing you could openly resent, but —

And you sometimes lost track of the situation and answered as sister to sister . . . and felt put in the wrong because of that ten shillings. But if it was helping Mary? And it was. But you can't remain at mental sacrifice pitch for twelve hours out of the twelve.

To Gertrude, Grace, the small child intermittently seen in a velvet frock and white boots, sashed and silent in a

South Kensington drawing-room, had grown into a woman who had wilfully acquired tiresome adult ways (how children do pick things up!), apeing her elders in resentments, prejudices and fads.

To Grace, Gertrude materialized as a driving, undemonstrative woman of sixty-six who, keeping within the law, traded on family anxiety: old enough to be her mother without giving the sense of righteous authority.

There was Arabella. Somebody one also knew very little but who still diffused a half-remembered atmosphere of jollity.

Grace pondered the move of writing to her, ransacking her memory for details of this sister and trying to decide from the result if Arabella would make her comfortable ... of course Gertie's house was more convenient for calls at Ramillies Terrace, but another string to one's bow wouldn't be a bad thing at all.

Arabella answered from an unfamiliar address at Haslemere.

'My dear, of *course* I'd have put you up for a bit until all this Worry is over, but I'm in the thick of moving in myself. Now that Francis has sent in his papers it looks as though we shall have a Home at long last. House small but pretty and very Surrey-ish — all little grass-plots and white posts and chains, and our Maltese embroidery looks delightful in the drawing-room.

'Neighbours, I *think*, are going to be pleasant, tho' so far I've only *really* got to know the one next door, young, with two dear little girls. Their mother is hunting for a governess for them with no success, so far. N.B. I suppose *you* wouldn't care to take them on?!! It's really only a sort of light job and she must have *a lady*. She'd be simply enchanted and it would be more like being a friend of the family, and with me next door, my dear! Of course if it bored you you could chuck it at any time. £1 a week. Does it smile?

'I'm almost sure we're going to like Haslemere, tho' it will take a bit of getting used to, i.e. the fact that here we don't know everyone as a matter of course as one did with the regiment.

'I do trust Mamma is improving — '

11

Grace worried for days over that letter. It was not so much the plan which temporarily had much to recommend it, as its implications. If Arabella was beginning to regard one in the light of an employee it meant that one was now a person to whom such suggestions could be made. . . .

The shock of this social derating warred with conscience. £1 a week. Almost equal to one's own old dress allowance. Mary . . . yet if one said 'Yes' to the arrangement wouldn't it prove to have been a false economy of a particularly virulent kind, once back at home? No words that occurred to Grace could soften or conceal the fact that once, for a few weeks, one had:

Gone out to earn;

Taken a post;

Become a nursery governess;

Had had to 'turn to'.

One might, to oneself, live it down, but it would always be waiting to reassert itself at the back of one's memory.

And it would get about. Come between one's conversations over the tea-table.

As against all that — if one did bring oneself to — it would be a real change. One would meet New People. *My dear Auntie Q., I assure you that men seem to think that because you teach them to get round a ballroom you can be embraced*

with impunity ... because they were paying me for the lessons.
Paula, at the Christmas dinner table. The possibility of That
would of course be a point against the scheme. Of course. . . .

One would escape from Gertie, help Mary, get to know
another sister as one knew friends. One would mention
Arabella's letter, to sound the family; they might (one
hoped? expected?) put their foot down. One would
allude to it jokingly, but better not disparage it too much
in case family feeling ran in the Haslemere direction. . . .

Gertrude exclaimed emphatically that she thought it a
capital idea. It was Paula, returned from conducting a
now packed dancing-class, who said: 'Hope you have a
good time, Gracie old dear.'

'But, I haven't decided to go, yet.'

'No? Well it's up to you, of course. I shall be glad if
you choose to stay on here.'

'Thank you, dear.'

'Same time, children are great fun, you know; no need
to funk 'em.'

Grace avoided her eyes. 'Naturally one loves children.
Everybody does.'

'What? *I* don't, but I know how to manage 'em, and
they know it.'

'Oh Paula, of course you love them. Every woman does.'

'Gracie, that's simply not the case, beggin' yer pardon
an' thankin' yer very kindly. There are hundreds of
women (I'm one) who don't care one toot for them *as*
children and who require that they shall first be lovable.
That attitude is far the greater compliment if you think it
out. And incidentally it answers best. Children will
always behave better and work better for you if they sense
that they don't come under your management with a
large sentimental margin of credit from you, but must earn

it first. You'll be telling me next that motherhood is woman's highest calling!'

Grace had been going to do nothing of the kind about a subject concerning which her whole being clamoured agreement, but her silence answered for her.

'Whereas when people say that, what they really mean is that motherhood is the only thing women are *known* to be able to achieve — a physical function. But that's not a vocation.'

It was no use. Grace, Paula saw, was hurt: eighteen months between their ages, and Grace eternally of the epoch which shied from abstractions, bogged down comfortably in second-hand thought, believed in God without being able to advance one single reason why or displaying any desire to understand Him, instead of investigating Him with the open-minded interest, basically complimentary, that one extended to any modern movement or invention.

One had grown fond of the little aunt, saw that she wasn't at her best cuckooing it with relatives, a point mother and Caroline had overlooked. Grace probably lived by her affections, a likeable mistake. All one's eggs in one basket. Her response to demonstrations was so pathetically instant ... not had much of a time at home, perhaps? A type which got itself overlooked because it wouldn't push itself forward and hadn't any physical façade if it could.

'Oh! What a *dam* fool nature is!' exploded Paula.

Grace, as so often over her niece's pronouncements, made no attempt to follow that one.

III

Grace would go to Haslemere. Mary approved, with concerned reservations. 'See that they give you hot milk at eleven, dear, and tell Mrs. Railton that you're used to at least one good walk a day. If she should be tiresome over anything, drop a hint to Arabella and she'll pass it on. It's so much easier, when people are friends. Send home at once for anything you need and I'll ring up every other day because the call may be expensive, and if you don't absolutely like being there let me know, and we'll think of something else. (The Hellards, I'm certain, would have you for a bit, and they only live out at Chiswick.)'

The letter from Arabella, affectionate and discursive, came four days later. 'Mrs. R. fixed up with a gov' nearly a fortnight ago. *Why* didn't you cut in sooner? . . .'

Overwhelming relief or disappointment? Grace didn't know. But one *had* been prepared . . . done one's best . . .

Gertie (or did one fancy it?) was looking thoughtful and glum. The Hellards . . . and one was absolutely sick with wanting peace and home life again.

IV

Grace's forty-fourth birthday was drawing near and the summer holiday question beginning to be discussed by the Randolphs, not very freely at first, because of Grace. Gertrude finally said: 'I suppose you could stay on here, my dear, only the maids go on holiday and might be tiresome without me at the helm. I'd take you with us only I really don't see my way to it — Clarence has had to fork out a bit to Bob to help him in his business, but we'll stand you a fortnight somewhere, at some nice private hotel perhaps, if Mary's rather dipped, as I suppose she must be.'

A fortnight at a private hotel. Alone. Grace wilted. And refusal might offend.

Paula, aware of tension between her mother and aunt, listened and watched and three days later came to Grace in her room.

'Look here, I think I've found the very thing for you. The mother of one of my kids rather wants somebody like you to take it off her bones over August. No lessons at all, of course, and luckily she — Mrs. Vince-Wells — is going to a nearby place. Hove. She isn't offering any payment. It's rather a picked job, you see, and I didn't press that side of it on purpose because I saw that it'd be a better thing for you. She's more than rather a snob and believes in me because I've got some titles in my dancing-classes.'

Grace murmured disparagement but Paula went on: 'She's large and smart and fifty-ish and was meant to be a really topping sort only her husband began to make money. When she bought her first car she started a lisp, but that's rather worn off now and only breaks through in places when she remembers it. She'll probably ask you 'Have you theen the peypers to-dey?' when she hands you *The Times*, but I remember her when she called people Deeree and Gurls and said Reelly? (it's reahlly, now). Heaps of people can't bear her because she's just not clever enough to stop boasting by implication of her titled acquaintances and income — oh it's *such* a pity! She does it in a rather special way so that they don't know why they leave her house feeling inferior and infuriated. The result is that she hasn't an intimate friend in the world though she's a mass of rather hysteric emotion and to hear her you'd think she walked down Park Lane with one arm round the Foreign Office and the other round the Admiralty. If ever we have another war, Gracie, she will knit and weep with the highest in the land. No titled sorrow will be safe from her. And then she'll probably set to and do something really fine.'

343

'But, do you think she'll consider that I'm quite what she is looking for?'

'Oh yes. Daughter of distinguished Army officer (was Grandpa distinguished? Anyway, he will be). She won't give you any trouble but play a lot of Bridge and lose a lot of money and not appear until midday, five minutes before her maid commits suicide. Go and see her. She has a large house in The Boltons.'

Grace, bewildered, accepted at once. This sort of thing was being rather like a bad dream, and from those one woke suddenly.

CHAPTER XXI

I

'So you're Miss Randolph's aunt? You're not a bit like her, are you?' Grace flinched, taking disparagement for granted.

'She's quite wonderful with children, isn't she? I was saying so to Lady Onthorp only last week — you know her daughter's pets, of course? — grandfather was killed in the Egyptian affair and when I heard, I just gave way. Everybody said that I got more sympathy than the widow! And I commenced to think "Well really, Florence Vince-Wells, you must be a very popular person to get all this attention. You know my Netsy?"'

Miss Netta was believed to be in the garden and her mother got up and called from the french window.

'Netteh! *Nett*eh! Come heer deere when mother calls!' Netta, a dark, nervous child, overhandled and socially precocious, flagged into the room.

'Yes Muvvah,' she droned, her eyes raking the stranger.

'Come *in* and shake hands.'

'But Muvvah — '

'*Nett*eh!' Mrs. Vince-Wells turned to Grace. 'I don't know I'm sure what you think of us, we usually have lovely manners. You know, when Archie Hemelsted — Lord Daggenhaw's youngest — such a nice young fellow — doing marvels at the India Office — only thirty — I mean, when the veterans come in and see him running the *whole* show they simply say "Who's the baby?" — he was down for lunch the other day and he said "Well Mrs. Vince-Wells, Courts simply not in it", and I said "My dear boy it's evidently a Case". He *roared*. Come *along*, deere!'

345

Grace Scrimgeour was to discover that Mrs. Vince-Wells could secure obedience, but at the cost of a disproportionate squandering of nervous energy and noise. It had silenced Netta but her phlegm was superficial. Long ago she had loyally adopted all her mother's alarms together with her social outlook. If she fell and grazed her knee she screamed in concert with her mother and it became a neck and neck race for bandages and iodine. At Hove she had for Grace a complete list of all those things which, tested, had unnerved her, and, untested, might.

'Muvver says it would frighten me. We mustn't see it.' Other children disliked her, and about the enormous Christmas and birthday parties given for her, mothers confided to each other that 'Florence hadn't the touch'. On the subject of the holiday, Netta now asked, 'Is there anyone there to *know?*' Mrs. Vince-Wells turned to Grace, closing her eyes. 'Only thirteen and hits the nail on the head! What are you to do with them? You don't pley Bridge, Miss Scrimgeour?'

Grace was sorry. Mrs. Vince-Wells became immediately and immensely tactful. 'Well of course I think you're perfectly right. One can't do everything, can one? I wouldn't pley myself only you know what it is. When people come for week-ends its just "Where's Florence?" I say this house is turning into an absolute hotel.'

'Muvver, Joker's loose.'

'Jowkeh? But deere, Phelps *can't* have forgotten — ' Mother and daughter flowed on to the lawn where a slim collie was seen to shudder out of sight under the bushes, a hasty smile of affectionate craftiness upon his lips.

'But how did it *happen*, deere? Jowkeh! Jowkeh! If it's Phelp's fault — he goes. Just as the *entire* lawn's been returfed. You're not telling Mummie a lie? *Nett*eh? ! !

346

If you've let him off the chain you go to bed and stop there, at *once*.'

The child got her tears in first by the fraction of a second. 'You know mummie *al*ways cries when you lie to her. Ring for Colmer.' Like rival actresses mother and child sincerely strove for the emotional scene. Grace, amazed, saw that the woman was genuinely weeping. Netta was removed, drenched.

'I *al*ways know when she's not telling me the truth and it gets the servants into trouble. I lost my footman through that — you don't know of one, I suppose? They come to be interviewed — dozen a day — they all seem to want to come to me — and I always say "No, you're not experienced enough" (tell from the *manneh*, you know). But I think I've spotted the man. Been with the Bishop of Avonminster ten years. Well that speaks for itself, I always say. Came to me — very correct — good appearance — and began to throw his weight about, about the Bishop. At once. I said to him, "Now look here: this isn't a Palath and it's not the size of a Palath, but if you come heere you'll be working — for — *Mrs. — Vince-Wells*." Closed him up.' She became human. 'Well, it's very charming and nice of you to come with us and look after my Bubsy, you'll have *every* comfort — I always say: well, you've got your faults, Florence Vince-Wells, but you do know how to do people. We shall go down by car of course. I'll get them to phone you all the arrangements.'

11

Except for leaving Mary, anxiety about Mamma and the fact of having struck forty-four, it was a pleasant holiday. Grace appreciated the servile attention, private sitting-room and the superexcellent menus. Netta, of course, was rather the fly in the ointment . . . but if (and Paula had confirmed it) the child was universally unpopular, it exonerated one's conscience and *amour-propre* in making no headway with her. What she was now, so she would become in an intensified form, Grace decided; that left you a merely physical shell to take about. One could not even tackle the problem of moral culture by discussion with the mother, since all faults, direct and indirect, derived quite obviously from herself, and one shrank from the cautionary 'Don't'. Mrs. Vince-Wells said that for two, all day long, over trifles and urgencies alike, so that the prohibition had long lost value.

'Will it be good for me to dip my head right under, Miss Scrimgeour?'

'I mustn't go in, here. The beach shelves so and they *can't* teach me to swim, muvver says.'

'You'll never learn, Netta, if you don't strike out for yourself,' Grace heard herself answer.

'Some children are like that. It's nerves,' Netta replied. And usually, in the end, Grace herself became infected with vicarious apprehensions, so that, half urging on, half warning off, her exhortations carried no weight.

Forty-four. The chosen friend-companion for a holiday at a luxury hotel. But — did the net result to the trippers look uncommonly like a paid attendant (not so young) in charge of the usual child? That side of things one fought and forgot, fought and forgot again.

'What's Luxemburg, Miss Scrimgeour?'

Grace, warm with embarrassment, glanced at the contents-bills of *News* and *Standard* and didn't quite know. 'It's a big place, Netta,' she improvised.

'Where is it?'

'Hurry up, old lady, or your mother will be worrying.'

She was not only worrying but in tears, walking, wild-eyed, about the hotel sitting-room.

'Oh thank God to see you both. My Netsy! Go to Colmer.'

She turned to Grace. 'Well — it's come! I know so *many* men in the War Office . . .' Grace saw that her chin was trembling and, ever suggestible, glanced out of the window to view the hostile battalions pouring on to the shore from warships lying at anchor. The esplanade was certainly emptier, and what people there were seemed to be hurrying, that was all.

'Mrs. Vince-Wells — '

'Of course we leave at once.' The ignoble funk upon her face faded as tears rolled openly down it. 'Dear Grace . . . it's such a comfort to have you. And I was actually planning a Bridge party for to-night!' Her arms round Grace she sobbed: 'One is so heartless . . . how people put up with me . . . the things one does.' She drew back, was frankly mopping her eyes. 'Well, Florence, after this, no more Bridge for *you* until All This is over — oh I know I'm a fool but I always was — the least thing — *floods* — and now This. Ring for the manager. Of course you return with us — I'll take no refusal. Phelps shall drive us home shortest way — *Deere, don't look out of the window!* You never know . . .'

Their departure was spectacular. The manager summoned and harangued on the best methods of protecting life and property by a Mrs. Vince-Wells beginning to weep again at her own words and his courage in carrying on. 'Oh my dear man, it's the thought of you people all *round* the coast, behaving as though nothing had happened,

I always say: "Well: there's nothing like an Englishman." '
The manager who had been naturalized for twenty years
politely assented.

'Anything I can do at *any* time — '

She tipped until they thought she was insane, broad-
casting incoherent invitations to the chambermaids to
come straight to her in any trouble. Both their hands in
hers she besought, 'Don't remember me as just a tiresome
visitor, just think of me as one of yourselves. You nice,
plucky things . . . and here I am just walking out on you —
let's face it — but I've got my baby to think of. . . .'

Her exalted mood carried her to London where she
cached Grace in The Boltons, deaf to any hints that Grace
might first wish to visit her own family; it would have
been anti-climax to her sincere passion to house and
protect before which urge no one was, for the moment, a
free agent. But (though her tears sprang anew) she was
forced to give place before the telephone call from
Ramillies Terrace which came through next day.

Mrs. Scrimgeour had died at six o'clock that morning.

IV

Once more the sisters were together, parting only when
Grace returned to The Boltons to sleep. So occupied with
the aftermaths of death, pathetic, sordid and irritating,
their feelings in odd moments of relaxation were more
those that filled them at the passing of Queen Victoria:
stunned, yet once removed from personal intimacy. After
all, calling condolers were informed, Mamma *was* eighty-
five . . . oh yes, she had put up a wonderful fight . . . quite
peaceful, it was thought . . . yes, opiates . . . doctors so
much more enlightened now. Worn out, crying a little,
Mary would say no more.

But even she could not protect her dead mother from criticism when her affairs were disclosed. Her daughters, of course, had never seen her Will and to discuss it in her lifetime would have been bad taste and heartlessness. On the whole, Mary thought, in the light of her own knowledge of Mrs. Scrimgeour, she had exercised restraint in face of what must probably always be a temptation to bestow money when you no longer need it yourself. . . .

It was the relatives less immediately concerned who were indignant. The bequest to that children's hospital would have to go through, they agreed sulkily, but the thousand pounds to Robert Bridgewood stuck, Gertrude said, even in her gullet. She dined the family solicitor and over coffee frankly tackled him.

'I know Robert Bridgewood is my own son-in-law and of course there's no denying that he owes us money we can't afford to sneeze at, but I'd be willing to waive that if my husband agrees, as I'm pretty sure he would. Robert *must* see — '

Mr. Mowbray put his cup aside. 'The point is really this, Mrs. Randolph: it's not a question of unofficial generosity, you understand. We must assume that Mr. Bridgewood, not unnaturally, will refuse to extend it, therefore you can only make an appeal *ad misericordiam* to him. If he refuses, all your sisters can do is to bring an action by which they seek to prove that at the time of making the Will your mother wasn't in her right mind.'

'My dear man, where finance was concerned I don't believe she ever was!' But, facetiae apart, she saw that line was blocked. She thought rapidly. 'This Will: when did she make it? Was it the only one?'

'It was the only one, except in respect of these two codicils, the hospital's and Mr. Bridgewood's legacies. She added those in 1899.'

351

'Fifteen years ago,' commented Mrs. Randolph. She was thinking, 'Just about the time that she began to take a fancy to Bob'.

V

The Scrimgeours themselves alluded to it, but briefly. Mary said: 'Gertie thinks that Bob could be persuaded to stand aside.'

'I'd rather be shot than ask him to,' rapped Queenie. Her acrimony had reached a height easily to be mistaken for pride.

'I quite agree. Gracie?'

Grace shook her head. 'Mamma evidently wished it even if he would agree,' she reminded them.

VI

The Bridgewoods talked it over. 'Gran never told me. I'd no idea of it, Carry.'

'No. I suppose it's all right or she wouldn't have done it.' He looked at her steadily. 'You know we're off in three weeks —'

'My good lad, naturally I do!'

'They say they'll keep my place open when and if I return.'

'Least they can do.'

'Well, they may have closed down themselves by then, y'know. Anyway, it'll mean pulling in your little horns quite a considerable bit while I'm away, and I just want to mention that unless I miss my guess you may live to be jolly thankful for that thousand.'

CHAPTER XXII

I

IT was just at the moment when, the funeral over, Grace was thinking, 'At last I shall be at home again and there will be room for me — always,' that Mary had to let her know that their house must be given up. 'I'm afraid, dear, that there's no doubt that we've not been left as much money as we expected.'

Grace had not expected anything in the sense of a fixed sum; she had merely taken for granted that they would all be provided for, in a slightly smaller house, perhaps, now that mother and nurse were gone. It was to Mary's manner and tone that she bent, those which gave her her first little dingy fear. Queenie was listening too with a look of sour pre-knowledge. 'You see, to pay these legacies we shall have to sell out, Mr. Mowbray says, and it seems to come to this, that we shall only have slightly over one hundred and fifty pounds a year each. We shall have to think how best to manage and where to live, but if we're very careful we shall pull through, all right.'

Queenie stirred, said: 'I'm sorry, I've been thinking it over and that won't suit me.'

They waited painfully. You never knew, with Queenie. She was looking craven and determined, apologetic and unhappy. And ill. Her sisters granted that. 'I want to have a place of my own, perhaps a little cottage in the country. I want to get *away*. And I'm going to buy an annuity.'

A year more of the lease of the house in Ramillies Terrace to run and by the time it expired, Mary and Grace regretful at leaving yet craving freedom from its exactions and tyrannies. They gave up the house-parlourmaid first, then after endless discussion and with a sense of incredulity, the cook, making do on the daily charwoman. Eggs, bacon and sausages they learned 'saw to themselves' and there was always the standby of sardines and other tinned food. The charwoman sometimes gave them good-natured hints for recipes that they were largely unable to follow. Their efforts in the kitchen were magnificent aids to dyspepsia and the rationing that was to set in later an uninteresting instructress, and a harsh, but if meat, eggs, potatoes and fats were scarce there was still a fine choice of patent medicines on the market.

Sunday evenings were an untold relief. On that day you could go for supper to the relations, listening with only half an uncomprehending ear to the complaints of the married sisters and nieces upon the subject of the foulness of the menu and the current cook as you ate the good, good food prepared by an expert in her degree.

Birthdays grew a significance that was not alone of sentiment. There might be a cheque. 'It's extraordinary what things cost and *nothing* to show for it', Mary, who had kept house for years on sufficient means, sometimes marvelled. But some things she and Grace could and did economize upon with a sense of tangible achievement; pleasures and holidays, of course, and clothes. Evening and semi-evening dresses began to be drawn into that category which, waving a long farewell to current fashion (out of date before half worn) 'made do' all the year round.

Their hostesses didn't like it. 'Miss Scrimgeour, Miss Grace Scrimgeour', and the entrance of that black velvet and bottle-coloured taffeta . . . did they live in the things?

Too new to the profession of impecuniosity, the entering Miss Scrimgeours did not know that once guests by their clothes become too familiar to fellow guests, so recognizable as to lead the visitors to ask each other whether, after all, their hostess's circle is not a somewhat limited one, their own social twilight has set in. Invitations dwindled insensibly; credulous and simple, it took Mary and Grace a long time even to realize that a rather unusual space separated one invitation from another. The point taken, they attributed it to their own lack of repartee, above all to the fact that they could make no return of hospitality. A cutlet for a cutlet. Just or unjust, they had been accustomed all their lives to existence on those lines. The next invitation would arrive in due course and out came the black velvet and the bottle-green taffeta. One economy Mary was unable to make. Books must be had from the circulating library; the annual subscription did not exactly make a hole in her resources, it only helped to lower her standard of living. Like that you didn't notice it sufficiently for self-reproach.

III

They had two invitations for Christmas, and several for luncheon and tea.

'We *ought* to have Mary and Grace, of course.'

'But — '

'Oh I know they don't shed much lustre — '

'But — '

'And it's their first Christmas since the old lady cashed in.'

355

'But—'

'My dear, *I* don't want 'em, but they're poor things.'

'Oh well ... lunch, then, but I bar dinner.'

'I don't expect they have much of a *time*—'

'Oh—all right, tea, then, but not lunch. They'll *have* to go at six, but I *can*not sit holding my jaws together half the afternoon.'

Arabella wanted them for a week at Haslemere, Gertrude to spend the whole of Christmas Day. The campaign became an exercise in relative expense. Gertie would mean presents to Clarence, Pauline, Gertie herself and Bertie which, opened under the eyes of the family, must be rather better than if sent by post; Arabella, family presents plus fares and tips to servants. It must be Gertie, but one craved for Arabella and her new house, cook, environment and companionship, and—it could be Arabella if tips came in time. People never thought of that when they gave you money, and, as Mary said, he gives thrice who gives quickly. Tips were rare, there was now hardly anybody left to send them, or perhaps the idea was that adults would be offended? Or that you had to give more in proportion to their age? If they but knew! Mary would conclude, wryly humorous. And it was quite terrible when people, stretching a point by using their imagination, gave you books; never the one you wanted and usually by an author you didn't read. The good, good money wasted! It was odd that talk of money sent one's thoughts back to Lady Mell, still for the Scrimgeours personally unknown, a name, a splendid background of country mansion and a fir-tree at Christmas, lumbering into Brecknock Gardens on a lorry.

'She must be an immense age by now,' said Grace.

IV

They had moved into three rooms in West Kensington with telephone on the landing, use of bathroom and landlady's cooking. The woman was gratified at the sudden praise. . . .

The remains of their furniture, after Queenie had been set up, gave them an illusion of home until they looked out of the windows, and once more they had that leisure to which they had been brought up.

The War claimed it. At first they had discussed the question of paid work, only to find that even if they could stand up to working by the clock they were unqualified. Even sacrifice demanded efficiency. In face of the adventurous flood of young womanhood pouring into London in search of patriotism or money or men they withdrew, intimidated. From parsonage, market town, country house, from slum and shop and service, the women were streaming to better themselves. From goodness knew where flocked those officially registered as women and still wearing skirts, whose alleged sex stopped above the waist (and sometimes below it) in an orgy of bass voice, boiled shirt, stiff collar and cropped hair, who should and would and could have been in the firing line did not a traditional chivalry which they never wanted prevent them; pretentious, laughable and socially offensive, they were putting in the best work allowed them in a hypocritic and bewildered world which, baulking at using them outright as endlessly plucky, tireless and enterprising cannon-fodder, elected instead to snigger behind the hand. At the other end of the scale were those about whose physiology there was no doubt at all. These drove the cars of Staff officers and preferred nursing the commissioned ranks. Somewhere between the two extremes were the Scrimgeours of England, flooding the less spectacular arena, faithfully bending over lint and wool, combing, teasing, cutting out and hemming khaki into sun-protectors for shrapnel helmets. They did not all put in an eight-hour day as did the Misses Scrimgeour. There was, after all, a social side, a home to order, and a husband and children to be considered. . . .

CHAPTER XXIII

I

WHEN Trans-Siberian Railways and Prussian Consols stopped payment Mary and Grace Scrimgeour were left with rather under fifty pounds a year between them.

Fear and its consequences is, in its symptoms, not unlike the progress of disease. Its manifestations veer from the tragic, the repellent to the bathetic in which tricks are played upon body and nerves that culminate in unromantic results, affairs commonly dosed in privacy and about which there is a conspiracy of silence.

Their first sensation was a stupefied acquiescence until the details came in. Terror, nausea — and other things — found good material in the Scrimgeours, weakened as those from large families must be by recurrent loss, sapped with war work and undermined by indigestible food ill-chosen and badly cooked. They could not even take to their beds; rest involving attendance was now a thing which must be paid for. The full implications of the situation would present themselves gradually, one cannot take in all sides of disaster at once. Meanwhile, there were enough ... everything you wanted, fancied or needed brought to a dead end, other things you took and gave up in the nick of time, because for that moment you had forgotten your circumstances.

Their memory often played them false in those first weeks. Economy was not enough when outfaced with the enemy of lifelong habit waiting to pounce, lurking to betray them into matter of course expenditure, from a pair of gloves to a packet of hairpins. It was the thinking twice

359

over purchase of sheer necessities that first showed them an unexpected side of poverty.

Indecency. Rather like a lack of privacy, or insufficient facilities for washing . . . curious, and interesting, if you had heart and leisure to examine it all round, and just as you thought you'd got the knack of it you were attacked from another side, found yourself committed to an elementary course in helplessness which was watching the other one lack. Grace, needing beef jelly after influenza, Mary without books. They became loving liars, struggling to find comfort in believing each other. 'Truly, dear, I couldn't swallow it. It seems as if all one really wanted is just tea.'

Mary considered her sister, then agreed and left the room quickly to ring up a number. They telephoned at once to the relations for the necessary comforts — in those early days. It seemed the only decent thing to do. They belonged to each other and one must not risk the health of common property. . . . It wasn't altogether easy, this technique of request, it grew, indeed, progressively difficult. One began rather to listen for certain inflexions in the answering voice. But, it was for Gracie.

It was for Mary.

11

'Of course we shall all have to do something', Gertrude Randolph said to her husband and Arabella, up for a day's shopping. Arabella agreed instantly. 'And we'll have to round up Georgie as well and get her to fork out her share — though one hardly *likes* to ask her, now Henry has gone.'

'Well really, my dear. . . . I know, but I don't quite see

why widows should be exempt; she's got her pension and the boy's safely in the army.'

' "Safely"!'

'Well, you know what I mean, that she hasn't got to sink money in floating him in business, as we had to with Bertie after Oxford. I think we ought to give her the chance to help.'

'Well, it's rather hard luck on Charlie. You call him Georgie's "boy" but he's nearly forty, and he's sure to have to help out with this, and suppose he wants to get married?'

'I know, but we're all scrubbing along on less, what with this infernal income-tax — good Lord! some man told me the other day that in 1912 it was one-and-tuppence in the pound. And we had money in Prussian Consols, too.'

'Most people of our class seem to have. "A good sound investment" . . . and they were talking of "The German Menace" in nineteen-hundred. That carries one back.'

Clarence said 'In the last resort no investment's safe because at the back of it there's always apt to be the human element to upset the apple-cart; greed or vengeance or pride or downright lust started by some backstairs beauty. Look at Henry the Eighth and Anne Boleyn. He liked the shape of her nose (and other things) and it brought Protestantism to England. Fid. Def. on the new pennies and God knows how many R.C.'s ruined. Worth considering.'

'Don't let's. The question is: how much are we to be expected to do for Mary and Grace? Look here, Arabella, Clarence and I have been guaranteeing the rent but we told them quite frankly that it could be only temporarily. It's two and a half guineas a week for those three rooms alone.'

'What? Incredible! They could get a house for less!'

'Don't you believe it! Also heaven forbid! That'd mean

a char right off, and rates. Besides, you can't get small houses at a reasonable rental any more. Big ones, yes.' Gertrude put her elbows on the table. 'What I suggest is this, that they move into two furnished rooms and sell their furniture.'

'Two? Gertie! They *must* have a drawing-room.'

'Well, share a bedroom, then. They used to.'

Arabella was dubious. 'It doesn't sound very *homelike* ...'

'My dear, it's all beastly, but we can't consider that sort of thing. The only alternative is to give them a home ourselves, share 'em out between us. Like that?'

Arabella flushed. 'I — I'll always be glad to put them up for a bit when I can —'

Her sister's smile was indulgent and mocking. 'Exactly! You needn't say another word! To be quite candid, I couldn't stand it, myself. I'd rather pay for them to go elsewhere while we can, fond as I am of them.'

'What about Queenie?'

'We'll have to count her out, I'm afraid. She's bought an annuity — about a pound a week, and her cottage is six shillings.'

'Somehow, one doesn't associate Queenie with a money sense.'

'I don't think she has one, particularly, she was smothered by the family and furious at seeing the cash poured out on other people and half crazy to be quit of 'em, and it worked out that way.'

'She might take Mary. Most cottages have two bed-rooms.'

'She might say that about us. We can't expect her to do what we're unwilling to do ourselves. We're paying our way out of the situation. Queenie can't.'

Arabella got up. 'Well, I must be off. We can't decide anything until we hear from Georgie.'

When the front door had shut on her sister, Gertrude Randolph turned to her husband. 'It's a very regrettable thing, but all this has made me rather dislike Mary and Gracie. Poor dear Mary and Gracie. One's heart bleeds for them, but — dislike and surly exasperation.'

'That's honest, at any rate.'

'Honest . . . oh, I'm *that* . . .'

III

Georgina Brailsford was shocked and distressed at the news. She would contribute ten shillings a week 'while I can, Gertie my dear'.

Arabella's husband would give the same, Clarence Randolph grimly came forward with thirty shillings, Paula with five ('The *poor* little aunts! I wish I dared promise more'), and Caroline with two-and-six ('Here's ten bob for the first month. Is it to be a *permanence?*').

'Can't — whatsername — Grace *do* something?' asked Clarence. His wife looked at him. 'Fifty-seven-and-six a week promised, and just under a pound a week from the smash for the two of them . . . three pounds seventeen-and-six . . . yes. I think she'll have to.'

'I'M so occupied with War work and committees that I feel I hardly see the children, these days.' Lady Ebban bent to a note on her desk. 'Mrs. Vince-Wells tells me you're one of her greatest friends.'

Grace Scrimgeour looked astonished. 'Oh no! Surely not? Her child goes to the dancing-classes, my niece's, that is.'

Lady Ebban's social geniality vanished. 'Am I to understand then that you don't know Mrs. Vince-Wells?' Grace crimsoned at the tone.

'Certainly. I mean I *do* know her, but not intimately.'

'Miss — er — Scrimgeour, this note is a *reference*, I'm sure you will see its importance if you are to come to me.'

Grace found that her hands were shaking and put them, clenched, behind her back like a schoolgirl. 'I can't help what — what people say in letters. . . . I do know her, though I don't like her much,' she heard herself falter insanely. The eyebrows of Lady Ebban went up. Grace buckled. 'She's very *kind*,' she added hastily. There was a slight pause. 'She is a most generous woman,' stated Lady Ebban. She was annoyed at being put into the position of champion of Mrs. Vince-Wells who had recently been one too many for her in getting important people for her own charities more quickly. She studied Miss Scrimgeour again. Nothing to look at but obviously a gentlewoman, that was something, after the last one. Not too young, either; well again, no silly business if men came to the house . . . and wouldn't be wanting to go off and pick up inflated pocket-money at munitions or get into uniform to ogle lieutenants. Come to that, nobody but the stumers ever did become govs, anyway. How long, oh Lord!

This hiatus between nursery and school was always tiresome, but at least one was out all day and half the night, oneself, so wouldn't have to *vis-à-vis* the probable procession of meek faces and quenched hats at meals. Where *did* these people get their hats? Miss Scrimgeour's looked like something that Queen Mary had trodden on by accident . . . from a good shop but neither a hat nor a toque . . . a Hoque? . . . She roused herself.

'What salary are you asking?'

Grace started. 'I — well really I hadn't thought.'

'I can offer fifty pounds,' rapped Lady Ebban who would have given up to ninety but was exasperated at the hesitations of the applicant.

'Thank you very much.'

'That suit you?'

'Of course. I'm sure it must be right and fair.'

The elder woman was disarmed, reproached and irritated, but it was too late, now. She supposed one could come forward with the larger offer but if fifty pounds did . . . and one hadn't taken all that much fancy to Miss Whatsername. 'You've had experience with children, haven't you?'

Miss Scrimgeour — could the woman never answer a straight question with yes or no? — considered. 'I . . . yes, but not as a *governess*, you know, not teaching, except a little reading with my great-niece. I *was* going to a Mrs. Railton, at Haslemere . . . then of course there was — ' her heart stopped. She had forgotten the name of the Vince-Wells child out of sheer nervousness. The more one battled to recall it, the more one realized the bad impression this lapse would make, the more one's brain refused to stir. Grace's gloves were damp as she concluded ' — Mrs. Vince-Wells's little girl.'

'Naturally, it's because of that that you're here at all,

isn't it?' bantered Lady Ebban, and Grace smiled shakily. 'How'd you get on with *her?*'

'Oh, very nicely, on the whole. But that wasn't teaching, either, just as companion for the holidays,' Miss Scrimgeour meticulously reminded her prospective employer.

'My dear lady, haven't you ever taught *anyone?*'

Grace found a chairback and clutched it. 'No. I — never meant to keep anything from you. You see, I never *knew* I was going to be a governess.'

Lady Ebban tutted back further irritation and put her hand on the letter. 'Mrs. Vince-Wells says you're "brilliant" with children. Underlined.' She smiled unexpectedly. 'It seems to be one of her good days.' The thought of the coming conversation with her friend and rival had already put her into a warmer mood. 'Very well, Miss Scrimgeour . . . by the way, fond of children?'

'I love them.' The answer was swift and assured.

'Right. Now, I do trust you're not faddy about your food. I can't bear people who want stewed lettuce at eleven, I'd always sooner give them quail at the proper hour.'

'Naturally I shall eat what I am offered.' Grace saw the woman opposite her quite simply as a hostess guilty of bad taste and manners.

Lady Ebban laughed. 'That's all right, that's all right, only some of them are so impossible. Standing on their dignity, you know, and getting wrong with the servants.'

'A governess *is* a servant,' Grace said, baldly.

It winded her companion effectively. 'My *dear* lady . . . do you seriously think so? How incredible! How they'd love you for it! But *you're* a lady — '

'When one takes wages one takes servant rank,' answered Grace. 'That's the way I feel about it.'

'The way you were brought up?'

'I — I suppose so. I shall do my best to give you

satisfaction and to keep on good terms with the servants. They are dreadful trials nowadays, I know.' She stopped abruptly. One mustn't seem to be boasting of better circumstances.

I I

To her husband, Lady Ebban, dressing for a fancy ball in aid of the Red Cross in what appeared to be a jewelled lampshade ending in trousers that no Oriental gentleman of caste would permit for a second in his harem, remarked, 'I've landed another gov'.'

He made the usual perfunctory enquiry. Viewing her, he sometimes wished that Veda would consider the alternative of posting ten pounds to the Red Cross instead of spending twenty-five on a personal appearance for its support, but that, of course, would not be working for charity.

'What's she like? Oh, she's got a face, you know, and a nose, I believe, but she's a museum-piece out of a cradle, if you get me.' She stooped to the telephone, plucked the receiver and called a number. Her husband escaped to his study. 'Mrs. Vince-Wells, Lady Ebb — oh, is that you, Florence? My dear, I've just seen your rum little cuss . . .'

'My what, deere?'

'Your Scrimgeour gov'.'

'Bless her,' breathed Mrs. Vince-Wells, 'she keyme to me in the wey they all do when they want work and I had to tell her: "I've got half Mayfair here already. Free." Got the Channel girl . . . I said to her mother, well reahlly, Duchess, she may be a society star but can — she — cook? Settled *her*, all right.'

Against her will Lady Ebban found the old, exasperated sense of impression steal over her. Florence certainly did get things done and before her consciousness of being Mrs. Vince-Wells she was amply and provenly capable of telling off the relatives of dukes. The house in The Boltons, mainly given up to a social club for privates and N.C.O.s, was well run and a success. Florence in her present incarnation knew waste when she saw it and wasn't above identifying a dirty saucepan, which probably pointed to a family tree whose boughs, one had long suspected, were shaky. One couldn't even have her on the hip about cosseting officers only since she had flummoxed one by encouraging the lower ranks. One's only comfort was that, being Florence, she just wasn't clever enough not to boast about her all-men-are-brothers move.

'I thed to the girl — sables — very grand — you know — quite tossy — "My deere girl," I thed, "look here: these men aren't going to teyke you out to the Ritz and give you a jolly good time and they couldn't afford to if they wanted to. *You're* here to make *them* comfortable." Her face! Tears at once. One of the boys heard and he just came straight up to me and saluted and said "Well, Madam," he said, "if we had a few more ladies like you we should *all* get on better".'

'Yes — but about Miss Scrimgeour. . . .'

'You're taking her, of course.' Mrs. Vince-Wells's voice was off-hand and businesslike at once, forgetting to croon and breathe and drivel and lisp.

'Why "of course"? *You* didn't.'

'My deerie, I've *explained* . . . and I can't have her even for my Netteh as I've had to send her to a boarding-school — West coast, of course — that place where the Vavasour children went — you remember Diamond? The Beys. The men adored him — he was always about with Lord Brount — saw a lot of him at one time.

The fact was, my boys here got *encouraging* Netteh so.
I said to her: "Netteh, you're breaking Mummy's heart,
you're so odious." I said, "You may have got the best-bred
profile in London," I said, "but you're losing all your
friends." Only way. There's one thing about me: I'm not a
besotted mother. Vedeh, darling, they were simply *making
love* to her. You know what she is — bright as a sixpence
— always an answer — and rather The person in any
room she goes into — '

'Florence, I just rang up to tell you what a liar you are.'

'Eh, deere?'

'Why did you tell me Miss Scrimgeour was one of your
greatest friends? *She* says she hardly knows you.'

'What's that? Nonsense. My dear Veda, it was absolutely
imperative to get the poor little woman a good post and I
just thought — *of course! Veda!*'

'Thanks a lot. But is she *possible?*'

'My dear woman, she's a lady and better born than
either of *us*. You stand by her, she'll stand by you.
I have my faults but I *can* spot character at a glance.'

'Well, another time don't say the thing that is not, in
references.'

'Now look here, you'll take that back and *at* once.
I'm your friend and you know it, and *as* your friend I'll
tell you what nobody else dares to: you're a spoilt woman
and your children are spoilt. I spoilt Netta, but thank God
I saw it in time. If Miss Scrimgeour comes to you, you'll
not only have a bargain but a chance of turning your lot
into something worth while.'

'Well . . . damn your eyes, Florence.'

The voice down the telephone was already broken.
'Oh, I know that was unpardonable of me, but though
I'm crying my eyes out already I mean every word of it,
deere — '

GRACE wished the family had come to see her off at the station; not the men, of course, one didn't expect that. . . . The sight of Mary standing by the open door of the third-class compartment was the only comfort, did much to stifle a dulled resentment at the apparently complete obliviousness of all the others to the sacrifice one was making. . . .

There wasn't much to say. Sustained conversation, even if they had been capable of it, would be shattered by rumbling churns twirled by porters, 'Mind your backs, there' of the pushers' of laden trucks and the coughing and wheezing of engines. Mary turned and bought her fruit and chocolate from a trolley. Gloucestershire was a long way off but the restaurant luncheon was half a crown. For the third time Grace opened her handbag to reassure herself about the ticket and the letter of directions in Lady Ebban's splashing hand.

THE FIRS. ELLINGWORTH. TELEGRAMS: EBBFIR. PHONE: ELL. 16

She ran her eyes along the rack, counting the pieces she knew to be there: small suit-case, wicker basket containing sandwiches and flask of lemonade, umbrella . . . a shilling for the porter at the other end and nothing for the chauffeur, Gertie had said. You don't tip the house staff when you're going to be one of the staff yourself.

'Was the trunk put in, Mary?'

'Yes, dear.' They had both watched it labelled, had

hurried with it to the guard's van, seen it shunted inside, but you never knew.

'This is right for Ellingworth?'

'That's right, lady.'

'And no change?' Cook's had confirmed the through run a week ago but the station arrangements might have been altered in the time. . . . They had got to the station three-quarters of an hour ahead of time and Grace had lain awake half the night for fear of missing it and in general dread of the day. It was as the train was moving that a new thought struck her.

'Mary, oh Mary, we shan't be together for Christmas!'

It was Mary Scrimgeour's last glimpse of her sister, a white face, too thin, and the grey eyes filling.

Sitting tensely upright, Grace suddenly remembered that she had omitted to supply presents for her unknown pupils. Two of them . . . two shillings each, perhaps, would buy something . . . handkerchiefs . . a village shop . . . but if there weren't one? Lady Ebban was paying one's fare, but if she forgot it one couldn't bring oneself to remind her. Or two-and-sixpence one might be able to run to. Grace opened her bag and made a note in her diary.

II

A small station without a buffet: a shed-like bookstall (picture-books, perhaps? if one could leave the children and slip out of the house unseen and if the station weren't too far). Outside the wooden railings a glimpse of sage-coloured allotments and a spiral of smoke from a bonfire: vans with local names on their sides, reflected from the solitary lamp-post. Bugden, Family Butcher. (Would one pay the book there?) A large saloon car and a chauffeur at the wheel. Miss Scrimgeour waited for him to get out and become active with the luggage. He saw her and did so, but — hadn't he rather taken his time? Was his 'Miss Scrimgeour?' a thought brusque, or worse, companionable? She had a leaden headache and the journey had made her unable to walk quite steadily. The glass partition inside the car was open and the chauffeur, looking straight ahead, occasionally said things. It startled her. Nervousness was, as usual, having the effect of inducing a partial deafness; she longed to close the glass but feared to seem uncivil.

'Cold?'

She heard that, all right, and stiffened. It was true, what she had said to Lady Ebban about the position of the governess, but you couldn't, apparently, always remember ... this feeling of being the family guest must be overcome. She was cold, but for some reason unknown to herself heard her voice giving thanks and reassurances. Gertrude or Paula or Caroline would have asked briskly 'Why aren't you in the Army?' and received a civil answer, but one wasn't that kind of person. One kept silence too long and then let annoyance appear in one's voice. Ethelred the Unready ... or was it Ethelbert?

'William the Conqueror, 1066 ... 1087 ... 1100 ... 1135.' Grace's lips moved rapidly and then stopped, she always foundered after 1135, and at the thought of the lessons — *lessons to be given by oneself* — a wave of nausea swept over her.

She would study her text-books, chosen and bought by Mary, that very night, alone, in her bedroom.

III

'Good evening, I am Miss Scrimgeour.' It was the formula she had finally selected for the maid who opened

the front door. It damaged Miss Scrimgeour quite
considerably when a footman appeared. He was impassive before her stammered announcement of identity,
coolly summing her up (oh, stop this second-rate mor-
bidity! He's only a servant. But so am I, and he's aware
of that. Oh, *will* you stop it!) She made an effort. 'I
don't think I know your name.'

'Soames, Miss.'

'I beg your pardon?'

'*Soames*, Miss.'

'And the children, where are they?'

'I really couldn't say, they might be anywhere. Will you
come this way, please?'

He was the only human being in sight, the sole person to
welcome her, if you could call it that. Following him, she
was visited by an insane impulse to ask, 'What are they
like? Shall I be able to manage them?'

Silently they passed along carpeted passages. The house
and its appointments was not unlike its mistress, pretentious and without tradition. The Ebbans were a war-time
creation. Money had been obviously lavished, but there
was dust wherever space offered the drawn finger and the
flower vases were unfilled. Lady Ebban, in the London
flat, sometimes said that what with her social and
charitable calls she had to let the servants rave a bit.

Grace was pleased with her room, large, comfortable,
without personality, but the man had barely closed the
door when she was on her knees by her trunk, tugging at
straps, burrowing in its contents for known and tried
possessions. It was the first new trunk she had ever
owned, what she had coveted as child, as young woman
... the family had given it her as a parting present, for
Gertrude had looked at the Scrimgeour collection of
Victorian boxes scarred with the journeys of bygone

Augusts, battered by the moves from house to house, and said, 'She can't make her début with one of those old arks'. Now that Mary was in two rooms the new trunk held nearly every personal possession Grace had.

Never mind clothes. The photographs, first. Quite soon, bedside table and mantelpiece were humanized; father, mother and sisters must get to know the room as well . . . they and Grace would help each other. The drawers and wardrobe would be more than ample for her hats, dresses and underclothes.

Grace, her head thumping with blunt pain, hovered over the residue of her things; they had got stuffed in at the last moment, objects one didn't need but couldn't quite throw away and to which Mary could give no house room. Grace vaguely handled a china ring-stand, the velvet heart pincushion of the old nurse's. . . .

'*Boo!*'

Her heart turned over and her temples clanged with pain. The doors of wardrobe and coat cupboard were opening. Two children edged out and stood looking at her.

Shock and fatigue sharpened Grace's voice beyond her control.

'What on *earth* are you doing here?'

The girl, conveying alliance to twanged nerves, answered for them both. 'We came to see your things. The last one had funny things too. Mummy says they will hoard so.'

'That was extremely rude of your mother,' rapped Grace.

'I say, Mavis, look at this!' The boy had sauntered to the dressing-table and was handling the ring-stand. 'What *is* it?'

'I dunno.'

'Please put my things down at *once*. What bad-

374

mannered children you are! Haven't you ever been told — ' Grace with dismay heard herself embarking upon a homily and guessed that it would end lamely: already the right words seemed to be evading her ' — that — that it is very badly — bad — bred to worry people's things?' That was over. One really must try and acquire greater command over rebuke. The boy had put — almost thrown — down the ring-stand and called out 'Look at that!' and his sister joined him at the dressing-table. Grace writhed.

'Oh please, you two, leave my things alone.'

'What's *that?*'

'What? That's a pincushion, and now I want to finish unpacking.'

'Mummy's brushes are enamel and she's got lotser bottles. Have you got an enamel set, Miss Scrimgeour?'

'No, I have not.'

'Why not?'

'Because, for one thing, they are too expensive.'

'Mummy's was given to her.'

'I daresay.'

'I say, Mavis, those brushes've got tin on the back. . . .'

'That's silver, you billy!'

'Silver! Whoever saw silver like *that* . . . it's cracked. *I* could bend it.' The boy took the hairbrush in both hands. Grace struggled up blindly. 'Look here, I think you'd both better go. I shall see you later.' She rallied her forces. 'Go along! Shoofly!'

The children didn't stir and watched her, interested.

'What's a Shoofly?' stated the boy coldly.

'It means run along and I'll see you later — oh, will you *go!*'

It was the girl who whispered, 'Come on, she's — ' and shuffling and giggling they went out.

375

She was — *what?*

A disheartening beginning. Grace paced the room. She had not kissed either of them. Odd, that. Nor even shaken hands. Now that peace had fallen upon the room she could lash herself for deficiency, yet knew that given the same set of circumstances she would act again as she had done. She had even forgotten the boy's name, if she had ever been told it. *Are you fond of children?* But that, one guessed, was merely a question off the list, now that one had seen the dust and the house and the children themselves: like the 'Are you an early riser?' that Mamma used to ask house-parlourmaids.

She had been unsympathetic probably, and undignified. Pettish, certainly, but one's head ... the journey ... shock ... but there were, she decided, no extenuating circumstances when you were a senior in command.

1135 ... and arithmetic. ... Mary's books that one must put by the bedside so that one could learn, in bed.

She looked about and found an electric bell, hesitated, and pressed it. The long pause before a maid appeared she filled with self-rebuke and remote apprehension.

'Ah, good evening. I want to know when the children have their supper?'

'Dinner's at half-past seven.'

'But — oh, very well.'

The girl left the room. Dinner? For children of that age? And one had forgotten to ask the maid her name. And did one dress? Grace glanced at her trunk and grew hot. Neither the man Soames nor the chauffeur had unfastened the straps. Faint memories of her sisters' country house visits and of their overheard recollections returned to her. 'The maid put out my pink, though I'd meant to wear the muslin' ... 'It was such a blessed relief to find all the box unpacked for one though we had an awful hunt for our things!' . . . and these people had done nothing at all. But the mistress of the house was absent, that always told. And of course one wasn't a guest, now. (Oh, stop all that!)

I V

. . . and the girl hadn't said 'Miss', or had she?

Grace dressed rapidly for the ordeal below, was ready in a semi-evening dress forty-five minutes before time. She reached for one of the lesson books, found that every sentence had to be read three times and put it aside. The tour of the room ate up five more minutes. There was a balcony and a rustling in the stillness outside that suggested trees and the garden, and she stood there, peering out into the darkness, rehearsing little sentences, of comment, question, appreciation.

'What a coward I am,' she murmured aloud, and went downstairs. She found herself in the hall which, luckily, was lit. On the leather fender the girl Mavis was sitting. She looked up. 'Hullo, what *you* doing here?'

'Well, what are you, if it comes to that?' was the best that Miss Scrimgeour could contrive at a second's notice.

'Waiting for dinner. Din-u-ar.'

'I don't know where the drawing-room is. . . .'

'We shan't be using that unless Mummy comes down with a party. Nursery and morning-room for us. Hullo Derek! I'm just quacking to Miss Scrimgeour till dinner is ready.'

'Do you always sit up for dinner?'

'Hoo! No. But we like it, you get better things to eat, and when Mummy's not here we get the servies to wangle it for us. Look, I've dressed. It cost three and a half

377

guineas, from Harvey's. Is your brooch real diamonds,
or just paste?'

Grace's brain reeled. Here, at the outset, was a problem
to solve by oneself. She temporized. 'Does your mother
come down here much?'

'Sometimes, with Daddy or one of her young men or
people she's trying to hook in for her committees.'

'I hate her latest young man, he's a soppy thing,'
remarked the boy. The man, Soames, came into the hall
and looked humorously at the couple.

'Sound the gong, Soamy, don't just grin. Do sound it
properly or you can say "dinner is served" if you like.'

The eyes of the footman flickered to the new governess,
but she seemed harmless . . . he approached the gong.

I think we all know what a gong sounds like, Mavis.

You needn't trouble, Soames, we are all going in.

And yet, it was the first evening; hadn't one, perhaps,
already exhibited too many prickles?

Indulgence, for this one evening?

And the man was belabouring the gong to the shouted
encouragement of the children. Derek, with exaggerated
courtesy she should have mistrusted, and still clad in
distinctly sullied knickers and jersey, she noticed for the
first time, offered Miss Scrimgeour his arm. She took it,
smiling at the notion, and he whooped and pulled her
into the dining-room at a run.

It was an antick repast. Mavis took the head of the
table which left Grace at another loss, and oscillated
between adult remarks to Miss Scrimgeour and colloquial
disputes with her brother, while the frequent silences
were broken by giggles and glances of alliance, directions
of aped authority to the manservant ('You brought that
plate round the wrong side') while drawing him
companionably into the conversation.

'You needn't wait, Soames,' Miss Scrimgeour suddenly heard herself remark.

'I was about to bring the sweet, Miss,' answered the man, blandly abstracting it from the service lift that she had failed to see or hear.

If they laughed? . . . but with the incalculability of children her order had set them off on another tack.

'No, you needn't wait, Soames. You can go, on — on — on.' They extemporized a chant:

'Go on *Soames*,
Soames, go *on!*'

And:

'Mr. Soames
Went back to his homes
An' ate the dog's bones. . . .'

'Don't be *silly*, Derek. You'd better finish up your pudding and we'll go upstairs.' But the verse-germ had gripped them.

'Go up — stairs
after three bears
Eating *Pears*.'

'That'll do.' Grace rose. 'Who is that maid who answered my bell?'

'What? A maid, a maid, a maid . . . that's Elsie. She drinks.'

'Nonsense!'

'She *does*. Tea-an'-water!'

'Ridiculous child!' Grace strove to infuse a light note of affectionate raillery and felt a fool. Bed was all one wanted of life but one must keep up to the last, whatever that might prove to be. 'Now, it's getting very late, suppose we have just half an hour more and then go off to bed.'

'Eight's *our* bedtime, really.'

379

And it was already half-past.

'We ought to've been in ages ago!'

'Well, so I thought, young man. Suppose you go up now.'

'But you said in half an hour.'

'Then I must keep my word. But you must remember that I'm new to all this — '

It was an extempore appeal to logic and generosity for which the Ebban children, in common with thousands of their like who would probably develop into decent and creditable specimens, were as yet unready. Grace Scrim-geour could not know that it was one of the eternal tragedies of the governess, eternally faced with relays of raw material; seeing objectively a merely transitional be-haviour which she will eternally mistake for a reflection upon herself, coming as she does with the sowing, gone and forgotten at the harvest.

'You must show me all your toys.'

'What, *all* of them?'

'Well, some, then. Do you like soldiers? I used to love them when I was a little girl.' This was evidently a witticism and the boy laughed mirthlessly and uproariously. Grace regrettably followed it up. 'It must seem odd to you, my being a little girl.'

'How old *are* you?' asked Mavis.

'Well, never mind that.' She erred again. 'How old do you *think* I am?' The little girl was kicking the heap of expensive toys round the amazingly untidy nursery.

'What? Derek, look! If you stand on that engine it goes forward and then crushes flat. Try one of the carriages. Let's crush them all.' Then, with the exhausting irrelevance that Grace was learning to expect, 'Mummy says all governesses are the same age.'

All things end. Even the Ebban children were in bed

at last, though Grace guessed that the fact was mainly traceable to the exhaustion of over excitement. Noisy and futile, they had persevered until she rang the bell for Elsie, who appeared, sulky, from her supper, yet curious. Grace edged from the reeking room, closing the door when she heard the footsteps in the passage.

'Elsie, am I to put the children to bed?'

'Why yes, I suppose so. Miss Austen did.'

'I see. They are very difficult, to-night.'

'Spoilt little brats, both of 'em. Give 'em a good slap, I would.'

Grace's flagging partisanship awoke. 'Surely there are other ways!'

'Hang few, ask *me*. Lady Ebban gallivanting about — she don't notice the poor little beasts. Seen her in this week's *Prattler?* Laugh! In a charity tableau. Charity my foot.'

Grace stiffened. 'You'll understand I can't discuss her like that.'

Two servants, gossiping outside a nursery door. . . .

But the girl, as servants are, was pleasantly titillated by the faintest hint of emergency, and, shelving offence, virtually took over the bedding and bathing of the children, roughly efficient, genially abusive, liberal of threat, push and slap, she showed the new governess the stuff to give 'em.

CHAPTER XXVI

I

'*I can always go home.*' But she couldn't. And there was
— with a pang of fright she faced it — no longer a home
to go to.

Hand propping her forehead, Grace Scrimgeour
slowly gave a dictation. So little stood between herself
and the homes of strangers, for ever? A handful of
furniture in two rooms, and the years that might be left
of Mary's life. . . .

The children, crouched ungainlily over their exercise
books, looked up, staring, at Miss Scrimgeour's pallid
face. So, she had made an exclamation? One mustn't
let *that* grow on one . . . or the contemptible habit of
glancing at the clock which would signal the releases of
meals and walks. She had been in her post for an eternity,
a week.

The first morning had passed in a merciful confusion —
the straight problematic issues of lost lesson books, copy-
books, filled and unreplaced. Grace made her neat lists
while the children looked over her shoulder (irritating),
and gave vague or facetious answer to her attempts to
classify their attainment, leading you on to believe they
knew nothing at all and, suddenly, losing the thread of
their own humour, crying contemptuously that of course
they knew *that*. She had started them again at the
beginning, a little abashed and uncertain before her own
decision, when, flicking the pages of history and geography,
she came upon tell-tale sign-posts, of pencilled cross,
underlined fact and "to here' in an unknown hand.

Miss Austen. . . .

The children to her relief and gratification raised no particular objection; in the majority of the text-books there were explanatory notes, answers to sums, for which Miss Scrimgeour was boundlessly thankful. In scripture alone was she sure of her ground. They would have scripture every morning. Dictation and copies, to the governess, were a godsent clearing in a perilous jungle. Sometimes, in bed at night, on walks, at leisure, she even found herself retaining some educational fact on her own account . . . but the strain of fear and betrayal before her pupils robbed it of any human interest.

It was with an irrational sense of achievement that she found she had remained in charge for seven whole days. And she had effected one reform. No more late dinner. A reference to it, kept deliberately light, to the maid, Elsie, a letter to Lady Ebban who answered (this was less pleasant to remember) 'Naturally I look to you to cope with all that kind of thing'. It was all very well, but, Grace worried, might mean trouble for the servants when Lady Ebban came down herself, and for which the staff would unite in blaming Miss Scrimgeour. She need not, she discovered, have concerned herself. The episode went with Miss Scrimgeour's note into the waste paper basket. Lady Ebban had a famous actress to flatter into a special matinée.

Scripture	9–9.30
Dictation	9.30–10
History	10–10.45
Geography	10.45–11.30
	Milk and biscuits
Arithmetic	11.45–12.30
Grammar	12.30–1
	Luncheon

Varied by wild excursions into set compositions, themes recollected by Grace from her own childhood, and the fact that she had never been able to do them herself allowed to make no difference. Abstractions. 'Patriotism.' 'Autumn.' 'Our Navy.' She passed them faithfully, hopefully on. Perhaps children were more intelligent, now . . . perhaps they would prove to *like* composition . . . these subjects must be suitable or one would not have had them set to oneself. . . .

Arithmetic and grammar were, luckily, an almost equal ordeal to teacher and taught. Grace, dismayed, gave up any attempt at elucidating the apparently incomprehensible and learnt to fence quite adroitly with the question that was, fortunately, rare.

'We'll go into that, next time.' (*They would have forgotten.*)

'That shows me that you haven't been following, Mavis.'

'Well, what do you *think* it means? Use your brains, Derek.' Grace learnt also to lean exclusively upon the printed page. The grammar became her bedside book, her ghostly visitant and headache-in-chief. Each day she wrested time for a line to Mary.

Was there any known way of making parsing clear to pupils when it wasn't clear to mistress?

Could Mary find out the address where proper copy-books came from?

And what punishment could Mary suggest in a household where the threat to 'tell your mother' was invalidated by the mother's absence?

Mary sent a new grammar in which specimens (six of them!) of a parsed sentence were laid forth. 'It's dreadfully dull, dear, and don't give it them every day, poor wretches! Indeed, I think at their age — seven and nine, you said? — it is a subject which might very well be postponed. But if I might suggest it, cram it up on your own account. It's probably all valuable. Keep them *interested*. Oh, how important that is! I'm *sure*.

'... punishment is, of course, always difficult, and will *always* vary with the child (or should). In your circumstances the only thing to do is to refuse them play time until their lessons are learnt. But don't trust them too far! A sense of honour is a social sense, as I see it, and does not always appear at that age, tho' its apparent absence, I suspect, is no final indication of character. You will have to remain with them in the room, my poor dear! They *must* learn that you mean what you say. Use the threat of Lady E. as sparingly as possible. . . .'

So, Mary, of all the Scrimgeours the born teacher. Mary, at sixty-four.

II

Grace Scrimgeour remained at The Firs for two years, comfortably mistaking the scholastic rut that she had dug for herself and her charges for attainment; but the qualities which were herself, of loyalty, conscience, decency and integrity were not those that obtained marks upon the written testimonial, and she sometimes wondered why she had lost so much weight, was looking so thin, during her initiation in service.

Lessons. Walks in the woods and footpaths and the waning fear of cattle and lost children. Meals, and a very gradual realization that table manners were now included in her province. The bathing and bedding of obstreperousness that was hilarious without being amusing. Supper and the blessed, blessed reading and letter-writing in the nursery. *Alone.* Bed, and a mental running over of all those duties one might have overlooked: of lights left burning, taps running, airing clothes too near the fender, messages forgotten — and ever with an ear cocked for the cry of fear or temper or emergency from the night nurseries. That window . . . was it fastened?

Dearest Mary — but I'm *certain* I did it.

Letters to Mary. *Dearest Mary, I can't stand it. I am too lonely and homesick and sad. . . .*

Mary dear, oh do let me come back! Why should it have to be me to be sent away?

Letters in one's mind. Planned and never posted.

Oh well, *go* and see after that window, if you won't believe me!

My darling, soon I shall see you again and you will kiss me. A letter (never written), to whom?

And by an effort of will one didn't go to the looking-glass.

III

The Ebban children, their governess discovered with each passing month, had every costly distraction upon the current market; a sand pit (with shed for buckets, spades and tin moulds), safety boats upon an artificial lake of a uniform depth of three feet, a wigwam in a clearing and elaborate Indian costumes, a garden house with sun parlour, pedal motor cars with electric headlights, and swing divans on the lawn. That the children themselves took the whole outfit for granted never failed to surprise Miss Scrimgeour. Such things in her own childhood would have been bliss unimaginable, but even if in the seventies the nursery had been so catered for she felt

these things would not have come her own personal way.
. . . Charlie, now; father would have tried to get them for
him, allowing for the fact that willy-nilly a London house
stems a father's generosity even to his son. Over the
matter of fact acceptance of their possessions Grace missed
the point that the Ebban children were as radically
conventional and unimaginative as the gardens and
house, which had been laid out and furnished by reputable contract. The great point to her about the choice of
amusement was that it was often successful in taking
initiative from herself in devising time-passing activity,
and that, for just so long, she could be free of body and
mind, idle of tongue and limb. Even spoilt children are
natural, sometimes, and even young Ebbans play. . . .

Fearfully, gradually, with smiling protestations and
shoulder glances a-many, Grace Scrimgeour enjoyed the
toys herself. Their location was well-hidden, only an
occasional stooping gardener in sight, and should chauffeur
or Soames appear, it would pass, with them, for a valiant
effort to amuse the pupils. Her qualms and conscience
at rest, Miss Scrimgeour would wedge herself into the
little motor, feel for the pedals and start, the keen air
barely displacing her neat hair that only strong sunlight
showed you to be a trifle faded. A rush down the slope
of the second lawn, picked little ankles revolving like
catherine wheels, and she would reach the level, slowing
down, her thin cheeks pink and eyes enormous with
enjoyment.

Between the playthings, evasion, occasional sharp
directions from Lady Ebban herself and the long-distance
guidance of Mary, Grace weathered a couple of years.
And then Lady Ebban, coached by her husband, 'decided'
upon a preparatory school for Derek and a fashionable
boarding-school for Mavis.

Grace listened to the explanation. It sounded reasonable enough, indeed Mary had thought for months that
the boy was overdue to leave the nursery, but that did not
prevent Grace's secret conviction that the scheme was
traceable to herself as a failure, any more than she could
determine which feeling, of relief or dismay, was uppermost in her mind. It was the sense of personal inadequacy
that drove her to an overwrought leave-taking of her
pupils, believing that their response would be test-case
and vindication.

Derek looked surprised, gave her a limp hand, and
said, 'I'm going to school'. And Mavis: 'Good-bye,
'sScrimgeour. Derek! Soamy says there's gipsies on the
Common!'

The car passed the front door, crunching down the
drive.

Grace stood, once more, upon the platform, trying to
remember it, but of course she was now on the departure
side. The bookstall faced her; after all, she had never
bought anything there. . . . The train drew towards
London and she ran her eyes over her hand luggage,
counting it.

I V

Grace was out of employment for three months: heaven
to be with Mary. Grace had not yet acquired the whole-
time fear of dwindling savings. They had made oblation
to economy by the plan of sleeping Grace in the sitting-
room, but the landlady objected. Very luckily there was
an available room in the house and Arabella gave Grace
a fortnight at Haslemere, would have put her sister up
for longer but that Grace must keep in touch with

advertisements for governesses. It meant either that Grace should retain her room in Mary's lodgings in which case the sight of Arabella became extravagance, or risk relinquishing it and, in the event of hearing of a post, of having no place to which to return. The sisters gave up the room and appealed to Gertrude Randolph to stand by to shelter Grace if the need arose. Gertrude instantly pointed out that she could not undertake to guarantee a vacant visitors' room at no notice and at any time and that the giving up of the lodging 'just for a stay with Arabella' was 'a definite pity'. It left Mary swayed by the justice and logic of the Randolph cause and unconvinced that in the dog-fight of conflicting economies (for Grace got free board at Arabella's) she could possibly have acted otherwise. The matter did not increase the sisters' mutual affection or respect. To her husband, Mrs. Randolph, rasped with pity, exasperation and remorse that it irritated her as the party in the right to be suffering, said, 'Poor Grace is really becoming the most appalling problem.'

The appalling problem, waiting like a tramp to be moved on, recognized only that nobody wanted her except Mary, who couldn't have her.

v

Between them, their married sisters were able to help Mary and Grace with cast-off clothes.

Grace never forgot the day the first boxful arrived, the wonder at what must, incredibly, be a present which was not for Christmas or birthday: the identification of Gertie's handwriting, throwing off the lid, reading of the note. 'I'm sure these will be useful to you.' Mary and Grace, silent, avoiding each other's eyes . . . then the abrupt little light remarks which didn't quite ring true, 'Gertie evidently has mistaken us for the Old Ladies' Home.'

It was Mary who hit upon the saner line that was to be adopted over subsequent bundles. 'How nice of her! That's a good silk, I remember admiring it. I should think that nearly all these things would come in for something or other.'

Grace followed suit. 'Anyway, we can always put them away until we decide what to do with them.'

It was curiously painful. And yet, each sister was internally arguing, they *had* passed on clothes in the old days in Brecknock Gardens and thought nothing of it. A large family of girls . . . then why feel it now? Because Grace, as the family afterthought, had never had the experience, and Mary for over fifty years had been used to her own original garments and the privacy and self-respect of that which is made for your own body and no one else's.

Their acceptance of the clothes had unexpected results. One was the discovery that not to wear them offended the majority of the entire family ('It reflects on *us* so to have Mary and Grace going about looking all anyhow, and then people think that we aren't helping them, which is *maddening*'). The second was the discovery of how the passed-on gown can influence social opportunity. It wasn't *likely*, Mary pondered, that people would invariably recognize it in drawing-rooms of friends known also to the relations, but it was at least possible.

Mary's instinct was for refusing all invitations. It was not until the day that she came upon Grace and saw she had been crying that philosophy took charge. Grace saw herself caught, committed beyond escape to explanation.

'It's the clothes. They make life so *dull*.'

And Mary suddenly answered, 'I've just this minute realized that when one is poor, pride is literally a luxury one can't afford. Like caviare, and seats at the theatre.' But neither of the sisters got as far as the discovery that the wearing of other people's frocks and coats also robs of personality: that with the putting of them on an actual dimming of individuality can set in.

The governess. The spinster. The Aunt Sallies of life and standbys of British serialized humour. Submerged in other people's garments.

CHAPTER XXVII

I

'ARE you Church of England?'

'I shall want your references, of course. They will be returned to you. Never part with the originals unless they are over two years old.'

'I see you have been out of a post for six months. That's rather an interval, isn't it?' The remark was statement rather than query and Grace reddened disastrously.

'Six months and a half, to be exact,' she answered.

'Well, we won't split hairs . . . What was the reason?'

It stung Grace. 'I can't help it if people don't want governesses,' she blurted with the rising voice of ragged nerves.

'I mean, why did you leave it?'

'I didn't. I mean, I *did*, but — '

Miss Collis sat back, waiting. By force of very silence she wrenched speech from her latest client, that truth so factually damaging and against which there was no plea of extenuating circumstance.

'I — was — supposed — not — to — be — able — to — — keep — order.'

'Oh well, that's not so good, is it? Of course you must see that the majority of mothers value that side of things far more than getting the children forward in subjects.'

Grace saw and knew it already. The Tarrant children had, she told her sisters, listening with lips slightly compressed, been exceptionally naughty. Deep in her heart she recognized that actually they were only unruly children that a competent person could have dealt with, and she hadn't been competent, and the reason for that was the now five-year-old episode of little **Derek** and **Mavis Ebban**, and their manner when she parted from them. It had confirmed her self-depreciation. She had argued herself out of it quite successfully perhaps fifty times and it came up fresh as a daisy to confront her nights.

It had worked another havoc: of causing Grace Scrimgeour to begin to believe that, after all, she did not love children. It sometimes seemed to rob her of her secret strength, of all dignity and of the only faithful love of her life.

Yet when, at the Tarrants, she knew beyond doubt and evasion that even if she should marry the union would be a childless one, she had wept in a grief and terror that she would never forget.

It had annoyed Mrs. Tarrant quite a lot.

11

The office was very neat, with walls lined with portable shelving and letters of the alphabet catching your eye everywhere from sliding racks and index files. You were supplied with a stand into which your umbrella could drip, and a chair facing the desk so that you need not stand to answer questions — very-nearly-home touches for which your eye learned to look. You became grateful for things. An office girl of sixteen had once handed one the *Daily Mirror* . . . young enough to be one's daughter . . . granddaughter . . . and one went on feeling under twenty, at appointments. But not looking it.

'And you are — how old?'

'Fifty. Fifty-one in the summer,' Miss Scrimgeour corrected herself. The eyebrows facing her rose a fraction. That would, Grace thought, not mean surprise at the information. Never that.

'Well, thank you, Miss Scrimgeour. There is really nothing more to discuss.'

Grace was outside the door. She had wanted, and meant, to ask outright, 'Have you anything in view for me?' Why not? What was it that always tied one's tongue? The fear of giving trouble. It made one feel guilty. But that wasn't businesslike. The woman was there for a definite purpose and so was Grace. Next time one would be more sensible. Next time ... one always vowed that. Meanwhile one was always outside the door. One ought to be over all this nonsense by now. Miss Collis's wasn't the first scholastic agency one had visited. It was Paula who had put one on to them when private advertisements came to nothing. Gone were the days when one went to situations through private recommendation and with the confidence-giving link of family friendship for one's employer. It was the loneliness of the quest for places that wore one down so, never anyone to go with even if they were willing and free, and of course to arrive at an agency with a friend would look ridiculous.

There were etiquettes. Grace, friendly, confidential, had been rebuffed once or twice, for sometimes she had found herself not the only applicant for the same post. She gave up her turn always, because some of the women looked so very tired and it was important to appear fresh and bright before whoever might prove to be in the inner room. To give way to people older than herself was a natural instinct hard to conquer, for some of them *were* older. Grace warmed to them for that assurance.... But it was mistrusted, this ceding of your turn. 'No

thank you!' the last woman to whom she had hesitantly
made the offer had rapped, suspiciously. Painfully Grace
worked out the reason, gave it up, and frankly asked the
secretary-typist, a nice young woman of the lower middle
class, who had smiled at her. Miss Hammond said,
'Well, you see, the last one in always has the bigger chance,
or thinks she has. First impressions telling is all hokum
really. It's much more often the last one that sticks in
the mind, especially if the client's in a hurry to fix up
quick.'

'I see. I'm sorry. I didn't mean — '

'Oh no. That's O.K. But it's a bit of a bother for us,
too. Gets the names mixed when you're called if you go
in out of your turn.'

III

Always, after an appointment, Grace got into touch
with Paula Randolph: Paula, always kind, cheerful and
(comparatively) young when one considered the sisters.
The action was a sensitive desire to convey to her niece
that she herself was sincerely trying to become independent. Paula listened for years to the incoherent account,
warm of praise at a successful issue, bluffly comforting at
failure or dismissal. Sometimes, she thought, it was
really about time that the poor little aunt learned to
stand on her own feet. Gracie was what you could only
describe as a 'doorstepper', a lingerer in draughts for the
speaking of the last interminable word, a sticky adherent
to the telephone receiver. In self defence one had sometimes to be a shade brusque. 'Yes, I quite understand,
Gracie. You're going on Tuesday and it's settled. I have
the address and now I really *must* go — '

Sometimes, if tired or depressed, one thought of Gracie

in terms of disparaging emblem. 'These mid-Victorians.'
'That generation,' and the fact that one was of precisely
the same epoch made no difference at all. Some women,
and Gracie was one of them, just couldn't adapt; there
they were, oil-paintings nailed securely into their frames
for everlasting, and if they wouldn't cling so how much
more brightly would one's affection glow! Poor old
Gracie ... but poor old all of us, if it came to that.
Money was getting tighter all round, since the War, and
investments failing or falling. One had sickening moments
in which one saw clearly that Gracie, and even Mary and
certainly Queenie would be much better dead. Mother
had said it right out before father and oneself, but mother
was like that. For oneself, one retained a remnant of
semi-honest and untenable sentiment that stopped at
merely thinking the same thing.

Queenie: the family fell with a common spleen that
relieved the lot of them upon her, using the least-known
member for scapegoat, as seemed more decent. . . .
Queenie and her annuity, and then her cottage kept on
staging local collapses which her money couldn't meet,
and they all had to shell out for repairs.

It simply came to this: that if a family conference was
called, you never knew from month to month to what
extent your proudly-won savings were to be called upon
and jeopardized. You couldn't blame mother for being so
irritable. She'd been a trump to Mary and Grace all
these years, an unpleasant one but a trump none the less,
paying out the lion's share. Carry, damn her, had
buckled up and welched on the agreement after the first
two years.

Paula Randolph, in her private room leading off the
large parquet-floored hall in which her dancing classes
were held, pinched up her shingle and absently finished

her glass of sherry. She was going out to luncheon and a matinée with what she described as one of her waiting-list, an ex-officer, as usual out of a job, and with whom, at one time, she had half-seriously considered matrimony. Failing that (his idea) a *ménage*. Marriage was out of the question — too expensive, and the alternative she could not rise to, and said so. One wasn't a post-War flapper and it was no use pretending that one was. So-called free love that was commonly neither free nor love jarred finally and for ever upon one's Victorian foundations and it saved time to face up to that at once. The irony of modern life was that a silver streak or a greying head made no difference whatsoever to men's feelings for one, even the young 'uns. Indeed, genuine girls had rather slumped, it seemed, and the day of the middle-aged attractive woman was with us. In the very nature of things one's male contemporaries were long married, and fathers, or broke, and the young men couldn't afford the girls in legal dalliance if they'd wanted to, and so nobody was marrying at all and one had another glass on the strength of it. In any case, Harry was so hard up that one had to pretend to like ginger ale in case he sported a chivalry he could no longer afford and called for the wine-list. It was probably all a great pity, but then broadly speaking everything was.

Paula refilled her glass and sipped as the telephone rang. That would be Harry, profusely apologetic and after a possible job. She lifted the receiver.

It was Grace.

I V

It shouldn't have been annoying, but was. Paula regretfully heard her own voice sharpening, rising, as the long, familiar story came through to her ears. She interrupted it. 'It comes to this, then, Gracie: that you haven't got the post.'

'Miss Collis didn't exactly *say* I hadn't — '

'T'tt . . .'

Grace buckled at the tiny sound. 'She didn't seem to like it that I had been out of work for over six months.'

'But, my God, you needn't have told her.'

'I — I think I had to . . . about my references, you see . . . the dates. . . .' Paula sulkily conceded the point. 'One doesn't want to give a false impression,' Grace faltered. 'I told her, of course, that I hadn't given satisfaction.'

'Oh, for heaven's sake, Gracie!'

'Well, I hadn't. It would have been dishonest — '

'Oh *lor*! Gracie: you seem awfully keen on running yourself down, but are you equally careful to quote any appreciative things the mothers have said about you?'

'Well, one doesn't do that, does one?'

'Apparently not,' answered her niece grimly. 'I tell you, you can't afford these nice feelings, in business. If you were dishonest or in disgrace or anything of that kind it'd be another matter, but where so *much* hangs on your ability to get jobs you simply must *not* be squeamish. The best defence is attack. You say these confounded kids were unmanageable. Very well then. Breeze in and blow your agency up for sending you to an unsuitable place; say that you were abominably treated — you know the kind of thing.'

Grace murmured disclaimers. 'It wasn't perhaps only that. Miss Collis seemed to want — well, someone *specially* young for the new post.' Not even to Paula could Grace hint at the half-suspected age question otherwise.

'How d'you mean? A girl of twenty-two?'

'She didn't specify age.'

'You mean she asked you yours?'

Grace's voice was artificially cheerful. 'Oh yes.'

'Damned impertinence. Didn't it occur to you that the very fact that she couldn't guess it was a point for you? ... what you tell her?'

'That I was going to be fifty-one in the summer.'

'Oh dear good Lord, Gracie! You make me tired ... listen, I suppose you've dished yourself now, but another time turn it aside or take off five years. You're not disabled physically or mentally and that being so you've a right to your private affairs.'

'I hate lies, Paula.'

'My dear, you can't afford to hate 'em. They're only indefensible if they harm other people. And look here: take my tip. *Don't* tell the aunts, and above all mother, how and why you've lost this job. It'll only make 'em rabid.'

v

Eight more years of it.

Trains to catch, Miss Scrimgeour's luggage scarred with the impacts of wellnigh every platform of every terminus in London. A now experienced preference in stations: Waterloo where the sandwiches were large and fresh and the Bovril really hot; Paddington, where already one of the myriad of porters had once actually recognized her; Euston, unchangeably and warmingly nineteenth-century, remembered from a dozen holidays from Brecknock Gardens; the pleasant woman in the ladies' waiting-room at St. Pancras who kept such a good fire and to whom one could talk until the train drew in; a favourite seat on Victoria platform near an automatic fortune teller that Miss Scrimgeour was always unable to resist, and the discovery that her pointing finger was still arrested at the fortune last promised the governess five months before. . . . Stations that were thus made homely, others that one dreaded: hot in summer, cold in winter, vast, noisy, draughty, smelly. The small recurrent triumph of securing an unreserved corner seat. Even now she still counted and recounted her luggage and parcels, it was in fact becoming a worse habit than ever. Once, twice tallied to her own admitted satisfaction, and then the nagging, mysterious compulsion to repeat the process.

The ancient fear of new posts, new faces and habits was now augmented by a seasoned apprehension as to her own creature comforts and the lacks which might be awaiting her in the new place, aspects of living that once had never occurred to her. Fears of a noisy bedroom, of one too far from bathroom and lavatory, of having no writing-table, of tepid hot-water bottles and dishes that disagreed with her, of stray, possible dinner parties and the absent guest in whose place one might be asked to sit, and the question of full evening dress. Fears that grew stronger with time and were deeply distressing to one who all her life had learned not to give trouble to others (but one would certainly 'speak' about the writing-table), above all disturbing when every passing year made more imperative the finding and keeping of situations.

And the greatest fear of all: the dread of being ill in the houses of strangers, always at the back of your mind, waiting to pounce so that thinking of it brought on those very symptoms your nerves were fighting against and you felt like a screwed violin string that might snap at any second.

The unfamiliar bedroom, the untested, unwilling

service, sulky parlourmaids bringing bowls of soup ...
the lying there aware that above all you had no tradition
of affection in that family and were, save by courtesy and
the impersonal claims of humanity, nobody's business,
your illness no longer an anxiety or grief but a mere upset
to the household, by one who wasn't earning her money
and keeping her share of the bargain.

Inevitably it had happened once or twice. That
children's birthday party to which 'your three' must be
taken, the car arriving from one country house to another,
the pallid governess squeezed in between velvet suit and
pastel organdies of the chattering children and the growing conviction of their chaperon that she was going to
feel ill at any minute. And the catastrophe at the very
table, crackers strewn round the stout iced cake bristling
with pink candles, Miss Scrimgeour in attendance at the
backs of chairs, ready to hand sponge fingers and jam
tarts: the sight and smell of them perversely nauseating.
And she had actually looked forward to the party and the
gala spread and sweets, the entertainment in the cleared
drawing-room and the bran pie — even governesses and
nurses were 'remembered' these days in the distribution,
especially at the Christmas parties.

Gloves, a small handbag, sometimes even the human-
izing bottle of scent. And she had suddenly buried her
face and retched into an exiguous handkerchief before
blindly stumbling from the room. The faces, resigned and
civil of the hostess, disgusted and avidly curious, of the
nurses, and she was set aside like an umbrella in a wrap-
littered bedroom until the car arrived.

That was at the Hallidays, in Berkshire. The Beeches?
Beech House? No, Beech *Hall*.

Twice in the platform life Grace had passed acquaintances going by in trains to their own situations: a tall woman she had had a talk to in the agency, seen now as a quiet, restrained profile of the type that used to be called 'interesting' gazing ahead at the empty seat opposite; a stoutish little body of persevering expansiveness and easy, well-worn facetiae whom Grace had seen in the agency and later met by accident over a crumpet and tea in the nearest Lyons after the interview. They had actually been able to exchange a few sentences of mutual delighted amazement before Miss Milsom's trunk was wheeled into a subway and she had rushed after it. Given security, they would have had nothing in common; now, it was different, and the sight of each other's remembered hats warmed them both for miles as they were rushed in different directions.

You didn't know where they were going or how they fared. Unreasonably it saddened you.

CHAPTER XXVIII

I

ARABELLA GRAHAME bit her penholder until it cracked
and added one more sentence to her letter to her sister
Georgina, crossed it out and sighed. It was maddeningly
difficult to compose, because one was still decent enough
to feel thoroughly mean at what one meant and hoped if
possible to achieve.

'Georgie, my dear,
    'I want to let *you* know first that I really don't think
I can possibly go on with my share of the money for Mary
and Gracie. I feel quite awful about it, but if you'll
stand by me and back me up — '

They had always paired off together, as girls, excellent
friends ever, and their marriages had made no real
difference, only given them more to write to each other
about.

' — and back me up.' Against Gertie and her comments, would be instantly understood by Georgie. It was
of course no use putting one's contemplated defection
upon the grounds of widowhood because dear old Georgie
had been a widow for years and gone on paying up like
a Trojan, and now Clarence was dead they were all
widows together. But widowhood *had* made a big
financial difference and it was no joke at all living on an
Army pension and finding your own rent in a poky little
London flat, since the house at Haslemere was now too
large for you.

Old age was expensive; your confounded body played
you false in a dozen ways that led to the cheque book.

Teeth, and plates that cracked or didn't fit, glasses that fell and crashed into the fender at thirty-five shillings per crash, rheumatism and acidity that called for gallons of Urodonal at twelve-and-sixpence per large bottle. . . .

' . . . I don't know what we all expected about Mary and Gracie, but I for one can honestly say that I hadn't quite bargained for having to fork out *indefinitely*.'

And then there was Queenie and her cottage. One had had to offer to help a bit there with dilapidations.

This letter to Georgina was no impulsive move. For many years one had mentally planned it, inveighing against the injustice of moral compulsion to support others. It wasn't such a large sum, in itself, twenty-five pounds a year, but it 'made all the difference', especially these days, with life beginning to feel insecure, and little credit, financial or social, to be any longer had, so that one was frightened at standing perpetual guarantor to anyone. And Mary and Gracie were one's juniors. . . .

Wasn't it more *honest* to throw in one's hand? And shouldn't a fixed dole promised from a fixed income decrease pro rata with the diminishment of that income? Now that Francis was gone?

One must try and memorize that point, for Gertie.

The relief of Mrs. Grahame at Mrs. Brailsford's reply, a fervent agreement heavily underlined on every sheet, was quenched when, reading on, she discovered that Georgina, fired by her sister's initiative, was proposing to attempt precisely the same thing.

'And you *won't* weaken, will you, Arabella? Gertie is *much* better off than we are — '

Lifelong Tories, the sisters planned the campaign of uncompromising Socialism.

Mrs. Randolph instantly called a meeting, and the available and suitable members of a large and affectionate family met and fought for two hours, scarlet with temper, white with anxiety. Present were Arabella Grahame, Georgina Brailsford, Gertrude Randolph herself and her daughters Paula and Caroline.

It began with an admirable tea, gossip and good fellowship. Marriage was no doubt praiseworthy and certainly necessary, but the old sisters, well over the upsets and social de-rating of widowhood, returned at the end of life to an ease of exchange which matrimony had long denied them and that came more natural to all. Once more, as when upon their girlhood shopping and calling expeditions, they were human beings.

It cut both ways. Gertrude, as hostess, got her blow in first.

'So you feel you can't afford your share for Mary and Gracie any longer, Arabella?'

'I've felt it for a long time. I'm *dreadfully* grieved about it.' Mrs. Grahame felt herself looking foolish and nervous and mean under the still brilliant black gaze of her eldest sister.

'And Georgie has come to the same conclusion', meditated Gertrude. 'Both at once. An odd coincidence.' Georgina cut in hotly. 'One's got to stop *some* time or another, Gertie, and to make out that we're doing it just out of stinginess is *most* unfair and unkind of you.'

'And, after all, Carrie was the first to stop *her* share,' Arabella supported her.

The battle was joined. Carrie almost whined 'I paid up *regularly* for two years — '

'Two years! And we've been paying for — how long? Fourteen? Sixteen?'

'Well really, Aunt Georgie, it was a bit thick to expect me to help at all, I think. They're only my *aunts*.'

'Thanks, my child.'

'Well, you know what I mean, and Bob thought it a bit thick, too.'

'If it hadn't been for Bob getting a thousand pounds out of your grandmother, Mary and Gracie mightn't have been in this fix at all,' rapped Arabella.

'Well, he didn't ask for it! And what we'd have done without it in the War wants telling, and you know how it is with ex-officers; no jobs and his firm closing down. How would you like to have a husband selling cars on commission? You never know where you *are*. Twenty-five pounds one week and then nothing for months.'

Paula said: 'There is something in that, Aunt Arabella.'

'Oh very well, very well. We'll count you right out. But about our share, Gertie, it isn't so much the *amount*, though it's that too, as the way it keeps on falling due. I try and put the money aside in quarterly dollops and then some absolutely unforeseen expense crops up and I have to borrow it, and that means drawing an extra cheque. And if I *do* put the money by it turns out not to be enough because of Queenie — '

'Can't we put Queenie into two furnished rooms in the village? There are sure to be some, with some nice woman . . .'

By the time they had thrashed that out, the rooms in the village were of an extreme comfort and the landlady a very nice woman indeed. Gertrude considered and nodded. For the time, they were all at one, a family habit where Queenie was in question.

'That awful cottage! It tumbles about like an acrobat.'

'Perhaps the owner knew it did and that's why she got it so cheap.'

Paula interrupted. 'Look here, mother, it'll make Aunt Q. miserable if you move her.'

'We can't afford to think of that.'

'Very well. What you've got to do is to find out whether the expenses of repairs will be less in the long run than the rent of two rooms in the village. *If* the rent comes cheaper, I suppose she'll have to go. I've stumped up all I could for Aunt Q., but I think to push her out now is an appalling thing to do, personally.'

'But the repairs, Paula', keened Arabella, 'they hang *over* one so — '

'I know, Aunt A., but I think it's rather brutal of all of you.'

'Well really! If you feel that, perhaps you could prevent it by contributing more yourself.'

'Aunt Georgie, I *daren't*. I don't want to make a promise I mayn't be able to keep.'

'But that's what we *all* feel!'

'You haven't my expenses. I don't charge much for my classes, my pupils may drop off, meanwhile the overhead goes on for ever. Pianist to pay, salaries and commission on private lessons to pupil teachers, rent, light, heating, telephone, stationery, new music — I *daren't*.' Mrs. Randolph thumped with the silver knobbed stick that was such a help in getting her out of chairs. 'Then it simply comes to this: apart from Paula's two-and-six a week and help with Queenie, and the pittance from Mary's investments, and the pound a week and her keep that Gracie gets, I've got to bear the entire burden of their support.'

Although it was what they had hoped, it sounded so bad when stated like that that Arabella and Georgina automatically buzzed unhappy disclaimers. Gertrude killed them. 'Well, I can't do it either and frankly I won't. It's true that my income is more than either of yours, but my expenses are larger, too.'

'Bertie?' faltered Arabella.

'Bertie has taken over Clarence's share, and he jibs a bit at that and one can't blame him,' caustically responded Albert's mother.

'But, Gertie, we *can't* go on . . . not as much, anyway. . . .'

'If *one* gives less we should *all* give less.'

'You can't reduce Paula's contribution, *much!*'

'Too bad, Aunt Arabella. I've explained — '

Thump!

'Well then, Mary must economize further. I always said she had too many books — '

'Couldn't we put her into *one* room?'

'And with the clothes we give her — '

'There's still shoes and stockings, they *cost* so.'

'She can't go into one room, with Gracie everlastingly liable to be out of a post.'

'Then we must put her up between us until she finds one.'

'You know I've no spare room — '

'Then it'll have to be myself, as usual, I suppose. She can have Clarence's room now I've turned over the spare to Paula for a sitting-room.' Paula remarked evenly: 'And about the money side?' She was partly horrified, partly reconciled entirely to her aunt to see Georgina's hands go suddenly to her face, that rather unfamiliar face, weathered by the wear and tear of India to a tan that the English climate had reduced to a yellowish buff.

Tears? Paula casually moved, masking her, but the little, unmistakable sound of grief told her she was too late. Perhaps it was best. Bring things to a head. And when all was said the aunts *were* Victorians. She moved, as casually, to the window. As so often happens when one's emotion is publicly detected, the realization aggravated the outburst, and Georgina Brailsford was sobbing now, quite openly.

'My *dear!*'

'It seems so awful. I *know* you'll all think I'm avaricious and hard, whatever I do in the future. It'll always be remembered . . . the things I've said this afternoon . . . *and* Arabella. She doesn't *really* mean it, either. One's so *fond* of Mary and Gracie. It's ghastly to be thinking of them like this. . . .'

Gertrude said quietly: 'We've all done it, Georgie. I have. Ask Paula. *And* Bertie.'

Again Paula softened. Mother was good stuff, had enormously the qualities of her defects. She said: 'I'm in it too. There are times when I could *hammer* Gracie.' But the indistinct voice went on monotonously, and although the hands were in the speaker's lap now, tears continued to well and roll. 'It's the way it *clips* life so, this having to keep other people, even when you love them: the little things you must go without, you don't notice it at the time, if the things are really trifles, but it *just* prevents one from opening out in a slightly larger way. . . .' She turned to the silent audience. 'When I die — if Arabella and I go before Mary and Gracie, and we're bound to — our pensions stop. And Gertie's got her family, who must come first. My children happen to be married, but Arabella's girl didn't. . . .'

Arabella said: 'I often lie awake, *sweating* at what's to become of her. She'll have so little when I go, and one can't save much, with three sisters round one's neck.' She looked ahead. 'Twenty-five pounds a year for six-

teen years I've given them. That's four hundred, taken
from Vera. . . .'

Gertrude Randolph jerked her head at her daughter.
'Get out the cocktails and sherry. I will say this for the
century: one can get tipsy without losing one's character.'

III

Edges rounded from nerves and temper, cold hands
and feet beginning to glow, the sisters resolved that Arabella and Georgina reduce their contribution by five
pounds each per annum, Gertrude to continue hers at
the old rate and Albert his: that an eye be kept upon
Mary's expenditure and that the Queenie problem be
gone into and a very firm line taken if necessary.

CHAPTER XXIX

I

Miss Collis considered a letter. That Mrs. Wrenne again, wanting another governess. With long, accurate memory she reviewed the number already supplied. Five, in thirteen years. Another baby on the way? When mothers wrote that their houses were 'a little disorganized just now' it usually meant that. Would the woman never stop? And the Wrennes couldn't afford it, if the reports of one's returned governesses were to be believed. Wrenne Polden wasn't, apparently, one of one's star bookings. Uncomfortable, one of these old country seats that, when they weren't converted into schools, Brotherhoods, hostels for hikers, museums, pulled down outright, bought by vulgarians (but rich) or sold brick by numbered brick to America were still lived in by their rightful families and kept up, if you could call it that, on a few hundreds a year with everything scamped. The governesses didn't like it. Cold passages, stairs, draughty bedrooms, low salary . . . children of all ages — a regular swarm in the holidays, back from public and boarding schools. And the village too far from London to make it possible for the governess to journey up to town for a bit of a rest or change, granted she had friends to go to, what with the price of the fare. And then there was the reported business about the master of the house. Flirting. Two of them had declared they hardly liked to be alone with him, half indignant, and a bit of a simper as well. One took that with a grain of salt, as the saying went. The wish was probably father to the thought. One had had a complaint even from Miss Nutley who was quite the lady and knew what was due to her and didn't hesitate to name it if anything wasn't what you could call proper and nice about the place. And really, as she had said, the Wrennes had no title, their seat wasn't a listed show-place with a day open to the public, so you didn't even gain anything *that* way. . . .

The Wrennes were an old family, but it didn't *show* in testimonials. The master of the house, it seemed, was a nephew, and elderly at that, and Miss Nutley herself had passed the remark that it seemed to go more with Eton collars and schooldays, and Mrs. Wrenne was just Mrs. Wrenne, as plain as Mrs. Smith. *The* seat, she said, was up North, and Wrenne Polden, in Somerset, just another family property.

One would like to tell Mrs. Wrenne that there was no one on the books 'quite suitable'. Polite, but sarcastic if you thought it over . . . but there was the fee. Every fee counted, these days, when people didn't seem to be engaging governesses like they used. If Miss Prendergast or Miss Nutley or Miss Spalding came in one would *mention* it, but tell them straight out they wouldn't care for the post. One liked to set aside the best places for those three.

Miss Collis mentally ran through the possibles among the ruck of her governesses, the not-so-young and the less competent — skimmings of the ledger and card index. Not so young . . . less competent . . . of course! Miss Scrimgeour!

No danger there from Mr. Wrenne, poor soul! But was she in a post? A swift reference to cards PRS showed that she was not, and Miss Collis rang up the number of a house in Victoria Road, Kensington. A Mrs. Randolph.

II

Miss Scrimgeour appeared within an hour, but what a Miss Scrimgeour! Miss Collis, furtively peeping at that wrecked face, the eyelids thickened with weeping, was shocked and slightly exasperated. No brightness was bad enough, but getting upset was ageing and Miss Scrimgeour couldn't afford to look even a year older than she was. Her looks were quite impossible to ignore and Miss Collis said: 'No bad news, I hope? Sit down. That's more the style!'

'It's my sister, Mary, you know. She's been taken ill — pleurisy they think, and it means a nursing home.'

'Oh dear, dear! That's bad, isn't it? And the expense, no doubt. . . .'

'My sisters are helping with that, well, *helping*, they are paying for it all.'

'Well, that's a great thing, anyhow. I *had* got a post for you but under the circumstances I quite see you mayn't be able to take it.'

'Mayn't be able to? But I *must* take it.'

'Oh well, that's famous. Only I thought, of course, you'd want to be with your sister.'

The silence in the office began to be discomfiting and she wished Miss Scrimgeour would face her instead of standing by the window, her head bent like — like people at eleven o'clock on Armistice Day.

III

She even omitted to count the hand luggage on the journey to Somerset. People died of influenza and pleurisy, and perhaps if Mary had had more care, better food, larger fires, this wouldn't have — but that led to this crying that was so difficult to stop. One's pupils, now . . . the new place . . . another village. . . . She had been very cheerful right up to the moment one had had to leave the nursing home. Better there, on the whole, than Gertrude's house.

New place, *new place*, NEW PLACE.

If anything happened to Mary (*new children to whom one might become attached*) the old dependence would be over. It would come cheaper if Mary . . .

Village. A nice, picturesque VILLAGE.

I V

In the arched tithe-barn two of the Wrenne children awaited the arrival of the new governess. Their mood was fatalistic and reasonable. 'I think you will find them self-reliant and easy to look after,' Mrs. Wrenne had written to Miss Scrimgeour, before quoting the line to her husband with a bashful grin. 'It makes the dears sound so *God-fearing*,' she explained, 'and that is bound to reassure anyone called Scrimgeour. What does Scrimgeour remind you of, Julian?'

'An unoiled lock.'

'N-no. It's more an isabella-coloured dish-clout being tightly wrung, and when it's only clammy, but not till then, its been thoroughly scrimgeoured.'

The letter had done no more than justice to her children. In common with so many of the present-day young they were also responsible persons, respecting the financial difficulties of their parents, accepting that Basil and Dallas went to Marlborough at the price of corridors of rooms at home being shut up, and co-operating in the matter of clothes because to thrash about in darned pullovers kept Jane at boarding-school, an attitude repaid in the holidays by the three seniors in sinking the age-question and a pooling of amusements. By this system you neither received nor expected bonuses for being eldest or youngest and boasts about either unavoidable condition were discountenanced with dispassionate kicks. Julian Wrenne sometimes harangued his assorted audience ranging in age from seventeen to six upon what he called 'the inherent and essentially unintelligent snobbery of this age-fetish, this lust for a predominance that, so far, can only be based upon grounds purely chronologic', and would conclude, 'It is no more intrinsically admirable of Basil to be at a public school than it is derogatory for our poor Tummy here to be clad in rompers. Basil wore them once — yes! I see the catch, so you needn't shout — and Tummy will be at Marlborough when his brother has passed on into spheres of ill-paid uselessness. It's all a matter of time, and now — '

'— to God the Father and the Son', piped Tummy, hopefully.

'No, pigdog. Let's go to the Shop and lay in some bull's-eyes.' Similarly, circumstances had conspired to make the Wrennes active in domestic affairs in a house for which local service was not easy to secure and difficult to keep. Exacting in its demands, there were insufficient hands for the great mansion always; 'outings', as its mistress optimistically continued to advertise, were 'liberal' and meant an almost illimitable choice in walks down lanes which, if beautiful and characteristic of the West of England, did not ultimately lead to the picture palace, and of entertaining in the conventional sense there was none, or nothing to be counted upon that led to the slipped note from the departing guest. In autumn the larder was impassable with game, but for the rest of the year the butcher's bill was curiously small for such a numerous family, a fact perfectly known all over the village, and if the dinner-service was Crown Derby, the sweets it dished were what the master of the house sometimes called an abomination before the Lord.

v

The walls and arches of the barn had been scoured by time to a uniform silvery grey, its height and structure carrying out the ecclesiastic idea until you heard from within the Wrennes taking their pleasure. Esmé, clutching a lower beam, was practising what she called a trapeze act against the day when she should become the highest-paid star in the circus of Captain Bertram Mills. The act at present was at the stage of many puffing pullings-up so that her head, with luck, appeared over the wood, but her ring costume was planned to the last spangle. Evelyn, upon an upturned crate that had once held Christmas oranges and whose top was lined with dominoes, was giving yet one more encore before a packed audience at the Quebecsteinbert Hall. In the more florid passages of perfect technique and revelation of command over the instrument, the dominoes fell off in all directions.

'Ouff. . . . I can't do any more. This training is very severe.'

'*That* was a Beethoven Concerto. I will now play you a rather nice thing by — by Casabianca. It is called 'Have No More Fear', or something, and is Op 36, dedicated to Madame de — de Stael. I wonder what "Op" means, Es? Would it be "opera"?'

'No, that's all singing.'

'I'd love to compose a real Op. I'd call it Op 11.'

'Why?'

'I dunno. I like eleven, besides I'm it. I do wonder what Miss Scrimgeour's doing. D'you think she'll be eating sandwigs in the train?'

'Too late. She'll have almost got here. Sandwiches is Wiltshire. Or she might have had lunch on the train.'

'That's two-and-six. *We* never do. What worries me is in case she doesn't like the beasts. Nutley hated Bourchier.' The bulldog at sound of his name stirred a twisted ear and looked truculent and self-conscious, like a prizefighter signing an autograph album.

'She'll have to *pretend* to like him. Nutley did.'

'It won't be any use. Bourchier always knows. He was ashamed of Nutley for being afraid of him, weren't you, my stink-bomb?'

CHAPTER XXX

I

'Miss Skinjaw, I've come to know if there's anything you want. The bell is ravver a long way from the kitchen and we're underhanded just now.'

Grace Scrimgeour, her hands in the depths of her trunk, sat back on her heels and looked. A boy of about seven or eight, fair and pink and earnestly polite, but somehow not suggesting shyness. She rose, extending her hand. From the first she had wanted to kiss him, and remembered another small, fair boy, pale and overhandled. . . . Charlie at the same age. She shook hands instead, stiff with shyness herself. 'That is very kind of you — '

'I'm Tummy.' She looked enquiry. It seemed that the actual name was Thomas, and that once in church the vicar had preached upon his namesake, and being a little precious had alluded throughout his sermon to the subject of his discourse as Thumas. 'And then he shouted "and when they got into the upper chamber, Thumas wasn't there", you see. But *I* was, and so I got called Tummy. I'd ravver, if you don't mind — I say, if it isn't rude and like pointing, what a pretty footstool!'

'It's a pin-cushion, Tummy, it belonged to my old nurse.'

'No! Did you have a nurse, in the olden days? That's very intursting. Isn't it lovely?'

II

She lived with the Wrennes for three years and for the first time knew what it could be to be a vital member of a

418

family yet an individual. Tummy alone would have sealed her to them for life. From being a beloved person he became her secret justification and restorer of dignity. She saw at last that the long procession of children who had passed through her hands had not only meant nothing to her but a livelihood and so killed her personal faith of child-worship, but that, the faith once dead, it had been outraged by everyone to whom the satisfactory reply to the routine question 'Are you fond of children?' was a condition of engagement.

Here, with Tummy and Esmé and Evelyn, she became herself and at her most definite. Neither unconsidered junior of a household that took her character for granted without enquiry nor the hired policeman of her latter years, she fledged wings of initiative, even made suggestions for retrenchment and amusement alike. Her gratification and pleasure when they were discussed, thoroughly and dispassionately, and often adopted, was ridiculously great. Physically, she revelled in the large rooms, high ceilings and tall, wide windows that gave you green and growth from every one you lingered by. She thought that the proportions of the house should have been intimidating, but shyness was impossible in this family. There was room and to spare for everything but that. Like any emergency, the dilemma that was the mansion in relation to its staff drew the family and its dependents together. Questions of expense were discussed by everyone, anywhere, and the governess's bogey of her own inadequate wardrobe was exorcized. As for Alison Wrenne, you could not long remain closed to a mistress who, looking like a dishevelled Romney, added the housebooks on both fingers, whispering and drumming as she sucked a sugarstick.

The still recurrent terror of the first days in the school-room was over. The Wrennes, Miss Scrimgeour discovered, were, when interested in any lesson, curious to a degree hitherto inexperienced by herself and before which she constantly faltered, grew pink, and fell back upon her trusty armoury of hitherto successful evasion, until the children discovered that they were making her uncomfortable and desisted with sub-table kicks. Esmé and Evelyn discussed it later.

'We don't want Scrimmy to go.'

'Go? Who said she was going?' Esmé was indignant, though all that morning's trouble had come from herself.

'She may have to if mother thinks we aren't learning anything, like with Miss Prendergast. We all barred Gastly, but that was just accidental.'

'Oh . . . but we don't have to *swot*, do we? I hate that. It's like being made to feel good in church.'

'No, but when you begin to see Scrimmy turning pink, change the subject and I will too, or say you understand, or something. It isn't as though we had exams.'

'All right. I see. But I only asked her about Lot's wife and she said herself that it was a mystery that nobody understood, so that doesn't count.'

'Yes, but you went on hammering about the salt and that's not being a gentleman.'

Together they plotted the peace of mind of the little governess. The system did not always run with smoothness and once Evelyn unguardedly asked 'What is thirteen times twelve?' and catching her sister's accusing eye, 'Oh, it doesn't matter at *all*, Scrimmy', and Esmé had a narrow escape with an overheard remark of her father's. 'Scrimmy,

love, what is "Relativity" — *really?* . . . but never mind.
It all comes back to me now!'

Tummy was, for his sisters, less easy to drill, but then
his lessons, they recognized, were also much simpler than
their own and should be quite within dear Scrimmy's
scope. . . .

He would look up and put a soiled and tentative paw
upon the governess's arm. 'May I be a nuisance, Scrimmy?
but I can't *do* this.' And five minutes later, 'May I be
another nuisance — ?'

IV

For the first time Grace had found pupils who were
deeply interested in *her.* Their questions and criticisms
about the Scrimgeour family she found warming, sensing
that the instant and sometimes unflattering comment was
the worst of the business. Expanding, she even found
herself criticizing a little, surprised at the light thrown
upon her past. Within a year there was not a Scrimgeour
face or history unknown to the children, and where bald
facts halted they invented futures for the family, futures
still profoundly influenced by the known past and the
row of photographs in their governess's bedroom.

'Mrs. Georgina is awfully dashing just now and has
bought a new bustle and is driving spanking greys tandem
in the park.'

'Miss Queenie has been very difficult again, to-day,
and had a scene with the vicar's wife in the middle of
the *lane.*'

'*I* like Arabella', from Tummy, 'she keeps boxes of
chocolates in her boodor and waves the gentlemen away
with a lace hankie. She is very hard to see because she is
a famous beauty. I hope she'd see *me.*'

'And she "goes to the harp" at parties. Onkle-ty blip, onkle-ty blip — '

'N-no, I wouldn't say she had ever been a *beauty*,' ruminated Miss Scrimgeour with a conscientiousness that enchanted her audience, 'more *striking*, perhaps.'

'Oh Scrimmy, you're a darling!'

'And does she accept jewellery from — you know, guardsmen and dukes and then they kiss her door-knocker and shoot themselves?'

'Dear Esmé! she's *an old lady!*'

They accepted it, half dismayed, half invulnerable; to them the essential Arabella Scrimgeour (no husband) was a belle of the seventies, eternally dashing, eternally fair, and for ever fixed in a chosen point in time. Julian Wrenne wrote a limerick to her.

> When the toast of the town, Arabella,
> Broke her ankle on *her* new umbrella,
> A masher from White's in sidewhiskers and tights
> Kissed and cherished the ferrule, poor fella.

Tummy, very red in the face and short of breath, wrote her a Christmas letter:

'Dear Miss Arrabella,

'This is to hope your Xmas will be a plesent one. We think of you a lot from your old admirar *Tummy*.'

Arabella, long primed by Grace's letters, replied:

'Dear Mr. Wrenne,

'Your amiable letter has, in my Seasonable correspond-ence, a *most* welcome place. Sadly indulgent and frivolous as I am, I have acquired a new Silk Gown in the fashion-able shade of "elephant breath" and shall wear it at a select assembly to which I am bidden in the New Year.

'May I hope that your festivities will be enjoyed by all your Family?
'With my cordial greetings to your Papa and Mamma,
'I subscribe myself
'Yours sincerely obliged
'Arabella (Grahame.)
'By favour of Miss Grace Scrimgeour.

V

Above all, they had helped Grace over Mary, for the test of death had come to the Wrennes in the first year of Grace's service.

Mary Scrimgeour died in the nursing home and Grace had not been with her. Unexpectedly, Gertrude wrote. The doctor had confidently hoped to pull her through, but, of course, her age had weakened resistance. All the sisters wrote at length, even Queenie, realizing perhaps for the first time the by-products of exile that were their youngest sister's. Between them — even Queenie had managed a few shillings — they sent Grace her mourning. It was a heartbreak so complete that it brought on what Grace for years had dreaded, and she became an invalid when on duty. Mrs. Wrenne sent a wreath of flowers from the gardens, they made it up in the schoolroom. Julian Wrenne said sadly: 'You must choose what you like to send up, Scrimmy.'

'You are so wonderfully kind. I shall remember what to leave for the Flower Show.'

His hands were on her shoulders. 'Scrimmy, we don't think of the Show — this year, please.' He considered. 'And, look here, Alison and I both agree that it's better to talk about Mary quite naturally. What I mean is: don't

create a bogey of her, let the kids go on inventing their
sagas about your family — what was the one about Mary,
by the way?'

Grace managed a smile. 'That she stole books from the
Times Library.'

'Ah . . . well, let her go on stealing 'em. I always feel
(mind my pipe?) — it's letting people down to pull faces
and lower one's voice about 'em. It's robbing them of
their personality, and setting up a dislikeable image of
perfection. Your sister would probably hate it, she seems
to have been a character. Lots of fun on the q.t. I wish
I'd known her. But, point is, let's keep her going. *Who
dies if memory lives?* . . . there's a lot in that.'

Given the emotional circumstances, her answering look
was very easy to misunderstand.

She sadly saw that she had entered into possession of the
plain woman's sole privilege of looking upon the beloved
without arousing suspicion. Already in need of no humble-
ness she was unable to regard her feelings as a calamity to
herself or the wife in the case. Rivalry was for ever incon-
ceivable. . . . With nothing to gain, it gave the active,
flitting governess a curious boldness that in a younger and
attractive woman would have inevitably made for trouble
sooner or later. The assuagement that was touch . . . little
affairs of pats upon his arm that would pass for a facetious
application of goverential authority . . . his possessions: a
gold mine there, when you were living in the same house.
She had surprised herself at her slyness when, one Christmas, she had by saving for weeks bought a camera for
Esmé, and, very bright and humorously executive, had
shoo'd them all on to the lawn for a family group. Clever,
that. The head of Julian, by Alison and behind Dallas,
had been enlarged in London. The village photographer
might have gossiped. It lay at the bottom of her trunk

waiting, nightly, to welcome her. She would pore over it with a sense of eavesdropping. The tie he was wearing, knotted in just that way on just that day, had been for ever preserved for herself by the pressure of a thumb, a magnifying glass brought out the detail . . . for a few seconds out of his life he had been looking at Grace Scrimgeour of all the women in the world. A man I knew once. My friend, Julian Wrenne. But not for the mantelpiece, this photograph, or at least until some future time when one minded less. Very old age, they say, deadened this sort of thing.

Sometimes, huddled close to her hot-water bottle in its cover of blue wool (material from Evelyn, knitted by Esmé) Grace gave thanks that she herself was not consumed with jealousy of Julian's wife. But, was it natural not to be? One was so inexperienced. Alison Wrenne was (so kindly) one's personal friend and also herself, and if one strained one's ears every night for his steps in the corridor it was with a longing for a sight of him, for a few words, for the wholly unimaginable good-night kiss that was an emotion self-contained and spreading no poison. Each closing down of night was a small death, the certainty of sightlessness for seven or eight hours. One must try to sleep better, 'drop off' sooner. Will-power. Meanwhile, there was always to-morrow and its possibilities; a talk, a different arrangement of words in a sentence . . . odd how terrible was the power for giving heaven or the other place of the exact allotment of words. Choose your words carefully. Grace had sometimes said that to children at English composition. For the first time she knew what it meant.

CHAPTER XXXI

I

SHE realized the reason why Julian's home had not in-timidated her, why, if it came to that, there had from the first been an almost remembered familiarity between its spirit and her own; it was — so nearly — the imagined house of her thwarted girlhood: the English mansion, half Dickensian cheer, half eternal attention from competing men with which picture she had beguiled the Christmas dinners in Brecknock Gardens, a house of log-fire and mummery, eternally blanketed in the silence of its snow. Wrenne Polden even had the flagged terrace, and if the snow was non-existent and the entertainment home-made, it was still the dwelling of the man she should and would have married. Grace smiled a little grimly at last at the men in her girlhood life, if you could so describe them: men, acquaintances who had never desired her at the right age and had left her to blunder to her man, at fifty-four, happily married to a woman whom she cared for and respected and whose children she loved.

II

It was the least characteristic and valuable aspects of Julian Wrenne that roused her admiration; the master of the house in stained overalls hewing timber, in climbing-irons lopping branches in a meadow, gun under arm off to shoot over stubble, exploits which later appeared as fire-wood and dinner for the household. Except as a facet of himself it meant little to her that essentially he was a thinker, shoved by circumstances into action, and the fact that fourteen feet from the earth he would argue the character of Hamlet or the poems of Rupert Brooke with whoever might be standing below was accepted by Grace Scrimgeour as a trimming.

'Mind you, I'm not saying for a moment (*crash!*) that the Sitwells, especially Osbert — heads below there!' and a branch creaking and slashing down, Miss Scrimgeour shivering with apprehension for him and none at all for herself in the air of an autumn morning.

'*Please* be careful, Mr. Wrenne!'

'Scrimmy, don't *palpitate* at me. The vapours have gone right out. It's heartburn and acid fermentation, now.'

III

In her love and gratitude for their trust, the home of which they had made her a member: in payment for their acceptance of her face and uninteresting clothes, she threw herself into the Wrenne's affairs with a nervous passion that ignored the protests of her body. After the death of Mary, one of her sisters had written offering Grace in the name of the family a weekly sum which would enable her to give up working, the offer that would have been heaven a year before and that now, with Mary gone and her energy of heart and limb and brain occupied to the uttermost ounce, she had refused with hasty pen, half her mind upon the next job and a corner of her eye for Julian Wrenne outside the drawing-room window.

In the following months she sometimes thought over Gertrude's letter, guessing at the sense of duty that had prompted the offer, the guilty, universal hope of her sisters that it would not be accepted.

Clear of Mary and Grace (though never quite of Queenie), Gertrude, Arabella and Georgina had made Grace that Christmas quite unusually good presents.

I V

'I do so envy you your nice Miss Scrimgeour, Mrs. Wrenne. *My* gov' is such a perfect lady!'

'I envy myself, too. They can be terrible as an army with banners.'

'Mrs. Wrenne, can you *possibly* lend me Miss Scrimgeour to take the children into Wells to the dentist? Miss Arkwright has started an ailing father.'

'You're coming to my garden party on the ninth, I *do* trust? And bring "Scrimmy", if she cares to. My mother wants to see her again. Miss Scrimgeour's the only woman round here who listens to her stories.'

'Alison, I'm going to make a most tiresome request for which you'll curse me, but it's about this fancy dress party at Lady Ailey's ... my two are going, of course, and Nanny's in bed with a chill and I'm all behind. Could and would you spare me Miss Scrimgeour to help? ... what? Oh, the usual pierrot and fairy queen, but they need sewing ... you're an *angel.*'

Within a three-mile radius there was in time scarcely a countryside nursery unknown to Grace. Sitting bent over sewing, standing at tables cutting out tarletan and satin in an agony lest the material be 'cut to waste' she learnt the politics and appearance of the upper storeys, seeking out (by permission) any old nurse who was still in service, talking to her, taking her little presents in memory of Nana. The work done, Grace would sometimes remain for a floor campaign of soldiers, her signal triumph with the children, and scurry home along the lanes and up the avenue, cheeks and nose pink with cold and pleasure.

Christmas, and the Wrenne's governess included in all communal work-parties in halls and morning-rooms for the making of paper chains, the contrivance of cottonwool mottoes and festoons of evergreen; autumn, and hard work in the orchard, picking, sorting apples and pears; summer, and Miss Scrimgeour helping behind trestle stalls at sales of work on neighbouring lawns, eagerly memorizing prices, less capably pressing her wares — somehow it was usually the woollen or 'useful' stall to which she was drafted. All this, plus long walks, lessons, mending, and even giving a domestic hand when the recurrent staff crisis arose and the local maiden departed sulkily, clambering over a stile with her wicker holdall.

So much had Grace Scrimgeour become a part of the house, so flattered and happy in the way the Wrennes — even the elder boys and Jane — expected her in all their outings and schemes, that it blinded Alison Wrenne no less than her governess to the facts. Grace herself saw nothing beyond a growing dismay, at first a suspicion stifled, of her own flagging powers.

'Jump, Scrimmy! The stones are wobbly here and the water's rather deep. . . .' 'We must run, Scrimmy, we've come a bit farther than we meant. . . .' An all-day picnic excursion, and Miss Scrimgeour to pack the lunch. One concealed the fatigue that had nearly made one vomit, and hurried, jumped, ran. Until the day when, very unobtrusively and falling a little behind the others, she had fainted in a wood.

'Tired heart. A long rest and no worries.' That was the death-sentence of the local doctor.

CHAPTER XXXII

I

'AND your age is — ?'

'Forty-five.'

The head of the scholastic agency looked openly incredulous as she surveyed Miss Scrimgeour, the latest addition to her waiting-list. She wondered for the fiftieth time why these women told such unconvincing lies, while Grace, her conscience frozen, thought of the years she herself had wasted and the situations forgone in the cause of absolute truth when a calculated reduction of age might have been plausible, while now, when her statement of years was inevitably disbelieved, she must continue to make it. The pause was an unpleasant one. 'You look very far from well,' remarked Mrs. Holden, accusingly.

'I have had a nervous breakdown,' answered Grace, off her guard.

'Oh dear, dear, dear . . . and your last post was over a year ago?' Miss Scrimgeour's eyes filled as she assented. Tummy was twelve now, and they had forgotten to tell her what form the celebrations had taken . . . the year before it had been a Grand Continental Circus in the barn . . . this crying was one of the worst features of convalescence. The doctor had been rather sharp about it, advising the patient to take another six months' rest. It was the fainting had frightened one so: one was always fearing to do it again, and give more trouble. 'And I am therefore very anxious to get another place.'

'Is there no possibility of your going back to this Mrs. Wrenne, who gives you such a really excellent testimonial?'

Grace's trapped mind worked quickly. Alison Wrenne, in intermittent, affectionate touch with her, had pressed

430

for her return, had even warned the new governess that the post might be a temporary one. The thought of return to that house had filled Grace with joy and an anxious despair. She knew that in fairness to the family she must never go back, was not up to the demands it entailed; guessed at sufficient of her own nature to be aware that the loving 'and you shall take it easy, dear Scrimmy' was impossible to her character. In the evasions and lies that the securing of work now made necessary at least she would hold to one act of integrity. But the decision, the writing of the letter, had set Grace back for months. Yet, if one told Mrs. Holden, 'the post was too much for me' that would damage one's chances elsewhere. Grace was in debt to her sisters so extensively that a life-time of employment might not work it off; their payment of her nursing home, lodgings and that fortnight at Cromer had been a gift, but always in one's heart one hoped to repay it. And she must work, apart from the honour question. With the conversion of War Stock from five per cent to three and a half, Grace was not only robbed of her last hope of a home life, but that allowance the family had once half-heartedly offered her was for ever impossible. It had affected even the Randolphs, had scared Georgina and Arabella into living together in a flat with a cook-general and morning woman. From now until the end Grace must live in the homes of strangers, her ability to secure that privilege dependent upon health, quickness of ear and brain, activity of limb and durability of sight. You had to read so much print when you were in the teaching world. Three-quarters of the women waiting in the agencies wore glasses. It was partly age, of course . . . but luckily spectacles and pince-nez were easily removed and concealed outside the door in one's handbag.

She managed to say, 'The air didn't suit me,' and saw

431

too late that the statement was a false move. Governesses didn't complain of the quality of the climate. It gave them a reputation for being 'difficult'.

II

In the end it drove her back to Miss Collis. She had shrunk from application to her old, first agency because of her appearance, hoping illogically, as she had hoped in her youth, that her face to a stranger would appear fresh, and younger and healthier. Once again she was forced back into the reverse consideration, that a known face would be remembered as it used to look, in this instance four years ago.

Miss Collis condoled, with only a vestige of an impatience with which Grace, raw with self-contempt, was in sympathy. But — three years in the last place . . . this super-testimonial from that Mrs. Wrenne. . . .

Within ten days she had 'fixed up' Miss Scrimgeour in London itself. Mrs. Bullivant, in Brunswick Terrace, Kensington.

III

'11 Brunswick Terrace,
'Kensington, W.8.

'Dear Madam,

'I am sorry to have to tell you that Miss Scrimgeour is leaving me at the end of the month.

'In my opinion she is completely unsuited to teaching children on modern lines. One of my daughters, as I wrote you, is studying for her Matriculation and with this schedule the governess you have sent me is unable to cope at *all*.

'I agree that her reference was an excellent one. In the

432

circumstances it is difficult to understand how a completely unqualified and uncertificated woman secured it at all and I can only imagine that Mrs. Wrenne's was a nursery post.

'What I require is a young and cheerful woman, and one if possible with a college education. . . .'

I V

Miss Scrimgeour's taxi rolled slowly away from the quiet road of broad-pillar'd houses in the direction of Kensington High Street.

She had telephoned her niece, Paula, two days ago when the blow fell, that which was also release from daily terror of detection and which no evasion or show of authority could surmount. The elder Bullivant girl was sixteen — demanding, a worker with a goal in sight that one had never had oneself, she would pass her examinations but not under the coaching of Grace Scrimgeour.

The taxi was slowing down again and every delay sent up the price of the fare; Miss Scrimgeour leant forward anxiously, peering at the dial. Paula . . . she had been (very understandably, one recognized it) a little crisp over the telephone. 'Oh . . . yes, Gracie . . . put you up? Well — I — oh, I'll *manage* it . . . but could you give me some idea for how long?' And Grace couldn't.

She mentally ran over the day ahead. Luncheon, and settling into her room in Paula's little flat, taken after the house in Victoria Road had been given up; unpacking, and perhaps some little tasks to be done for Paula; when you were rather often an uninvited guest it looked better to keep on the move . . . an early bed if it was convenient, then to-morrow and its visit to Miss Collis who would possibly be annoyed with one about Mrs. Bullivant. It

was only occasionally in flashes that Grace knew terror
of the future.

That night in the small, strange bedroom, she stood
with the photograph of Julian Wrenne in her hand, explaining to it her inability to keep the Bullivant post,
whispering because walls were thin of her sick longing for
a settled life of free will and privacy. But to-night the
photograph had nothing for her. She had waited for that
moment all day, and over-expectation had defeated its
own ends. The print was becoming smeared. Copying
from an enlargement was expensive. Esmé would have
destroyed the negative. Grace put it back in her trunk.

v

Miss Collis was annoyed. These misleading testimonials
were maddening and ultimately did the agency no good,
but even she demurred at suggesting the only situation at
present on her books that was suited to an unqualified
woman. Mother's Help. A Mrs. Green in North Kensington. 'You may find it not quite what you are used to,' she
forced herself to say, remembering the shrill, offended
tirades with which the place had been refused.

'I'm surprised, I'm sure, at your offering such a thing to
a lady,' Miss Rivers had said.

'Rather insulting, perhaps,' insinuated Miss Wilson.

'I'll take it, of course,' said Miss Scrimgeour.

VI

A trampled street off Portobello Road, a cul-de-sac in
a run-down locality looking deceptively quiet and fated to
be overrun with brazen-voiced children who put lighted
squibs through letter-boxes on the fifth of November, and

434

otherwise with peg-tops, conker, hoop and ice-cream
cornet followed the seasons.

Mrs. Green herself opened the door. The shock was
mutual. It was Miss Scrimgeour, finally, who put her
prospective employer at her ease, as she looked at the
grenadier with yellow hair and unfriendly eyes.

'I'm Miss Scrimgeour, from Miss Collis's agency.'

'She sent *you?*'

'Yes.'

'Well . . . I don't know, I'm sure. What I wanted — it
was an advert. in the local paper, but you know what
agencies are; snap you up and put you on their books — '

'*Do* they?' answered Miss Scrimgeour, who had haunted
agencies for over twelve years.

'Come in, will you?'

They were in a room separated from the adjoining one
by open folding doors; in spite of its proportions it contrived to be fusty and inadequate. 'Can't get straight easy
with all the children about. Torments for muddle. Well,
as I was saying, I wanted a strong capable girl — '

'I see. I'm not that, of course, but I should try to give
you satisfaction. I have a very good reference.' She began
to grope in her bag for Alison Wrenne's letter but stopped
as the woman cut in.

'Oh, references! We all know what *they* amount to.'

'You doubt my word?'

'It's elbow grease I'm out for and to have baby kept
quiet. Well . . . I haven't heard of a girl, they all want to
live out, these days, if you care to try it. One thing: I
hope you aren't finical about your food?'

'I hope — '

'Ten shillings a week.'

It was half what Grace had been receiving but every
shilling must be hoarded. Her Post Office savings book

had long been her Bible, handled with pride and reverence, read with far more comfort. It lay in the bottom of her trunk under the photograph. Two things to live for. Gertrude Randolph had left her fifty pounds and it had all been swallowed up by doctors, medicine, tonics and lodging in that year of enforced leisure after Wrenne Polden. Grace had triumphantly made it over to her sisters as payment for her cost; it had seemed a big sum to her, but, Arabella privately lamented to Georgina, was only a drop in the bucket, even without the expense of Gracie's illness. Ten shillings a week for a year, not the price of a furnished room . . . but of course Gertie had her children to consider.

VII

Hastily-cooked food, chops lying tepidly in their fat, puddings dried by too high a flame, vegetables put unwashed into saucepans and served sogged with water soon accounted to Miss Scrimgeour for the pale peevishness of the Green children, a symptom that their mother to a chorus of howls cured with cuffings and threats, the baby, heavy and resigned, on her lap at meals, fed with 'tit-bits, like a little man'. Mr. Green, a clerk in the offices of a gas company, off-hand with his wife's new woman at introduction until he heard her speak, then flattening himself awkwardly against the wall as they met about the house, calling her Madam — it slipped out, once, and she was merciful to his hot, resentful confusion.

Fires to lay, a job that had, so far, not come her way and with which she struggled, at night in bed planning the business as a General his campaign. To-morrow one would try less paper and the wood *on* the cinders —

Beds to make, and here she was an adept, from the days

with Mary in Ramillies Terrace. 'You don't want to make
such a job of it, we shall be all night, this rate. Just
smooth the undersheet and pull up the clothes.' But Miss
Scrimgeour continued to make a job of it. The back door
to be answered, and the colloquial greeting of the tradesmen's boys withering on their lips at sight of the small,
grey-hair'd figure, at her quiet thanks. She glowed at a
friendship with the baker's lad that sprang from his shrill
carolling of a song.

> 'OW, there's nuffing half so sweet in life
> As love's — young — dream'

shouted the youth as he sorted loaves with a grimy hand.

'I remember that so well,' remarked Mrs. Green's help,
'my sister used to sing it.'

'Ar? Got it on the wireless. Them ole Variety stars.'

'Oh *no*. It was long before the wireless, about 1880, and
it wasn't a new song, then.'

'Go on!'

His name was Arthur Blundell, and Grace came to look
forward to his visits. Sometimes they would even sing a
little together, in the area, Miss Scrimgeour very pink and
smilingly accepting correction. Marketing in the High
Road in the afternoon, and Grace with a string-bag, a list,
a folded note (if one lost it!) and the baby's hand-carriage
to push, and the flittings from counter to doorway to see
that he hadn't been stolen or got upset, so that you kept
on losing your turn; and the battlefield that was each
crossing, and the problem, never solved, of hauling the
baby-carriage bump by bump up the front door steps, a
gymnastic feat that left you a little giddy and started those
palpitations which went on sometimes for an hour. But
the worst feature of this post was the lack of privacy by
day or night, for here Grace Scrimgeour must share a

room with an inquisitive child, mercifully at school for long tracts of the day. Against her Grace learnt to keep her trunk locked. It was the one familiar object in that room, its key her amulet. And with it all, Grace could not feel that she was satisfactory. There were times when she knew herself flagging, letting go here and there in exact perfection of performance ... the day she pared the potatoes without rinsing them, made a bed in the Green manner ... trifles which, bringing a fractional immediate ease, nagged her half the night. Sometimes over larger affairs it was noted and exposed, but Mrs. Green did not guess the instinct that drove her employee to conserve every ounce of energy, nor Miss Scrimgeour's realization of the sacredness of the physical body that, working, could earn money.

VIII

Grace had concealed the nature of her work from the family through some twisted pride in her unchosen profession and a desire not to bring home to them too sharply her present way of life. It would look like begging — 'You had better not try to see me at this place. Mrs. Green does not care for me to have visitors,' she wrote to sisters and nieces.

Two invitations came at Christmas, from Arabella and Georgina to a little family dinner, and from the Wrennes. The temptation to accept the latter nearly defeated her for all it would mean of affection and beauty, decency and reinstatement, if only for one week. She handled her savings book, mentally rifling it, and put it away. There would no doubt be a greater claim on it than love.

Paula would lend her the fare, but Grace was sickened with indebtedness, of loans that had, in the end, to turn into gifts.

At night and in her spare time she must contrive her little, shameful presents, *must* withdraw a few shillings. While you could make a present to anyone you were still in the running as a human being. Julian only a card, for 'ladies don't make presents to gentlemen', it had been one of Mamma's axioms. Grace practised her message to him on paper. With affectionate wishes — thoughts? . . . with my affectionate wishes, Scrimmy. One dared not use the word love, but wrote it on the scribbling block.

A few sweets for the Green children — anything, but in the newspaper shop at the corner her sharp eye, days ago, had spied a toy left over from heaven knew what of inertia of window-dressing or changing juvenile taste, among the net stockings, jars of sweets, packets of cigarettes and strings of tinsel; a glass ball containing a castle which, when shaken, became softly smothered in snow. Toys of imagination however cheap always enchanted the Wrennes, and their parents.

Her savings book depleted, Grace almost danced along the pavement. It was quite amazing how thirty shillings in your purse could change the face of a day, how, when you were down to a few pence from the weekly dole you allowed yourself, flatness set in from the moment of waking, and creeping inertia that affected spirits and output. Lordlily she scanned the shop windows.

Her provisional acceptance of her sister's invitation had, after all, to be cancelled. Mrs. Green and the family were going out for the day, 'and I always say it's no holiday to *me* if Baby comes along too'. She did not absolutely insist upon her help remaining at home, she merely trusted in the inability of a lady to stand up for her rights and no nonsense. Her confidence was not misplaced. But Miss Scrimgeour might have a glass of port and a fire in the bedroom.

Grace would have no family dinner and perhaps it was as well. Now that Mary was gone the spirit of Christmas had gone too, and Grace's position in this house could cause embarrassment to her hostesses. It would, she consoled herself, be a staid little gathering, of her elderly nephew, Albert, Paula if she was willing to please her old aunts, and Caroline and Robert very doubtful while there was a restaurant to fling about in. Young people — Grace still thought of her great-niece and nephew as that — could not, it seemed, suffer the old, and as for *their* children one never saw them and the bond was now intermittent hearsay.

But Grace would have her Christmas. Locked in her trunk were the package and letters from Wrenne Polden, an envelope with Tummy's tipsy handwriting on the top (even now he couldn't form a neat R in spite of the copies one had set). There was no letter from Julian — from Mr. Wrenne — but there would be a message inside Alison's. One would open them all on Christmas night when the house was empty and quiet, and put out the photograph with a sprig of mistletoe, bought for that purpose, against it, and one must keep an ear alert for the return of the Greens. . . .

IX

There were a few street revellers on Christmas night whose strident cries and singing almost roused a woman who had overtaxed even her power of joy at certain messages of remembrance. She slept with her head on the table while in its cradle a pale baby drowsily complained.

A fortnight later Miss Collis, openly impatient, was saying: 'It really begins to look as though you ought to try for some lighter post, Miss Scrimgeour.'

CHAPTER XXXIII

I

OLD Miss Widdowson enjoyed her food and ran her eyes over the menu while the head waiter dabbed with suggestive finger and another waved a hand facetiously servile at her unresponsive Pomeranian. Micky, Miss Widdowson's companion had to admit, was at least well behaved, he had not the character to be anything else. Silent, bright-eyed and querulous, he accepted the decorous antics of a servant. The animal was accustomed to eating in public; so by this time was his mistress's companion, sitting there wishing that the choosing of the meal might last for ever. When it was selected, the embarrassment, never to be overcome, set in of raising one's voice in public so that people heard and stared and—an agony which gave one dyspepsia for the rest of the day — smiled slightly and turned to table partners with undertoned remarks. The companion had not a good 'deaf' voice and knew it; when she raised it it became thin and shrill and made her cough, so that she had to keep a box of lozenges in her handbag. If one could eat in peace! If one could eat in *peace!* The food was so good, so wonderful after landlady's cooking and Mrs. Green's. But that wasn't what one was being paid for. One was here to crack one's voice and get throats sore and dry and to become conspicuous and be ever so slightly ignored by waiters. If one could train oneself not to *mind*. . . .

'The restaurant is very full to-day.'

'Eh?'

'The restaurant — h'm — is very — '

'What? I didn't quite catch.'

'Very full. The *restaurant*. Plenty of people.'

And even then Miss Widdowson had turned away to the waiter beaming at her side.

'I hev remembered what Micky laike. Dere! Goodt dawg. He look at me, zo, an' know what I bring. Hier-komm, Micky!'

He got half a crown, always, and the head waiter heaven only knew what. Her entry into some restaurants was the cue for clustering attentions, one man to shoulder Micky's cushion and lead, another to carry the dog, a third to find a good table with the minimum of delay and a fourth hurrying up for an informal chat, with cheerful stoopings of all to her deafest ear. Somehow the Staff invariably contrived to make Miss Widdowson hear the first time, her companion worried. The very fact of sex seemed to act as a conductor. Already Miss Scrimgeour was beginning to talk too loudly to everyone, herself, and people didn't like it. Sometimes Miss Widdowson had her better days and would complain, 'Not so loud! I'm not quite deaf! It's only that I can't always catch what you say.' It was vanity, Miss Scrimgeour realized, in time. Deafness, it was to be understood, was not an accompaniment of age, but a slight misfortune like an ill-shaped nose that might happen to afflict anyone. The pathos of the re-curring pageant escaped a Grace Scrimgeour consumed with her own problems. She did not even guess at the gnawing loneliness of an old woman whom life had reduced to pleasure in recognition by waiters, who was bereft of all but creature comforts. In a situation essen-tially identical, it occurred neither to mistress nor com-panion to make friends with each other. Served at every hand, they toiled and flitted the great house in a stately London square.

Officially, companionhood is light work, clean, dignified, healthy, admirably adapted to unskilled and necessitous gentility and making no inroads upon anything but that easily ignored abstraction, the nervous system. It is a form of occupation that by its nature renders it scarce and overcrowded; it is almost inevitably in the gift of the elderly and the ailing, of age with its caprices of sudden, irrational demands and dislikes, its dismaying habit of death.

The employment of Grace Scrimgeour gradually became casual. The agencies were filled and refilled with companions, ageing themselves, and softened by comfortable living, perkily cocksure, some of them, of an immediate similar position, and, flown with savings, refusing the firm offer, only to return in a week, a month, pallidly apologetic, explaining, 'Miss Collis had misunderstood . . .'

Miss Scrimgeour, willing to accept any offer, was often able to pick up their leavings. One post, of temporary reader and shopper to an elderly globe-trotting American, took her to her old home in Brecknock Gardens.

By closing eyes and ears to the murmured conversation of the guests, shattered by the shrill cries of the boy pageing wanted names to the telephone, she was able for a few seconds to fancy herself back in the bird-fluttering drawing-room, with the rustle of *The Times* and *Morning Post* translated into Mamma's perusal of the fashion-plates. Over by the window nearest the balcony now stood a desk with writing materials, bent to by an elderly retired Colonial official. That would be Mary, making up the house-books.

Grace's employer had the bedroom once occupied by Queenie and Agatha. Grace herself was allotted a smaller room that structural alteration to the house had mercifully rendered without a past; as far as she could judge it would be one of the maids' rooms cut into two. More than once Miss Scrimgeour was within an ace of blurting the truth to Mrs. Elmer Morse: 'I used to live here, it was my home,' and bit back the confidence. One mustn't seem to be boasting, it might be so regarded, instead of the aching desire for reminiscence that it was. Mrs. Morse was imperious and demanding but kind-hearted; an admission of past estate would seem to hint that one only came to her in desperation, and the ideal companion gave the impression, always, that compatibility had drawn and kept you by her side. . . . The page had bustled in again. 'Mrs. Faulkner! Mrs. Faulk-ner.'

Just touch the bell, Mr. Elmslie.
Sandwiches, Major? I've remembered your favourites.

Some of the seated visitors, abstractedly turning the pages of *Punch* and *Tatler*, may have spared a second to wonder what ailed the little grey-haired woman who had suddenly put her hands to her eyes.

III

Even intermittent employment did not always carry with it the security of board and lodging. Grace began, only a little anxiously at first, to live upon her savings. When the space of time between one post and the next was protracted she had to appeal to Paula Randolph. Caroline and Robert could spare neither space nor money for her and Albert had gone to live abroad in a warmer climate, though a desperate letter to him had produced ten pounds. She had even wildly considered an appeal to Queenie, but Queenie had been forced to give up her cottage, and, now too old to live alone, was in rooms in the village.

Grace was sixty-five. Her dividends had shrunk to a few shillings a year. She had seven pounds in the post office. She was too young for the Old Age Pension and too old to earn a living wage.

IV

It is possible that Paula Randolph, business woman and temperamentally realist as her mother had been, bore the heavier burden of fear. Her aunt Grace, she guessed, was of an epoch bred to expectation of dependence and succour, and against all evidence would continue to believe in the social fairy godmother. 'It looks as though it boiled down to us two as far as helping Gracie is concerned,' Paula had written to her brother, Albert; 'you know what Bob is, always in and out of jobs. Frankly, old dear, I'm in a funk about the whole cursèd business.'

Albert Randolph, entrenched in the South of France, was full of common sense. It was very distressing about poor 'Aunt Grace', but he was opposed to the promise of anything of a permanent nature. At any moment circumstances might arise which —

He would not forget his aunt, was indeed enclosing a cheque, and was there not some pension or fund for just these cases?

Manlike, he failed to appreciate the anguish of uncertainty from irregular payment. Paula must keep her eye on the calendar and make good Grace's rent and chance reimbursing herself. Only one year younger than her aunt, she had given up the dancing school for some years. Actually, dry-rot had set in with the swamping of London by the Russian ballet, a horde that was to breed its mob of imitators from what *The Dancing Times* called the Madame Bunkums of the profession to those who knew their job and set for ever a standard that was to weed out the unfit. The indulgent imbecilities of the 'fancy' dance had vanished, and the children set to barre and centre practice, learning for perhaps the first time the five correct positions for arms and feet. Working with the best material in the world, the experts took a hand, and even Pavlova had opened an Academy at sixty guineas a term. Neither Bunkumist nor expert, Paula sensibly threw in her hand. Her income materially reduced by a War lasting until 1918, she was living upon an income derived from paternal foresight dating from 1840.

Pity, she discovered, was not akin to love, and she began to dislike Grace Scrimgeour enthusiastically. She envied the male detachment of her brother-in-law, Robert Bridgewood, as reported by Caroline. 'Keep right out of it, if you're wise. Once these helpless sort of people get their claws into you you'll never be free of 'em.'

His wife looked upon the advice and saw that it was good. The maid was told: 'If a Miss Scrimgeour rings up, I'm out.'

Sometimes Miss Scrimgeour called in person, and Mrs. Bridgewood was not at home. Grace, still faithfully trying to 'keep in touch', did not know that her relations now dreaded even the sight of her handwriting.

CHAPTER XXXIV

I

FROM her furnished room in Pimlico, Grace Scrimgeour, after setting it in order and laying in what stores she could afford, waited every day in agencies. Her reason had ceased to hope for another suitable post but instinct loyally kept up the fiction that she was employable; her conscience in any case would have goaded her to the offices. Also, waiting to be interviewed and the walk there and back filled in the day. Time had become the enemy Grace grappled daily to kill. Living in one room, deprived even of the feminine prerogative of domesticity: eggs do not take long to boil nor sardine tins to open . . . you made the bed and swept and dusted; you absurdly looked forward to the shopping and to what the chances of the morning might bring, to a word with some fellow housewife — a real one with a perambulator, to being served by that young man who always had a smile for you. You went home to a room very dreadfully still and waiting for your initiative, left as you had left it, making a great business of putting the loaf away in its crock, the butter in its dish, the sardines in the cupboard, then, assembling best clothes, came the agency, and back again, virtuously tired. Grace would lie on her bed watching the clock for it to be time for a cup of tea. If one broke the rule and had it at four o'clock one might be tempted to have more at four-thirty, and tea was one of the heavy items, like shoes. Other people's shoes seldom fitted and nobody seemed to give one stockings, it was always hats and outworn jumper suits. Very, very kind, but it did make one

447

look rather odd at the agencies, so smart about the head, so run-down at heel . . . an effect one had observed about the others, sitting waiting their turn. The high-light was half-past seven in the evening. Then, winter or summer, there was the reading of the newspaper to look forward to, with even the politics devoured to spin it out. That, and the postman who always might have a letter for one which would flick this nightmare back into its shades. Then bed, and a conscience inevitably silenced. Yet even bedtime tended to become earlier and earlier to make the day less long, and in winter to save on light and heat and stun the craving for something new to read.

The summer nights were pretty bad, needed a lot of mental effort to get through. People walking in couples or groups hurt one so. Grace wondered exactly what would happen if she leant from the window and called 'May I come with you?' Nothing sensational, she knew; plenty of these pairs would consent, only a little taken aback, and companionship might develop. People were so kind, if you had the courage. But you hadn't, and never would have. And yet, association with them was now so perilous. Grace had found that out, even with old, rarely met friends. It was the money question. 'Just lend me sixpence, Gracie, for the waitress', and you hadn't got more than fourpence with you, every penny mortgaged. 'Let's go in and get some sweets' . . . 'We must meet soon; we might go and have lunch somewhere', and Grace, longing for the meal and the meeting, refused, always, because it might after all mean that the friend meant you to pay for yourself. Sometimes a friend would say, 'Meet me at Leicester Square tube', or some other point distant from the lodgings, and Grace evaded that as well ('rather busy just now, arranging about another post'). She knew herself unable to walk to and from the rendezvous. If people would only *think!* But the whole point was that they mustn't guess, because that ignorance of theirs kept one still their friend. . . . Grace had already proved the general truth of this, had eagerly made acquaintance with a young woman in the room above her own.

II

From Daisie Lemoore Miss Scrimgeour had received what a woman more worldly-wise would have recognized to be a liberal education; being Grace Scrimgeour, she listened rather than learnt, side-tracked by the cheerful manner in which information was conveyed, as a child nervous of a kitchen mouse will appreciate the wolf in a fairy tale.

'It's the rent that gets you down,' said Miss Lemoore. 'When it gets to *that* point I just walk out while Mother Push is in the kitchen. Police can't nab you for that, not without the landlady gets a lawyer's letter and ten to one she won't take the trouble.'

'Never take digs near a big railway station, it brings a very low lot, and the landlady's on the extra look-out for her money.'

'I tell you: when I want a square meal, know what I do? I go to a restorong where there's two floors. On the ground I have my dinner, see? then I go down to the smoking-room 'n have a cup of coffee. Two checks. When I go out I forget the dinner one an' pay the coffee into the desk. When I want a bit've something to eat here I go to the grocer an' buy half a pound of something cheap and then take off the counter. You wooden be*lieve* how easy it is. Get done sometimes, though, if he don't have to go away for what you want. Got a pot of that patty, yesterday. Kind of liver paste, French. Seven-and-nine, I ask you!'

To Grace, the Lemoore was not an example of what in last resorts her own sex can be brought to, but an isolated and entertaining eccentric. Miss Lemoore, misled by Miss Scrimgeour's neat room, language, face, voice and manner, paid instinctive tribute of faith in the little woman's silence about her own exploits and began to borrow money.

Grace helplessly gave the first requested shilling, 'for that bloodworthy old meter' and returned to her own room to rail at herself in terror. The shilling was given back but not for ten days of suspense, suspicion and worry. The gas often gave out when an egg was still nearly raw. She refused the second loan, nervous before a potential debtor. After that, she resented and avoided Miss Lemoore. People without money were a menace.

III

The commonplaces and very decencies of life became personal enemies. If you cannot walk to relations the S.O.S. for money hangs upon stamp or telephone call, and a penny buys a roll of bread. One morning she discovered that her tablet of toilet soap was used up. She had to wait until the arrival of Paula's cheque next day to buy another.

IV

She discovered odd and unexpected sides to loneliness: the fact that, of a large family, and later, in service in prosperous or full households, the letter-box of a lodging-house, frequently empty, could depress her, and that now

of no fixed address, she herself no longer received catalogues and circulars. She learnt the craving for a pet, but
you can't condemn an animal to one small room and the
hazards of the street; also, dogs needed licences and birds
seed and sand. Suffering for company she must deny
herself such chances as offered lest her hoard be threatened
or worse, her needs exposed.

She missed, even now, a voice of concern, reproof or
alarm to meet her on her return.

'Gracie! You're sopped through!'

'Did you remember to take an umbrella, dear?'

'Run upstairs and change at *once*.'

The absolute silence of her room reminded her that, at
last, she was her own mistress, free to catch chills and do
the foolhardy thing. In a kind of defiance of it she would
sometimes pull off her shoes and deliberately omit to put
them by the fire to dry.

v

She had one adventure in that year. It swooped upon
her when she was least prepared, showed her for all time
that the resignation she had believed herself to have won
to was a delusion, that Grace Scrimgeour, a tame and
colourless thing dead to world, flesh and devil, still had its
terrible resources of emotion, those feelings that belonged
to the young and the charming woman. Julian Wrenne
had met her head-on in a street near the agency from
which she was returning, thinking of some news picked
up that afternoon from another woman disappointed of
work — some Organization that gave pensions to people
of her own class who could not find employment; a woman
whose desperation at failure had contorted her face and

driven her to an outburst which Grace hoped that one day
she herself could forget . . . a gentlewoman with a landlady
to return to and no Paula to intervene, losing combatant
in some scene from which one averted the eyes of the
spirit. At the extra shock of meeting Julian Wrenne,
Grace had nearly fainted on the pavement as every remembered personal trick and tone of voice enclosed her.
He had glanced at her casually, then with sharp attention.

'It's not — *Scrimmy?*' What he said for minutes afterwards was wiped for ever from her memory. He suggested
tea and she allowed that, it was a natural invitation which
one could accept. She had thrown herself into questions
about his family, from passionate interest no less than from
some defensive instinct to postpone his own enquiries.

'When are you coming to see us, my dear?'

That was easy to answer, even sheltered women with
money had their previous engagements. . . . 'Well then,
I'll come round to your place.' That trapped one. Her
mind photographically reproduced the room she had left
two hours before . . . and had she or had she not omitted
to put away that unwashed plate, and the stockings over
the chairback? And draw the screen across her washing
place? Even if he weathered her environment, failing to
take in its implications, he might draw the truth from her.
Pretend a telephone call and then go out by another door?
But she knew herself not big enough to leave him: famished
for his face and voice she must continue to play with
explosives.

'I am leaving my present address, Mr. Wrenne,' she lied.

He looked at her. She was praying he might accept it,
yet longing for his disbelief. And — would he remember
the voice she used for prevarication? So often she had
helped an overdriven Alison by outfacing unwelcome
visitors. But he bested her again. 'Where for?'

'I — I haven't quite decided.'

He considered her. 'Scrimmy dear, excuse me, but is anything the matter?' She denied hastily but was dismayed to feel her eyes filling. 'Is this a final veto? Mayn't I come and visit with you and do my bit of knitting while you tat?' Julian — Mr. Wrenne — appealing for her company when the very fact of his having entered her room for five minutes would transform it for ever after; that room she had never had the heart to individualize, so crowded with lodging-house furniture that her second box of personal stuff could not even be unpacked and was, by permission, upended in the passage.

'Better wait until I'm more settled.'

'Oh, that. Yes, of course. Scrimmy, I'm wondering so hard whether you're merely in your usual to-do of slaving for everyone or just a damned liar . . . now listen: you must give me your word not to lose touch with us. Please.'

She promised glibly, and gave herself up to looking.

CHAPTER XXXV

I

THE FAVOUR OF YOUR VOTES IS EARNESTLY SOLICITED ON
BEHALF OF
MISS GRACE SUSAN SCRIMGEOUR
(BORN 1870)

*Youngest daughter of Army Captain. Has been governess and
companion. Age and nervous debility has made it impossible for
her to continue to earn. Through depreciation of investments she
has now practically no resources. Is being kept by relatives and
now in very urgent need of help. The case is known to and
recommended by:*

Miss Netta Vince-Wells,
Miss Widdowson.

II

'Of course these things take time, Lady Mell, but I don't
anticipate a very long wait, in your case.'

At this reassurance, the old, fine-drawn woman turned
at the door and gave the speaker a sub-acid smile. 'Even
in our ashes we can pull wires. I dined last night with
Lord and Lady Frowen, at Frowen House, and asked the
whole table for some votes. I was the success of the evening! What a shocking thing is social influence! But many
thanks indeed, my dear. Far be it from me not to wish to
hasten the day of my election. You've been most considerate to an old 'un. No red-tape nonsense. She
appreciates it. I will say au revoir, then.'

The door closed and the Almoner of the Distressed

Gentlefolks' Protective Association, a keen-faced woman of sixty-odd, returned to her desk. 'It's Miss Scrimgeour, isn't it?'

'Did you say "Lady Mell"?'

The eyebrows facing Grace rose the fraction of an inch. 'Yes. And now — '

'You must think me impertinent, but my father and mother knew a Lady Mell. She sent us a tree every Christmas.' The Almoner's face softened. 'Then you two must meet. Perhaps at our Sale.'

'Oh, she wouldn't know me. We never saw each other.'

'She's an old dear: takes our help exactly as we want the candidates to, and you wouldn't believe how some of them face up to it, as though taking charity were a disgrace. One woman told me she'd been brought up to consider it so.' It was a test-speech that escaped Grace's perception, she merely looked ruminative.

'A disgrace? . . . I think it's much more disgraceful to be a burden on relations.'

'Ah.'

'You see, one has *tried* . . . pretty hard. Doesn't that make a difference?'

'We think so . . . now, Miss Scrimgeour, your leaflets will be ready in a very few days. You couldn't let us have the names of a few more sponsors, I suppose?'

'There is a Lady Ebban — '

'Good. Anyone else?'

Miss Scrimgeour looked obstinate. 'No.'

'Very well. Now, as an adopted candidate you'll receive five pounds at Christmas, and now, even until you get your annuity you will be entitled to draw what clothes you may need from our wardrobe.'

Grace flushed. 'You are so kind. I shall be glad to.'

'And if you ever need help about spectacles or dentures

there is our Consolatory Fund. We'll always do what we can. By the way, if you are lonely — I can understand so well, coming as you do from a big family — we can always arrange with the nearest G.P. Branch for one of our ladies to drop in and see you.' The Almoner looked up with a faint grin. 'And by that we do *not* mean sending a gorgon to read the Bible to you and peer into your saucepans. Nor. will she arrive without asking your permission first.' She rose, and Grace with her. 'It may take time to get you your votes,' she cautioned. 'Some of our ladies have stood for as many as six elections — that is three years.'

III

' — in declaring this bazaar open.'

And, actually, Miss Blanche Preston herself had come up and spoken to one as she was leaving the Town Hall. That *would* be something to tell Tummy, who was reported to be stage-struck. . . .

One couldn't, of course, afford to buy anything at the stalls, but the spring flowers cheered one, and there was a good luncheon and tea to look forward to. Grace Scrimgeour gripped the tickets. Perhaps, as the waitresses were probably ladies, they wouldn't accept a tip? But one had foreseen that and there was threepence in one's purse. And *if* they were ladies one could have a bunch of polyanthus.

PART FOUR

AND AFTER

GRACE SCRIMGEOUR, flitting between one room and the
next, would stop dead, forgetting her errand, and let her
eyes take in for the thousandth time her familiar goods and
chattels.

Two rooms. Hers. For life. The marvel of it never
failed. Because it was her birthday and therefore high
summer there was no welcoming fire, but the flowers in
every vase made up for that and the sun searched out even
Nana's pin-cushion, faded, and studded with its rusty pins.
A pity about the fire; Grace would have liked to have
heaped the goodness of every season upon her expected
guests, as it was she scurried back to survey the tea-table
once more, counting every item, seeing that every cake
and sandwich was present and correct, then impelled to
repeat the tally. . . . She thought, cockily, it was a pity she
hadn't bought a larger pot of *foie gras*. Julian — Mr.
Wrenne — was so fond of it, but the man in the grocer's
had assured her that her pot would be ample even for six
people, and she had been almost annoyed with him.

'Don't hurry about, take it easy'; the doctor had said
that when she consulted him about what she called 'these
palpitations'. But her heart would have to take its chance,
this afternoon. She could be careful ever after.

Seventy to-day, and she didn't feel it, didn't even look
it, because she supposed, for so many years now she had
looked older than her age. Two years, now, since she had
become an annuitant of the 'G.P.' Twelve-and-sixpence
a week, for life, clothes, and help in illness, and, as if that
were not enough, the railway had begun to pay dividends
once more. Just over two pounds a week, for life. It was

wonderful how much more genial it had made one to the
whole world, less short in temper, less censorious in one's
judgments, less suspicious. Paula — even Caroline and
Robert — were kinder to one, and even came to pay one
little visits, these days, so no doubt Grace had been wrong
ever to criticize them in her heart. . . .

Time was no longer the enemy with treats now made
possible; an outing to the cinema and studying the latest
film idol and comparing him unfavourably with Julian —
with Mr. Wrenne, and sometimes, by saving, or plunging
with that five pound Christmas Box from the G.P., a real
theatre could be gone to, and all day Grace would brood
sybaritically over the preparations for her own comfort:
keeping the fire in, putting out hot-water bottle and
dressing-slippers, choosing fillings and cutting sandwiches
for the jaunty theatre supper on her return. The theatres
had troubled her a little, at first, as being wrong, and unfair to the Association that was helping her to live, and she
had written to the Secretary, who had reassured her in
the kindest way.

11

Armoured in relief and gratitude, it was only on
occasion that personal loneliness got under her guard.
But there were still a few friends left and with a little pre-
caution, outings with them, teas and even suppers for
them could be braved. It was so pleasant, the hurly-burly
over, to have them, to study them, seeing them for the
first time as personalities unswamped by thronging sisters.

And the Almoner had evidently spoken, for Lady Mell
herself — so very old, but what a naughty tongue, quite a
rattle, like Georgie! — had written, and a friendship had
begun.

She was nearly eighty-seven, she said. It meant that, after all, in the days of Brecknock Gardens and the Christmas trees, she must have been what, to-day, would be called still a girl. Not thirty. Yet Grace and Charlie in the nursery had always thought and even spoken of her as 'old Lady Mell'.

And still it was only ten minutes to four . . . the Wrennes couldn't arrive for quite another twenty-five minutes. It was so wonderful of them to come when their days in town were so rare! Grace sat down to savour it. It meant that they were fond of her, and that included Julian. She stroked the cat, a large tabby who opened one glassy eye, said 'Krrr-lank' and instantly cast himself into a posture more favourable to stomach-massage. The Wrennes had promised to take Muffin if anything happened to her and the landlady had their address. Grace could not absolutely trust the big beast to anyone else. Julian called him 'The Chingford Scorcher' from Muffin's habit of wild pedalling when tickled, and Alison had said what a dreadful little bounder he would look in a cloth cap at the wheel on Sunday.

How flat one was going to feel when the tea-party was over . . . must try and not think of the Wrenne's leaving. Firmness. Think of other things. The quarterly cheque from the Association had arrived two days before, and when you were able to save a few shillings a week you could make plans, pretend you were going to take a room in Queenie's village to see a little of her before booking the ticket to another county, to Somerset. . . . Queenie wouldn't mind, poor Queenie! that large, sallow old woman; fretful and forgetful, she was succumbing to age, unlike Gertie who was indomitable to the last.

So there was her holiday to look forward to, in a fort-night, and the return home to Muffin, arching and smiling in the doorway. Christmas, wonderfully soon after that, and the bazaars. Grace loved the toy departments and their special features: 'A visit to the moon' in a machine with a humorous Guide, or magic caves, and always at the end a present from Santa Claus or a Moon Fairy, a box wrapped in pink or blue tissue paper. And all for a shilling. It was very childish and silly, she told herself, but one *did* enjoy opening the present though one always was careful to tell them it was for some little girl at home. She would watch the shopping mothers surrounded by school-boy and schoolgirl sons and daughters, linger near, trying to see the crackers they chose, picturing their Christmas table. Then off again to another stall.

She looked at the clock, and the discovery that it was four-fifteen made her heart thump so that the room seemed to grow black. In any minute now . . .

She would never forget the day that, knowing herself secure at last, she had written to the Wrennes about it all, describing her new rooms — really positively boasting — and the avalanche of affectionate reproach they had sent down on her for her unkindness to them in hiding every-thing she had been through. Even their children had written and Tummy had called her a beastly cad, and said she was 'no lady'.

The front door bell rang.

III

It had come — the departure of her guests, but by that time Grace Scrimgeour was in such a state of wild, inner excitement that there was no room for regret, and, in any case, only two weeks to wait. . . .

'A noble tea, dear Scrimmy. God! how I've gorged.'

'Same here. Do have another birthday soon!'

Her eyes, Alison Wrenne noticed, were blazing; always her best feature, one remembered.

Julian Wrenne put his arms round Grace, kissing her warmly.

'Good-bye, my dear — but only for a very short while.'

She didn't answer, had stumbled? His grasp tightened instinctively as she fell forward, against him.

'Alison . . .'

His wife knew that tone, had heard it at least once before . . . to that groom who had lost his temper with a horse at schooling. . . .

IV

'. . . But she was perfectly well, at tea,' he was repeating to the hastily summoned doctor.

'She's had some shock, not necessarily an unpleasant one, but I warned her once against over-exertion and — '

'But, I tell you, she — '

'It was a tired heart. They often go, like that.'

'But, right up to the time we were leaving — '

They stood together, murmuring arguments about the happy little form lying on the sofa.